Brand of the Hunted

Charles M. Barker

A Black Horse Western

ROBERT HALE · LONDON

© 1963, 2003 John Glasby
First hardcover edition 2003
Originally published in paperback as
Brand of the Hunted by Chuck Adams

ISBN 0 7090 7240 6

Robert Hale Limited
Clerkenwell House
Clerkenwell Green
London EC1R 0HT

Typeset by
Derek Doyle & Associates, Liverpool.
Printed and bound in Great Britain by
Antony Rowe Limited, Wiltshire

1
Riding the Wide Range

At first the trail to the east had been deserted, empty as far as the eye could see, but now there was a small, scarcely seen cloud of dust in the far distance where it came in out of the mountains, to cross the wide, stretching wilderness of the dusty plain.

Neil Roberts sat easily in the saddle, hands resting loosely on the pommel, eyes narrowed a little against the glare of the sun now climbing up swiftly from the eastern horizon, red turning yellow, soon to become white as it approached the zenith, when the waves of heat would lift over the range and the dust-devils would cavort and whirl madly around the buttes.

He was a limber man with a rider's looseness about him, about every move of his tall, lean body the grey eyes half-hidden beneath the lowered lids, the crinkly hair just show-ing beneath the wide-brimmed hat that kept some of the sunlight off his face. All of his features were angular and solid, and his shape was lean and stringy, the shape of a man who lived in the saddle, whose home was the great rolling distances of the prairie and whose ceiling was the sky.

The rising whorls of dust, perhaps ten, maybe fifteen

miles away, drew closer, the only evidence that whatever it was out there was moving. But as they drew closer, it was possible to make out some form of shape in the grey dust.

The tiny dots, barely seen at first, drew themselves out from the shimmering heat waves, moving slowly in single file, big wagons each drawn by four powerful horses.

From that distance, it was impossible to make out how many there were in the train, but he guessed there must have been close on sixteen or twenty of them, heading west along the trails which cut through almost a dozen states, through some of the roughest and most dangerous country in the world; not only dangerous because of the miles of arid, alkali desert, high mountains that had to be crossed, great rivers in full flood; but because of the other dangers which lay hidden in that country. Men who would stop at nothing to destroy the wagon trains, the big cattle bosses whose cattle roamed the wild wilderness of the prairie, and then the border gangs, the men who lived off the wagon trains, murdering and plundering.

And at the end of the trail, for the fortunate few who made it, the Promised Land – California, a land so they said flowing in milk and honey, where gold nuggets as big as a man's fist were to be had for the taking, and where the soil and climate were so good that whole cities were springing up virtually overnight as people moved in from the east.

He forced a quick grin. He was a man who could grin whenever the going became tough, whose smile was inclined to touch not only his mouth but his eyes too. Yet he was also a brooding man with something that often showed at the back of the cold, grey eyes; as if a hidden devil lay somewhere in their depths from which it would sometimes leap up unbidden, naked and threatening, only to sink down again behind the veiling lids.

A quick glance at the sun told him that the wagon train would not reach him much before early afternoon, even if they pushed their horses to the limit, which did not seem likely.

He put his mount down the gentle slope towards the bank of the river, where there was shade from the tall trees that grew along the water's edge. Alighting, he lay flat on his belly upstream from his horse and drank deeply of the cool water, then filled his canteen, an action born of long years in the desert when each drop of water was a precious thing.

Going back towards the trees, he seated himself in the shade of the tallest, resting his back and shoulders against the broad trunk. In the distance, his mount moved lazily along the river bank, drifting to graze. He pulled his hat down over his eyes, stretching his lean body out.

He woke when the heat of the sun shone full on to his face again, sat upright, looking about him, knowing that he had been asleep for some hours. The sorrel was still there, twenty yards away, grazing peacefully and, in the distance, the dull cloud that almost shrouded the wagon train was now less than a couple of miles away. He could just make out the faint calls of the drivers and the outriders as they urged their flagging horses forward to the river.

Back to the east there lay only desert for more than fifty miles and Neil knew that the horses in the train, and the cows they were bringing too, would have smelled the water by now, would be straining at the traces.

Standing up, he whistled to his mount, swung himself up into the saddle, then put the horse into the water. In the middle of the river, where the current flowed strongest, he could feel it push against the horse's chest as it breasted the current, at times forced to swim across.

On the other side, he rode towards the lead wagon, giving the sorrel its head. Down a slight slope he went, reining as he came alongside the wagon, staring up at the barrel-chested man who rode it, sitting easily on the lip of the seat. A big man of sinew and muscle and bone, with flaming red hair and a beard to match, reddish and ragged. The floppy, wide-brimmed hat was pulled down well over his forehead, but sweat ran in rivulets down his face and the white alkali dust, burning and stinging, had worked its way into the folds of his skin, mingling with the perspiration until it formed a streaky mask from which his eyes peered out, black and piercing under the thick, tufted brows. There was a rifle, a Winchester, Neil noticed, thrust into a leather scabbard on the side of the wagon within easy reach of his huge hands.

'Clem Jackson?' Neil called, as he turned the sorrel, riding alongside the other, his mount easily matching pace with the wagon.

'That's my name,' growled the other in a deep voice that seemed to come booming all the way from the lowermost depths of his chest.

'Mine's Neil Roberts. Perhaps Weston mentioned my name before you left.'

'Roberts.' The other nodded slowly, ponderously. 'We were warned to keep a look out for you, didn't expect to run into you so soon.'

'I figured you might run into trouble around this neck of the territory and came along as fast as I could. There's bad country ahead.'

'Figgered that might be so.' The other's glance strayed towards the Winchester. 'Didn't intend taking any chances. We've put all we got into these wagons, and we don't aim to let anybody take them away from us without a fight. We're headed for California and, by God, that's where we're going.'

'I'm sure you'll make it, but it won't be easy. In the meantime, you've probably noticed there's a river dead ahead, less than a mile further on. You could make camp there, plenty of water for your horses and cattle, and I could have a pow-wow with you. There's a lot of things I ain't got quite straight in my mind yet, and if I'm in to take this train through the country

8

up ahead, I'd like the answers to some questions.'

For a moment he saw the hesitation in the other, then the huge frame relaxed and the man grinned.

'I like you, Roberts,' he growled. 'You're the kind of man I could trust. They told me that much when we started out, but I never take a man on trust, no more'n I'd take a horse or a wagon. I like to look them over first and make up my own mind.'

He flicked the bull-hide whip over the horses, urging them on, but by now the animals had got the scent of water and needed no urging. The Conestoga wagons rumbled forward, wheels creaking on their axles as they bumped and swayed over the rough, uneven ground. Up ahead the water shone and glistened in the bright, harsh sunlight and the whooping of the men riding scout told that they had already reached it.

Half an hour later the wagons had been drawn up in a wide circle on the eastern bank of the river. They would not ford it until the horses had been watered and everything had been checked. The river was deep in the middle and the current strong.

Seated opposite Clem Jackson, Neil ate the beans and bacon which had been handed him on a plate slowly, chewing easily on the appetising food. He had lived for so long on jerked beef, eaten cold, washed down with water, that this food, and the hot coffee that went with it, filled his stomach well.

'You reckon's there's a chance of getting through along this trail, Roberts?' asked Jackson suddenly. He glanced up and eyed Neil shrewdly with his dark, brooding eyes. 'They warned us that it wouldn't be easy this way, that we ought to have taken the northern trail. But that would have added a hundred days to the journey, and it's bad country there, especially if we're caught in the winter.'

'That's right.' Neil nodded in agreement. 'But I ought to

warn you of what lies ahead of you if you still want to take this trail.'

He waved a hand almost negligently towards the east, back along the trail they had just come. There was a grim trace of amusement in his tone as he said:

'Back there you drove these wagons across more than fifty miles of alkali desert, and most of you probably figgered that if you could do that, you could do anything. But that was nothing compared with what lies in that direction.' He jerked a thumb to the west.

'Doesn't look too bad to me once we ford the river,' muttered a short, dark-hared man.

'Maybe not. But it ain't the country you'll have to fight there. Plenty of water between the big rivers, plenty of grazing, too. And plenty of trouble. Mebbe you never heard of the Shermans and the Hollards.'

'Nope, can't say I have,' went on the other with unconscious arrogance.

His words sounded too sharp and distinct, the tone just a mite too clear for Neil's liking. But he kept his temper, knowing that a Western man had a looser and easier way of speaking. He guessed this man came from way back east, maybe thought he knew everything there was to know about the west and wasn't inclined to accept advice.

Neil smiled in a wintry way, eyes deliberately as bleak as his voice.

'This is cattle country, mister. Stretching for the next three hundred miles to the west and more than twice that distance to the south and north, is all cattle land. Probably a hundred thousand head of prime beef cattle, all belonging to one of two men – Jesse Sherman or Matt Hollard. They don't like nesters, or even men like yourselves just passing through. This is their land, even though you might say that it was got illegally. But they hold it by force of arms, they have got their own bands of outlaws, hired gunmen whose job it is to shoot down anybody trespass-ing here and stop anybody like you from moving through.'

He grinned faintly.

'I suppose it's true to say that most of the time they're at each other's throats, rustling and killing. But they'll band together to fight any wagon train that tries to make its way across their land.'

'Then we'll fight,' grunted Jackson.

He reached out, picked up the long-barrelled Winchester holding it tightly in his hairy fists, the knuckles of his hands showing through the skin, glistening in white bone with the pressure he was exerting.

'Do you think that you can fight those men, professional fighting men, the scum of a hundred towns, men wanted by the law from here to the Mexican border, but safe so long as they work for these men?' He shook his head very slowly.

'Are you suggesting that we turn back, or maybe that we try to go around them?' asked Jackson tightly. He met Neil's steady glance with a brief show of impatience.

'If you don't want to turn back – and I figger that ain't likely seeing that you've come so far – then we'll have to go straight ahead. No point in trying to drive this wagon train around that territory. It would take the best part of seventy days to do it, and there's no guarantee you'd be safe even then.'

'So we drive straight on,' growled the big man.

Very slowly he relaxed his grip on the rifle, let it fall to the soft earth beside him. He picked up his mug of hot coffee, tilted it savagely to his lips and drank deeply of it, some of the scalding liquid splashing over his arms and bare chest, but he did not seem to notice it.

'Just so long as everybody in the train knows what they're letting themselves in for,' said Neil quietly, and evenly.

'They knew the danger before they agreed to join the train,' muttered Jackson thickly. 'They all agreed to come along and they elected me to be wagon master. They take their orders from me now. That's the way it's got to be.'

'Can you speak for all of them?' Neil glanced at him in surprise.

'That I can.' He nodded his head ponderously. 'And I say that we drive straight across this territory, and to hell with the Shermans and the Hollards, and their hired gunmen.'

Neil shrugged negligently.

'Very well.' He drained his coffee. 'If that's the way you want it. Better rest up your horses for the rest of the day out here. We can ford the river first thing tomorrow morning.'

'That makes sense,' agreed the dark-haired man. 'Ain't no sense in putting tired horses into that current.' He threw a quick glance at the sky, clear and cloudless. 'Weather's going to stay fine. Ain't likely to get swollen in the next few hours.'

The big man paused, then nodded, got heavily to his feet and went over to sit on the wagon tongue.

In the heat head of the afternoon, a deep and clinging silence lay over the camp. It was possible to make out the gurgling of the water over the smooth stones near the bank where the river ran faster. Lowering very slowly to the west, the prairie sun threw down the heat that was reflected from the desert in dizzying waves.

Men and women forsook the open for the shade inside the wagons, but even here there was a deep and sullen heat, nowhere was it possible to escape from it. It was something that had been their constant companion since they had entered the desert to the east some four days earlier.

Not until an hour before sundown did the heat pressure ease. Then the wind came sighing in from the north-west, blowing off the tall hills in the distance where they stood out on the skyline, a cooling wind that brought the men and women out of the wagons, around the fires which had been lit in the open.

Down by the river's edge Neil Roberts washed some of the

dust from his face and neck, feeling the cold water sting his skin where it had been burned by the sun, rubbed raw by the alkali dust.

Around the fires they were cooking bacon, boiling coffee in the big pans, ladling it out into mugs, the smell of the steaming liquid lying over everything.

Neil pulled the lashing of his jacket tighter about him to keep out the cold night air. He rubbed a broad thumb against the butt of the Colt at his waist, stared across through the leaping flames at the leader of the wagon train.

'You said you had some questions you wanted to ask, Roberts,' boomed Jackson loudly. 'Go ahead. Ask them. I'll tell you all I can.'

'There's not much.' Neil shrugged, chewed reflectively on a strip of bacon. 'I know where you're headed – California. But why do you want me to lead you?'

'You're a fast man with a gun,' said the other bluntly. 'They told us that if necessary you shot first and talked later. You're the kind of man we need on this journey if they spoke the truth. Some of the dangers you've told us of, but there are bound to be others. We've heard something of what happened to the other trains that tried to get through. Some of 'em didn't even get as far as this. We passed some on the way here, back there in the alkali.'

Neil nodded, narrowing his eyes a little. For a moment he wasn't listening to the big man seated on the opposite side of the fire, and his eyes were fixed eastward on the flat, rolling face of the desert where the whiteness of the alkali seemed to shine eerily in the fading light of evening. He, too, had seen the remains of the small wagon trains that had tried to push their way westward and had met their fate out there in the terrible, heat-wavering wilderness where the days were scorched slices of hell, and the nights, long hours torn out of the arctic cold. The small trains, perhaps half a dozen wagons, had tried to cross without sufficient water, possibly without any real idea of what they were facing, of the only way to go; and they had died. Months later men had come across the remnants of the wagons, with the bleached bones lying beside them, all that was left of men and animals.

Now, any wagon trains heading west were larger, more than a score of wagons, plenty of water in the barrels they carried, all of the men armed with the latest weapons, repeating Winchesters, Colts, ready to meet trouble along the way.

'You can consider yourselves lucky if you've managed to get this far without trouble,' he said flatly. 'The going isn't likely to be as easy from now on.'

'We're ready to meet anybody who tries to stop us,' said the big man quietly. 'If we have to fight these hired killers you speak of, then we'll fight them. We're not looking for trouble, but if it comes …'

He left the rest of his sentence unsaid, but there was a tightening in his tone, a hard, grim determination.

'It will come, take my word for it.'

Neil glanced at the man beside him, then beyond the men at the fire towards the women and children clustered around the wagons drawn up around the fire. Perhaps the men were ready to fight it out with hired killers and the border gangs, he thought tightly, but what about them? His grey eyes were cold as he allowed his gaze to wander around the camp.

Night closed in swiftly from the east. For a brief moment the setting sun, hidden behind the mountains, touched the crests with a flash of red light as if a fire had been lit at the rear of the world. Then the darkness swamped it out and the stars were clear and crisp in the heavens overhead.

The horses settled down for the night, the handful of cattle they had brought with them lowed softly for a little while, then they too became silent. But the fires still burned among the wagons. Several of the men were still awake and guards had been posted.

Lying in his blanket, Neil listened to them, talking softly among themselves, as the long dark hours passed slowly, and the brilliant stars counted out the minutes in their slow wheel across the vast span of the heavens.

As he lay there he tried to think ahead, to assess the dangers which he knew would be lying in wait for them. For the next two hundred miles or so he could foresee the danger, but being able to foresee it did not necessarily mean that they would be able to overcome it.

The country to the west, whether it belonged to Sherman or Hollard, had a reputation for sheltering wild ones. Men quick with a gun, men who would shoot to kill on the slightest excuse. A wagon train such as this would be regarded as easy picking to them.

At the prospect of this he felt his skin tingling, prickling with a faintly uneasy apprehension. Once, in the red firelight, he turned to study the tall, big figure of the man who stood for almost an hour on the edge of the camp staring out towards the west, out across the wide river which they would ford in the morning at first light, and if there were any doubts in Jackson's mind about the outcome of the drive that stretched in front of them, none of them showed on his face. He seemed confident that they would win through, even though he probably accepted the fact that some of them in the train would inevitably die.

There was no movement by the big man as he stood on the edge of camp. He seemed utterly absorbed by what he was seeing in his mind's eye, out there beyond the stretch of the river. Neil drew a deep breath, pulled his blanket more tightly around his shoulders. The fire was dying a little now, the cold of the night creeping into his bones. Except for the guards, the wagon train slept.

The next morning, after eating breakfast over the rekindled fires, they began the crossing of the wide river, putting the horses into the water even before the sun had lifted clear of the eastern horizon.

Evenly balanced in the saddle, Neil sat and watched the lumbering wagons through narrowed eyes, alert for trouble. This was always a dangerous moment as far as a wagon train was concerned. Few of the men on the tongues of the great covered wagons were experts, and in the middle of the river the water was deep, the bottom difficult and treacherous, although fortunately the current was slow. It was hard driving, arms straining on the lashings and reins as the water breasted against the horses in a curling whiteness of foam and their feet slipped on the sandy bottom.

A dark-haired man dressed in leather yelled a sharp order as the water came over the tongue of the wagon on which he sat, the horses surged forward, thrusting against the river. Sam Jessup, Neil remembered the dark man's name from the previous evening when he had sat with the others around the blazing fire, listened to their talk, their hopes, their fears, their confidence that they would eventually win through to the rich yellow land of Southern California.

'Keep them moving!' Neil called to the rest of the men as the wagons rumbled ponderously into the river, began the long pull across to the further bank. He knew with a sure instinct that if one wagon faltered here, it could mean they would lose it in the mud.

There was another man, short and inclined to fatness, driving Jackson's wagon now, and the big wagon master was riding a high-spirited horse, urging the lumbering wagons forward, his loud, booming voice bellowing even above the rumble of the wheels on the dust of the trail. He turned in his saddle, came riding over towards Neil, his face expressionless.

'Once we cross the river, it ought to be good driving country,' he observed, nodding his shaggy head in the direction of the flat, rolling ground that lay on the other side of the river.

Neil nodded speculatively, remained silent, his face tight.

'You still worrying about those cattle men who'll try to stop us?' growled the other harshly.

'I am. We won't see them, not at first. But they'll see us. It'd be impossible not to spot a wagon train this size. They'll try to kill us before we've gone a score of miles.'

The last of the wagons crossed the river, the horses straining in the traces as they hauled it up the far bank. Neil and Jackson waited until it was safely over, then put their mounts to the water, took them across.

The train had formed up, was moving slowly across the smooth stretch of country leading towards the rising curve of a low hill. There was no sign of a trail here, no place where the ground had been beaten flat by the pounding of countless hooves over the earth.

Around them everything lay quiet and still, with a watchful, waiting quality hanging over it, and Neil felt the muscles of his chest tighten a little in response to the silence. He thought without pleasure of what lay ahead of them, knew the hundred different kinds of danger and death which faced them here in this wild country, and more especially in the Badlands that lay further to the west.

But before they reached that terrible terrain they had first to make their way over the vast stretch of prairie. He threw a wide, sweeping glance around him, eyes narrowed a little against the vivid red glare of the rising sun, alert and watchful for the first signs of trouble.

The heat of the day was beginning to lie over the land around them now, the distant horizons shimmering as the dust devils cavorted over the plain.

Neil spurred his mount, rode out ahead of the train, knew that Jackson was close behind him. They reined their mounts on top of the curving crest of the hill that looked down on to the wide valley spread out before them, a vast stretch of land that lay all the way in front of them towards the mountains in the far distance where the red rays of the sun were just touching the ragged peaks with splashes of crimson.

'They'll have their beef cattle somewhere about,' he remarked tonelessly. 'Ought to be some of their men here, too, keeping an eye open.'

'You mean the Shermans?'

'That's right. Matt Hollard's spread is a hundred miles or so to the west of this one.'

'I'm not interested in Hollard, or Sherman,' said Jackson. He pointed back towards the straggling wagons. 'All I'm concerned with is getting that wagon train to California. You getting scared now that we're close to trouble?'

Neil lifted the reins and set his right foot hard in its stirrup, watched the hardness in the other's face, the wariness at the back of his eyes. With an effort he controlled the anger that had risen deep within him, choked it down, relaxed his hands where the right one had hovered for a fraction of a second just above the gun in the holster.

'I'm not afraid for myself, and you know it, Jackson,' he said tightly, forcing evenness into his tone. 'But there are women and children back there in those wagons, and we surely have to take them into consideration.'

'I'll answer for every one of them,' declared the big man dispassionately.

He turned his head, looked out over the plain, then stiffened abruptly in his saddle, nodded towards the open valley below them.

'Looks as though there may be trouble sooner than we think.'

A small curtain of dust moved towards them, down on the plain, and Neil saw the three riders spurring their horses in their direction. He nodded in agreement.

'Sherman's men,' he said tonelessly. 'They may decide to give us a warning to turn back while we have the chance; but it's more likely that they'll try to gun us down, then ride back with the warning to Sherman. Once they get there, a score or more will ride out on Sherman's orders to destroy the train.'

The three riders set their mounts at the slope of the hill, rode up to the crest. The horses they sat were lean and hard, the saddles worn. Each man wore his guns low and their eyes checked the two men sitting there, then flickered in the direction of the slowly advancing wagon train down below on the other side of the hill.

'You know that this spread belongs to Jesse Sherman,' murmured one of the men silkily. 'He doesn't like home-steaders moving across it.'

For a long moment Jackson stared at the three men facing him.

'We're driving straight across,' he said flatly. 'Do you figure on trying to stop us?'

For an instant there was a perplexed consternation on the face of the first man, then his eyes narrowed to mere slits and he sat a little straighter in the saddle. His eyes were as empty and emotionless as those of a snake, and the thin cruel mouth was compressed to a mere slit.

'Reckon you two hombres have made a big mistake,' he grated harshly.

Not once did his gaze leave Neil's face, and it was as if he had instantly recognised that it was he, and not the bigger man, who was the more dangerous of the two.

Neil said: 'Suppose you prove that, mister,' speaking in an even steady voice.

This one, and possibly the other two, would be fast men with a gun, he reflected. All three were undoubtedly profes-sional killers, deliberately hired by Sherman to do any dirty work like this for him. Men he could trust because only here, in his employ, would they be safe from the law. There would be wanted posters of these men in sheriffs' offices all over the territory, rewards out for them, dead or alive.

There was also an easiness about the way in which the three men sat their mounts and waited, quite obviously certain that they were facing a couple of men far slower with their guns than they were themselves.

The man's eyes were fixed on Neil's face, unblinking, steady. The other was one who watched a man's eyes for a sign that the other was beginning his draw. That way, thought Neil, he got the signal a split second before his opponent's hand began its downward move. It gave him an edge, one which had probably been sufficient to keep him alive so far through a dozen gunfights that he might otherwise have lost. A cocky gunfighter, with a strange warped sense of pride, who would not draw first unless he was sure that the man he faced was probably faster than he was.

Neil could almost read the uneasy balance of the other's thoughts, the rapid weighing of his chances. Then, suddenly, the man's stretched patience was gone. His hand moved, striking down for the gun at his belt with the speed of a rattler and, as he moved, so did the two men with him, their hands moving almost in unison.

Even as their guns lifted into line, two guns threw death at the gunmen, both guns blazing as one. The first man went down grabbing at his chest, the gun tilting from his hand, hitting the dirt a second before he did. The other two sat for a moment, bolt upright in their saddles, expressions of stunned amazement on their hard features. Then they slumped forward in their saddles, arms hanging loosely over the pommels for an instant before they, too, fell and lay still, their mounts shying away. Then there was silence; a dark silence that crowded in on the two men at the top of the low hill.

Slowly, eyes wider than before, Jackson turned to face Neil, then dropped his gaze to where the smoke still rose from the twin guns in the other's hands.

Roughly almost, Neil pouched them, sat forward a little, elbows on the saddle, staring down at the still things on the ground only a little distance away. Guns had spoken on that quiet hill overlooking the vastness of the plain, guns held in the hands of a master craftsman, hands which had moved faster than the eye could follow and had shot to kill.

'If you're thinking that this might stop the others from attacking us, then you're wrong,' said Neil softly, and his words fell into the deep and muffling silence all about them. 'Sherman will see us all dead for this – and even if we do get through, we'll have to face Matt Hollard and his gunhawks.'

Jackson gave a quick little nod, then tightened his mouth.

'We'll face 'em,' he said, with a growing confidence in his voice. 'And I take back all I said about you being scared to go on.'

'I still think you're a fool.' Neil's voice was still quiet. 'This is some of the worst country in the whole of the United States, and by the time we've crossed to the border the weather will have changed, it'll be winter, and only a fool would attempt to cross those mountains once the winter snows start.'

'We'll face up to that when it comes,' muttered Jackson.

He pulled hard on the reins, wheeled his mount and rode back down the slope towards the wagon train.

Moving past the hill, the wagons drove westward. The sun climbed up into the zenith, a flaming disc of fire, burning their skin, the heat shocking back at them from the plain in dizzying waves.

They nooned in the lee of a tall canyon but there was no shade there, and men sweated and cursed, drooped in their saddles, rubbing the white dust out of their eyes.

There was mesquite and low cactus here and, further on,

from the edge of the camp, Neil could make out where the scrub oak began, dense growths which could give conceal-ment to a whole army of gunhawks

This was a place of weirdly etched buttes and narrow gorges, fluted and carved by wind and sand, a rugged and inhospitable stretch of country legally belonging to no man, but claimed by Jesse Sherman, anxious to protect his stretch of grassland some distance to the west.

The drive began again during the afternoon. There was no place there to make camp that day and both Jackson and Neil were anxious to move on. Deep in the choking dust through which the horses made their way and the wooden wheels of the wagons rolled, the train moved forward in single file.

Jackson had taken his place on the seat of the lead wagon again and at times he waved encouragement to the others following behind. There were women seated beside the menfolk, Neil noticed, sitting tall in the saddle as he rode a little distance away, women who carried the long-barrelled repeater rifles in their hands, women who would not be afraid to fight alongside their menfolk if the going got tough.

But he still felt a little uneasy in his mind. Whether or not they were prepared to fight, whether or not they had more rifles and six-guns among them than the band of gunhawks that Sherman would undoubtedly throw against them, he doubted the ability of these people to fight against profes-sional killers, and there was also the one inescapable fact that even if they did succeed in driving these men off, even if they managed to fight their way through, not only Sherman's coun-try, but Hollard's spread further along the route, by that time their numbers would be so depleted, their stores at rock bottom, that the survivors would lack the courage or the stom-ach to fight off the raiding border gangs who were even more dangerous than the gunhawks they were likely to see here.

On top of that, there would be the long winter days up in

the mountains, seeking a place to camp, shelter from the raging blizzards that swept those icy slopes, and then— But what was the use in going on, thinking along those lines? If everyone paused to consider the difficulties that faced them, no one would ever have ventured out into this wild, untamed country in the first place.

He shrugged off the thoughts, rested himself more easily in the saddle, let the sorrel pick its own gait. When a man had a long way to ride, the best way was the slow way.

As he rode, his eyes three-quarter lidded to shield off the all-pervading glare, he saw all there was to be seen right out to the shimmering horizons, and he speculated long on the shape of the buttes or the twisted course of a deep ravine with steep razor-backed sides, seeking out any places where a man with a rifle might lie concealed, his mind drawn inward in the manner of a man who often rode alone.

For the men rolling west with the wagons, it might appear that this was good country, and that the country that lay directly ahead was even better, with rich green grass, watered by great rivers, territory where there could be a coolness that one could not find out here in the middle of the scorched wilderness.

For him, however, the opposite was the truth. With the trees and grass there would be danger. There it would be impossible to see far, and death could be very close and a man would never suspect its presence until it was too late.

And there was another danger, one which came from the cattle that roamed these prairie lands. They were unused to the wagons, would be moving on their muscle, and the slightest wrong move, or the slightest prompting by Sherman's men herding them, could begin a stampede. His mind baulked at the thought, racing ahead, visualising what could happen if this slow-moving wagon train found itself in the path of a stampeding herd. There would be nothing whatever left of them by the time those countless tons of muscle and

23

beef had smashed their way through the wagons.

He set a spur against the flank of his sorrel and rode forward, watchful, recognising the places where danger might lie in hiding, but the long heat of the afternoon passed without incident. They saw nothing that moved on the plain around them and, at their backs, the dust settled slowly, dust kicked up by the hooves of the horses and the churning wheels of the wagons.

There had been dust and heat and a blazing sun, but now, slowly, that sun was descending towards the undulating skyline of the west where the tall peaks of the mountains still seemed as distant, as far off, as ever. Neil estimated that they had moved perhaps ten miles that day, good going considering the fact that most of the wagons had a couple of cows tethered to the back, and at best the wagons themselves could move only slowly and ponderously on their creaking axles.

Night came out of the east. The sky overhead purpled, then grew dark, and the stars stood out in their thousands, a vast curve of powdered light right down to the far horizons. Twin fires blazed in the camp, but now that they were well inside Sherman territory, Neil placed more men on watch and himself rode the perimeter of the camp, knowing that there would be little sleep for him that night, not with the ever-present possibility of a surprise attack lying heavy on his mind.

Jackson and Sam Jessup moved forward to join him in the cold darkness. Caught in silhouette by the faint light of the half-moon, horses and riders blended as dark shadows across the uneven ground. Neil sat quite still and waited.

'You reckon there might be trouble during the night?' asked Jessup quietly.

'Could be.' Neil nodded. 'This isn't the best place to make camp with gunslingers like Sherman's men around. They'll have found those three men back there by now and soon they'll come looking for revenge.'

The big man was silent for a moment, pondering on the

other's words. Then he shifted himself in his saddle.

'Just what kind of a man is this Jesse Sherman?' he asked, staring off into the darkness that lay all about them.

There was a quick glance from Neil.

'He's ruthless, determined. Came out here just after the finish of the war. They say he came from somewhere up north, but nobody knows much about him. Built up a cattle empire from almost nothing; and a man has to be ruthless to do a thing like that. He knows that sooner or later there'll be nesters moving in, that the Government will break up the big stretches of land, and he's determined to resist that with every means at his command. And if that means bringing in every gunslinger and killer this side of the Rio Grande, then he'll do it. He'll offer them safety so long as they stay on his land and obey the orders he gives. They do all of the killing for him and make sure that nobody tries to settle on the land, or even to cross it as we're doing now.

'In return, he keeps them from the law. They don't have to keep on runnin' and driftin' from state to state, always one jump ahead of a United States Marshal.'

Jackson mused on that for some time, then nodded his great head.

'And Neil Roberts – what kind of a man is he?'

Neil hesitated for the barest fraction of a second, almost as if caught off balance by the question. Then he shrugged his shoulders nonchalantly.

'Sometimes I discover myself wondering about him,' he said soberly. 'Wonder why he does what he does. Why he kills as he does – and where he's really going. Then again, I wonder if he'll ever get there, wherever it is.'

There was a loud bellow of a laugh from Jackson. He gave a quick nod.

'Like I said when we first met, Roberts – I like you. And after what happened on that hill back there, I'm glad that

25

you're with us and not against us.'

Behind them where the fires were dying slowly, there was a faint snicker of a horse, a sudden movement, then silence once more.

Neil continued to sit tall and straight in the saddle, staring around him, eyes probing the darkness, looking for any faint shadow or a vaguely seen cloud of dust in the distance; ears straining to pick up the faint thunder of horses moving over the flat prairie, but there was nothing, and gradually he forced himself to relax.

He had figured that if Sherman's men had found the bodies of their three companions up there on the hill, perhaps ten, twelve miles to the east, they would follow the easily seen trail of the wagon train and attack after dark, when they would have the advantage of surprise. The fact that there was no sign of them worried him more than if they had swung in from the east and ridden down on the sleeping train, guns blazing. He rode on, circling the wagons in the darkness, the cold seeping through into his bones.

2
Danger at Noon

Morning, and the train moved out of camp, rolled on to the west. It was hard driving for the men and women on the wagons, hard, monotonous and mean. The dust of the hard ground, lifted by the ploughing hooves of the horses, hung thick and white in the air, worked its way into the folds of the skin, itching and irritating, gummed up the lips and burned the eyes so that it was impossible to see properly at the end of the first hour.

Already the heat pressure was rising swiftly, but this time, Neil noticed there was something different about the sun. It no longer shone brilliantly in the east. Instead, there seemed to be a dullish, eye-searing haze surrounding it, a haze that spread up from the horizon, thickening as the minutes dragged themselves into hours. The air was utterly still and windless, an expectant calm that began to eat at his nerves as he rode the edge of the trail.

The sky in front of them now carried an answering glaze as if the blue polish of the sky had been scoured and braided, giving it a curiously threatening look. He turned his horse, rode in closer to the wagon and their straining teams.

At the rear of the train, where the dust hung thickest in the air, he rode alongside the wagon, eyes slitted against the sickening glare. There was a woman riding on the tongue, holding the reins tightly in her hands, and beside her a boy of perhaps eleven or twelve, freckle-faced, bright-eyed. Neil noticed the way they kept flicking their glance towards the heavens, knew that they, too, had noticed the storm that was brewing down there close to the horizon, that they were as worried about it as he himself. ———

Virginia Millais and her son Johnny had, according to Jackson, joined the train at Boston, were going west to join her husband in California. It was a long and hard journey for a woman and a boy, he reflected, as he rode alongside the wagon, watching the way in which the woman handled the team, noticing the rifle cradled in the boy's arms.

He leaned forward with one arm resting on the rope-burned pommel while the woman turned and eyed him with a faintly apprehensive smile on her lips. She gestured to the south-west.

'What do you think that means, Mister Roberts?' she asked quietly.

'Trouble, I'm afraid,' he answered slowly. 'There's a storm coming up, Ma'am, a bad one. I reckon it ought to hit us around noon at the rate it's travelling. We may be lucky and get only the fringe of it, but that's going to be bad.'

'It looks ominous.'

'Dust storm,' nodded Neil musingly. 'Often blows up in these parts at this time of the year. Better make certain that you keep the canvas tightly closed or you'll spend the rest of the journey trying to get rid of the sand in there. It will help, too, to keep your faces covered with kerchiefs, or you'll find it difficult to breathe when it does hit us.'

They nodded.

'Do you intend to stop the train when it comes?'

Neil shook his head. 'Won't do any good to stop, Ma'am. We'll just keep them moving. That way we'll get through it quicker. But whatever happens, make sure that you keep up with the others. If you drop behind and lose sight of the wagon in front of you, you'll be lost in minutes, and when the storm blows itself out we may never find you.'

He spurred his mount, rode swiftly along the line of wagons, giving the same warning, the same advice, to each of the drivers, making sure that they understood, sitting his sorrel while they tied down the canvas. He doubted if any of them had been through a real dust storm before, if any of them really knew what it was like, those millions of swirling yellow grains, hurled by a shrieking, howling wind that blew endlessly and with a terrible force, cutting into a man's body, making it almost impossible for him to move forward against it, even if he bent himself into the wind. It would be almost as bad for the animals. They, too, would be forced to keep moving into it. He threw a wary eye in the direction of the approaching storm, felt a wave of apprehension go through him.

An hour passed. Still the storm had not reached them, the air hung heavy and oppressive, with the stillness that came before the storm.

Neil reached the head of the train where Jackson sat huge and square on the tongue of the wagon, a bull of a man, the hands that held the reins heavy across the backs, with black hairs along the wrist that glistened in the diffuse sunlight.

'I've told them all to close it up,' Neil said tightly. 'We're going to get that storm in less than an hour now, and it won't be easy to see when it does hit us. I don't want to lose any wagons.'

It was almost as if the other hadn't heard the words. His eyes looked due west, reaching out over the flatlands to where the mountains lifted sheer towards the sky on the horizon. But now they did not stand out clearly as they had on previous days, their outline etched darkly against the blue heavens. Now it was difficult to see them at all. Occasionally it was just possible to glimpse a tall peak that thrust itself up

29

out of the flatness of the plains. Then it would be lost again as the dust storm blotted it out completely, erasing it as if some painter had come along and made some swift strikes with his brush, wiping it off the broad canvas.

In spite of the fact that he knew what to expect, that he had ridden storms such as this before, Neil felt himself tensing in the saddle as the curtain of yellow-white haze swept closer. Now it was so near that it was possible to see it moving, to see the strangely intermingled draperies that formed within its diffuse boundaries; rather like the sheets of dark rain that could be seen whenever the summer thunderstorms rolled in over the mountains, but more subtle and ominous.

The wind began to rise, plucking a little at the sleeves of his jacket, lifting the sand and dust from the ground all about them, hurling it over the plain in a faint sheet of yellow.

At their backs the sun had climbed higher into the darkening sky, but although it was now virtually at its zenith and the heat pressure lay on everything like the press of some hot, invisible hand, it was difficult to see the sun clearly. It was hidden now behind the thickening cloud of sand that came sweeping in from the far horizons. It was a long silence that clung about the wagon train now as it rumbled slowly forward at a snail-like pace, the wheels creaking and groaning, the axles grinding, the occasional slap of the reins against the rumps of the horses. The silence was made even more ominous and pronounced by the faint but rising shriek of the strengthening wind. Neil rode back along the train strung out over nearly half a mile of prairie, urging them to close up, shouting his warnings now at the top of his voice to make himself heard above the sickening howl of the wind in his ears.

The storm was on them with a suddenness that took everyone by surprise. One moment it seemed to be hanging back, lying low on the western horizon; the next it had closed in on them from all sides, blinding, searing the flesh wherever it was

30

exposed, clogging the mouth and nostrils, making eyes useless, the countless millions of irritating grains working their way into the folds of the skin, into the necks and sleeves of tunics and dresses, finding its way into a million crevices along the wagons. The horses stumbled forward, weary animals, moving into that terrible yellow wall of sand and dust.

Head lowered, his bandana over the lower half of his face, eyes narrowed to mere slits, trying desperately to draw pure air into his aching lungs, Neil rode up and down the entire length of the train, keeping it in motion, knowing inwardly with a sick certainty that the moment one of those wagons stopped, or got itself bogged down in the drifting sand, they were finished. He would have to call a halt then, and at the moment that was the last thing he wanted to do. So long as he could keep them moving forward, it lessened the time they would be in the middle of that terrible storm.

How long it would take to blow itself out he did not know. Sometimes they lasted for less than an hour, at others they could blow for the best part of a day. The ground was as level as a table, and there were no hills where they could shelter while the storm blew itself out around them.

The racing yellow cloud snapped across the last sliver of blue-grey sky and the sun was blotted out entirely now so that they moved in a strange and frightening half-world of dimness and discomfort. There was a terrible savagery in that storm as if nature were daring men to defy her, to put their strength against hers. Primitive and raw, the dust storm swept along the whole length of the train, a solid blanket of grains hurled by the wind. It was old to him, having experienced it before, but still frightening. The wind was a roaring thunder in his ears, blotting out all other sound. He fought to keep his head lifted, pushed his sight as far as possible into the yellow-ness that surrounded him. Less than ten feet away he could just make out the canvas top of the nearest wagon, swaying

31

from side to side as the driver, crouched down low on the tongue, urged the horses forward as fast as they could go. But already they had slowed to a crawl and nothing on earth, Neil knew, would encourage them to go any faster now. He tried to see the wagon directly ahead, could see nothing at first, then barely made out the vaguely seen shape that appeared and then vanished tantalisingly between great gusts of dust.

It was going to be very difficult, if not utterly impossible for them to keep together. He knew that with a sudden certainty and felt a sharp sense of loss at the back of his mind, tightening the muscles of his ribs.

Turning his mount, he rode back along the trail. The wind was now at his back, he was riding with the storm, able to breathe just a little more easily. He passed four wagons, glimpsed the men and women huddled down on the seats, holding on for grim death as they humped and swayed from side to side, the fear-crazed horses hauling savagely on the reins so that it was all the men could do to keep them in check.

Neil felt the sickness in the pit of his stomach growing as he made his way to the very end of the train. He passed the last but one wagon, then pushed his way forward, eyes peering under the lowered black brows, searching for any sign of the last wagon in the train, for Virginia Millais and her son. He picked his way forward slowly and carefully. It was out of the question to try to pick up the sound of the wagon above the high-pitched shriek of the wind in his ears. He had to rely on seeing it through that whirling, sweeping wall of yellow.

The minutes lengthened and still there was no sign of the wagon. Was it possible that he himself had worked his way off the trail, that he was moving around in a circle, unable to orientate himself? Had he passed within a few yards of it and yet not seen it, not even known of its presence there?

He turned his head in every direction, trying to make out anything that moved, a sense of terrible urgency riding him now. He knew that he had to find that wagon within the next five minutes or the chances were that he might never find it again. There was no sign that the storm was abating, blowing itself out; the wind still blew with a fierceness that snatched away his breath, and there was no let-up in the fury of the storm.

Four minutes later, when he was on the point of giving up, of turning his sorrel back into the teeth of the storm, trying to search in another direction, he caught a fragmentary glimpse of something dark, something only vaguely seen on his right. Swinging the head of the sorrel towards it, he kicked in his spurs, felt the horse bound under him, feet sliding a little in the loose sand underfoot.

A moment later the unmistakable shape of the wagon materialised out of the yellow gloom, directly in front of him. He could just see the figure of the woman, her face swathed in a broad handkerchief, still gripping the reins. The wheels were barely moving, the two horses straining clumsily and awkwardly.

Scarcely pausing to think, Neil turned his stud, brought the sorrel alongside the wagon, then slid out of the saddle, coming up beside the woman in a single, smooth movement. He took the reins from her as she moved, unresisting, further along the seat. There was no sign of the boy and Neil guessed that he had taken shelter from the storm inside the wagon.

A moment while Neil's hand flicked the long whip against the hides of the horses, a moment while they seemed to hesitate. Then they strained forward and the wagon began to roll more quickly, edging its way in the direction Neil judged the rest of the wagon train to be.

It was quite impossible to see the trail, impossible to guess if they were headed in the right direction. All he could do at that moment was to keep the horses moving into the storm, trust that the wind had not changed direction, and that the rest of the train was still doing the same. There were so many things which could go wrong, he knew, and the chances were great that once the storm lifted they would find themselves isolated, with no sign of the wagon train.

'Where in God's name are the others?' called the woman. 'We lost sight of them just after the storm began.'

'They'll be just up ahead,' he shouted reassuringly, trying to look confident in spite of the growing sense of uneasiness in him. 'All we can do now is ride out the storm, wait for it to die down. Then we'll join the others. They won't be able to make very good time, either.'

'I told Johnny to stay back there, out of the way.'

She leaned forward a little, only the slits of her eyes showing over the kerchief.

Slowly they moved into the heart of the gigantic storm that swept over the wide, stretching distances of the plain, the sky darkened, the triumphant sound of the wind a harsh, endless shriek in the ears, the rustling of millions of individual grains of sand grinding along the wagon, tearing at the canvas, threatening to rip it into shreds. Even the ground underfoot seemed to be sliding and shaking as if the sea were rippling about them, long waves moving in and then vanishing behind the wagon. It was an incredible thing, a frightening thing, nature gone wild and turned insane.

The long minutes passed, still the storm blew about them in its full and awesome fury. Neil found it becoming more difficult to breathe, and every breath that he did take burned like fire in his aching lungs, pounded in his throat and chest.

No sight of the other wagons in the train, no distant sound in their ears for all lesser sounds were blotted out by the terrible shriek of the wind, the grating of the sand on the metal and canvas of the wagon. It was impossible even to talk, for the words were torn from their lips and tossed into the yellow haze.

Out of the corner of his vision, Neil saw the woman's face, lowered against the whirling dust, tight with fear and apprehension. He could guess at the thoughts that must have been

34

passing through her mind at that moment. They were lost. They did not even know if they were still on the trail. There were no landmarks they could see, and it was as if they were utterly isolated in that tremendous, howling wilderness of yellow dust and alkali.

'What can we do now?' The woman turned and shouted the words in his ear, bending close so that he might hear her.

He shook his head. 'Nothing for the moment. We'll just have to ride out the storm and hope we can pick up the others once it blows itself out. Maybe it would be easier for you inside. I'll call you if I need you.'

She shot him a thankful glance, turned and moved into the wagon, pulling the thick canvas tightly over the opening. Neil turned on the tongue of the wagon, holding the leather tightly in his hands. The horses moved forward slowly now, fighting their way through the dancing, swirling haze that roared about them, choking and blinding. His own sorrel moved alongside the wagon. It needed no rope to tether it to the back.

There were long moments now, minutes which dragged themselves out into individual eternities of uncomfortable straining, choking agony. Leaning forward against the thrusting pressure of the storm, Neil pushed his sight through the yellow haze, looking for any sign of the other wagons.

Deep down inside, he knew that it would be unlikely that he would catch any glimpse of them until the storm died, blew itself out. Even then there was the possibility that he was driving the wagon in a tight circle, was now miles from the others. There was the chance that they, too, had become scattered, even though he had impressed on them the necessity for keeping close to each other, within sight of the wagon in front.

In the past too many wagons had been lost entirely in dust storms such as this whenever they blazed their way over the stretching wilderness, and they had not been found until months, perhaps years, later, with the bleached bones telling

35

their own pathetic story of men and women who had died many miles from the nearest waterhole, who had wandered through the sun-caked desert until they had died of thirst.

If there was a hell anywhere, he thought savagely, surely this was it. This terrible curtain of choking dust which never once let up in its mad whine, which shut off all sight, worked its way painfully into the folds of the skin, mingled irritatingly with the sweat that coursed down the cheeks and along the muscles of his back and chest, worked into his clothing so that there was not a single inch of his flesh which was not on fire with the itching particles that tore and chafed at his body.

Back inside the wagon it would be little better. It had been a futile gesture telling the woman to go inside. The sand would find its way everywhere, and within minutes of the storm blowing up and swallowing them in its yellow mist, the interior of the wagons would be covered with sand and alkali, not a single inch escaping.

The wagon lurched as one of the wheels hit an upthrusting boulder. For a second it threatened to tilt over on to its side, and Neil fought savagely to right it. His eyes were blinking as he tried to see in front of him. They were driving over rough, uneven terrain now, not the kind of smooth, flat ground he expected on the trail. Another lurch as he fought for control. Then the canvas at his back parted, was twitched aside, and Virginia Millais peered out at him. Her eyes were wide now, staring up at him in a brief moment of brilliance.

Suddenly frightened eyes. Then her gaze flickered towards the rearing canyon walls that suddenly loomed up in front of them, crushing in on either side of the wagon. Neil sucked in a sharp breath, cursed himself for not realising this possible reason for the sudden increase in the shrieking howl of the wind. That sudden sharp jump in its speed ought to have warned him that the wind was moving along a constricted path, that they were entering a narrow gorge.

Clumsily, awkwardly, the wagon moved between the red sandstone walls. He tried to see where they were going, knowing now that the only thing he could do was to let the horses pick their own gait, choose their own path, rely on that strange animal instinct which might guide them through this new danger.

'Get back in there,' Neil yelled at the top of his voice. He pulled hard on the leather as one of the horses reared, threatened to bolt. He did not even bother to turn his head to see if she had obeyed him. Everything now depended on them being able to ease their way between these tall walls of sandstone, trusting that it was not a box canyon, that at the end of it they would find a dead end.

The wagon lurched as the rough surface of the canyon wall slid by less than an inch on one side. His sorrel had dropped behind. Perhaps it had already taken fright and bolted into the storm. The thought crossed his mind briefly, then he thrust it away. If that had happened, there was certainly nothing he could do about it now.

Somehow they had to work their way out of this canyon, out into more open country. There, with the immediate danger lessened, it might be possible for them to ride out the storm. That they were well off the trail, he now realised. But there was nothing for them now but to go on and trust to Providence that they were not too far away, that they would find themselves in sight of the others when the storm passed.

Thunder from the roaring sweep of the wind. Thunder from the millions of red and yellow grains. His ears hurt with the sound of it. His eyes burned as if they were on fire, the dust having worked its way under the lids, blinding and sore every time he blinked.

If only it were possible to see, he would have felt easier in his mind. It was the fact that his vision was limited to less than five yards that added immeasurably to the danger.

Then, as suddenly as it had begun, the storm was leaving. Neil lifted his head slowly. The whine of the wind was no longer quite as loud or as shrill as it had been just a few minutes earlier. For a few seconds he had the impression that it was nothing more than his imagination. Then he found that he could make out the far end of the canyon, that directly in front of them the floor of the ravine widened, the rearing walls moving away from the trail, and fifty yards ahead lay open country. The sky was noticeably lighter now. The ominous yellowness was fading appreciably, and he could make out the position of the sun overhead, a dull patch of light that was growing brighter with every passing second.

He pushed the kerchief tighter around his face, breathing through it. As a filter against the whirling grains, it was remarkably efficient, but it tended to become clogged with the alkali, rubbing his cheeks and chin raw and making it difficult to breathe through it after some minutes.

Narrowing his eyes, he stared straight in front of him. As he watched, the dark yellow curtain rolled across the sky, the ochre colour changed swiftly to blue, and the sun came out, harsh and brilliant, glaring down at them from the broad heavens. Jerking the kerchief from around his face, he sucked in deep breaths of clean, pure air, expanding his chest as he drew it down into his lungs. Gradually the tight ache in his body went away, he found himself able to see more clearly, although there was still a dull red haze hovering in front of his vision.

They came out into the open country and he reined the horses, standing on the wooden tongue of the wagon, shading his eyes against the harsh glare of the sun, peering in all directions, looking for the other wagons in the train. Virginia Millais stepped out through the opening in the canvas. Her face was streaked with sand and dust, and it had worked its way into her long hair. She licked her dry, cracked lips and rubbed at her cheeks absently.

'Can you see any sign of the others, Mister Roberts?' she asked in a throaty voice, blinking her eyes against the glare.

Slowly he shook his head.

'We must have wandered some way off the trail, Ma'am,' he said. 'Wouldn't have thought they would be too far away. The storm would've slowed them just as much as it did us, and this is pretty open country hereabouts. Ought to be able to spot 'em if they're anywhere within fifteen miles or so.'

'I don't see them.'

'They've got to be around somewhere.' He clambered down from the wagon. 'We'll have to find 'em before dark. By morning they could be clear into the next state, and then we'll never catch up with 'em.'

'What do you intend to do? You're not leaving us here, are you?'

There was a note of apprehensive fear in her voice now as she looked at him anxiously. Neil had moved away from the wagon, then he turned.

'Have no fear of that, Ma'am, but I reckon there ain't no chance of picking that train out from down here. I was thinking that maybe if I was to climb up to the top of that ravine I might get a better view over the country around here, might be able to pick 'em out more easily. There's just the chance that we made even better time than they did, and they're still moving up behind us. If that's so, we won't see 'em until they get level with us, and it might be dark by then.'

He turned and began to make his way up the steep, rough slope where the sheer walls of the canyon lifted out of the flatness of the desert. Behind them, in the direction they had just travelled, it was impossible to see anything, for the ravine blocked off all vision. It was hard work, climbing that steep slope. His fingers clawed and hooked on to outjutting spurs of rock as he hauled himself up, feet searching for tiny footholds where he could find them. More than once his feet slipped from under him and he was forced to hang there by his hands, shoulder muscles aching with the tearing strain of taking his whole weight on his arms.

Whipping himself around, grasping tightly at the ledge of rock above his head, he swung outward into space and downward, feet sliding off the inch-wide ledge on which he had been standing. For a split second his fingers threatened to loose their hold, sending him pitching downward to the floor of the canyon some forty feet below him. He dropped until his chest scraped hard on the jagged rock, the impact knocking all of the wind out of his body. Desperately he fought to retain his hold, heaving himself upward with all of the strength in his arm and shoulder muscles, drawing agonising gulps of air down into his straining lungs.

His vision blurred for a moment. Then he managed to get one elbow hooked over the sharp edge of the ledge above him and hung there for what seemed an eternity – but which could only have been a few seconds – his feet digging against the hard surface of the sandstone, toes kicking savagely as he struggled to make a hole for himself, a slight foothold in the otherwise completely smooth surface.

Swiftly he pulled himself up a couple of inches, until he had his other elbow over the ledge, and for the moment he had anchored himself securely to the face of the canyon wall.

Gradually, moving his toes up and down, he found lodgement for his feet, lifted himself slowly and gently, an inch at a time, his arms and elbows taking the strain from the very insecure foothold he had found for himself. A pause, then he gathered his strength, gritted his teeth tightly in his head and made the upward lunge that carried him on to the ledge, where he crawled to safety.

Sitting upright, he brushed the filming of sweat from his forehead with the back of his sleeve, then glanced above him. The top of the canyon was now less than twelve feet away, but here the rocky wall bulged outward a little, like a huge wave of stone, frozen just at the very moment of breaking. It was not going to be an easy matter easing his way around that shoulder of rock, he reflected, but if he wanted to reach the top it had to be done, and there was no sense in sitting there and thinking about it, wasting precious minutes.

He glanced down for a moment and could just make out the shape of the wagon standing where he had left it, with the figure of Virginia Millais staring up at him, her head tilted back in the sunlight so that she could see him better. He saw that the canvas flap of the wagon had been thrown back and Johnny Millais was peering up at him too, eyes shaded, squinting up against the harsh glare of the burning sunlight.

He drew in a deep breath, flexed his hands for a moment, then rose carefully to his feet, stood quite still for a moment on the narrow ledge, finding a firm and secure foothold before he made his final attempt on the rocky face.

Gingerly he edged his heels back until they were poised over the very edge of the ledge, shuffling them a little until he was sure of his stance; then he moved around the blistered, bulging face of rock, body flattened against the sandstone, his belly drawn in until it seemed to be touching his backbone.

Inching sideways, he found the narrow gully he had hoped might be there, knew that it would be relatively simple to work his way up it now. Pulling himself up with caution, he finally reached the top and threw himself forward, rolling a little way to make certain that he was well away from the lip of the canyon, before sitting up and staring about him.

Far off to the south-east he could just make out the misty cloud of the storm as it receded over the face of the desert. It stretched across a vast stretch of country and, from that distance, it seemed to be in no real hurry to move.

Then he lowered his gaze and almost gasped out aloud in his relief. Down there, perhaps two, three miles away and, as he had half-suspected, behind them, were the other wagons, a string of dark dots, partially hidden in the dust of their own drag, edging forward, one behind the other. He reckoned that in less than half an hour they would have drawn level with the canyon, but about a mile to the south.

Relief from the pressing feeling that they were completely lost was so great that for several moments he could do nothing but stare out at them, holding his breath. He guessed that, having to maintain contact with each other and knowing that the danger of getting lost was ever-present, Clem Jackson had deliberately slowed their pace. He let his breath go in a long sigh, waved an arm to the woman down below, saw her lift her right arm in answer. Then he began his descent. Going down was, if anything, even more difficult and hazardous than the climb had been but somehow he made it without mishap and walked over to Virginia Millais.

'They're over in that direction.' He pointed. 'About two miles away. I reckon we ought to meet up with them in an hour or so. They'll probably spot us the minute we get clear of these rocks. They've been hiding us until now.'

She nodded slowly and the utter relief showed clearly on her face. Her hand brushed some of the dust from her cheeks and lips, and she blinked it away from around her eyes.

They went back to the wagon, Neil hitched his sorrel to the back, and they moved off, heading into the sun glare. The heat lay like a vast pressure over the mesquite-dotted desert now and he reached down for the canteen nearby, offered it to Virginia first, then took a deep drink himself feeling the warm, brackish liquid trickle down his throat in a slow, refreshing stream. His dry, parched mouth absorbed a lot of it even before it reached his throat, but after a moment he felt better and his swollen tongue moved more easily around his mouth and lips.

They rode out from the deep shadow of the canyon, headed for the other wagons which could be clearly seen now. It was too far away for either of them to be sure whether they had been seen by any of the others, but as they drew nearer Neil saw that the line of wagons was turning slowly, heading in their direction.

Then they were near enough to make out the large figure of Clem Jackson, seated on the front of the leading wagon, his huge hand lifted in greeting. They came up to the others, Neil pulling sharply on the leather.

'We thought you were lost,' boomed Jackson's loud voice. 'What happened back there?'

'Lost contact with you during the storm. Only thing to do was to keep on going and hope to find you again when it blew over. We finished up in that narrow canyon yonder, but I managed to spot you from the top. We must have drifted some ways from the trail.'

The other nodded his huge head in agreement. He turned his head and stared towards the west, where the mountains in the distance were as far off as ever, still snuggling down on the skyline, dull blue in the streaming sunlight.

'Where do you reckon we ought to make camp, Roberts? This don't look too good a place to me, not with that ravine less than two miles away. Anybody could be hiding there, and we'd know nothing about it.'

It was true; they would have to continue driving the tired animals further, through all of the heat of the long afternoon and the early evening. He wondered how far the horses would go before they fell in the traces. The storm would have taken far more out of them than was visible on the surface. The biting, scouring sand grains would have worked their way into the animals' throats and lungs, tearing, clogging and abrading. If they didn't rest up soon, get plenty of water, it might mean the end of some of them.

'Keep them moving,' he said quietly. 'We'll camp as soon as we get to an open space, or near water.'

3
Trail West

Night reached across the heavens from the east and the train camped on the banks of a small, shallow stream that came bubbling down between high banks of hard mud from the north. On the far side the ground rose steeply and became more rugged, and here and there were patches of dense forest, first-year pine as far as Neil could make out – and this presented more danger to them. True, it would offer them shade from the burning, blistering heat of the sun and the ground underfoot would be easier, but there was too much shelter for any of Sherman's men, too close to the trail, so that they might attack without warning. It meant that they would have to ride with eyes and ears open continually, that he would have to scout ahead of the train as it rumbled slowly west through this country. They were getting closer to the Sherman ranch now, and they could expect trouble, big trouble, at any time, once they crossed the stream. But for the time being, for that night, this was undoubtedly the best place they had found so far for making camp.

The men drew lots for the first night guard and the quiet voices of the unlucky pair could be heard in the darkness on the edge of the camp. The fire burned low and then went out unheeded. There was no point in keeping the fire going that night. Although the Conestoga wagons themselves would be readily spotted, even in the darkness, a fire would give away their position to watching eyes quite easily, and there seemed little reason for pinpointing their presence as accurately as that.

There was action down at the water's edge as men scrubbed the dust and alkali from their bodies, the cold water burning and stinging their skin where it had been scorched by the sun through the thick, coating of dust. Jackson cursed softly as he rubbed at his arms and face, then straightened, shook his head like a dog coming out of the water, slicked his hair back with the tips of his fingers.

'This storm was somethin' I never want to go through again,' he growled throatily. He looked across at Neil. 'You bin through one of 'em before?'

Neil nodded. 'Several times,' he affirmed. 'Always they seem to get worse. Could be that it's because you forget what it was like the last time and you always seem to think that it wasn't too bad.'

'Don't reckon it will be like that from now on. We seem to have left the desert behind us.'

'There's still danger ahead.'

'Sherman's men?' The reply was a question.

'That's right. They may decide not to attack us until they're sure they can finish us. They won't be partial to risking their own necks when they can ambush us somewhere along that trail and cut us down without too much risk to themselves. and those trees up there will make an excellent place for an ambush.'

'That's more'n likely,' agreed Jackson.

He rubbed himself dry. They walked slowly back to the camp where the fires were little more than glowing embers in the darkness.

'I'll ride out at first light. Take a look-see, just in case.' He stood in front of the dying fire. 'If my hunch is right, they'll follow us for a little way into those trees. An Indian would lose his way out there in the desert if he tried to track us down and, after that storm, our tracks would be completely wiped out. That desert was made for fellas on the dodge.'

Jackson grinned broadly. 'You're right.'

He sank down on to his haunches by the glowing embers. The words were flat and cold. Neil sat down opposite the other and watched the huge man's eyes grow a mist as they stared out into the cold darkness, out over the stream, over the hills beyond as if he could see clear out over that vast and wild, untamed country, clear to the borders of California.

What was the other thinking, Neil wondered. Why was he so anxious to get to California? Men had found gold there, he knew, rich red gold, and there had been the usual rush from the east, wagon trains setting out across the face of a continent, thrusting the frontier westward, rolling it back across the page of American history. There had been this sudden movement from the East to the West, many thousands of people all heading in the same direction.

True, there were inevitably some who turned aside, found a place to their liking, and stayed. There were countless others who never made it at all. But some got through, though it could not be said that the trail westward had yet been blazed. Perhaps that was what Jackson was hoping for. To be the leader of the first large wagon train to blaze the trail westward.

'You still figure that you're doing the right thing, bringing this train out along this trail?' he asked softly, keeping his gaze fixed on the other's face.

Jackson looked up and there was something about his features which surprised Neil. It was as if a tiny devil had jumped up behind the other's eyes, stood there exposed and naked for a long moment before sinking back down into the depths again, out of sight. Then the big man's lips thinned, drew closer to the square teeth. 'It's the only thing we can do now,' he said harshly.

'I suppose that you realise you're risking the lives of

46

everyone in these wagons?'

'I only know that I warned them all of the difficulties they might have to face and that if they paid to join the train, then I'd lead them all the way to California, but they had to stick the trail. There was to be no turning back no matter how hard it got, or how tough the going was. They knew that and they all agreed before we set out.'

'But I wonder whether any of them really knew what lay in store for them. I know, because I've lived out here most of my life. I know the kind of men you'll find here, hard, ruthless men, most of them with no respect for the law, men who would kill and think nothing of it if it meant they got their own way. And there's nothing surer than that these men don't want any nesters here.'

Jackson set his lips into a tight, thin line.

'The country is growing up, Roberts. Sooner or later, everybody has got to be made to realise that. If we're to be a nation at all, the country has got to be settled, and by men and women like those in the wagons, not by the killers and outlaws who're here at the moment. The Government realises this, which is why they're making the land available to settlers.'

'Mebbe so. But the settlers are going to have to fight for every inch of that land, and most of them don't stand a chance against professional gunmen. You know that as well as I do.'

'Sure I know it. But there ain't a thing I can do about it. I'm being paid to lead them out to California. That's what I aim to do and I don't mean to let Sherman, or any of his hired killers, stop me.'

Neil lifted his brows a little, then shrugged. He got heavily to his feet.

'I hope that none of us regret it,' he said. He shrugged. 'I reckon I'm going to catch up some sleep.'

He got his blanket and rolled himself into it, lying close to the fire, with his Colts within easy reach of his hands. Jackson remained sitting by the dying fire, staring morosely into the red embers. Despite the other's bold front, Neil guessed that he was inwardly uneasy, that he had been turning over in his mind many of the things he had mentioned. They had been plain lucky so far, luckier than they had deserved. Either those three dead men back there had not yet been missed or found, or Sherman's boys were playing it safe, taking their time, knowing that they would have plenty of opportunities to strike before the wagon trail let the Sherman spread.

In the morning, before most of the others were awake, he saddled his sorrel, then swung up, put his mount to the stream and forded it swiftly, pulling up the horse on the far bank. Here there was a slope of sparse, dry grass where the desert seemed reluctant to release its hold on the territory, stretching its dry, bony fingers across the water.

Presently he rode among the tall, straight trees, felt the cool, sharp smell of the pines in his nostrils. It was cool here for the sun had not yet risen and the dawn was merely a brightening line of silver grey in the east. The place held a strange fascination, almost as if there were a secret there, but as he rode, keeping his eyes and ears open, he found nothing there, certainly nothing to indicate that anyone had ridden that trail recently.

Coming out into the open again, there was a gentle slope leading down into a wide, open plain and, in the distance, he could make out the cattle, a large herd, possibly two thousand head, grazing on the rich grass.

He sat saddle for a while, studying his situation, looking keenly about him. There was no sign of any herders with the cattle, they seemed to have been left to their own devices, which struck him instantly as odd. A herd that size would have men guarding it, unless Sherman was extremely sure of himself, knew that there would be no trouble.

But there was another thing which made him feel a trifle uneasy. The trail led down into that wide valley and the wagons would be forced to make their way past the herd. Those cattle might be on the mean side and would not be used to wagons.

Shrugging the thought away, he turned back into the brush. Maybe at that very moment Sherman was planning to save him the trouble of trying to get the wagon train past those cattle.

It was grey dawn when he rode back into the trees, and he heard the sound in the near distance very clearly. Swiftly reining the sorrel, he leaned forward in the saddle, straining his ears, waiting for the sound to be repeated, but there was no further noise and he could see nothing. But he had been certain that he had heard a man's voice yelling orders.

Then, looking upwards, he discovered a man seated on the lip of the trail, high among the trees, less than three hundred feet away. Even as he stared at the other, the man brought a rifle to his shoulder, took quick aim and fired, the bullet striking the dirt of the trail wide of Neil's position. The sorrel flung up its head at the sharp, flat report of the rifle, then Neil had dug in his heels, making a run for it towards the nearest clump of trees, head low, lying over the saddle to present a more difficult target to the bushwhacker.

Another shot drummed through the air very close to his head and buried itself in the trunk of a nearby tree, slashing the brown bark away and revealing a deep gash in the trunk. Then Neil had flung himself from the saddle before the other could take aim again, his Colts whispering from their worn leather holsters, snapping into his hands, in spite of the jarring agony of the impact of hitting the ground, knocking the air from his lungs in a loud gasp.

He rolled over on to his side, brought up the guns and snapped a couple of shots in the direction of the man. The marksman on the rim of the trail continued to pump shots methodically into the brush close to where Neil lay, trying to seek out his target, laying a pattern of bullets into the rough foliage. It was clear that he had lost Neil for the moment, but the lead was flying disturbingly close and Neil knew that it was only a matter of time before the other hit him, or the sound of rifle shots brought more of these gunhawks running to the scene. It would not take them long to surround him, cut him off from the rest of the men with the train back across the stream.

The firing ceased for a moment. The marksman would be taking time to reload, he figured. Maybe he was working his way closer, too, trying to improve his position, get within sighting and killing range.

In the mesquite, the daylight brightened. Soon the sun would bound up from below the horizon, flooding everything in its harsh light, and he would find it more difficult to get away then. He sucked in a deep breath, crouching down among the thick, tangled undergrowth, then slithered forward, eyes alert, trying to pick out the position of the other.

Far off he thought he heard the drumming of approaching horses and knew that this could be some of the other's friends riding up. If he stayed there the chances were that they would circle around him and take him from the rear while the first man kept him pinned down.

Pouching one of the Colts, he carefully parted the thorn bushes in front of him and peered through the opening, slitting his eyes, trying to catch an upward glance at the rim of the trail where the other had been a few moments before. He could see nothing there now, knew instinctively that the other had slipped away, was possibly much closer now and, with that rifle, would be able to stop him at a much greater distance than he could with only a revolver.

Taking off his hat, he balanced it on a short stick, pushed it up slowly, then pulled it down swiftly as the single shot rang out from less than a hundred yards away and a little to one side. There was a great hole drilled through the crown of the hat proving that the other was no mean marksman and that he had circled much further than Neil had anticipated.

Swinging around, he loosed off a couple of shots into the undergrowth. There followed no sound, and he guessed that neither of his bullets had found its mark.

Moving to one side, he began to circle himself, keeping to the right of the hidden marksman. His sorrel was standing a little distance away near a clump of trees. Careful as he was, the other must have heard the slight sound for more shots rang out and the fire sang though the trees, following him. He scuttled for one of the trees, flung himself down behind it, steadying himself. He knew now exactly where the other was, not too far away, certainly close enough to be reached by a revolver bullet. Still no sign of any more of these gunhawks. But he guessed that even then they were spurring their mounts forward as fast as they could ride, heading in the direction of the shooting.

Knowing the kind of man who had tried to shoot him down from ambush, Neil felt a cold wash of anger sweep through him, drowning out every other emotion in his mind, changing him, chilling him. Patience made rock out of him as he crouched there so that it seemed he could have waited for ever for the other to betray himself and make the wrong move. It was waiting that would break the other down, he felt sure of that.

Unfortunately, the other would also be aware that several of his friends were on their way, would arrive on the scene, too, and if he could keep Neil pinned down during that time, they stood a good chance of picking him off with little risk to themselves.

Somewhere, close at hand, he heard a horse begin to thresh, knew that it was not his own but that belonging to the man who had tried to kill him. He thinned his lips and grinned tightly in anticipation. At last he heard a sharp sigh come from the other as he let his breath go from between his lips. Swiftly Neil brought up his Colts in that direction, fired off a short volley into the brush, then went forward, slowly and cautiously, guns held ready. It had been that sudden need for air which had

51

betrayed the other's presence, and the man seemed to have realised that almost instantly, for scarcely had the rolling echoes of Neil's shots died away than the other began to fire in his direction, shooting blindly and recklessly, without taking proper aim, hoping perhaps that if he fired a sufficient number of bullets, at least one of them was bound to find its mark.

Some part of his mind counted the other's shots, then he had plunged into the dense undergrowth, feeling the long thorny strands tug at his legs as he strode forward. He meant to make his man back away until he was forced to come out into the open space on top of the trail's rim, where the other had stood before when he had first opened fire. Once there, the bushwhacker would make a perfect target.

'You made a big mistake trying to gun me down, stranger,' he called softly, skipping to one side as the shot he had been expecting snapped through the air close to where his head had been a split second earlier. The other could not have many more slugs left in his rifle, would be forced to reload, unless he cared to rely on Colts. A pause, then Neil heard the other suddenly crashing through the brush as he turned on his heel and took to flight, back through the trees to where he must have tethered his mount.

He made out the scrape of the other's body through the tangled bushes, then caught a fragmentary glimpse of the gunman as he darted across an open patch of ground among the trees. Neil laid his gun along the running figure and squeezed the trigger gently, felt the Colt back against his wrist, saw the man fall forward on to his face and lie still.

Running forward, he went down beside the other, turned him over. The man was a stranger to him but he had the stamp of the gunhawk written all over his squat features. It hadn't been a long wait, but those other men would be close to the trail now, wouldn't have been wasting time getting to the scene of the shooting. He caught the bridle of his own mount, swung himself up swiftly into the saddle and rode out along the trail, crouching low in case there were any shots headed in his direction.

A spate of shots whistled past him as he rode. Then he had swung around a bend in the trail, was out of sight of the crowd of gunmen at his back. By the time he reached the stream most of the wagons were already over, the horses pulling them up the steep bank, rocking and swaying the Conestogas from side to side as they dragged them, dripping from the water.

The sun had risen now, was lying close to the eastern horizon, big and red, full of the promise of more heat to come, but not yet with any real indication of the full heat which would develop around high noon.

Jackson came forward, looked at the dust that was heavy on Neil's jacket, where it caked his sweat-stained pants. Neil tilted his canteen to his lips, drank deeply.

'We heard shooting up there in the trees,' said the big man, speaking almost casually. 'Trouble?'

'Afraid so. There was one of those hombres waiting for me on top of the trail overhang among the trees. I reckon he's dead now, but several of his pals came riding up just as I got away. They'll be waiting for us in the brush.'

Jackson considered that, rubbing his flaming red beard, then he nodded ponderously.

'Reckon that since we know where they are, we might as well get moving.' He lifted a hand to halt the onward moving wagons for a moment. 'What would your advice be? Stay here and try to fight 'em off if they decided to rush us at the stream?'

'Depends on the men in the wagons, if they're willing to fight. Can they be trusted to handle their guns??'

'I reckon so. Don't worry none on that score. They'll fight.' A huge hand dropped on to Neil's shoulder as he slid from the saddle. The other's laugh was loud. 'I'll warn everybody what to expect, tell the women and kids to keep inside the

53

wagons, and to stay down. That canvas won't stop a bullet.'

It was a blunt speech, but then Jackson was a blunt man. Neil waited while the other strode along the line of wagons, speaking to the men seated on each, saw the women and children move inside, saw the men reach out and loosen the long-barrelled Winchesters from their scabbards, check that they were loaded and ready for use. Jackson came back, taking a long-bladed knife from its leather sheath. He tested the edge with his thumb, balanced it carefully in the palm of his hand for a moment, his face dark. Then he glanced up sharply, his lips twisted into a vicious grin that was almost a snarl, showing the square teeth.

'Right, Roberts. Let's go!'

A wave of the huge right arm, then the wagons began to roll forward, away from the stream, wheels and axles creaking, the canvas tops shaking and swaying from side to side as they moved over the rough, stony ground, climbing up to the tall trees that dotted the earth on either side of the trail.

In among the trees were huge, massive boulders which hung over the trail. Neil had spotted these on his ride out that morning, could guess where the killers would make their attack. It was possible that they would not be expecting the wagons to roll into the trees now that he knew that they were there, and the gunhawks would be debating whether to move down to the stream and attack them there. On either side of the slow-moving train rode grim-faced men on horseback, the outriders, their Colts in their hands, eyes flicking from side to side, alert for trouble, ready to meet it no matter from which direction it came.

The column had formed, the leading wagon reached the top of the stony rise and moved for the trees. Neil could feel the tenseness rising in him now, could sense the tightening of the muscles of his arms and chest. He switched his gaze from side to side, looking for the first glint of sunlight on the shiny steel of a rifle barrel that would give away the

54

position of the waiting gunmen.

There was the feel of eyes watching their every move. Jackson motioned to the riders to swing forward. No point in taking too many chances if they were to get through without too many casualties.

Neil spurred his stud forward, heels kicking into the horse's flanks. He was followed by Tom Jessup and the other men of the outrider team. A gun flared among the rocks, half-hidden by the fringe of trees. The harsh, flat sound bucketed in the clinging stillness that lay over everything, breaking over the rumble of the horses and the wagons. One of the riders close by suddenly clutched at his shoulder where a red stain began to bubble through the cloth of his shirt, dribbling between his fingers. He swayed in the saddle, managed to stay upright, dropping back towards the wagons.

More shots bucketed out of the rocks. Neil narrowed his eyes, swung the sorrel round sharply, brought up his Colt and loosed off a couple of swiftly sighted shots, saw a dark figure hidden in a cleft among the boulders suddenly throw up its arms and pitch forward, sliding down the smooth face of the rocks to land on a narrow ledge some ten feet above the trail.

Fanning out around the rim of the wagon train, the other riders joined in, racing past the slow-moving horses that hauled the Conestogas, heading for the bend in the trail where the shooting was coming from. A bullet drummed over Neil's head as he crouched low over the neck of the sorrel. Then he reached a spot less than five feet from the trail's edge, flung himself down out of the saddle, and moved swiftly into the trees, pushing his way forward through the tangled brush and scrub. The other men were slipping from their mounts, urged on by Jackson.

One of the gunhawks lifted his head, tried to bring up his rifle to line it up on Neil's chest, then collapsed backward as the other's bullet found its mark. Behind them, the men in the wagons were firing too, adding the weight of their rifle fire to the sharper, more frequent sounds of the Colts.

Neil sank to the ground, flattened himself under a clump of mesquite, mindless of the tough bare branches that scratched and raked his face. He kept angling towards the left, detouring to get the extra cover, edging around the boulders among which the gunmen were hiding. When he was sure he had moved far enough to get around to the rear of them, he turned back, edging down the steep slope that overlooked the trail. Using what concealment the mesquite bushes afforded, he worked his way cautiously down the slope. The roar of the guns was a vast sound in his ears and occasionally a slug would tunnel through the branches around him and bury itself in the ground close to his body. Coming downslope into the deserted area to the rear of the boulders, he moved more carefully now, crawling forward an inch at a time, keeping his head low, judging the position of the gunslingers from the volume of their fire. Nearby a horse snickered and he froze instantly, keeping his body pressed tight towards the earth, listening for the faintest warning sound from dead ahead of him, which would tell him that the horse had given him away.

It came so suddenly, so close to him, far closer than he had imagined, that his taut nerves vibrated like plucked strings.

'Keep firing at those wagons, damn you! The rest of us will take care of those men in the trees.'

Neil sank to the ground, checked his guns. For a moment he lay quite motionless, his scalp still tingling at the narrow margin by which he had escaped blundering into the others. They were less than two feet away, directly below him, and now his straining ears picked out tiny sounds. A grunt and a low curse as some of the rifle fire from the wagons hummed and ricocheted off the boulders.

Cautiously, he began to ease his way forward, snakelike, through the tall coarse grass that grew at the top of the rocky incline. A kind of haze formed in front of his eyes as he held his breath, then risked a quick glance over the top of the rocks. The whining scream of a ricochet, fired from the wagons, screeched past him less than a foot away, but he ignored it. There were seven men directly below him, and one man stretched out full length on the rocks to the right. One glance was enough to tell him that there was nothing to fear from this man, he had been caught by the fire from below.

Very carefully he got to his feet, saw the men at the wagons lower their rifles as they spotted him, outlined in the harsh glare of the sunlight. For a moment he noticed the outlaws directly below him pause, obviously puzzled by the sudden cessation of firing from the train. Then one of them, more sharp-witted than the others, turned his head swiftly, then relaxed imperceptibly as he saw the twin Colts levelled at him.

''Jest turn around slow and easy,' Neil advised. 'I don't want to have to shoot any of you in the back, but I will if you make me.'

Slowly the men turned to look down the barrels of the guns Neil held at his sides. The barrels were still; stone steady. No use for any of the men to take the gamble and hope to outshoot him, but for an instant the thought crossed the mind of one of the men, lived briefly in his eyes. Then he shrugged, tossed his gun on to the rocks as the others did likewise.

'That's better.' Neil went down into the level patch among the rocks. Already the other men from the train were moving in, their rifles held steady on the gunslingers, covering their every move. Three of the men had been wounded and stood clutching their shoulders; one man badly hit, a film of whiteness under the leather of his face, the blood bubbling through his fingers with every breath that he took. He stood swaying against the tall rocks, strength and life bubbling out through the deep wound.

Keeping them covered, Neil called down to Clem Jackson,

and the giant of a man came climbing upward, moving with an agility that belied his tremendous size.

'What do we do with them, Roberts?' he grated. 'I never was one for shooting down men in cold blood, although I doubt if that goes for these *hombres*.'

Neil eyed the six men casually, saw the look of fear that showed in one man's eyes.

'You wouldn't do it,' muttered one of the men sullenly. 'Three of us are in bad shape. We're through. You wouldn't shoot now?'

'You tried to gun down helpless women and children in those wagons down there,' said Neil softly. There was an overtone of menace in his voice.

'We only carried out our orders,' said another of the gunslingers.

'Whose orders?'

Sullenly again: 'Jesse Sherman's.'

'We figured that. Any reason why he should send *hombres* like you out to kill innocent women and children?'

'This is his land, my friend,' said one of the wounded men with a snarl. 'He don't allow any wagon trains to move over it.'

'I understood that the Government were turning over most of the land to the settlers,' murmured Neil quietly. He snapped his gaze from one man to the next.

'He reckons that he bought it ten years ago. We can't argue that point with him. Besides, he's a big man in these parts. We're only paid to carry out his orders, and if he says we're to run any wagon trains off his spread, that's what we gotta do.'

'Reckon that if we had any sense, we'd shoot the lot of you. Rattlers like you don't deserve to go on living.'

'They'll ride back to the ranch and warn Sherman of what has happened if we let them go,' said Jessup harshly. He held his rifle warningly in his hands, his finger crooked tightly around the trigger.

'It's a mighty long way to the ranch from here, best part of five days' journey on foot.'

'You ain't going to—' started one of the men, then fell silent as Neil swung his gun once more to line the barrel up on his chest, stopping all further argument.

'Better check where they left their horses, set 'em loose. These *hombres* can walk home. I reckon they'll be footsore by the time they get back to Sherman's ranch.'

'But Simms, Carter and Sneddon are wounded, they need a doctor fast,' argued one of the men. He slitted his eyes, starting forward.

Tension crackled in the heat that lay over the trees, flowing though the branches, over the tumbled rocks. Neil's eyes were bright with challenge, hands rigid around the guns, fingers crooked over the triggers, ready. Another step by the gunhawk would have started those guns hammering. Anything or nothing if the tension lasted another ten seconds. Then the other stopped, stepped back, face sullen, lips twisted with hate.

'That's better,' nodded Neil tightly. 'Didn't reckon you were such a damned fool as that.'

'You're goin' to regret this, mister, ' growled the other harshly, the voice rasping from the depths of his chest. 'One of these days we're going to meet again, and the next time you won't have the drop on me. Then I'm going to kill you.'

'Maybe you'll get that chance,' grunted Neil. He lifted his gaze a fraction of an inch, saw the big man climbing over the rocks, searching for the horses. A moment later he heard Jackson's loud yell, followed by the stampeding thunder of hooves as the gunmen's mounts galloped from out of the trees, down the slope and across the plain. Jackson came back, gave a brusque nod.

'Reckon they won't be roundin' up those mounts in a hurry,' he said in a satisfied tone. 'You figgering on letting 'em go now?'

Neil nodded slowly. 'I guess so.' He turned to the others. 'Take your friends with you and get moving.'

It was simply said, but the words carried the promise of death if there was the slightest argument on the others' part. There was none. The gunslingers recognised the threat in the veiled tone. Slowly they made their way down through the rocks and boulders and into the trees. While the men from the wagons retrieved the guns which the gunhawks had discarded, Neil went back to his horse and mounted up. The wagons began to roll, bumping and swaying along the narrow trail between the tall trees. The timber was old first-growth pine, thick and massive at the butt, tapering in a smooth and flawless line towards the interwoven top covering which here made an almost solid umbrella against the sunlight. But if it kept out the light, it did not keep out the heat, and very soon sweat formed a film on his features, running down into his eyes and along his neck.

Far away he heard one solitary starved echo, a sharp blast of sound that might have been a gunshot, but he could not be sure, and it was not repeated. The tall, red-barked trees ran solemnly before them and somewhere over the thick arch of tangled boughs the noon sun blazed like an inferno fire, hidden by the green of the leaves, but here, under the trees, the air was blue-shadowed and still, with the hot smell of the pine needles in his nostrils. They broke cover by early afternoon, came out into the vast green plain that stretched away to the west. Far in the distance the cattle grazed, placid as yet, but how they might react to the wagons as they approached was something no man could have predicted, and there might be riders with the herd who would cause more trouble.

They held to the curve of the high ridge for as long at possible before dropping to the plain, heading west towards the distant herd on the shoulder of the low hills. Back of them, the mountains lifted to the unsullied arch of the heavens. Overhead the sun was lowering, westering, keeping its heat. Now that they were out in the open the heat struck them more forcibly than when they had been among the trees.

The wagons moved in single file, rumbling out of the trees at Neil's back as he sat the sorrel, pausing to turn and look behind him, running his gaze over the line of Conestogas. Ahead of them the sunlight shone on sleek backs and waving horns that caught and reflected the sunlight like polished slivers of glass. Around them now was a silence that was so deep and heavy and still that it seemed easy for a man to be able to reach out and touch it. A silence that was enhanced, rather than diminished, by the faint creak of the wagons as the horses plodded slowly over the soft earth and grass. Neil gigged his mount, rode in a great circle around the train, pausing to warn each of the outriders in turn of trouble. He had the feeling that it would come very soon, but from which direction he was not sure. Perhaps from that vast herd which they would soon pass, perhaps from the men who might be riding it, perhaps, although he did not think it likely, from the men they had left behind among the trees, left to walk back to the ranch or their nearest companions.

A quarter mile. Half a mile, and now they were well into the plain, moving out and away from the ridge at their backs. For a long while they rode in silence, men and women engrossed in their own thoughts, remembering the firing back along the trail, thinking how easy it would have been for some of them to have been lying back there with bullets in their bodies, looking ahead even to try to visualise what might lie in store for them, some eyeing the herd that moved like a rippling black wave over the side of the hill.

'We'll have to keep riding until we're clear of that herd,' Neil told Jackson, as he rode alongside the lead wagon, turning his head a little to eye the other. 'They look mean, could be trouble if we tried to camp too close. Besides, they'll have riders out

61

fanning around them, especially after dark. Reckon they'll be just as mean as those critters we met back on the trail.'

Jackson nodded musingly. 'The horses are tired,' he observed. 'You reckon it would be wise to push them too far?'

'We've got to.' He knew it sounded hard, but there was no other choice open to them.

'If you say so.' Jackson flicked the long whip over the horses. The other wagons followed. Neil threw a swift glance at the sky. Another four, perhaps five, hours of daylight left. Then it would be dark, but they would have to keep the wagons moving that night, long after nightfall. Deliberately he edged the train away to the left of the herd, hoping to pass more than two miles from it. Perhaps he was being over cautious, seeing danger where none existed. It was not likely that Sherman would send out his paid killers to watch a herd, even one of that size. He could usefully employ them on better business. The men riding the perimeter of the herd would be ordinary cattlemen, skilled in the way of handling cattle, but not equally skilled in the ways of handling guns.

If he was right in this, there might be little danger. If he was wrong, then all hell might be let loose on the plain, a hell that moved on four feet, that held needle-sharp horns, a squat, evil head, and a ton or so of solid beef and muscle behind it. There was an odd edge of tension to his body as he sat the saddle, pushing his mount forward, eyes flicking from the wagon to the herd, and back again.

4
Stampede!

Slim Farrel had a dark, saturnine face, dominated by a thick black moustache and dark brows which slashed across his features like a black line drawn by some artist's swift stroke of the brush. His shoulders were broad and he had a deep, powerful chest but thin, spindly legs which looked as if they could scarcely support his own weight. He was a cattleman who had herded cattle across most of the vast continent until he had grown tired of the business and thrown in his lot with the wagon train, seeking fresh horizons to the west, further along the trail than he had ever travelled before, hoping to settle down in California. He now drove one of the wagons with the train, a man who kept himself to himself and did little talking along the trail.

Now, however, he had quite a lot to say. The wagon train was camped on a stretch of level ground by a narrow river that ran along the perimeter of the grasslands. Neil had set a hard pace. It had been an unwelcome decision, but an extremely necessary one. Not until they had left that herd behind was he satisfied that there was little danger to the train. They had seen nothing of Sherman's men with the herd, but there was the feeling that they had been watched all the way across the plain.

'Likely you're wonderin' why I insisted on making you

travel so fast and hard this afternoon and evening,' muttered Neil.

'You scared of that herd back there?' queried Jessup. He raised his brows into a straight interrogatory line.

'Could be. Sherman knows we're here, I've had that feeling for a long while ever since we crossed the stream this morning.'

'If he wants to kill us, there's one sure way he can do it,' put in Farrel. His sharp blue eyes peered through the darkness, brows furrowed. There were years of knowledge in his brain, knowledge of cattle, their little meannesses and ways.

'Just what do you mean, old-timer?' asked Jessup. His eyes held Farrel's.

'That herd back there. It wouldn't take much to start them on the prod, set them stampeding in this direction. I'm a Texan. I've ridden herd more times than I care to remember. I've seen 'em at their best and at their worst. And I didn't like the look of that herd back there.'

'And you figger that's what they mean to do?' murmured Jessup. He seemed to be thinking over the possibility in his mind, as if the thought had never occurred to him before.

Farrel shrugged. 'I don't claim to read the minds of Sherman's men, but if I wanted to get rid of a wagon train and I had that damned great herd poised back there, just ready to move, I'd know just what to do.'

Jessup rapped his knuckles irritably against the pommel of the saddle lying on the ground close beside him. His strong teeth tore a strip of beef from the bone in his hands and he stretched one leg to ease the ache of his muscles. 'If they do decide to do that, this ain't the best place for the wagons to be.' A breath whistled in and out of his flared nostrils.

Around the fire nearby there was the murmur of voices. The others were preparing to settle down for the night. the children had been put to bed in the wagons and quietness was settling over the camp. The fire crackled and there was movement in the dark shadows that moved beyond the flickering glow of the fire.

'I'll check the horses,' muttered Jackson harshly. He got heavily to his feet and moved away from the fire.

Jessup waited until he had gone, then said softly: 'I don't like this, Roberts. A stampede is something I never bargained with when I said I'd make this drive, and I'm sure that goes for most of the others, too. A gunman I can stand up to and fight, but a thousand head of beef cattle on the run – that's something different. We wouldn't stand a chance against them. They'd run down the train and leave nothing once they'd passed over us.'

He turned to Farrel. 'You reckon that could happen? You know these steers. Would they start a stampede?'

'It only needs somebody to fire off a handful of shots in their ears and they'll start to run. They're damned funny, unpredictable creatures at the best of times. A thunderstorm could blow up and the heavens open with the sound of all hell being let loose, and they won't stir an inch. Then loose off one shot and they'll start and nothing will stop 'em.'

Jessup looked in doubt into the darkness. There was a sharp tenseness in his body. A moment later Jackson came back. 'Nothing moving out there. The horses seem skittish, though. Something worrying 'em. They can sense something.'

He looked in doubt towards Farrel. The darkness was sharpened by the bright pinpoints of the stars glittering in the jet cloth of the heavens. Outside the camp there seemed to be a tremendous loneliness crouching there – a deep and tense loneliness which must have been a common thing to man right at the beginning of the world when these plains were first made. A fear-filled loneliness that ate at the nerves until they were drawn tight through the limbs.

Gradually the fire went down, leaving only glowing embers that pulsed with brief flashes of orange flames whenever the air caught at them, fanning them into brightness. The men and women in the wagons slept. The night air held a sudden chill. In his blanket within a few feet of the dying fire, Neil slept and not far away the horses dropped their heads. Perhaps two hours passed, then another. The moon lifted from the eastern horizon and threw a pale wash of yellow light over the scene. Inside his blanket, Neil stirred, then came fully awake, sitting bolt upright on the cold, hard ground, straining with every sense to pick up the sound which had woken him. For several seconds he sat there, peering into the moonlit darkness which lay around him.

Moments passed and still he could hear nothing. But something had woken him. There was no doubt about that. This was a feeling he had experienced many times before in the past and every time there had been something definitely wrong, and he knew it would be foolish to ignore it. Beside the fire he could make out the sleeping forms of Jackson and Jessup. Had he been mistaken? Was it just one of the ordinary sounds of the night which had woken him. Perhaps one of the horses snickering in the near distance on the edge of the camp – a log falling into the heart of the fire?

The slight sensation of apprehension in the pit of his stomach eased. He stretched a cramped leg forward to ease the tightening of the muscle of his hip. Then the sound came again and he was on his feet in an instant, head turning to the east from whence the sound came. A cattleman himself, he recognised it at once. A moment later he was shaking Jessup and Farrel awake, then moving over to where Jackson lay under his blanket.

'*Stampede!*'

Farrel yelled the single word at the top of his voice. A moment later he had fired a couple of wild shots into the air, the sharp, cracking echoes heard all over the camp. For most of the men in the wagons there was no need for warning.

*

Those who did not know from their own past experience could guess only too well what stampeding cattle meant. Countless tons of solid beef and muscle on the move, slashing horns and lowered squat heads. All of the meanness that could be found anywhere on God's earth rolled into one vast avalanche of lunging and bellowing, fear-crazed beasts. The herd could only have been three miles away, and yet even from that distance it was possible to hear it crashing into action, the ground beginning to shake. Neil leapt for his horse, swung the saddle up and tightened the cinch with swift movements of long practised hands. Then he was up in the saddle, Jessup and Farrel beside him.

Leaning down, he yelled to Jackson as the big man moved towards his own horse. 'We'll try to head 'em off. You'd better get into the lead wagon. Head them out of here. The ground's far too open. Get them across the stream and on to the other side. There's rough ground there a mile or so ahead. Try to make for that and get everybody into the lee of the hills.'

Jackson gave a quick, brusque nod of his great head to indicate that he had understood. He ran for the wagon, leaving his own horse to make its own way over the stream. Around the wagons themselves there was feverish activity. Fortunately everyone had heeded the warnings given by Farrel the night before and the horses were readily hitched into the shafts. All were awake by now. It was doubtful if anyone could have slept. Not after those twin bucketing shots from Farrel's gun and the growing thunder of the stampeding herd in the distance. Neil bent forward in the saddle, knees pressing tightly to keep his seat as the sorrel moved forward into the night. An animal trained for this type of work, the stud knew exactly what to do. Horse and rider became as one as he headed the sorrel away from the dying embers of the fire. Jessup and Farrel on either side of him, dark shadows in the pale yellow moonlight that washed over the plain, lighting on the sluggish water of the nearby river. But Neil had no eyes for that. The people in the wagons would have to make the best time they could and depend upon Clem Jackson to get them over the river and into what safety they could find on the other side. Certainly, so long as they remained where they were, they were in terrible danger. That stampeding herd would stop for nothing, and certainly the river would prove no barrier to their onward rush. It was doubtful if they would stop for the rocks up ahead.

Two other riders detached themselves from the train at Jackson's harshly yelled orders and galloped after Neil and his two companions. They rode loosely, reins hanging loose, their arms swinging, making no attempt to guide their mounts. Somewhere ahead of them came a tidal wave of tossing horns, heads, hooves and tons of muscle. Neil felt the tightness growing in his chest. Dimly, over the thunder of the stampede, he heard the sharp barks of guns blazing, knew then, even if he had only suspected it before, that the herders with those cattle had deliberately started the steers on the run, knowing that they would trample down the wagon train where it was camped on the river's edge. He tried to push his gaze ahead of him, to pick out the black surge of the herd as it came forward. In the moonlight, shadows were tantalising things, not once materialising so that he could see things clearly and properly. He reached the tip of a low rise, reined his mount, lifting his right hand to check the onward rush of the four riders with him. His feet found the stirrups as he paused there, peering directly ahead of him.

'There!' Jessup yelled the word savagely, pointed a finger into the darkness.

Neil narrowed his eyes, looked in the direction of the other's pointed finger, then sucked in his breath sharply, felt the muscles under his ribs tighten convulsively. No time to look about them now. No time even to try to think. That vast sea of dark shadow was already streaming over the plain, heading in their direction. He did not doubt that the stud he rode could quarter across the face of the rushing herd and still outrun it. But there were the wagons at his back to think of. Somehow they had to try to turn the tip of the herd, to divert them from the path they had already chosen, turn them around and try to send them plunging along the bank of the river, heading them south. If they could do that then they stood a good chance of saving all of the wagons. If not—

He did not allow himself to think of the consequences of failure. He had seen too many herds stampeding not to know what happened to anything that was unfortunate enough to get into their path.

A swift glance behind him and he saw to his relief that the wagons were just beginning to get under way. The first had moved down into the water, was crossing the river. But he knew instinctively that they could never make it in time unless the herd were turned. Any chance of stopping those animals had gone the moment those gunshots had been fired behind them. Strange and moody, utterly unpredictable, they had begun to move.

No time to worry about the wagons now. Swiftly he pulled the Colt from its holster, gigged the mount. It leapt forward, down the far side of the slope, down towards the thundering mass of the herd. Beside him rode the other men. If there was any fear in their minds at what they saw directly ahead of them, nothing of it showed in their actions. There was no hesitation now on their part. Swiftly Neil swung the sorrel so that it was racing across the edge of the herd, while with his left hand he gestured to the men with him to swing around, to follow his lead in everything he did. Success or failure, life or death depended on split second timing here. One false move on their part and they could be trampled down by that sea of horns. Lunging and bellowing the herd came on. The riders with them were far to the rear. They had started the fear-crazed beasts on their way and were now hanging back, keeping themselves out of danger.

Jessup rode swiftly, cutting towards the side of the herd. His gun was out and he fired savagely, straight into the faces of the animals alongside him. Above the thunder of the thousands of hooves it was impossible to make out any other sound. Neil reached the tip of the crescent, where the foremost steers formed a vast bulge, racing ahead of the drag. Behind them came the mass of the herd, following blindly on the heels of the leaders. If only they could turn the steers that led the herd they might stand a chance. The thought pounded on and on through Neil's mind as he headed the sorrel straight for the fanning group, his gun spitting flashes of orange flame into the eyes of the beasts close to him, seeking to crowd them over to the right, to divert them from the path they were taking.

But it was as if the devil had got into them that night. They were being driven on by the fear of the guns which had roared behind them, startling them, setting them running, out across the open face of the plain, out towards the river. No barrier there as far as they were concerned. Again and again the other men were firing and loading, clinging to the backs of the bucking horses with tightened knees. It was mean and cruel work. Dropping a steer here and there in the hope of forcing them to change their course, to set them swinging in a wide arc. Jessup slashed at the faces of the charging, plunging steers with his coiled riata once his guns were empty, yelling harshly and savagely at the top of his voice. Nearer at hand, Farrel, old to this game, continued to thrust his mount against the bulging side of the herd, adding the fire from his guns to the din.

Gradually, as the minutes passed, there was a wave forming along the length of the herd. But a swift glance told Neil that it would be too late. They could not hope to hold them, even to turn them completely along the nearer bank of the river.

A bunch split out from the main herd, went careering out across the dark plain, just visible in the flooding moonlight as they raced away, bellowing and lowing in anger and fear. Neil watched them for the briefest fraction of a second, then let them go, turning his glance back to the others. There was no danger from that small bunch. They would go on running until they stopped from sheer exhaustion and by that time they would be miles away from there. He doubted if they would cross the river. It was the big body of cattle that worried him.

Now they were less than half a mile from the river bank. A quarter of an hour was gone, a period made up of minutes which had ticked themselves away into a roaring, bellowing thunderous eternity. The mad eyes of the steers could be seen in the shadows of the shaggy heads. The horses were doing their best, the guns were still flaring at the crazed beasts, but it was making little difference.

Turning his mount, Neil rode swiftly for the river. Behind him the roaring herd came full pelt across the plains. Somehow he had to reach the wagons and try to get them under cover. Not that he doubted Clem Jackson's ability to do the best he could. But the other lacked his experience of this country, did not know it as he did. All hell couldn't stop that herd now. He hit the water at the run, felt the current crash against the sorrel's chest as it began to move over.

For a moment the horse lost its footing on the smooth bed of the river, on the stony bed, went floundering forward, its neck arched, almost under. Then, with a tremendous effort, it found its feet again, righted itself, crashed on until it reached the opposite bank, plunged up it into the rocky, rough ground that lay beyond. The last of the wagons was on the trail on the far side, rocking and swaying from side to side as the horses plunged and heaved on the traces. How long those wagons would take that kind of punishment he did not

71

know. But it needed only one of them to break down now, and it would be impossible to save it from the death that came close behind, a surging, terrible sea of death.

Water dripping from his pants, he clung to the back of his stud, raced it along the trail after the wagons. Fifty yards, a hundred. By now, he thought, not turning to see, the herd must have reached the river. Jessup and the others would have reached it, too, would be doing their best to turn it. The river was the last obstacle in the way of the stampede. If they did not manage to turn it there, they had no chance in hell of doing it anywhere else.

Half a mile away lay the craggy hills. There lay the only safety they could find. The lead wagon was almost there, but the others were strung out over more than a quarter of a mile, dashing forward as hard as they could go, the men and women in those lurching, swaying Conestogas knowing full well what would happen to them if they stopped now, if they didn't make the rocks. Behind him, breathing down the back of his neck, the herd came on, closer and closer with every passing second. A swift glance over his shoulder and he saw that the leaders were over the river, that the others were in the swim. His heart sank within him and he groaned aloud as he saw the danger. The men were riding close to the plunging, snorting animals, still firing their guns in their faces, still hoping to cut them over the plain to the south. He knew that they had very little chance. The distance was so small that the leading steers would be upon the last wagons before they reached safety.

Guns were spreading death among the plunging, roaring steers. But there was a limit to what a handful of guns could do. That limit had been reached.

Drilling his spurs into the flanks of his sorrel, he sent it racing along the dark trail, knowing that the slightest slip could mean the end for him. But the sorrel was a sure-footed creature, picked its way easily through the boulders which lay scattered over the trail. As he rode he peered ahead, trying to pick out the shapes of the wagons clearly. Too close ahead, they were moving too slowly. He sucked in a deep breath, pondered his next move. He knew that Jackson had understood everything he had told him, knew that the other would do all that he could to get the train under cover of the rocks. But the horses were tired, the wagons were cumbersome things, and it was dangerous to try to drive them as hard as this. Over the smooth ground of the desert to the east they might have got away with it, but here on this rough, stony ground disaster was always very close.

It came with the suddenness of a bolt of lightning. Not the last wagon, but the one immediately in front of it. One minute it was on the trail, racing forward, the canvas top shuddering, the wheels churning in the rocks. The next it had plunged sideways as if a giant had struck it, hurling it to one side.

Neil forced a sharp groan through tightly clenched teeth. One of the rear wheels had split, must have hit a boulder the wrong way and, at that speed, the shattering force of the impact had been more than enough to smash the wheel to pieces. The end of the wooden axle was digging deep into the hard ground, scraping forward as the horses continued to pull on the traces. Another few yards and it would go over. But before that could happen the frantically struggling horses succeeded in snapping the leather of the traces, and the team ran free, surging forward into the darkness. The wagon turned sharply at right angles and came to rest across the trail. Savagely, Neil urged his mount forward. Out of the corner of his eye he saw the black mass of the herd over to his left. They had crossed the river back there and were running free and wild over the rough terrain here. They were no longer on to the trail but swinging over the ground to his left, directly on to the smashed wagon. He knew with a sick certainty that there was nothing he could do to prevent them from getting there before he did. They were sweeping forward now in an irresistible wave. Somehow he got the sorrel alongside the leaders, turning his Colt on them, firing savagely and blindly into their faces. Even at that last moment he had the feeling that it might have been possible for him to turn them just that necessary fraction so that the black tide might swing past the wrecked wagon. The last wagon in the train had somehow pulled clear, had gone bucking and swaying past, although it was still in terrible danger. Steers went down before his flaming guns, but there were always others to move forward and take their places, trampling down those which had been killed. Another shot, a vivid splash of orange flame and a steer dropped dead. Swiftly he tried to bulwark the smashed wagon by building a wall of dead steers in front of it, a dam of flesh and bones and curving horns to keep away the cattle which came behind.

The man who had been driving the wagon had been tossed out when the wheel had gone. He lay on the trail a couple of yards away, face downward, his arms and legs out flung. He did not move, and it was impossible to tell whether he had been killed outright by the fall or whether he had simply been knocked cold. Aiming with an almost unconscious movement, Neil dropped two steers next to the fallen man, but it was no use trying to form a barrier there. The dark wave descended on them and the figure of the man lying in the dust was blotted out in a massacre of stamping hooves.

The wagon itself lay directly in the path of the crazed animals. As he drew alongside he debated whether to clamber on board and risk his life doing so, or whether to try to mill the herd about him. A moment while he slashed at bawling, lunging heads, their wicked, needle-sharp horns missing his legs and thighs by inches. Then the wet folds of the canvas collapsed as the tremendous weight of the herd surged over it. Wood split and splintered under that massive onslaught. He thought he heard a woman scream, a thin lost sound in the night. But he could not be certain in that bellowing, savage roar that filled the whole of creation.

Turning the sorrel, he pulled it into the side of the trail. The rest of the herd thundered by, dust rising from their pounding hooves, choking and clogging at the back of his throat and nostrils. His eyes were filled with grit and it was almost impossible to see anything. Certainly he could hear nothing but the sound of that stampeding herd roaring past him. The body of a steer slid against the sorrel, threatening to crush it against the solid rock face nearby. Deftly Neil clung to the saddle, kept his hands tight on the reins. No point in trying to drop any more of the animals. The damage had been done. All he could hope for now was that Jackson had got the other wagons into some kind of safety, some refuge from the black avalanche which threatened to roll over them all and annihilate them utterly.

There were suddenly more shouts in the night. Jessup and Farrel and the others, moving forward along the curving side of the herd where it bulged as it was fed by the mass of animals crushing forward from behind. As the herd curved away from him, Neil urged his stud forward, away from the sheer rock face at his back.

'*Hiiiya! Hiii-ya! Git over…. Git over!*' The shrill cries echoed in his ears as the rest of the men surged along by him. They must have known that now there was nothing more they could do. The herd would continue along the trail until they were exhausted, when they would stop. If the wagons were not under cover now, then they were finished and nothing in heaven or on earth could save them.

As the minutes passed there came a lessening in the crash of the herd as the last of the stragglers went by. The guns stopped their hammering roar. No point now in continuing to fire. If they hadn't got the leaders, the rear would never change their onward rush. Once the herd had moved by, he made himself go forward to where the smashed and splintered remains of the wagon still lay in the middle of the trail. It was now something virtually unrecognisable. The canvas had been torn to shreds that fluttered in the breeze, and the wooden upright had been splintered and crushed, the wheels torn from the axles and ground into the dirt. Yet there was still someone alive in there. Neil heard the low groan quite distinctly, although a second fled before his mind accepted the fact that everyone had not been killed outright. It seemed inconceivable to him that anyone could have lived through that pounding rush but—

Within seconds he had slid from the saddle, was yelling at Farrel to join him. His hands tore with a desperate urgency at the sodden canvas strips that covered the debris. Blinking his eyes, he tried to see in the gloom. Farrel dropped to the ground a couple of yards away, came running forward, gave the trampled red thing in the middle of the trail only a cursory glance. Then he was on one knee beside Neil, tugging at the weight of the splintered wagon.

'Reckon there's somebody trapped inside there – still alive,' muttered Neil harshly. 'Heard 'em cry out a moment ago.'

'Hell, they can't be unhurt,' said the other. He shook his head slowly, wonderingly.

Neil knew what was in the cattleman's mind. Under that stamping wall of bone and muscle, nothing could have escaped unscathed. He pulled hard at wood and metal. The groan came again and he was able to locate the sound in the darkness. Then his outstretched hand touched a woman's head. She moaned and sucked in her breath hard. His fingers drifted over her shoulders then down to her arm, and he felt the shudder pass through her at his touch.

'She's here, Farrel,' he said tightly. 'I think her arm is broken. It may be trapped under the beam. Better try to lift it. Careful now!'

Together they lifted the heavy beam which pinned the woman's arm down. She uttered another loud moan, then was silent. Neil bent, listened for a moment, then nodded as he heard the harsh whistle of air rasping in and out of her lungs. She had fainted. In the circumstances that was perhaps the best thing that could have happened. Now at least she would feel nothing when they came to move her.

Carefully they managed to free her, to lift her clear of the wagon. In the dull wash of yellow moonlight, Neil recognised her. Claire Vance, riding with her husband to a new life in California. He felt a sharp tightening of his throat muscles. That would be Tom, her husband, lying out there among the rocks a few feet away. Whatever happened, she must not come round and see him.

'Let's get her away from here,' he said tightly, 'before she wants to know what happened to her husband.'

'What about kids?' asked Farrel harshly.

'None. Damned good thing, too. They'd have been killed in this mess.'

Carefully he lifted the woman on to his saddle, then led the sorrel along the trail to where the wagons had moved towards the rocks. The herd had gone, thundering onward in a straight line, in their blind, blundering rush which would carry them for many miles before they finally halted. At the back of his mind there was a sharpening sense of anger, a blinding thing, which urged him to deliver the woman to the train and then turn, ride back and try to hunt down those murderers who had started that stampede. But common sense told him that not only would those men have moved off into the darkness of the plain, but he would be needed more urgently at the wagon train.

They made slow progress along the rough trail and by the time they reached the rocks the train had begun to move back out into more open ground again. They had been lucky, fantastically so. Far luckier than he would have ever thought possible. Jackson had located the small side canyon halfway along the rocky path through the hills and had somehow succeeded in turning the train into it. Here they had been

77

perfectly safe from the thundering hooves of the steers as they plunged past along the main trail. But there were a few steers scattered on the trail near the entrance to the small side canyon which told of a desperate fight to keep the crazed animas at bay and prevent them turning.

Clem Jackson stepped forward as Farrel rode up, then turned and eyed Neil curiously as he walked forward with the woman lying over the saddle. His thick black brows went up into a mutely questioning line over the dark eyes.

'She'll be all right once we've fixed her arm,' Neil told him quietly. 'At least I couldn't find any other bones broken. But the wagon was smashed completely and she's lucky to be alive.'

'What about Tom Vance?' boomed the other.

Neil shook his head slowly. 'At least he never knew what hit him. He was thrown from the wagon when it hit a boulder and split the wheel. He must have died at once. If he didn't, then he was unconscious by the time the herd got to him.'

'I'll get one of the women to look after her.' Jackson gave a quick nod, then reached up and lifted the woman down in his huge arms as if she were a baby and had no weight at all. He carried her into the rocks where the rest of the men and women were gathered. They had all had a shaking experience and it would be some time before they got over it, Neil reflected. But for Claire Vance, things would never be the same again. There would be no new life in California for her now. She would never even know what had happened to her husband, and for him there would be no proper grave. He felt a sudden weariness in him which was something more than the tiredness that came from the long night and the endless battle with that stampeding herd.

'One more piece of trouble like that and the train will be finished before we've gone another fifty miles,' said Farrel. He built a smoke, stood quite still watching the rest of the folk sitting among the rocks, oblivious of the cold night air that blew about them. It was as if they could sense the tragedy of what had happened, knew that someone had died during the night, and for them, as for Claire Vance, it would never be quite the same again. They had seen death in one of its more terrible aspects, death in the form of a thundering, bawling wall of steers, something primitive and frightening, old to the cattlemen, but new to the others.

Neil sighed, dragged himself to his feet. There was stubble on his chin and the back of his hand rasped over it as he rubbed his face.

Jackson came back. He stood looking at the wagon nearby for a long moment, then said: 'We may have to rest up for tomorrow morning and carry out some repairs, Roberts. There'll be rims to be fitted to the wheels of some of the wagons, and fresh axles put on at least two of them before we go any further.'

'It might be best if we did rest up for the morning.' Neil nodded. 'I don't think there will be any further danger from the herd. By morning it will be miles away from here. But as for the men with it, that's a different matter. We'll need to be on our guard in case they try to attack us. I figure we may even get a visit from Sherman himself with some of his hired killers.'

'You know this man personally?'

'We've met before,' Neil admitted. 'The same goes for Hollard. I reckon those two are in cahoots now that they know we're moving across this stretch of country. They'll do anything in their power to stop us.'

Daybreak found them huddled around the fires. A cold wind had blown up after midnight and the clouds which had begun to gather, blotting out the yellow face of the moon, brought rain and discomfort. There was hot coffee in the boiler over the fire and they ate their breakfast hurriedly, before starting repairs to the wagons. The threat of danger still hung over them all. It was a tangible thing that could be felt and men had only to look up to where the two men were standing atop the tall columns of rock nearby to know that it might come at any moment.

Claire Vance was lying in one of the wagons, her arm fixed in a sling. Neil had climbed on board to take a look at her twice that morning, found her each time staring up at the sodden canvas over her head, her eyes open and wide, with only a vague emptiness in them. She neither turned nor seemed to hear him when he spoke to her and, after a few moments, he climbed down from the wagon into the pouring rain, and went back to the others.

'You figure she'll be all right, Roberts?' asked Jackson harshly, the second time he came back. 'I saw her a little while ago and she didn't seem to know I was there.'

'Shock,' said Neil briefly. 'It can do strange things at times. Maybe she still thinks that her husband is alive. Sooner or later she'll come out of it, and that will be the time when the pain will strike. I've seen it happen before. The mind pulls itself behind some dark curtain and shuts itself off from reality. As soon as we get away from here and that arm of hers heals a little, we'll get one of the women to break the news to her.'

Jackson nodded. They went back to work on the wagons fitting the new rims to the splintered wheels, checking the axles, the canvas and the traces. The rain continued to fall in a dark, hazy curtain from the heavens, so that there seemed no place where they could find dryness or comfort. Weary men who had been awake all night. Gaunt and haggard men who shook the rain from their hats and pulled their coats and jackets more tightly about their bodies as the cold wind blew down from the north, down from the distant mountains that loomed on the skyline, just a little closer now.

Shortly before noon one of the look-outs on the rocks yelled harshly. Neil glanced up at the man as he pointed to the west. Then he scrambled up the rocks to where the other stood, his gun whispering from its holster.

Ten riders had checked their mounts on a rise of ground to the west, men who looked out towards the hills. They seemed to be men who had ridden hard and ridden fast. The leader lifted a hand, urged the others forward again, and in that moment Neil recognised him. Jesse Sherman. There had been no mistaking that tall figure.

'Looks like trouble,' he said casually to the man standing by his side. 'I'll warn the others. You stay here and keep an eye on them.' He made his way down the rocky slope again, uneasy and apprehensive. For the moment he knew that these men did not intend to attack them. Had that been the case, they would have moved up unseen, keeping to the rocks and ravines which split the country in that direction.

'Sherman and some of his killers are headed this way,' he told Jackson. 'I doubt if they mean trouble just now,' he added, as the other reached for his Winchester. 'But I'm interested to know why they've come like this.'

Almost without direction, his hand loosed the gun in his holster. There was the sound of horses in the near distance, riding towards them, then the riders, bunched close together, came into view, Sherman leading them. He reined his mount a few yards away, stayed the men with him with a gesture of his hand. There was a sneer over the darkly handsome features as they stared down at Neil.

'Somehow, I figured it would be you, Roberts, leading this wagon train over my land.' There was a touch of menace in the other's cold voice. 'I reckoned we would meet again some day.'

'There ain't no law that says a man can't move over this stretch of country,' broke in Jackson in his loud, booming voice.

'I'm the law in these parts,' said Sherman tightly. 'All of this country that you can see, right to the horizons, belongs to me. If I say that you can't cross it, then the law backs me up. Could be you'd like me to send some of my men into Twin Creeks and get the sheriff out here.'

Neil grinned sardonically. 'There ain't much doubt in my mind, Sherman, that the sheriff there will do exactly as you tell him to. If he don't, then it won't be hard to replace him.'

'Just what are you insinuatin', Roberts?' snarled the other. For the moment his right hand hung poised over the gun at his hip, his eyes holding the promise of death in them.

'Just try it,' said Neil warningly. 'You'll be a dead man before you can get that gun clear of leather – and you know it. And if you're banking on one of your gunslingers getting me first, I reckon it might pay you to take a look around you. There are rifles pointed at every one of you and these men won't hesitate to shoot you down like the rattlers you all are. They ain't forgotten the way your men set that herd on to them last night. We lost a good man then, and there's a woman lying back there with a broken arm and her husband gone.

'These folk ain't asking much of anybody. Only the right to keep on moving until they get to California – and neither you, nor anybody else is going to stop 'em.'

He saw Sherman's gaze slide from side to side, saw the other stiffen a little and then drop his hand swiftly to his side as he saw the grim-visaged men who stood around the trail, the Winchesters and Colts rock-steady in their hands, their fingers bar-straight on the triggers. There was a long moment of silence on the trail. Close at hand a horse snickered, but that was the only sound that broke the clinging, heart-stopping stillness. It needed only one of the men with Sherman to make a wrong move to start those guns hammering, to fill the air with death.

With an effort Sherman forced himself to relax. A smile spread slowly over his features. 'I ain't going to forget this, Roberts,' he said softly, tonelessly, his voice oddly flat. 'I got a score to settle with you from way back and I intend to do it. You won't slip through my fingers this time as you did before. As for this wagon train, you're all fools if you believe this man and think that you will get through to California.'

'Your herd didn't finish us, and the same will go for your men if you try anything,' Jackson said harshly. 'We mean to ride through here to the mountains and you ain't going to stop us.'

'We'll see about that. If it's trouble you want, then by God you'll all get it. You'll begin to wish that you'd stayed back East where you were safe before I'm through with you.'

Before any of the others could speak, he had jerked the reins in his hands with a savage motion, wheeling his mount cruelly. He rode off along the narrow trail, the men following him. Slowly the thunder of their horses died into the distance and there was only the endless sound of the rain as it hit the hard rocks around them.

Neil drew in a deep breath and ran a dry tongue around equally dry lips. He stared at Jackson. 'I reckon we'd better get everything ready as quickly as we can and move out soon. I won't feel safe until we hit Twin Creeks. That's on the edge of Sherman's territory.'

'Reckon we can get supplies there?' asked Farrel. 'We're low on flour.'

'If we get through I reckon we can,' said Neil dully. He turned and went back to the waiting wagons. Throughout the rest of the morning and the long, grey, wet afternoon, they worked, ignoring the rain, the cold and the discomfort. The rain continued to fall endlessly, huge drops that soon turned the trail into a stretching river of mud. Overhead the clouds were low and thick, piling up from the western horizons in large masses. There had been no sign of the sun all that day, no sign of any let up in the rains. By late afternoon they were able to hitch up the horses and start the wagons rolling.

5
Twin Creeks

It was ten days later and nearly two hundred miles by the time the wagon train rolled into the township of Twin Creeks. In the hot dusty sunlight the town seemed asleep with the heat haze of high noon hanging over it. The wagons had stopped half a mile from the edge of the town and Neil and Jackson had ridden into the town to check on supplies. They reined their mounts at the end of the long street that stretched clear in front of them to where it moved all the way through the town and out the far side. The buildings had been erected on either side of that single street, stores and saloons, hotels and livery stables.

It was a town that was similar to hundreds of others in the west. A frontier town which pinpointed where the tide of civilisation, moving westward, had halted at some time in the recent past and men had set up a community here, to act as a bulwark against the Indians, who had ridden these plains long before the white man had come and wrested the land from them. Now, even though the white man had come, the place was still almost as wild as it had been in those early days when the frontier had stopped right there and there had been nothing beyond, to the west, but empty desert and unexplored mountains, herds of buffalo that roamed the plains in their millions.

The lie of the land on either side of Twin Creeks was of two different types. To the east stretched the rough country which merged gradually into the lush grasslands of the Sherman spread, with low rolling ridges that blended perfectly with the background. Westward lay the tall hills, a rugged country of rock and sharp-cut ravines, here pinnacles and boulders and buttes were all jumbled together, tumbling over each other as they lay spread out to join the tall mountains that spiked the horizon. The town lay in a wide hollow between these two strikingly opposite terrains, with the clear water of the two creeks that ran down from the hills to the west and gave the town its name, shining brilliantly in the hot sunlight.

Neil's eyes searched along the apparently deserted street for any sign of life. There were some. Men who sat on the board-walks, in the shade of the single-storey buildings, their legs up on the wooden staging on the edge of the street, their hats pulled well down over their eyes. A handful of horses stood lazily in front of one of the saloons, tethered to the hitching post, their heads dropping in the sullen, oppressive heat.

Slowly the two men rode along the main street, eyes alert. It was not so much the look as the actual feel of possible danger that sent little warning currents surging through Neil's body. There was no doubt that they were exciting some curiosity from the people there. It was quite usual for folks to stare at him and he did not find it in the least disconcerting, but now he guessed that most of them were staring at the giant of a man who rode beside him, the hair and jutting beard making him look even more huge than he really was.

The wide brim of Neil's border hat extended well from the crown on all sides, keeping the heat off his face and the glare of sunlight out of his eyes. He sat the sorrel quite relaxed, but although he scarcely seemed to move his head, it might have been noticed that his eyes were never still, that they flickered continually from side to side, taking in everything, missing nothing.

There was only one two-storey building in the whole town, the hotel which stood halfway along the street, a wide gallery around three sides of it. A tall man stood on the gallery, his legs spread wide as if bracing himself against some sudden lurch of the building which might pitch him down into the street below. He gave the two men a swiftly appraising glance, then turned sharply on his heel and vanished from sight. Probably, thought Neil tightly, going to warn someone of their arrival in town. There was bound to be someone anxious to know when they got there. Here, in Twin Creeks, it was possible that he would be recognised and he did not doubt that his name and reputation were well known to most of the people here.

He gigged his mount again, then motioned towards the nearby saloon. Jackson nodded, licked his lips, turned his mount, reined in, in front of the hitching rail. He slid easily from the saddle, then fell in with Neil as they went inside, away from the heat.

The saloon was almost deserted. A couple of men were seated at one of the tables near the windows. Four more were playing cards at the far end of the room, but that was all. Neil made his way towards the bar, eyed the bartender through narrowed eyes. He did not recognise the man, doubted if the other knew his identity, but the same might not go for any of the men at the tables.

'Whisky for both of us,' he said. 'Leave the bottle. It's thirsty work riding out there.'

The bartender brought the bottle up from beneath the bar, set it in front of Neil, then placed the couple of glasses beside it. His eyes were narrowed a little and he seemed plainly puzzled. 'You been riding the trail long?' he inquired.

'Long enough to work up a thirst,' Neil told him casually. He threw the whisky back. It burned his throat a little but washed some of the dry dust out of his mouth and sent a wave of warmth through his stomach. 'Where could we eat in this town?'

'If you ain't too particular about the food, I reckon I could fry you up something. Potatoes and beans and some bacon.'

'That'll go down fine,' said Jackson. He poured himself another drink and held the glass in his hands for a long moment staring down at the amber liquid in it. None of the men in the saloon had stirred since their entry, and Neil guessed that they had not recognised him, were not concerned with a couple of strangers who came riding into town.

'There's a room through the back if you'd care to go inside,' said the man behind the bar. 'I'll have the meal ready for you in ten minutes.'

They moved into the other room. There was a plate at one of the tables with a slice of steak on it, cut through in the middle, with a cup of coffee, half-finished, beside it, steam still rising from it. Neil eyed it sharply, but gave no sign to the bartender that he had noticed. Not until the other had pulled the heavy curtains back over the opening did he catch a tight hold of Jackson's wrist, motion him to silence, saying in a hoarse whisper:

'There's something wrong here. Somebody was inside this room a couple of minutes ago, must've seen us come in. He's slipped out now, whoever he was, maybe to warn the sheriff.'

'More of Sherman's work? You said that he ran this town – and the law here.'

'Could be. Maybe they figure that with us out of the way, the train won't be able to go on. Maybe they reckon it might turn back, or even stay here.'

He swung his eyes to the curtains over the entrance. A load of buckshot through there and it would mean the end of Jackson and himself. Swiftly he cast his eyes about for another way out, knew that there had to be one, because the man who had been in there a couple of minutes before had clearly slipped out without them seeing him. Then his gaze lit on the door at the far end of the room, a door almost completely hidden by the wooden cases that had been carefully piled in front of it. Very cleverly done, he thought, some of the anger beginning to rise in his stomach. His hands tightened savagely as he pushed back his chair and rose swiftly to his feet.

This play had been deliberately engineered by either Sherman or the sheriff here in Twin Creeks. By now they would be heading for the saloon. There would be some charge trumped up against Jackson and himself, and before they knew what had happened, they would find themselves locked up in the jail here. Then they would either be lynched by the mob, deliberately stirred up by Sherman, or shot in the back trying to make a break. Any chance they had of getting back to the wait-ing wagon train would be gone. He pressed his lips together into a hard, tight line across the middle of his features.

Outside, beyond the curtain that blocked off all sight of what was happening inside the saloon itself, he heard some-one talking in a low voice. Then there were other voices, the sound of men moving into the saloon. Turning, he gave Jackson a quick glance full of meaning, saw the other reach down to check the guns in his holsters, then give a quick nod to indicate that he understood perfectly what was in Neil's mind. A second later Neil reached out and jerked the heavy curtain aside, stepping forward into the saloon.

There was a small knot of men just inside the door. He recognised Sherman, a curious expression on his face. Behind him was a short, stout man with a hard face and the star of a sheriff pinned to his shirt. Sherman was in the act of speaking to the sheriff when Neil moved into the room, eyes taking in every detail of the saloon, from the man in the white apron standing tensely at the back of the bar, to the two groups of men still seated at the tables. Even as his gaze flicked over them, they pushed back their chairs and moved away into the far corner of the room. Evidently these men were not part of the deal, wanted nothing of the gunfight which they sensed was in the offing, getting out of the line of fire.

'Looks to me as though you're trying to find somebody, Sherman,' said Neil, in a steady, even tone.

For a moment he saw that he had taken the rancher off his guard, that the other was a little unsure of himself, saw the flicker of uncertainty at the back of his eyes. Then Sherman nodded sharply, back on balance once more, dangerous, tricky. He said thinly: 'That's right, Roberts, I warned you back on the trail that you and the wagons you were leading were trespassing on my land. The sheriff here is to see that the law is carried out.'

'The law?' There was a note of deliberate sarcasm in Neil's tone now and he moved forward a couple of steps away from the heavy curtain, aware of the huge figure of Jackson at his back.

'That's right.' The portly figure of the sheriff stepped forward, a little hesitantly. He eyed Neil a trifle nervously. 'You ain't allowed to go driving a wagon train across that land. You were warned by Mister Sherman, yet it seems you went ahead in spite of that. The law says that the wagons, and all goods that they contain, may be confiscated and taken over by the person who had been wronged. In this case, I reckon that's Mister Sherman. In addition, it says that you and the leader of that train can be arrested and charged with—'

'Save your breath, Sheriff,' snapped Neil harshly. 'I ain't ever heard of those laws and neither has anybody else. The Government has given settlers the right of access to the trails that lead to California, and there ain't nobody who can dispute that. If anybody else says different, then I reckon he's just been bribed by Sherman here.'

'Now see here,' began the other harshly. There was a filming of sweat on his flabby features now and Neil could see him glancing towards Sherman as though seeking advice, waiting for the other to back up what he said. 'I'm the elected sheriff in Twin Creeks. If you try to resist arrest, then I'll have to take you in the hard way. Are you coming peaceable, or not?'

Neil shook his head very slowly. 'You ain't got no right to arrest us, Sheriff, and you know it.' His smile was thin and deliberately menacing, and it never touched his eyes.

Sherman said harshly: 'You're only making things worse for yourselves, you know. There are plenty of us to take you in, more men out in the street. Why not see sense and realise when you're licked?' In spite of his words, there was a look of angry defiance in his eyes.

Neil thinned his lips. His fingers were spread wide stiff, like the branches of a tree, hovering only a little way above the twin guns in his belt. He knew that the eyes of every man in the room were on him at that moment, wondering what he intended to do. He knew that the sheriff wasn't too happy about the thought of trying to take him in, even with those men backing him up.

Out of the corner of his eye he saw the bartender edging sideways a little, trying to make the movement as slow and as unobtrusive as he could. He could guess at the reason for the other's actions and he knew that the showdown would come within a minute or two. There would be a shotgun somewhere behind that counter and that once the bartender had his hands on it, he would use it. But first, the other would wait to see what move Sherman intended to make. The blast of a shotgun could make a terrible mess in that confined space and the other would not want to use it unless as a last resort.

Neil grinned at the Sheriff's discomfiture. 'Seems like that man of yours at the back of the bar is tired of livin'. Reckon you ought to warn him that he'll be dead before he can lift that gun out.'

This was more or less what Neil had expected, and yet he knew that Sherman was still hesitating. Maybe the other had figured that if he brought along enough men there would be little chance of the two men making a fight of it. That could be the reason he had come himself, to see that nothing went wrong. Perhaps he was even now beginning to regret that decision. He would know of Neil's reputation and would have realised that if lead did start to fly there, he was right in the middle of it – and such a thought, such personal danger, would not be to his liking. He preferred to send his own hired killers out to do the dirty work for him, to risk their lives, but never his own.

'Thinking about it, Sherman?' put in Neil softly. 'I reckon that you'd better make up your mind pretty quick if you're going to back up your words or stand on one side and let us pass. Because I'm going to count up to five and at the end of that time either shuck your gunbelts or go for your guns. The choice is up to you.'

The rancher glared at him truculently but did not reply right away. Neil saw him run his tongue around his dry lips, then flicker his gaze towards the man standing behind the bar, his hands still in sight on top of the polished bar where Neil could see them. Neil put a hard stare at Sherman, then let his glance slide to the sheriff. The other pulled out a red handkerchief and mopped at his streaming brows. Almost as if it had been a signal, Sherman leapt back, throwing his body to one side, his hands streaking for the guns at his belt.

It was a good draw, a fast draw, but it could not match that of the man who faced him. Even as Sherman threw himself to one side, striking the floor and rolling a little way towards the door, the bullet struck him high in the shoulder, and he uttered a shrill yell of pain, the gun dropping from his nerveless fingers. The other men went for their guns, clawing for them, reacting just as Neil had expected. The initial action had startled these men. For an instant they were motionless. Neil shot now without hesitation. He knew who these men were, knew that they were low-born killers, men like those who had deliberately sent that herd stampeding on to a defenceless wagon train, killing Tom Vance and making a widow of his wife. Two of the men were driven back as the bullets slammed into their chests, their faces relaxing into expressions of frozen amazement, their bodies knocking against those of the men standing behind, sending them off balance, spoiling their aim. A bullet hummed very close to Neil's head, smashed the mirror at the back of the bar into a thousand gleaming fragments.

He caught a glimpse of the bartender leaning to one side, reaching for the shotgun, determined to join in the fray. Then the other suddenly stiffened, seemed to jerk up on to his toes as if reaching instead for the ceiling over his head. His body slumped forward as Jackson spun and drilled him neatly through the head, sending him jerking over the bar, where he lay sprawled with his arms dangling limply in front of him.

Quite clearly Sherman had expected his men to gun down the two men who faced him. Only this was one time when it wasn't going to work. The guns that spoke and roared in that saloon were handled by one of the fastest men in the west, and Jackson was not too far behind when it came to handling his long-barrelled weapons.

The blood began to pound through his ears and along his veins as he thumbed back on the twin hammers, sending bullet after bullet crashing into the men in front of him. They flopped to the floor of the saloon. One man tried to crawl away, still reaching for the gun which had been knocked spinning from his fingers. Without any mercy in his mind at all, Neil shot him down. Now there were only two men left on their feet facing Neil and Jackson. One man stumbled forward, clutching at his stomach as Jackson fired. The other suddenly let go his guns, stepped back a couple of paces and lifted his hands over his head. His face lost colour, became like putty and his eyes took on a startled look of fear.

Neil said easily: 'Just stay right there, nice and easy, mister.'

He saw the man's adam's apple bob up and down as he swallowed thickly, still keeping his hands lifted. On the floor, Sherman pushed himself on to his knees. Blood flowed from the wound in his shoulder, staining the perfect whiteness of his silk shirt. He pressed his fingers tightly over it, but the redness continued to dribble between them and he gritted his teeth with the sudden pain of it, lips pressed tightly together, eyes narrowed to mere slits, as he glared at Neil, then turned his eyes slowly to look at the men who lay beside him.

The fear in his eyes faded slowly, to be replaced by a look of anger, a crafty look that Neil noticed at once. Then there was hatred there, a vitriolic hatred which Neil could not recall having seen in any man's eyes before.

'Reckon you overplayed your hand,' he said softly. 'Seems like you might be needin' a new sheriff around here, too. The last one made the mistake of trying to draw when the odds were stacked against him.' Neil went forward and poked at the short, fat figure on the floor with the toe of his boot. But the sheriff did not move and there was a vacant look in the eyes that stared up at the ceiling, a dead and empty look.

He could see Sherman's thoughts through the rapidly changing expression on the rancher's features. Incredulous disbelief, then the raw and naked fury again as he realised that his men had been killed, shot down by two men who were past craftsmen with a gun. His face was white. Through tight lips, he said harshly and with a savage emphasis: 'I told you when we met the last time that I'd kill you, Roberts. I still mean that.' The words were flat, emotionless things in contrast to the anger written on his chalk-white face. He was still trembling with rage. 'I'll hunt down that wagon train with every man I can lay my hands on, I'll burn it to ashes and destroy every man, woman and child who rides with it. I don't care whether it happens tomorrow or whether I have to follow you all the way to California. I'll finish you, Roberts, and everybody with you.'

'Better get on your feet and move outa here before I lose my patience and plug you,' said Neil with a faint snarl. 'I ain't forgotten what happened when that herd was stampeded against the wagons. I'll never forget that. And I want you to remember this. The next time I see you, whether you've got a gun or not, whether you're wounded or not, I'll shoot you down like the polecat you are.'

Slowly, painfully, the other pushed himself to his feet. He moved over the sprawled bodies on the floor, passed the man who stood with his hands raised in the air, said harshly: 'Stop looking like a goddamned fool, Henson. If he meant to shoot you down he'd have done it before now.'

Reluctantly, keeping his gaze fixed on the gun in Neil's hand, the other lowered his arms, then turned and followed the rancher out of the saloon. The batwing doors swung shut behind them. Neil walked to the door, stared out into the hot, dusty street that ran the full length of the township of Twin Creeks. There was that odd tightness back in his mind now as he dropped the gun back into its pouch. There would be no more warnings on either side. The lines were drawn as far as Sherman and the wagon train were concerned, and the fight was in deadly earnest now. But that was the way it had to be and, inwardly, he knew that it was the way he preferred to have it. Now he knew where he stood, knew that once Jackson got back and told the others what had happened, he would have every man in the train behind him, ready to fight if they had to, because now they would know exactly what they were up against. The chips were down and this was the only way they could ever hope to win.

Sherman walked slowly across the street, the other gunman close on his heels. In front of the glass-panelled door of the sheriff's office directly opposite the saloon they paused, held conversation for several minutes, sometimes pausing to glance back in the direction of the saloon. They were too far away for Neil to be able to pick out any of their conversation, but he guessed that they would soon ride out of town and pick up any other gunslammers that Sherman had on his ranch. Then they would come a-riding after the train. With the humiliation of having been shown up in front of people from the town, and thirsting for revenge, the other would not wait long before making his play.

Sherman untied his horse from the hitching post, mounted, then swung away down the street, dust kicked up from the hooves of his mount obscuring him as he reached the far end and then swung out of town, back along the trail to the east. The gunman who had spoken with him had paused, turned to watch the rancher ride off, then he went inside the sheriff's office and closed the door behind him. For a few moments Neil deliberated that move, then decided that there would be no more trouble from that man for the time being. Evidently Sherman had left him behind in town to keep his eyes open and report back to him everything that happened, particularly when the wagon train moved into town and then continued on its way west. Twin Creeks lay on the very boundary of Sherman's vast cattle empire. West of the town, where the country changed, reaching out as far as the distant mountains, lay the Hollard country. Matt Hollard, a man tarred with the same brush as Sherman.. Two sworn enemies, but he had little doubt that when it came to letting a wagon train move across their land, they would temporarily forget their differences and band together against a common enemy.

'You reckon that he'll come riding after us like he said?' asked Jackson, as they went outside on to the wide boardwalk, stood looking about them for a long moment, with the heat of afternoon lying over them.

'I'm sure he will. He'll never rest until he's killed us all.

Maybe it would have been better for everyone if I had shot him back there and finished it then.'

'Could be.' The other looked at him from shaded eyes, then his lips twisted into a curling smile. 'But we'll cross that bridge when we come to it, my friend. There is no point in worrying about these trifles.' He clapped a huge hand on Neil's shoulder. 'Now we must see if we can get any supplies. It may be that everyone here is so afraid of Sherman that they won't sell us anything, even though we have the money to pay for it.'

This proved to be true in the first three stores they tried. It was not until they entered the fourth, a smaller place at the far end of the street, that they had any better luck. The middle-aged woman behind the counter eyed them curiously as they went in, glanced at the guns which hung low on their hips, then stared up into Neil's face as if trying to read what she saw there.

'Howdy, Ma'am,' Neil spoke pleasantly. 'We're from the wagon train to the east of town a mile or so back along the trail. We need some supplies, thought you might be able to sell us some.'

She continued to eye him for a moment with a look of frank puzzlement on her face. Then she nodded her head slowly as if in secret understanding. 'There was some shooting down at the saloon a while back,' she said softly. 'I don't suppose either of you two gentlemen had any hand in that. They tell me that crooked sheriff and a dozen or so of the killers who go under the name of deputies around town were gunned down.' She raised her brows a little, the ghost of a smile playing around her lips.

'Reckon you heard right, Ma'am,' murmured Neil, quietly.

'I thought so. Ain't much I don't hear. They also say that Jesse Sherman was wounded in the fighting and that he's ridden out of town swearing revenge on the men who did it.' Her eyes were shrewd and bright. 'Can't say I've liked that man or what he does around here. Anybody who takes a gun and teaches him a lesson deserves everything this town can give him. Though I doubt if you'll find many people here who'll be willing to help you. They're all too afraid of what Sherman and his men will do to them if he should find out.'

Neil nodded. 'We've already discovered that for ourselves, Ma'am.'

'I thought so.' She paused, then said quietly: 'Well, what is you need?'

'Many thanks, Ma'am,' Neil grinned. He gave her the list of supplies they needed. 'It's good to know that there are some folk at least who aren't afraid of Sherman and what he stands for in these parts.'

'He's an evil man. He'll kill you if he ever gets the chance. Don't underestimate him, whatever you do.'

'We won't,' said Jackson loudly. 'He's ridden out of town but left one of his men in the sheriff's office. Reckon we'd better get back to the train and warn them before it's too late.' He tipped his hat to her, bowing a little from the waist.

Outside, they loaded the supplies on to the waiting horses, untied them from the rail, then swung up into the saddle, heading out of town. Out of the corner of his vision Neil noticed the white face of the gunman staring at them through the window of the sheriff's office, watching them as they rode out of town.

At the wagon train the news spread like wildfire, but strangely there were no dissenting voices when Jackson put the position to them, told them that they had decided to ride west, to finish the drive. But there was a certain hardness in the others now. Neil noticed it, not only with the men – for he had expected it there – but the women too, were hard-faced, as if they had been stung by something so that their pride had been touched. He knew now, with a conviction deep within him, that there could be no turning back for the train now.

These people were solidly behind him, would fight every single inch of the way to the California border, facing no matter what lay ahead of them with that singleness of purpose which came from the knowledge that they had right on their side and that whatever happened they would triumph over evil.

'What's the terrain like west of here?' asked Jessup harshly. He chewed on a plug of tobacco, teeth working on it endlessly. He gave Neil a shrewd glance.

'Rugged, I'm afraid. It's Hollard's land but he won't stop Jesse Sherman from riding over it and bringing his killers with him if he knows why Sherman is trailing us.'

'Never figgered he would. Seems the cattle bosses ought to have their tails cut a little. Wonder why there ain't been no Texas Rangers moving into these parts, maybe a straight marshal or two.'

'They'll be along one of these years,' Neil told him. 'Until then, whenever you come up against a crooked sheriff working in cahoots with these killers, there's only one thing you can do. Fight them yourself.'

'Sure. And if they catch you, there'll be a wanted poster out for you, and they'll telegraph your name and description to every sheriff's office in the territory. Even the straight lawmen will be on your trail then and you don't stand much chance proving your innocence to them, do you. Not only the lawmen, but the bounty hunters, too.'

Neil nodded his head slowly, eyes clouded a little with memory. He left the other and went over to where the sorrel stood waiting. That was how it had been with him several years before. The outlaws had moved into town, bringing their own brand of lawlessness with them, setting up their own sheriff. They had tried to run his father off their small ranch on the outskirts of town, and when Neil had shot four of them down and sent the rest running off with their tails between their legs, he had been arrested and tossed into jail on a charge of murder.

Fortunately, he had still had some friends in town, and one dark and moonless night they had overpowered the two men set to watch his cell and busted him out of jail. He had ridden hard for the ranch, only to find it a smouldering heap of ruin and ashes. His father's body lay in the yard by the well they had dug. The outlaws had ridden back with him out of the way and shot his father down. There were four bullets in his back and he hadn't even had a chance to get a gun to defend himself. It was then that Neil had sworn to hunt down the men who had done that deed, even if it meant searching for them throughout the whole of the territory. But it hadn't taken him as long as that, for they had taken over the town then, set themselves up as the law there. He had gone on a bloody trail of vengeance which ended when ten men lay dead in the dusty streets and there had been only one man left – Jesse Sherman.

Almost of its own volition, his right hand moved down, touched the butt of the gun in its holster, fingers running over the smooth metal, almost caressingly. Killing Sherman had become his own special burden now. It was something which had changed him utterly from the man he had used to be. It had burned most of the humanity out of him, seared through him like a living flame, taking with it any tendency towards mercy and justice. It had made him tough, had forced him to practise with the guns until he had become the fastest and most feared man in the territory. Now he had the reputation of a killer, and yet had never shot a man except in self-defence, and then only men who deserved nothing more.

But he doubted if that reputation would ever leave him. It was something he could never throw off, something indelible like dirt that stuck to a man and changed his entire life, turned a man from a peace-loving citizen into a dedicated killer with a purpose.

How many of the people riding with this train guessed

that, he wondered. There was no doubt in his mind that some of them knew he had a past, perhaps had figured out for themselves that he was wanted by the law, but so long as he made it possible for them to get through to California, then they were prepared to forget that, overlook his past. While he regretted the necessity of bringing Sherman's vengeance down on these people, he knew that he had had no other choice left open to him. Jackson knew that too. He threw a swift glance to where the big man was hefting large bags of flour and beans into one of the wagons. Soon they would be ready to move out. The heat of the day was past and it would be getting cooler. The country that lay directly ahead of them was not easy ground to cover in wagons, and he knew that it would be thirty, maybe forty days before they crossed it and came into the foothills of the tall mountains that formed a vast barrier to their progress.

By then it would be nearing winter, the first snows would be falling up there among the peaks and the narrow passes. There were two passes over the mountains, and they would have to choose one of them. Whichever they chose, it was going to be difficult to cross the mountain barrier, a nightmare of snow and ice, raging blizzards that could bury them.

With an effort he put the thought out of his mind. A lot could happen before then. There were other dangers to be faced, swollen torrents as the rains swelled the rivers, the border gangs who preyed on the wagons that managed to get that far; and, above all, Jesse Sherman, thirsting for revenge, hunting them down with hatred in his heart.

6
Night Ride

Four hours after the long wagon train pulled through Twin Creeks, heading west along the rough trail, a small party of men left the Sherman ranch and rode across country, heading in the same direction, but much further north so that their paths would not cross. Leading the men, Jesse Sherman, ignoring the wound in his shoulder, from which the bullet had been taken that afternoon, his teeth gritted against he pain and his face grey from loss of blood, sat taut and straight in the saddle, gripping the reins with an unnatural tightness with his good hand. The deep-seated anger and the need for revenge drove him on. The doctor who had extracted the lead from his shoulder and patched it up had warned him against leaving his bed for two weeks, had told him that he might not live if he persisted in his wild idea of riding out that night with some of his men, running the risk of opening the wound again, starting the blood flowing into the bandage around his shirt.

Five miles to the west of the ranch they crossed the boundary between his land and that which belonged to Matt Hollard. The uneasy truce which had existed between the two men lasted only so long as neither side made any wrong move along this boundary, but Sherman knew deep within himself that there would be armed men watching every inch of the trail from that point on, and there might be a bullet waiting for him before he could get to the ear of Matt Hollard.

But such was his anger at what had happened back in Twin Creeks that he had thrown all caution to the winds, had deliberately decided to take the risk of being shot from ambush. Before he had ridden out he had debated whether to go alone; knowing that if he went with a bunch of armed men such as this, it might appear that his was a warlike, provocative mission and not a peaceable one as he intended. But he had decided against this. A couple of men might think twice about opening fire on them if there was a large party.

He debated on the wisdom of even approaching Hollard with his proposition, and wondered how the other would take it. But Neil Roberts and that wagon train had moved out of Twin Creeks, was headed west, and if he wanted to stop them, if he was to fulfil the threat he had made, that he would shoot down every man, woman and child in that train, then he would have to cross Hollard's territory to do it, there was no other way open for him. He knew how Hollard hated settlers and nesters just as he did, and there was the chance that the other might listen to reason, might be willing to forget the feud which had existed between them, at least until he had carried out his promise of destruction.

He glanced out of the corner of his eye at the men who rode with him. Grim, determined killers, men he had chosen carefully and well. They would obey every order that he gave, would have no compunction about shooting down unarmed women and children. In fact, he thought with a touch of grim amusement, they might even prefer things that way. It would minimise the risk of any of them being shot down in return.

Two miles further on they crossed a narrow trail which led up into the dark fastnesses of the hills, and he turned his mount deliberately on to it, so that within minutes they were climbing the steep, switchback courses that swung around the side of the hills, looking down on to the rough open plain below. Here they were forced to ride in single file, and as he neared the Hollard ranch he felt his nerves beginning to jump uncontrollably. A lot would depend on Hollard now. He was a strange and unpredictable man at the best of times, a man it was unwise to cross. But he might be inclined to be a little more co-operative now when it came to destroying this wagon train and he knew that Roberts killed some of Hollard's men at some time in the past. It was more than likely that the other would be glad to get rid of him, once and for all.

The wind had built up to powerful gusts here and there was a storm blowing up on the horizon, with brief flashes of lightning running along the dark skyline. Overhead the clouds were gathering, a dark curtain that came sweeping across the sky, blotting out the stars, sending the first heavy drops of rain down on to their heads and into their faces.

Gritting his teeth as a spasm of pain lanced along his arm, Sherman drew his heavy coat tightly around him, knowing the foolishness of trying to hurry along a trail such as this where, in places, only a mule was sufficiently sure-footed to be absolutely safe.

Half a mile on the trail widened, and Trudeau, the ranch foreman, rode up alongside, his face in deep shadow.

'I got the feeling that we're being watched all the way, Mister Sherman,' he said gruffly.

'That's more than likely. They'll have seen us ride in from the ranch over the boundary, but they won't be sure of what we want. That's why they'll hold their fire until they get any orders from Hollard, and I'm figuring that he'll be more than curious to know why we're riding out to see him.'

'You reckon he might agree to your proposal,' Trudeau asked. His voice was quiet and calm, the voice of a man unafraid.

'I don't reckon he's got anything to lose.' Sherman turned quickly. The wind switched from side to side now that they were more in the open, away from the shelter of the lee of the hill, hitting them from one side and then the other like the angry switching of a mare's tail. The rain began to pour on to their heads now, sweeping in sheets down the side of the hill.

'We've got to move if we want to hit the ranch before the storm gets any worse,' Sherman growled. He felt the weakness growing in his body and there was a mist in front of his eyes, a mist which came from the weakness in him, from the blood which had flowed from the gaping hole in his shoulder before the doctor had managed to plug it. The bandage, which had been bound tightly over it, was still warm and sticky where fresh blood had soaked into it, but the anger that drove and spurred him on would not let him rest, would not allow his body to get the sleep it craved so much. There was a lot he had to do before the night was over, and all of it began with Matt Hollard.

They reached the end of the downward trail, came out among the tumbled rocks at the base of the hills. The trail was a grey scar over the darkness of the plain that stretched away in front of them, dimly seen through the driving rain. The heavy drops fell from the brim of his hat, pattered against his face, half-blinding him. The lightning, never ceasing now, speared across the western heavens, bringing the roaring thunder close on its swift heels.

They put the heads of their mounts into it, crouched low in the saddle now, bending over the necks of the horses, hanging grimly to leather as they made their way over the rough terrain.

In spite of their haste, the full fury of the storm swept about them before they reached the Hollard ranch. They rode around the brow of a tall hill which overlooked the ranch house and corral, and were moving slowly when the three dark figures materialised suddenly from the stunted bushes that grew on either side of the trail. Sherman reined his mount instantly, saw Trudeau go for his gun and stopped him with a sharply hissed warning.

'They've got rifles trained on us,' he said harshly. 'Keep your hands away from your guns. I'll deal with this.'

'Now if that ain't real sensible of you,' sneered a deep voice. 'Better ride up here aways, mister, and let me take a look at you – and no tricks, mind, it would be the greatest pleasure for me to put a bullet into you.'

Gigging his mount, Sherman rode forward, said in a soft level voce: 'I'm Jesse Sherman. I've come out here to speak with Hollard.'

'Sherman!' There was a trace of surprise in the other's voice. He kept the barrel of the rifle trained on the other's chest, then came forward a little way, clambering over the smooth, treacherous rocks, wet with rain. He peered up into Sherman's face, then nodded his head slowly, let his breath exhale in a thin whistle through his clenches teeth. 'Now why should you be riding out here to parley with Hollard?' he said, half musingly.

'That's no business of yours,' snapped Sherman. 'Just take us to him.'

'Well, well, now. You seem mighty sure of yourself, Mister Sherman. Maybe you're forgetting whose spread you're on.' The insolence in the other's tone was readily discernible, but Sherman forced himself to ignore it. He was in a very precarious position here and recognised the fact instantly. Even with his men with him, even if he did go for his guns and shot these three men down, there would be more than two dozen others on their backs before they could ride a quarter of a mile, and that was not going to help him with his problem.

'You going to take us to him, or do I have to find him myself and tell him that you tried to stop us from seeing him?' he asked quietly.

For a moment he thought he saw the tight look on the man's face turn nasty and there was a lot of meanness in him as he said: 'All right, mister. Follow me. I must say you were the last man we figured on seeing here.' He turned on his heel, boots rasping on the rock as he led the way down the slope of the hill, across to the corral and the ranch house. There were lights burning in several of the windows, and Sherman could smell smoke in his nostrils as he reined his mount in the courtyard and slid from the saddle, standing weakly by the animal for a long moment, sucking the air down into his gasping lungs as a wave of weakness went through him. Gradually his whole being steadied. He did not want Hollard to see how badly hurt he had been during the fight with Roberts. It might give the other man ideas about taking over the whole of the range in that part of the territory if he figured that he could get him at a disadvantage.

The gunman walked to the door of the ranch and rapped loudly, waited. A moment passed and then the door was flung open and Sherman saw a short, stocky figure outlined against the yellow light from inside. Evidently Hollard was not antic- ipating trouble otherwise he would never have outlined himself in silhouette like that, inviting a bullet from the dark- ness.

Hollard hesitated, then walked out into the pouring rain. A flash of lightning picked out his short figure as he made his way across the courtyard until he was standing in front of Sherman. His keen-eyed gaze flickered over the other as he stared at him, the rain streaking his features.

'Slim says that you want to speak to me, Jesse,' he said harshly. 'I reckon it must be something pretty important for you to come riding out here to find me. Better come into the house. We can parley in comfort there.' He turned his head and ran his gaze along the line of men seated in the saddle around him. 'I know you'll understand if I ask your boys to go with mine into the bunkhouse where they'll get themselves a bite to eat and something hot to drink.' A faint smile flickered around the edges of his mouth.

'Sure, sure, Matt.' Sherman gave a quick nod, following the other into the ranch house.

Hollard waved the other towards a chair in the well-lit study at the rear of the ranch. Then he lowered himself into his own chair, let his gaze drop to the bulge of the bandage under Sherman's coat. 'You look as if you've been hurt, Jesse. Not trouble, I hope.'

'Nothing I can't handle, Matt,' acknowledged the other. 'But I'd like your help in this.'

The dark, thick brows lifted a little over the deep-set eyes. 'My help? Now this must be the first time you've ever come asking for that. What sort of trouble is it?'

'Settler trouble and a man called Neil Roberts.' Sherman saw the speculative expression grow in the other man's eyes. Hollard leaned forward over the polished top of the desk in front of him, placed the tips of his blunt spatulate fingers together.

'Roberts. Sure, I seem to recall that name. He made some trouble for me a while ago. Shot some of my best men. I've always wanted to meet him face to face. Where does he fit in with you?' A certain hardness to the other's tone now.

'I want him dead and I want to pull the trigger that sends him into eternity, and I want him to know that it's me who's shot him.'

'Did he do that?' Hollard nodded his head in the direction of the bandage around Sherman's shoulder.

The other nodded slowly, lips tightening a shade. 'He killed some of my men and made me look a fool into the bargain, in front of most of the people of Twin Creeks. But there's more to it than that – a lot more. He's leading a wagon train west to California. One of the biggest collection of

107

settlers you've ever seen, and they slipped across my land before I could finish them. I had some of my men stampede a herd of beef at their wagons, but they managed to get into shelter before the steers hit. Now they've passed out of Twin Creeks and are headed over your land.'

Hollard jerked up his head at that. 'Over my territory,' he boomed, rising swiftly to his feet. He stood for a long moment, staring down at the other, then forced himself to relax and sat down again..

'That's right. I know you'd normally go after them yourself. But that's why I'm here. I've got something personal in this. I swore I'd hunt them down and kill them all and fire their wagons around their ears. I want your permission to ride across your land after them and carry out that threat.'

Hollard rubbed a hand down his cheek. There was a thin smile on his lips as he gazed directly at the man in front of him. 'Do you reckon that with that wound you're in any condition to ride out on their trail, Jesse?'

'I'm damned sure I can. I mean to kill Roberts and everybody who's riding with him, particularly a giant of a man called Jackson. No flesh wound is going to stop me.'

'You must hate this man Roberts,' murmured the other. He grinned quickly. 'I never did see eye to eye with you, Jesse, in the past, and that boundary has always been a bone of contention between us. But I guess I could stretch a point here. I have no liking for settlers myself.'

'I figured you might see it that way,' agreed the other. 'In that case, I'll be on my way. That wagon train could make plenty of ground during the night, and the sooner we catch up with 'em the better.'

Hollard gave him a quick, shrewd glance. 'You ain't thinking of riding on after them tonight? Good God, man, you've been hit. There must be a hole in your shoulder the size of my gun barrel and you've obviously lost a lot of blood even riding the trail to get here. They won't get far with this storm blowing up. I'd be surprised if they made it to the river by morning. My guess is that they'll make camp somewhere on this side of the bluff. That river can be real mean if she's full, and right now, with the heavy rains to the north, she's running hard and strong. Roberts is no fool. He won't put those wagons over after dark, not with the rain beating down in a solid sheet, the current running fast in the middle, and the lightning flashing fit to put the fear of all creation in those horses they have pulling the wagons.'

'Do you know Roberts?' inquired the other, getting unsteadily to his feet, trying to hold himself tautly upright, not to show Hollard just how badly hurt he was. There seemed no point in showing just how much in this man's power he really was. The friendship which the other had extended did not go very far below the surface. Deep down inside, Hollard hated him just as much as he disliked the other man.

Hollard frowned suddenly. 'I've heard a lot about him in the past three, maybe four years. Is there anything more to know?'

'I reckon that I know him better than any other man alive, maybe even better than he knows himself. He'll put that wagon train across the river even at the height of this storm and in total darkness, too, because he knows I'll be riding out after him, and he knows that I can have more men with me than he can stand up against unless he can choose his own defensive ground. That's why he won't really rest until he's over that river and there's one natural barrier between us.'

'Suit yourself,' growled the other harshly. 'It's your funeral. If you want to risk your life going after him right now, when I don't reckon you need to, that's up to you. Do you need any more men to go with you?' He looked directly at the other as he spoke, eyes lidded, speculative.

Sherman hesitated, then shook his head quickly. 'I figure we can handle them,' he said decisively. 'He shot down some of my boys on the eastern edge of my spread and I've a few men with me who want a chance to get him in their sights.'

A fresh gust of wind from up the mountain rocked the branches of the trees that grew on the edge of the spread around the ranch house as Sherman remounted and waited for the rest of his men to put in an appearance. They came straggling from the direction of the long, low bunkhouse to find him in an evil humour, sitting tight in the saddle, lips twisted a little in a dark scowl. The light from the doorway of the ranch showed Hollard standing there, a thin black cheroot between his lips, looking out at them.

'Get mounted!' he called sharply. 'We're riding on after that wagon train.'

A flurry of wind and rain caught his words and whipped them away into the darkness. His sodden clothing clung to his body as he leaned forward in the saddle. Behind him the men climbed grumbling into the saddle, urged their mounts forward, raking spurs over the horses' flanks. They pushed on along the narrow, winding trail that led over the low hill, and as he rode Jesse Sherman peered straight ahead of him, pushing his sight into the rain-soaked darkness, trying to pick out the man he intended to hunt down and kill. For a moment, with the rest of the men around him in a tight bunch, he reached down with his left hand and touched the hard, cold metal of the Colt, fingering it almost caressingly, lips tightened into a thin, hard line across the middle of his features. The rain beat down against the wide-brimmed hat and ran into his eyes, and he brushed it away with an irritated impatient gesture.

As they reached the top of the hill the wind built up into powerful gusts which tore at them from all sides. More than ten miles ahead of them lay the river, and Sherman felt the impatience building up in him as he realised just how much of a lead the train had over him because of that forced stop-over at Hollard's ranch. He felt certain that Roberts might decide to put the team into the water that night, refusing to let them make camp until they were all on the far side. Hollard's opinion that the train would hole up for the night near the bluff he did not believe for a single instant.

He drove the men with him, at a savage, cruel pace, punishing the mounts, forcing them to the limit. He knew that the men with him were grumbling at his insistence on continuing to ride in that weather, but he ignored them. They would obey every order he gave, no matter how foolish or unnecessary they considered it to be, because they had no other choice.

At the back of his mind, however, there was a nagging little thought which would not give him peace. Had he made a mistake in asking Hollard's permission to ride out over his territory? Would it not have been in his own interests to have simply cut across country after the train in the hope that they could do so without being spotted by any of Hollard's men? Now Matt Hollard knew that he was headed west after Roberts and the wagon train, knew that he had most of his best men with him, that his own ranch and spread would be virtually unguarded. There was nothing to prevent the other from mustering as many of his men as he could and riding out east, burning and destroying, as he had sworn to do so many times in the past.

It was only with a tremendous effort that he succeeded in putting the thought out of his mind and concentrating on the task in hand, riding down that wagon train and destroy-ing it utterly.

An hour passed. Then another, and still the rain poured out of the dark and overcast sky. The horses covered the distance quickly, but not swiftly enough for Jesse Sherman, who kept urging his men on at a breakneck pace, over rough country that would have tried the endurance of any mount in broad daylight; and now, at night, in that terrible weather, it was a hundred times worse for the tired animals and rain-soaked men. At times Sherman halted his group, held up his hand for silence and listened, trying to pick out the rumble of wheels on the wet earth, a sound which would tell him whether they were close to the wagon train. But he heard nothing, and the knowledge came to him that they had already reached the river, were possibly crossing it at that moment.

A night crossing – rain and wind and total darkness, with all of its hidden thousand dangers and fears. There was no moonlight to show the river in its full flood, the white, sweeping foam where it plunged over the needle-sharp rocks of the river bed, the logs which were being borne down by the current from further upstream.

Riding to the ribbed bank of the river where the plunging, sweeping water had eaten into the soil, Neil stared about him, taking in everything. Vivid flashes of lightning lit the scene, showed him the boiling, bubbling water in front of him, dull, cold brilliance against the dark background of rocks.

'You reckon it would be wise to try to cross in this storm?' Jackson came riding up, turned his head a little to peer directly at the man who sat tall and straight in the saddle at his side. 'It could be dangerous.'

'We've got to reach the other side before Sherman gets here with his band of killers,' gritted Neil harshly. 'We've no choice.'

'You think he'll come tonight?'

'He'll come, make no mistake about that. He'll be riding out on our trail right now, with as many gunhawks as he could collect. They won't stop until they've caught up with us. That's why I feel we have to put the river between them and us as soon as possible, certainly before morning.'

'I suppose you know best.' Jackson threw a swift, apprehensive glance in the direction of the raging torrent in front of them, then wheeled his mount and galloped back to the wagon train, waiting a hundred yards away. A flash of lightning showed them clearly to Neil as he glanced behind him, the wagons outlined brilliantly against the glare, the canvas tops gleaming white, the horses in the traces, heads drooping, the rain steaming off their flanks.

It would be men's work getting those wagons safely over the swollen river. The danger was there, hanging over them all. And behind them, drawing closer with every passing second, came Sherman and his gunslingers, thirsting for revenge.

Rain dripped in an endless curtain from the low clouds as the first of the wagons moved slowly, hesitantly, down the river bank and into the swirling water. It was characteristic of Jackson that he sat on the tongue of that wagon and drove it into the sweeping current himself. Neil would never have thought it could have been otherwise. Whatever else Clem Jackson lacked it was certainly not courage and he would never ask any man to do what he was afraid to do himself.

Slowly at first, then faster as though hurried along by the brief flashes of lightning and the booming roll of thunder as it roared over the hills, the wagon moved into the middle of the raging torrent. The horses plunged and reared at the tremendous weight of water, thrust down by the current, caught them on the side, threatening to hurl them sideways, to bring the top-heavy canvas of the wagon toppling down.

Neil sat tightly in the saddle, watched through narrowed eyes as the wagon moved deeper into the river. For a moment he saw the wagon sway dangerously to one side as a wheel struck a hidden rock under the water. The rushing water attacked it hungrily, struck with a titanic force; then, miraculously, the wagon righted itself, continued forward until it dragged itself, dripping, up the other bank.

One by one the other wagons in the train began the crossing. Neil watched tensely. At any moment danger could strike and a wagon, possibly more, could go tumbling into that foaming water and be washed away before they could get a lariat around it and bring it back upright. For a while everything went well. Most of the wagons had crossed, were safely on the other side. There were only four left to move over, four and Neil himself.

A half-hour. Twenty minutes. Then the last two wagons were moving slowly and unsteadily across. Neil waited for a moment, then put his horse into the water. It moved strongly forward, sure-footed, keeping its balance with ease. The tension grew in Neil's mind. It only needed one mistake, one piece of ill fortune and—

It happened suddenly and without warning and although he had half-expected trouble, it came with the shock of the unexpected. He heard the shouts of the men and women on the wagons, could just glimpse their white and frightened faces in the flashing lightning that seared across a heaven gone berserk. Then the last wagon suddenly tipped over to one side. The horses struggled in the traces, tried to keep their balance against the dragging weight of the overturning wagon. The shrill scream of the woman inside rose to Neil's ears.

'Hold those horses steady!' he yelled, shouting at the top of his voice, but the warning was drowned out by the peal of thunder which broke almost directly overhead, and the warning came too late, anyway, to save those in the wagon. Crashing into the water, it turned over and over, the white canvas, sodden with the water, curling and flapping about it as the current caught it and carried it unresisting downstream. The horses suddenly broke free of the leather, struggled upright, neighing in fright, swam for the further bank.

Turning his own mount, Neil plunged down towards the overturned wagon, his lariat whirling in his right hand. He caught a brief glimpse of the white arm upraised from the smashed Conestoga, tried to make a cast, but the wind caught it, deflected his throw and the noose fell short. Then there was nothing he could do. Those in the wagon were lost. Wearily he wound the riata, coiled it back into place. There was a deep weariness in him as he made his way to the bank.

Jackson came stumping back, rain puddling about his feet. He stared up at Neil, blinking the water from his eyes, wiping it swiftly from his face with the back of his hand.

'There was nothing I could do for them,' said Neil dully.

'I understand.' Jackson nodded. There was a curious expression on his face and Neil noticed the way he suddenly averted his gaze, as though afraid to meet Neil's directly.

Neil kept them on the move, knowing that the best thing now was for the people in the train to work and not to think of what had happened. Soon, perhaps in the morning, they would have time in which to realise that some of their friends had died during the night, their bodies carried away by the sweeping current.

Three hours later he called a halt. They were almost five miles from the river on a wide stretch of ground, raised a little from the surrounding terrain, to form a miniature plateau. Overhead the storm clouds rolled from horizon to horizon and there seemed to be no place where they could get dry. It was dangerous to light a fire, and they settled down, shivering, waiting for the grey light of dawn to bring an end to their discomfort.

Five miles to the east Jesse Sherman reined his mount, peering through the teeming rain, looking down at the river where it stormed between its banks in the darkness. Sucking in his lips, swaying in the saddle from weariness and weakness, he turned and gazed at the men who had ridden with him. Tired men who had ridden far and hard. But they had to go on. The river faced them and there was a dull ache in his body which refused to leave him now, something which had always been there since they had set out on this ride and which had grown over the miles and the hours.

'There's one of the wagons down by the bend a couple of hundred yards downstream,' said one of the men. 'They've crossed the river and could be miles away by now.'

'That wagon back there? What happened?'

The other shrugged. 'Must have hit a rock in midstream. Nobody still alive and I doubt if anybody got out of it. They never stood a chance. Roberts seems determined to push ahead, even if it mean killing some of 'em on the way.'

'He knows we're around, close on his heels,' murmured the other grimly. He pulled his cloak more tightly about him as gusts of wind pulled at his clothing.

'Do we cross now?' asked another man thinly. 'Since we're in this as deep as you are, I reckon we ought to know just why we're after this wagon train. I know you're intent on killin' Roberts. That's understandable. But what about the train?'

Sherman looked him over deliberately. He said: 'You seem to be acting damned big at the moment. Are you workin' for me, or aren't you?? Remember, I can turn you over to the law and then you're finished.'

'I'm working for you,' affirmed the other, 'but I'd like to know why we're going out to shoot up unarmed women and kids. I've a hankering for bigger game than that.' He spoke boastfully, fingering the gun in his belt, ignoring the rain that slashed at them. He stared challengingly at Sherman. 'I'd have preferred to have a gamer chance with some of Hollard's men.'

'You may get that chance before long,' Sherman promised. 'But right now we have another job to do. Go after that wagon train and finish it off. I don't want a single person left alive when we're done.' ———

The man nodded, relaxed a little. 'You must hate Roberts to do something like this.'

Sherman forced a tight grin. That was the second time that night someone had said that to him. Yes, he thought savagely, with a tightening of the muscles of his arms, he hated Roberts, meant to see him dead before morning. With a sharp yell, he urged the men into the river, putting his own mount into the storming current. The river was so swollen in the middle that they were forced to swim their horses, and the current carried them almost fifty yards downstream before they climbed the further bank.

The storm increased as they hit the trail and started west, their horses plunging and rearing in spite of all they could do to calm them. Such terrible pounding storms had plagued this stretch of country for centuries, had been one of the natural scourges of the west. Storms that blew up swiftly, clouds running before the wind, bringing solid sheets of rain, great splashing streaks of lightning bolts and such savage roaring thunder that they were one experience which startled newcomers to these parts and were never forgotten by those who had the misfortune to ride through them.

Sherman forced himself to hold on tightly to the reins, leaning forward over his mount's neck. The drenching rain never ceased to pound at them. The lightning showed them the trail, the streaking bolts searing across the sky in an almost continual succession.

He pushed his sight ahead of him as far as he could whenever the vivid flashes lit up the terrain around them, a wild and rugged landscape of tumbled rocks and tall canyon walls, etched and fluted by long ages of wind and rain, where

117

erosion had bitten deeply into the sandstone. Gusts of wind caught at them and threatened to hurl horse and rider from the trail, into the brush that rose up on either side. But by the light of the flashing lightning it was possible to see the deep ruts where the wheels of the heavy wagons had bitten deeply into the soft, muddy earth. Already they were filling rapidly with water. He kicked spurs along the flanks of his mount, galloped him into the darkness.

Half an hour later they followed the trail more slowly and warily. Sherman had the unshakeable feeling that the wagon train lay only a short distance ahead and he was not anxious to stumble upon it without warning. That could be asking for trouble if they had guards posted, although in this weather and after so long a ride, he doubted if the guards would be quite as watchful as Roberts would have wished. Still, there was no point in taking any unnecessary risks. Roberts himself and that great bearded giant might be on watch and they were a different proposition. They would never sleep while there was any danger to the train. He felt the tightness in his body once more, felt for the butt of the gun at his hip, and cursed the wound in his shoulder which made it almost impossible for him to use his right arm now. A half-cripple might stand little chance against a man such as Roberts, and yet he was determined that it should be his gun that killed the other and that Roberts should know he had pulled the trigger.

He turned things over in his mind as he rode, forming plans and then rejecting them almost instantly. He would have to rely on one of his men disarming Roberts. Then he would step in and take over. Every one of his men had explicit orders on that particular point. He wanted to kill Roberts. They had only to wound or disarm him. He would do the rest. His lips curled at the thought, at the sweetness of revenge.

Then they had topped a low rise and the vivid flash of

lightning which lit up the whole heavens showed them the scene below. Less than half a mile from where they stood lay the wagon train. There was no mistaking the white canvas that flapped sluggishly in the wind. A slight shiver went through him as he narrowed his eyes against the glare. Then the lightning died and the darkness was deeper and more intense than before. He could see nothing, his eyes still dazzled.

'There they are,' said Trudeau. 'Right where I would have figured they'd be. He's no fool, that *hombre*. He know the best place in the territory to put a wagon train where it's going to be most difficult to take 'em by surprise.'

'He's no fool,' grated Sherman, 'but in spite of that, he's soon going to be dead and I mean to be the one to kill him. Don't you forget that – any of you.'

'You figuring on riding in there right now, running 'em down before they know we're here?'

'Now I know you're a goddamn fool,' snapped the other. 'They'll have guards on look out. If you want to get yourself shot, just try riding in like that.'

'Then what do we do? Sit it out here for the rest of the night?'

'We go down on foot. Get rid of the guards first. Once they're out of the way the rest ought to be simple. Then we'll be able to take the train by surprise. That way, even Roberts will be unable to stop us.'

He lowered himself unsteadily from the saddle, stood for a long moment, ashen-faced, steadying himself against the heaving flanks of the horse, sheltered a little from the wind and rain there. The pain in his shoulder lanced through his body now and his legs seemed to be losing their starch, unable to go on bearing his weight. Somehow, he forced himself to move forward, one leg in front of the other, walking stiffly, slowly, keeping his blurred vision focused on the

119

wagon train in the distance, as if he needed something to maintain his iron will and determination to keep his tired, weary body moving.

7

Vengeance in Gunsmoke

Neil twisted in his blankets. Lying under one of the wagons, seeking some shelter from the teeming rain, some tiny sound penetrated into that part of his brain which never slept. It was only the faintest whisper of sound but it was sufficient to wake him, his right hand moving out towards the Colt, which lay in its holster within easy reach at the same moment that he eased himself up on to one elbow, wide awake, eyes peering into the darkness about him. He moved his legs a little then eased himself upright, standing by the side of the wagon, the Colts in his hands, every nerve stretched taut, every sense alert, seeking the source of the trouble, the danger. There was the soft clop of hooves in the distance as men rode close, then halted their mounts.

He wondered what had happened to the two men he had placed on guard. Probably asleep by now, wearied by that long ride, by the danger of crossing the swollen river, thinking there could be no danger for what man would ride after them in that teeming rain, with the heavens open above them. They had clearly overlooked the driving hatred which could exist in the soul of a man such as Jesse Sherman, a man who would ride through hell itself to get his revenge.

At the edge of camp he caught glimpse of Calder, one of the men on watch. He was seated on a large boulder, his Winchester between his knees, trying to build himself a smoke in the rain. A second later a coiled rope fell over his shoulders, pinning his arms to his sides, hauling him out of sight.

Neil's two shots, aimed high into the air, woke the wagon train. Then there was the roar of gunfire from all sides and he threw himself down behind the wagon with a savage curse on his lips. He ought never to have allowed those two men to have taken watch, he ought to have known that they would be half asleep, would not keep a good look out with the rain pouring down on them, with the belief that the nearest danger was many miles away, and would not catch up with them before morning.

He heard the bull-like voice of Clem Jackson yelling a harsh warning, saw him go charging forward between two of the wagons, his long-barrelled Winchester clutched in his huge hands, bringing it to bear on two gunhawks who came leaping among the rocks, firing as they ran forward. Bullets hummed about Neil as he picked himself up and flung himself forward. More pecked at the wet ground near his feet, or cut through the flapping canvas close to his head.

A dark figure stumbled forward from the direction of the rocks. Swiftly he brought the Colts to bear, squeezed the trigger, saw the other fall forward, the guns in his hands hammering savagely as he pressed down on the triggers with the last ounce of strength in his body. The brief orange flares from the guns showed in the teeming darkness. Then more gunfire had broken out to the rear of the wagons, and he knew they were surrounded.

Jesse Sherman's harsh voice yelled from the darkness; 'You're finished, Roberts. Better throw down your guns and come out here with your hands lifted. The same goes for everybody else. If you don't, then I'll have to kill everybody in the wagon train. You wouldn't want me to do that, would you?'

'You'll do it whether we throw down our guns or not,' yelled Jackson harshly before Neil could answer. A rifle shot bucketed though the silence as the other fired in the direction of the voice.

Now the men in the wagons were firing and some of the women had guns too, were shooting at the shadows of the gunmen hidden among the rocks in the darkness, aiming for the orange flashes which gave away the positions of the gunhawks. Sherman and his men were well hidden, had evidently crept up on the train in the darkness, hoping to take them completely by surprise, would have done so had Neil not picked out the faint sound of horses in the near distance.

Everyone was shooting now, firing and loading – firing and loading. Six-guns answered from the boulders. Near the edge of the train Neil ran forward, crouched over until he came to where Jackson lay on his stomach, pumping shots slowly and methodically into the rocks.

'Follow me!' he said harshly. 'We've got to take them out there, before they shoot down everyone in the train.'

Jackson nodded, understood in an instant, crawled forward after him. The lightning was retreating to the eastern horizon as the storm passed over. The rain was not so heavy now and there was a faint pencil of grey light in the east where the dawn was beginning to break. The air was still cold and beneath their bodies the ground ran with water.

Neil sucked in a long, heavy gust of wind, let it come out through his nostrils in slow pinches. Someone moved directly ahead of him and a moment later he made out the shapes of three men, crouched down behind the rocks. He touched Jackson's sleeve, nodded in their direction.

Some sixth sense must have warned one of the men of the danger for he whirled swiftly, loosing off a single shot that scorched past Neil's cheek, before Jackson blasted with his rifle. One man pitched backward with his arms outflung, hung against the rock at his back for a long moment, before sliding on to the rocky floor at the foot of the boulders. The other two tried to bring their guns to bear, died as Neil squeezed the triggers of his six-guns, felt them buck against his wrists. More ricochets whined off the rocks, jagged fragments of metal that hummed through the night.

There was confused shouting in the distance as more of the gunhawks came under fire from the wagons. Evidently the gunslingers had not expected this savage return fire and were finding things a little too hot for them. Out of the corner of his eye Neil saw two men darting back over the uneven ground to where their horses were evidently waiting. Neither of the men was Sherman. He began to wonder about the other. Sherman had been hit badly in the shoulder during that fight in the saloon back in Twin Creeks, and he must have lost a lot of blood. That, coupled with the hard riding they had evidently put in during the night, meant that he would be as weak as a kitten, would still be holed up somewhere among the rocks waiting a chance to shoot him down from ambush.

He crept forward to the end of the narrow chasm in the rocks, with Jackson following close on his heels, reloading the Winchester. The shouting went on. There was the sound of feet scraping among the rocks less than ten yards away to their right. A burst of gunfire, then a regular fusillade of shots pouring into the wagons. The gunfire rose to a smothering racket that seemed to come from every direction, with the echoes bouncing back from the rearing, rocky walls that lay about them. Drawing his breath, Neil fired into the rocks, saw a dark shadow lurch to one side clutching at a smashed wrist, the gun clattering to the rocks at the man's feet. He clawed for the other Colt with his good hand, but before he could draw it clear of leather another shot took him in the chest and he went down, to stay down.

Gradually the shooting was dying down. The gunmen with Sherman had no stomach for this kind of fighting, with the odds stacked a little too much against them. When it came to shooting down women and children, then they thought nothing of it, but several of their number had been killed, and even Sherman must have realised that they were in a tight spot. More slugs beat through the air as the gunhawks made one last attempt to locate Jackson and Neil, to drill them before they could cause any more trouble. But they might just as well have tried to hit a pair of shadows.

For several minutes shots sounded in ragged, uneven rhythm from the rocks. A man seated on the lip of one of the wagons suddenly gurgled and swayed to one side. Neil saw the woman behind him lean out of the canvas, grab him by the shoulders and haul him back into the wagon. Now the answering fire from the rocks had dwindled until there were only a handful of isolated shots that tore through the canvas or hammered off the wooden upright and shafts. Crouched down among the rocks, eyes straining to pick out any of the gunhawks, Neil heard the thunder of hooves in the distance, heard the horses move away over the crest of the small plateau and then towards the tall hills in the distance.

He drew in a deep breath and lowered the guns, then thrust them back into the holsters. Beside him, Jackson got to his feet, stood with his legs braced against the earth, staring out after the retreating horses. His shoulders moved, swaying a little, as his eyes continued to search through the drizzling rain. Then he gave a quick nod of satisfaction.

'I reckon they had enough,' he said dully. 'I don't figure they'll come this way again in a hurry.'

'I'll feel safer if I know what happened to Sherman. Take a look and see if he's dead. If he is, he'll be lying somewhere in the rocks. I'll go down to the train and check on the casualties there.'

Slowly he moved back into the ring of wagons. There was movement there now. Men who had been wounded by the flying bullets that had torn through thin, flimsy canvas, torn into flesh and bone and sinews. Women were busy tearing up long strips of cloth with which to bind up the wounds that bubbled red. Neil's keen gaze took in everything in a single, wide sweep. Several men had been wounded, but no one killed. They had beaten off Sherman and his gunmen, had whipped them in the rain-drenched darkness. He felt a wave of elation pass through him, a feeling that vanished instantly and utterly as a familiar voice behind him, from near one of the wagons, said:

'Don't make a move for your guns, Roberts. I've got the drop on you and I only need the slightest excuse to kill you.'

Very slowly, without turning, Neil moved his hands away from the guns at his waist. He knew that there was one gun trained on him at that moment, that he could not possibly draw and fire before the other man, weak and wounded as he may have been, fired and the slug found his heart. But for a moment the idea lived in his mind, then was forgotten.

'Better not tell any of your men to do anything foolish. This gun is trained on your heart and I can kill you long before they shoot me. That goes for the big *hombre* up there.'

Neil lifted his head a little, saw Jackson standing a few yards away, with the Winchester cradled in his arms.

'Drop it, Clem,' he said sharply. 'He means what he says.'

Slowly, reluctantly, the other let go of the rifle so that it fell clattering to the dirt at his feet. His eyes glared at the man standing behind Neil.

'That's being sensible.' There was a harsh laugh from the other. 'All right, Roberts, turn round now but very slowly and easy. I'm going to shoot you down like I swore I would, but I want you to be facing me when I pull this trigger.'

Neil ran his tongue over his dry lips as he turned very slowly to face the other. Sherman stood a few yards away in front of one of the wagons, a Colt in his left hand, the barrel trained on his heart, the other's hand rock steady in spite of the greyness of his features and the limp right arm hanging by his side.

'And what do you figure is going to happen to you even if you do shoot me, Sherman?' he asked, keeping his voice steady and even. 'You'll be dead the next minute, I suppose you know that. Your men have left you, run out on you. By now they'll be miles away and they won't be coming back to help you.'

Sherman thinned his lips, drew them back over his teeth. 'They've served their purpose now,' he said harshly. He swayed a little, then snapped up the barrel of the Colt sharply as Neil made a slight movement forward. 'I've been waiting for this moment for a long time. I want you to crawl and cringe this time as I had to do all those years ago.'

There was no answer from Neil. He waited, turned his gaze for a moment over the faces of the men and women standing around the wagons. There were no words from any of them. Not that he had expected any. No movement. Sherman drew a rasping breath in through his nostrils and stood erect with an effort. There was a growing red stain on the front of his shirt, a tell-tale bulge where the thick bandage had been wound tightly around his shoulder in an attempt to staunch the flow of blood.

'I'm going to kill you, Roberts.' It was simply said, and there was the promise of death in the other's eyes as he took a single step forward, his finger bar-straight on the trigger of

127

the gun in his hand, knuckles growing white with the pressure he was exerting. Neil braced himself for the impact of the bullet. His eyes locked with those of the man who intended to kill him, waiting, watching, probing for the sign which would tell him that death was on its way. Silence crowded down on the wagon train.

Then there came the sharp, searing blast of a gun. Involuntarily, Neil winced, stiffened, then stared as Sherman fell forward, the gun slipped from his fingers. Slowly, as though every muscle in his body was reluctant to fight against the need to hold him upright, he crashed to the wet ground.

Neil touched his lips with a dry tongue, went forward and stared down at the body of the man who lay in front of him, stretched out at his feet. Then he lifted his head and stared at the wagon directly behind where Sherman had been standing, saw the canvas part and someone step forward with a smoking rifle in her hands.

His eyes held in bewilderment on her as she stood framed in the opening. Then he recognised her, knew why she had killed Jesse Sherman, why she had taken that rifle which had belonged to her husband and shoot him in the back.

Very slowly, like a woman in a dream, Claire Vance lowered the hand which held the rifle and stood looking about her in stunned surprise. Out of the corner of his eye Neil saw two of the women move towards her, take the gun from her and lead her gently back inside the wagon.

Jackson came forward, tall and massive, looked down at the dead man with a hard expression on his pitiless features. Then he gave a slow, ponderous nod of his head. 'A strange kind of justice, I suppose,' he said slowly, choosing his words with care. 'But I for one can understand why she killed him.'

Neil gave an answering nod. 'She saved my life,' he said softly.

'Somehow, I doubt if that was the reason she did it. She

knew he was the man who was directly responsible for setting that herd on us when her husband was trampled to death by those stampeding steers. Perhaps she'll find some rest now, poor soul.'

The next morning they broke camp, moved out along the trail to the west. The storm had passed and the sunrise was one in which all of the colours seemed to have been washed clean by the rain, flaming reds and oranges which lit up the whole of the eastern horizon. In front of them, almost seventy miles away, the tall peaks of the mountains lifted clear to the blue heaven, their peaks glistening in the brilliant sunlight which touched them with a touch of red, while still leaving the bases in shadow.

Once they reached those mountains, Neil reflected, they would have to move up through one of the two passes open to them. He felt the tiny wave of apprehension flowing in him again. It would take them the best part of thirty-five days to cover that distance because, from his knowledge of the territory, the going became rougher the closer they got to that high range and their progress would be slowed to a crawl during the last ten days or so. By that time the winter would be on them and the first snows would be falling up there among the passes. If they were caught in one of the early winter blizzards, they might find themselves trapped, and even if they did manage to get safely over to the other side of those mountains, which formed a natural barrier along the trail, they would have the marauding border gangs to contend with, professional killers who owed allegiance to no one and preyed on any wagon trains which managed to get through as far as that.

They had only one slim chance of beating the winter snows among those high passes. He would have to drive the train hard, harder than they had been driven so far, and once again, as far as the others were concerned, the danger was one they would not readily appreciate. A man could see danger when it consisted of bullets drumming at him from the darkness around a ring of wagons, or when it lay in the swirling foam of a swollen river, built high by the heavy rains to the north. But talk of snow which might be there more than seventy miles away and it did not seem to present any real danger.

Fifteen days on the trail. Long days with short nights. Neil had set the hard pace, anxious to cross the plain as quickly as possible, driving man and beast to the utmost limit. They camped wherever they happened to be at midnight, woke with the first grey light of an early dawn, ate quickly, hitched up the teams and moved on again, keeping to the trail that led due west.

Seated by the blazing fire, on the night of the fifteenth day after their brush with Jesse Sherman, Clem Jackson said quietly: 'Some of the men have been grumbling about the way you're driving 'em, Neil. They figure that there ain't so much hurry that we have to drive more'n fifteen hours every day. By the time we reach the mountains, none of the wagons will be in any fit condition to make it over them. We'll have to carry out extensive repairs, and that will take time. You'll lose more time with that than you'll gain pushing them as you are doing at the moment.'

'Do you think I haven't considered that?' Neil spoke with an unaccustomed sharpness, then forced himself to relax. 'Sorry, but I guess I am a little jumpy.'

'You afraid of what we might find when we hit those mountains?' The other raised thick, bushy eyebrows, regarded Neil quizzically.

'Guess so. I made an agreement to get you folk through to California. We lost some on the way here, mostly my own fault. I had no right letting any of my personal feuds interfere with this, specially as far as Sherman was concerned. That's been the main cause of all our trouble so far.'

'You ain't got nothing to reproach yourself for on that account,' declared the other. 'We all realised that Sherman or Hollard would have killed us all if they had the chance. They're as much against settlers as they were against you.'

'If we run into bad conditions up there in the mountain passes, we may have to spend the whole of the winter this side of 'em. Reckon we don't have enough supplies for that, so the only chance we have is to keep on going. That's why I'm pushing everybody as hard as they can go. I'd like you to try to make them see that. I don't like keeping up this cruel, punishing pace any more than they do. But it won't be long before the first winter storms start up there.'

'Anybody tried to cross during the winter months?' The other teased a strip of beef with the tip of his long-bladed knife, then pushed it into his mouth and chewed on it reflectively.

'Some,' Neil admitted. 'They didn't get far if we can believe the reports that came back. The blizzards struck while they were crossing, caught them unawares, blocked the pass completely. None of 'em managed to get through to the plains on the far side.'

'And you reckon there's a good chance of that happening to us?'

'I reckon so. We may be lucky. The storms may be late in starting this year.'

A pause, then: 'But you don't think they will be? Is that it?'

'Judgin' from the rivers, they're pretty full at the source up there in the mountains. That's always a bad sign. Could mean an early winter.'

There was no more talk at the fire that night. With the long days on the trail, men snatched at sleep whenever they could. An hour lost in talk meant a tired man the next day, a man whose reflexes were just that shade slower than they ought to have been and that could spell danger.

Wrapped in his blankets, feeling the wind that blew off the mountains blowing cold against his body, Neil Roberts tried to figure out in his mind the best thing to do for the safety of the train. Had it not been for Jesse Sherman, they might have picked up more supplies back in Twin Creeks, might have enough to wait out the worst months of the winter, at least, before attempting the dangerous crossing of those tall, snow-covered peaks. As it was, they had very little left. Perhaps just sufficient to carry them through to the end of the trail, but little besides. There could be no question of waiting it out. Half of them would starve before the weather changed for the better and allowed them to go on with their journey, and he doubted if they could shoot enough to keep themselves alive.

No, they had to cross the peaks and once he had made that decision there was the question of which pass to choose. The pass which slashed through the upper reaches of the mountains directly ahead of them would be the very devil in the midst of winter, was certainly the shortest route, but the more dangerous. The other was easier to negotiate, but it meant swinging to the south, more than two extra days on the drive. He fell asleep with the thoughts still spilling through his mind.

Ten days later they left the trail, struck out across more rugged country leading to the south. Neil Roberts had made his decision. He told Jackson and Jessup of it as they moved off through the rough terrain, the wagons bouncing and jolting over the stony ground.

'We daren't risk taking the wagons over Snake Pass,' he said quietly, eyeing the big man who sat the tongue of the wagon beside him, his own sorrel moving alongside. 'A couple of thrown wheels up there and we would be bogged down for weeks before we could make repairs. At least this way we stand a better chance of getting through without mishap. The South Pass is lower, if there is snow it ought to be less severe than to the north.'

'We're in your hands as far as that is concerned,' muttered the other harshly. He stared ahead, his jaw jutted forward. They had covered several hundred miles now, and somewhere on the other side of that tall range of mountains lay California, the Promised Land, the country where the climate was always mellow and sunny, where the rich red gold had been found. It was enough to fire the imagination of any man, and watching him out of the corner of his eye, Neil could almost read the other's thoughts, knew that most of the men and women in the train were thinking along the same way now that they were approaching the end of their long journey across a continent.

In a way, he felt the empty coldness in his own mind. For him, it seemed, there would always be the wandering, the leagues of rolling grass or the white alkali of the stretching, flat deserts, a man hunted by the law, framed by a crooked sheriff, and always on the run.

'Do you reckon that the folk here can take that journey over the mountains?' he asked abruptly. 'So far, the going has been easy compared with what we'll find up there.'

'They'll take it,' said the other emphatically. 'They knew what they were letting themselves in for before they started out on this trip. You ain't reckoning on any of 'em wanting to turn back now, are you?'

'I was wondering about folk like Claire Vance. There wouldn't seem to be much left for her in California.'

The big man caught Neil's look, shrugged. 'You may be right. Whenever you set out on something like this, there's always somebody who has to get hurt. I suppose she was one of the unlucky ones.'

'How is she taking it now – after what happened with Sherman, I mean?'

Jackson pursed his thick lips. 'I got Virginia Millais taking care of her. She seems to have got over it pretty well considering the shock she must have had. You worried about her, Neil?'

'In a way. She's been through a lot and I feel, well, sorta responsible for her. After all, she did save my life by shooting Sherman. If she hadn't done that he would have shot me down in cold blood.'

'She's back in the fourth wagon if you'd care to take a look-see for yourself. Maybe you'd be able to get her to snap out of it a little.'

He gave Neil a queer look which the other pointedly ignored. Then Neil had swung his legs over the side of the shafts and dropped lightly to the ground, waiting while the other wagons rolled past him, kicking up the grey dust as they rumbled by. He waited until the fourth wagon came alongside, then climbed up on to the tongue. Virginia Millais gave him a smile of welcome, moved along the seat. He took the reins from her, slapped the rumps of the horses absently.

'We're heading for the South Pass,' he said quietly, pointing towards the tall peaks which were now close on the horizon. 'Once we cross that and move down into the plains on the other side, it ought to be plain sailing all the way into California. I'm sure you'll all be glad once this journey is over.'

'And the border gangs you mentioned. What about them?'

'We may run into trouble with them.' His eyes followed those of the woman to the tall peaks that glistened in the sunlight. 'It's hard to say. But we fought off Jesse Sherman and his killers. I reckon we can do the same with these men.'

There was a movement in the wagon at Neil's back and a moment later the heavy folds of canvas were twitched aside.

Neil felt his gaze being drawn to the golden-haired woman who looked out at him, her eyes turning to Virginia Millais and then back to him.

'They tell me that you're feeling a little better now, Ma'am,' said Neil quietly. 'I'm afraid I've never had the chance to talk with you, and thank you for saving my life as you did.'

There was an instant of pause, then: 'He was the man who gave the orders to stampede the cattle. He killed my husband just as surely as if he had trained a gun on him and pulled the trigger. He didn't deserve to live.'

'I'm real sorry about your husband.' Neil spoke hesitantly. 'He was a good man. It was a bad way for anyone to die.'

The woman's face did not change. Only her eye seemed alive. 'He's dead now, but life has to go on here whether we like it or not.'

'I understand. Perhaps when we reach California, it may be different. You may be able to start a new life there, pick up the threads and begin again.'

'Perhaps.' Her voice was merely a faint whisper of sound. Then it grew a little stronger. 'And you, Neil Roberts? What about you when we reach California? Do you intend to turn and ride back into this terrible country? Here, so they tell me, you're always on the run.'

'You seem to know a lot about me,' he said softly.

'Enough to know that you're no criminal, that the charges brought against you were made by crooked people, men who hid behind a badge and brought shame to this country.'

'I wish you could make everyone see that.' He spoke lightly, in a faintly bantering tone, but his words were deep and serious. His fingers had tightened a little, convulsively, on the leather reins in his hands.

'Then why don't you stay in California? Surely the past could never catch up with you there. It's new country, shut off from this place by the mountains. Like me, you're looking for

135

some place to start a completely new life.' Her eyes looked over him with a renewed interest, as if seeing the man for the first time.

There was silence while the wagon lurched forward over the rough trail, the creak of the wheels loud in Neil's ears. It was a thought which had never occurred to him. Perhaps this woman was right. Perhaps in California, hundreds of miles from here, he might find the peace he had been seeking for so long and there would no longer be the need to keep on running, moving on from one place to another, with only the wide arch of the heaven for a ceiling, his saddle for a pillow.

'You'll consider it?' There was a trace of insistence in the woman's voice as she looked at him.

For an instant his gaze locked with hers, then he gave a slow, brief nod. 'I'll consider it,' he said softly. 'But first we have to reach California and that isn't going to be easy. We've still a long way to go and if there is snow up there in the Pass, it's going to be ten times worse than anything we've had to endure so far.'

The lie of the land was far rougher now than anything they had yet encountered. They forded a wide river, shallow, but with the current running fast. Already in flood, fed by the rains and snow up in the mountains, it boded ill for a crossing of the South Pass. Now they were moving into the foothills of the mountains. High above them, crushing down with all of their tremendous, massive weight, the mountains looked up against the bright blue of the sky, their topmost peaks almost lost to sight. Then the tall trees which covered the lower slopes crowded in on them from all sides, and although high noon blazed somewhere above the leafy arch over their heads, here it was blue-shadowed and still, with the air cool and filled with the sharply acrid scent of the pines.

Presently they came upon the relic of an ancient wagon

trail, broader than that which they had followed from the plain, and they made good time with the horses pulling hard in the traces, the wagons rumbling forward, rocking gently from side to side. In places the trail wound around jagged rocks, then climbed to a long, bare ridge of stratum where they came out into the open, the trees thinning, then falling away from them on both sides so that the bright light of the glaring late-afternoon sun beat down at them with an intense fury that half-blinded them until their eyes became accustomed to it.

Halfway along the stratum they came across the remains of an old digging. There were two log cabins built by the side of the trail in the lee of a tall stretch of rock, but the roofs had fallen in and there was the mark of a solitary grave in the hard earth in front of a small clump of trees, the rough wooden cross thrusting itself up from the dirt like a vaguely accusing finger. Neil let his gaze wander over the scene, taking in everything until he was certain that the place was deserted and there was no danger there. In one of the trees an axe had been thrust into the bark, left there by the former occupant. At some time in the past, he thought, a man had driven that axe-head deep into the wood and then simply turned on his heel and walked away, possibly the man who had buried his companion in that lonely grave near the trees.

'Do you know this land, Neil?' Jackson turned from his seat on the lead wagon, holding the reins loosely in his huge gnarled hands.

'I've been here a couple of times before. There's a good place to camp about three miles ahead. We won't reach the pass for another three, four days maybe, depends on how fast we can travel.'

'You been all the way over and down to the other side?'

'I have, but not in the middle of winter. It may look easy right now, but when you're up there, in the middle of a blizzard, things look very different.'

By degrees the country roughened and, around them, the pines grew smaller, more stunted. They were climbing through the timber now, but the trail led them by many switchback courses, and Neil knew that the change would not be sudden, that only gradually would they notice the difference between the tree-covered slopes down here, where the air was still warm, particularly at high noon, and the rocky passes high up where the air was thin, and even if the sky was blue and cloudless, the air was cold and frosty; and the long nights filled with the bright and glittering stars were colder than any of these people had ever known.

They camped on the wide bluff some five hundred feet above the plain. There were crags and deep, knife-edged ravines all about them now and the wind that came sweeping down off the sheer side of the mountains was bitterly cold and struck through their clothing into their bones. The wagons were drawn up in single file and the two fires were lit in a shallow, narrow-sided ravine where they could not be picked out from the plains down below. Although Jesse Sherman was finished, there was still the possibility that Matt Hollard might come riding out on their heels, even though they had crossed his territory now.

They had held the wagons to the ridge during the latter part of the long afternoon, but now had dropped down into the ravines. Shortly before sunset they had crossed the narrow creek and there was plenty of fresh water for themselves and the horses. While the others ate their evening meal, cooked over the fires, Neil made his way to the edge of the bluff, checking on the ground. The land, he saw, was deceptive. They had passed out of one large canyon, up to this flat stretch of ground, and in front of them stretched another canyon, although the trail itself was still pointed at the summit of the mountains. Now they were on an island of height with a sheer precipitous drop of three hundred feet on one side of the trail directly ahead of them. He peered along it in the growing darkness, trying to make out details. It would not be easy to drive along that particular stretch of the trail, he estimated, and there was a very narrow trail running down the side of the precipice, a trail which could have been traversed only by a mule or a mountain goat. Certainly nothing else could have been sufficiently sure-footed to make it and he could see that this trail had not been used for a long time. Possibly it could not have been anything more than a series of footholds cut out by goats.

The cliff itself was rock and earth, growing a stunted kind of vegetation which clung tenaciously to it, sucking a bare existence from the dry soil with the solid rock only an inch or so beneath. The darkness fell swiftly as he stood there and the night air began to flow more swiftly off the peaks, sweeping down the narrow ravines. He shivered and made his way slowly back to the camp. Clem Jackson motioned him down beside the fire, his eyes drifting slowly around the looming rocks which lay about them at the shadows that crouched beyond the ring of red light thrown by the leaping flames. A platter of sizzling beef was placed in front of Neil, and the other waited until the platter was clean before saying quietly: 'What do you think of it? You did go to take a look along the trail?'

'We'll have to be careful when we pull out in the morning. There's a sheer drop of nearly three hundred feet on one side. One false move and that wagon will be finished.' He forced a quick smile, but there was no answering smile from Clem Jackson. The big man gnawed at his dry lips.

'There's no sign of snow,' he said finally, the words deep rumbling things that came from the depths of huis chest.

'The weather can be deceptive here. It can change without warning.'

Jackson shrugged, gulped his coffee. Jessup refilled his

cup and the big man held the cup between his hands, rolling it a little, absorbing the heat, then held the coffee beneath his broad nose, sniffing the fragrance and drawing it deep into his lungs.

'How soon before we hit the bad country, Neil?'

'Maybe three days. The trail winds around the outcrops of rock most of the way now. We'll have to move the wagons one at a time past the precipice. Once we're beyond that, we ought to make better time, although it's going to be uphill all the way now.'

Neil filled his coffee cup from the boiler and sipped it slowly, swilling it around his mouth before swallowing it. It brought some of the warmth back into his frozen body.

Later, getting up from the fire, he made his way back along the line of wagons. They stood in shadow now that the light had gone from the sky, but as he moved quietly past one of them there was a slight movement of the canvas and a voice came out of the darkness, a rich and husky voice that he recognised immediately.

'Neil ...' called Claire Vance. 'Neil, do you mind if I talk to you?'

8

The White Menace

Bending forward a little, Neil stared up at the questioning eyes of the woman who looked down at him from the tongue of the wagon. She drew her shawl more tightly about her shoulders in the cold night air. Then her hand reached out and she placed it on his arm.

'Do you mind if I talk to you, Neil?'

'No.'

He felt a curious tightness in his body as if his muscles were all drawing tight under his flesh. It was easy to forget Sherman and Hollard, to forget the life he had been forced to lead in the past, for ever running from the law, sleeping where he could, never knowing how long it would be before some gun, faster than his own, caught up with him and ended his life in a single, red-edged instant of time. He sensed her nearness and felt the strange warmth that seemed to flow from her hand into his arm, even through the thick cloth.

'Did you think over what I told you some days back, Neil?'

'About settling down in California, if we ever get there?'

'Yes.'

'I've thought about it a little.' He straightened up as she

141

sank down on to the hard wood of the wagon, sat beside him, staring up at the brilliant stars that powdered the heavens over their heads, frostily clear now. Soon, thought Neil tightly, those stars would be even clearer until the time came when they were utterly blotted out by the racing snow clouds.

'And you don't like the idea. Is that it?' Her voice was soft and low. There was no trace in her voice or face of the trouble that she had experienced on the drive, the loss of her husband and the time when she had shot a man in the back.

'I think it may be a good idea. But I wonder if a man like me could ever settle down and try to forget the past, or whether it wouldn't keep on coming up, standing between me and any peace I might find.'

'It wouldn't if you were determined to forget it. If you only wanted to put it behind you and kept it there.' She paused, then tightened her grip on his arm. 'If you want something hard enough, nothing in this world will stop you.'

'I only wish I had your kind of faith, Claire,' he said softly.

She leaned to one side. Her shoulder touched his and her weight rested on his arm. 'Do you know that's the first time you've ever spoken my name.'

'I never realised.'

'I hope you do decide to settle down there, and not come riding back to look for vengeance.'

'Why should you think I'm seeking vengeance now?'

'I'm not sure. I know how things were between you and that man I had to shoot. There was some kind of personal feud between you that could only be settled when one of you was dead. Now he's gone, but there are others back there who would like to see you dead, aren't there?'

He hesitated, knew that he could never lie to this woman, that she saw things about men more clearly than they realised. 'Yes, there are men here who won't rest until they've killed me. But Sherman was the worst. He was the last of the gang who framed me all those years ago.'

'And yet you're still running? Why?'

'Because the wanted notices are still out for me. Because decent lawmen believed the lies they spread around, believed them enough to put a price on my head. What chance do you reckon I'd have if I gave myself up and tried to prove that I was innocent of everything?'

'I think I understand. But California is a new country, a whole new world just over the top of those mountains. There are no crooked sheriffs there who know the name of Neil Roberts. And there aren't likely to be any riding out there looking for you – no bounty hunters coming as far afield as that.'

'I wish I could be sure of that.'

'When we get there – and I'm sure we'll get there one day, I hope you will be sure. You and I are very much alike, Neil. We both seem to be looking for the same thing, and this new country that lies ahead of us is the last and only chance we'll ever get. We both want peace, peace to forget everything that has happened and start with a clean sheet. It isn't going to be easy for a woman without a man out there. This is a world that men have made, and there's no place in it for a woman like me, not unless she wants to go up into the hills and shut herself away in some small hut where nobody can ever find her, or she goes the other way, becomes a bad woman.'

'You'll never be like that,' he said fervently.

'Someday I will. But before that happens there are so many things I want.'

Neil shivered, threw a swift glance at the clear arch of the sky about him. Already he thought he detected the touch of snow on the breath of the wind.

Carefully, one behind the other, the wagons edged forward along the trail. The men sat gingerly on the tongues of the wagons, guiding the horses slowly while the women and chil-

143

dren walked behind along the stony trail. In places the earth had formed a fresh slide across the trail, dirt not yet packed firm. There was no point in risking the lives of everyone, and Neil noticed the eyes of the women and children flicking incessantly towards the bottom of the canyon down below them less than three feet from where they walked, but three hundred feet down. There was water at the bottom, silver and thread-like, made narrow by distance.

One by one the wagons negotiated the precarious section of the trail. The women and the children climbed back on board, and they swung forward along the winding trail, heading up into the upper fastnesses of the mountains. The air grew thinner as they moved higher, thinner and colder. There were more narrow creeks to be crossed, high banks with loose rocks that moved whenever the wheels of the wagons crushed over them. Water foamed white over the boulders, splashed over the axles of the wagons as they crossed. Slowly the weather and the terrain was building up a picture of what lay in store for them, and Neil found the apprehension in his mind growing with every mile they travelled. Above them the towering peaks still lifted, high and seemingly inaccessible. It seemed incredible that they could ever get the wagons up there and, in places, the trail narrowed until it was all they could do to move the Conestogas through between the rough, rocky walls of the rearing canyons through which they had to pass.

Two days, three, and then on the fourth day there was no sun at first light. The dawn was a vague greyness that spread up from below them, touched the sky with a curious eerie light. Rolling out of his blankets, feeling the cold dampness on his body, Neil glanced up at the clouds that moved in swiftly from the north-east, blowing over the ragged peaks, and knew that there was snow on the way, that the luck which had been with them for so long had given out.

144

He folded his blanket, then moved over to the embers of the night's fire, kicked them with the toe of his boot until it broke flame, and piled more dry wood on to it until the flames leapt high and the boiler of coffee was sizzling over it. The others rolled out of their blankets, shrugged, and then stood up. Jackson rubbed the sleep from his eyes, then stared about him, caught Neil's worried look and walked over, stood with his hands outstretched towards the fire.

'Think it spells trouble, Neil?'

'Afraid so. Those clouds mean snow. We ought to reach this end of the pass by noon. Could be that we can be well into it before the snow comes. But there'll be a blizzard before night.'

'I figure you're right. What do you say to that, Jessup?'

The other nodded, pursed his lips tightly. 'This is country I don't know, Jackson. But I'll take your word for it. Want me to get the train moving as soon as possible?'

Jackson nodded. Soon there was the smell of sizzling beef and bacon, with beans scooped on to the platters. Breakfast was a hurried meal of silences, soon over. Then the train pulled out once more, moving through a country of almost unsurpassed grandeur; a beautiful terrain, a magnificent vista which seemed to defy the imagination. But in spite of its beauty, it could be capricious and deadly.

The people in the wagons stared about them with open eyes. This was something none of them had ever seen before, something new and strange. By noon, with the clouds still lowering over the crests of the mountains, they had reached the eastern end of the South Pass. In front of them the ground stretched for mile upon mile, almost level with the tall, towering rocks lifting sheer on either side of them, a vast natural cutting that stretched clear over the mountain chain. Soon there was no talk in the wagons. The first few white flakes drifted down in the wind.

Twenty minutes later the blizzard struck, a million white flakes that swirled about the wagons, obliterating the rocky walls on either side. Men rode with their heads down, shivering in their thick clothing. The snow worked its way down their necks in spite of the high collars and wide-brimmed hats, into their boots. The blast of the wind, seeping along the pass, threatened to hurl them back into the rocks, and the animals made little headway against it.

This was worse than Neil had expected. He had hoped that they would have made it halfway along the Pass before the blizzard struck. Another blast of chill air lashed at them, this time off the walls of the pass, hit so hard that the horses were forced to stop in their tracks and brace themselves against it, unable to move. Neil cursed harshly under his breath, lifted his head a little and tried to peer into the heart of the snowstorm. Already it was beginning to settle around them, forming a white layer on the uneven ground, even beginning to stick to the rocky walls of the canyon.

It made an even greater danger now, obliterating the rocks and boulders in the middle of the trail so that they could not pick them out in time, before the wheels ran over them, sending the wagons lurching and swaying from side to side. There was one thing, he thought quickly, if there was anyone following them it would blot out their trail completely.

'Do you think we can keep going in this?' shouted Jackson at the top of his voice. He bent from the wagon as Neil rode alongside. His body was almost covered in snow, his face covered by the hood which he had pulled down over his eyes so that only the shaggy beard showed, thrust forward aggressively.

'We've got to. It won't let up for days, possibly weeks. I know these blizzards. Once they begin, they just keep on going.'

Heads down, they pushed ahead into the storm.

Everything was a solid wall of white and it was impossible to see more than three feet in any direction. Overhead, the sky was a deep and ominous grey, with no let-up in the icy wind. Minutes stretched themselves into hours as the numbing cold bit deep into their bodies. Even inside the wagons there was no escape from the driving snow. It worked its way through the folds of the canvas, formed a deep layer on the tops of the wagons, threatened to tear the canvas. The horses trudged forward, heads down, moving by some strange instinct.

How they managed to survive the biting fingers of the wind, the driving snow which was piling high on all sides, it was impossible to tell. When night came it did not bring an end to their misery. Rather it was just beginning.

Jessup tried to build a fire in the lee of the rock, with the snow shrieking past, but it was virtually impossible. They huddled close to the flames and tried to get some warmth into their frozen bodies. Savagely the wind howled around them, threatening to tear the heavy canvas from the wagons, exposing their interiors.

'If we ever get through this, meeting up with those border gangs is going to be child's play,' growled Jessup tightly. He rubbed the snow from his face and eyes, shook his head numbly. 'I don't mind facing up to something I can see and fight, but how in God's name can you fight this?'

'You can't,' Neil told him, pushing his hands out towards the flames. 'You've got to accept it, try to go with it. Just tell yourself it would be even worse if we'd taken Snake Pass. If it doesn't get too deep, we ought to be all right. But if the Pass gets blocked before we make our way through it, then I reckon those of you who know how to pray had better start, because we'll need all the luck we can get. There's no turning back now. We've committed ourselves to getting through, and if it means fighting this every hour of the day and night, then that's how it's got to be. Better get that into your minds right away.'

He turned his head slowly, looked at one man after the other, trying to read the expression on their faces. There was a little fear there, he saw, a little apprehension, but at the moment it was all hidden under the terrible surface numbness that came from the constant battering by that icy wind and the driving clouds of snow.

Jackson got heavily to his feet, moved over to the cook-pot, pulled out a long strip of beef and thrust it between his teeth. With an equal slowness, he filled his cup with coffee and drank it down, then returned to his place beside Neil.

Calder, thin-faced and short, pushed his legs towards the fire, said harshly: 'I've got the feelin' that we're making a drive we'll never finish. No one told us that it would be anything like this. We'll never ride out this blizzard. We ought to have waited down in the plain until the winter passed.'

'Don't you realise it yet? We didn't have enough supplies to do that.' Neil spoke more sharply than he had intended. 'We'd all have starved to death before the winter was through. And there's another thing. There was the chance that Matt Hollard might be riding out on our trial, coming to finish what Sherman started out to do.'

Calder shook his head in a bird-like fashion. 'You've been scaring us with this talk about Hollard all the way here, Roberts. I don't believe most of it for one. Seems you may have some idea in your mind that by coming with this train you'll be safe from the law, which I understand is still on your trail. If you'd been forced to stay back there, they'd have come riding after you and then you'd have been taken back to Dodge or Abilene to stand trial. What was it they accused you of, Roberts? Murder, wasn't it? They say you shot down a couple of men in the street.'

By a supreme effort of will, Neil held in his surging anger. Keeping his voice lightly controlled and even, he said through clenched teeth: 'That ain't quite true, and I reckon you know it, Calder. Sure I killed some men a few years back, but they were crooked lawmen who would have shot me down without just cause. But the sheriff managed to get my name put out on the wanted circulars throughout the territory, and nobody seemed to inquire whether or not there was any truth or justification for it.'

'Seems we only got your word for that. You seemed mighty anxious to lead this train all the way through to California. I ain't denying that you seem to know this country, but I'm beginning to wonder why you came along. I ain't forgetting either that we've lost some good folk because of the fight between you and the cattle bosses here.'

'They would have killed us all if they had been able to,' interrupted Jessup harshly, turning on the other. 'We needed somebody with a fast gun who wouldn't be afraid to stand up to them.'

'Seems we really got somebody like that,' muttered Calder hoarsely.

'I'd hate to think of what might have happened to us if we hadn't,' said Jackson quickly. He turned and glared at the other, forcing him to a sullen silence. The logs crackled on the fire and there was an occasional hiss as the snowflakes whirled around the corner of the rocks and fell into the flames.

At first light the next morning they began to move out again. Tired men and tired horses. The snow lay more thickly about them now, almost two feet in depth, and was still falling, although the wind was no longer as strong or as blustery as on the previous day, but the snow still fell as thickly as before, and there were no breaks in the clouds, no sign of the sun.

For most of the day they travelled without mishap. Then, during the afternoon, they reached a spot where the ground became more open, the rocky walls which had hemmed them in all the way were no longer so close. In front of them the floor of the pass stretched in an unbroken sheet of white, the snow smooth and unsullied.

At the head of the train Neil reined his mount and lifted his right hand to halt the train. Slowly, reluctantly, the wagons ground to a standstill.

'What's wrong, Neil?' boomed Jackson, from his perch on the lead wagon.

'I'm not sure. Just a feeling, I guess.'

The other peered ahead through the thickly falling snow, staring out under thick brows, covered now with snow. 'I don't see anything wrong. Looks all right to me.'

'Maybe so. But there may be danger up ahead. In country like this there may be chasms splitting across the floor of the pass, and it only needs a horse to put his foot into one of them and we lose not only the horse but the wagon as well.'

'What do you suggest then?'

'You'd better stay here. I'll ride on ahead and take a good look-see. If there is any danger there, the sooner we know about it, the better.'

He gigged his sorrel. The animal moved forward slowly and carefully, picking its own pace. The horse was both tired and doubtful, seemed to sense that there was something wrong, increasing the feeling of apprehension in Neil's mind. The stud frequently stopped and had to be prodded forward before it would take another step. Turning in the saddle after a few minutes of this slow progress, Neil felt a momentary twinge of surprise, realising that he could no longer see the train, that it had been blotted out completely by the curtain of snow.

He could not have travelled more than twenty yards, and yet there was neither sight nor sound of the train. The snow utterly muffled any sound and he had the impression of being utterly and completely isolated, cut off, in a nightmare world of white.

On his left the edge of the trail suddenly pitched downwards into a deep canyon whose bottom he could not see. The sorrel gathered its feet closely together and began to mince a little, hesitant, winding itself around and around, trying to reverse its direction, until it was facing the way back to the wagons. Holding tightly to the reins, Neil forced it to turn and begin moving forward once more. They had gone less than fifty yards when the sorrel halted once more, stuck in its feet and refused to budge, no matter how he coaxed it. Slowly he slid from the saddle, moved forward gingerly on foot, placing one foot in front of the other, feeling his way forward, confident now that there was some kind of danger here, danger which he could not see as yet.

Then his left foot went from under him, slid away as there was no trail to meet him. Losing his balance, he toppled forward into sheer emptiness. Only the fact that he was still holding on to the leather of the reins and that the sorrel had dug in its feet saved him at that moment. Swiftly, with a savage instinct, his hand tightened on the reins and he felt himself jerked upward as the sorrel pulled up its head in alarm. For a long moment he hung there, suspended in mid-air, feet swinging loosely under him, unable to obtain a grip or foothold. His other foot had slipped off the trail the moment he had lost his balance. Somehow he managed to prevent himself from panicking, maintained his hold on the reins and slowly swung his body back towards the trail, holding his breath in his lungs until it hurt, praying that the sorrel would not move forward or they would both go crashing to their deaths in the chasm that yawned below them.

Slowly, speaking gently to the sorrel, he managed to swing his legs back on to the trail, sought for and found a precarious hold, dug in his toes and hung there, scarcely daring to breathe. Then, inch by inch, the sorrel moved back, away from the slippery edge, on to the firm ground of the trail.

Neil found lodgement for his feet, heaved backward and managed t stand up straight, slowly placing his weight on the rock. It was covered with ice under the snow, but there were a couple of upthrusting rocks, and somehow he succeeded in wedging his feet into them, fighting to maintain his uneasy balance. He walked back to the break in the trail, shuffling his feet now until he reached it, and knew himself to be on firm ground. Then he swung himself up into the saddle and urged the sorrel back to the waiting train.

'There's a slide back there,' he said brusquely to Jackson. 'Sheer drop into the chasm down on the left. Trail's broken there and we'll have to move around it before we can be sure we're safe. It ain't going to be easy, but unless we do, we're stuck here for good. Better pass the word along to the others. Then we'll move out. We've wasted too much time as it is.'

He rode back along the whole length of the train, giving his orders to the others. They listened in silence, their faces almost completely hidden by the broad hoods pulled down over their eyes, the hands muffled in thick gloves. He knew how they must have been feeling at that moment, bodies numbed and frozen, with scarcely any sensation in their hands and feet. Yet they had to be made to move on, into the teeth of that howling blizzard, along the trail where danger lurked at every turn, and to fall out of the train meant certain death for the people in any stranded wagon. There were many tales in this part of the west concerning wagon trains that had moved out over the mountains and had never been heard of again, had certainly never reached their destination. Whether they had perished up here in the wild passes or had been set upon by the border gangs and totally destroyed, the wagons looted of all their possessions and then burned by the gunslammers, no one knew.

At last they were ready to pull out and Neil led the way, moving close to the wagons, urging them to keep together, not to lose sight of the one in front. Ten yards in that swirling blizzard, tens of millions of white flakes streaming across one's vision and everything was lost behind that curtain of white.

Coming to the break in the trail, Neil paused, pushed himself upright in the saddle, then signalled to Jackson to move forward slowly, to swing away to the right, away from the edge where the rock fell away into nothingness, down into the stretching depths of the chasm that loomed on that edge of the trail. Had it not been for that strange sixth sense of his, something he had never been able to explain, but which had saved him so many times in the past that he had learned never to ignore it, they might have all gone plunging over the side into oblivion.

It was a dangerous, tricky business getting those wagons past the break in the trail. Neil had expected no trouble with Jackson, nor with Jessup. Both men knew how to handle horses, even when the animals, sensing danger, threatened to rear and panic away from the spot. But there were others in the wagons who did not have that experience, and Neil was forced to station himself on the very lip of that steep drop and allow the wagons to move past him. It only needed one of the horses to bolt and he would be finished, thrust off the trail by the panicking animal, knocked to one side by the careering weight and bulk of the wagon.

Then, after what seemed an interminable period, they were all past, moving on slowly into the swirling snowstorm, canvas tops swaying from side to side, but more slowly now with all that weight of snow lying on top of them.

Another camp that night with the cold dampness seeping into their bones. There was the misery of not being dry, of wet clothing clinging to their bodies, irritating and chafing at the flesh until it had been torn and opened by the roughness of their garments.

There was little wood here to light a fire, and once it went out during the later part of the night, the cold became more intense than anything they had ever known before.

Neil considered that up here in the pass itself there would be no danger from outlaw bands, or even from Hollard if he was following them, and he knew that it would be both dangerous and unnecessary to post guards to keep a look out for trouble. The men needed all the sleep they could get, and it seemed wrong to deny them it just because of the million-to-one chance that gunhawks might come upon them in the middle of the blizzard.

Progress was measured in yards most of the way. If they succeeded in travelling half a mile a day, they considered themselves to be making good progress. Primitive and raw, nature fought them with everything at her disposal, as if to show them how puny they really were, that if she wished she could destroy them utterly.

There were cold mornings and colder nights, men clustered around the fires when they had the chance, and now the stops along the trail were becoming more and more frequent as the men grew more tired and the horses needed the rests.

There seemed to be no end to the pass, or the snow. It swirled around them as they rode with their bodies hunched forward over the reins or the necks of their mounts, eyes and nostrils clogged by the beating snow. It seemed incredible that these small, feathery flakes could do so much damage, could be so devastating.

The folk with the train began to murmur among themselves, but although he knew of this Neil did not consider it dangerous. They had long since passed the point of no return, now they had to go on because to turn back would mean certain death.

Then, two weeks after they had entered the pass, the snowstorm abated. Now they were fighting their way through deep

154

drifts which, in places, threatened to engulf the wagons themselves, although fortunately the sheer walls of the pass had shielded most of the trail from the full fury of the storm. The sky cleared, the dark, lowering clouds blew away and, with the sudden change in the weather, they discovered that they were no longer moving level, but were descending down the further levels of the mountains.

They had moved through them, had weathered one of the worst blizzards in the South Pass, and were now dipping down towards the stretching, fertile plains that lay beyond.

Less than a hundred miles to the west lay the frontier with California. As if anxious to reach there, the men pushed their wagons to the limit now. The coming of the clear weather, even though the air was still cold, had brought a new life to the folk in the train. There was the feeling that they had surmounted every possible difficulty, that nothing could now prevent them from getting through, that they were safe from all trouble and danger.

Perhaps it was this which almost proved to be their undoing. Reaching the level plains, they moved on in a cloud of their own dust, still heading west, not once deviating from the trail.

They had come across almost a thousand miles of some of the worst country in the whole of the United States, had forged a trail across the continent which would prove to be the beginning of the tremendous movement to the west, would lead to the eventual population of the State of California.

There was laughter now among the wagons, laughter that seemed to ease the strain of the past few months when everything had seemed to be conspiring against them to prevent them from reaching their destination. Now they were in sight of it, and they felt certain that nothing more could go wrong, that if there were any more dangers, they could not be as bad as those they had already faced on the way, and they could meet them and overcome them easily.

Inside, Neil did not share their optimism. True, they had fought off the hired killers of the cattle barons to the east, they had met and forded rivers swollen in flood, and they had crossed the South Pass through a tremendous blizzard when it had seemed that nothing could possibly survive.

Now, in front of them, stretching for mile upon endless mile, as far as the eye could see, reaching out to the flat, distant horizons to the west, lay the great plains.

Riding ahead of the train, Neil turned in his saddle, feeling the sun warm on his head and shoulders, the dust on his face and cracked lips, getting under his eyes, blurring his vision. But anything seemed better than the snow up there in the pass. Behind him, stretched out over two miles of the prairie, the wagons were strung out in single file, rumbling forward.

But, looking at them, it was hard to realise that these were the same wagons that had set out from the eastern boundary of Jesse Sherman's territory all those long weary weeks before. Then they had been brightly painted, with white canvas stretched over the backs. Now that canvas was torn and shredded by the tearing fingers of the winds up there in the mountains and the soaking it had received during their crossing the great rivers to the east. The paintwork was scratched and scoured, and the men who drove those wagons were all changed too. Now they were lean, gaunt men with deep-set eyes, brighter though than before, eyes that had looked out upon the far horizons and witnessed the great open spaces of prairie and mountain. Men with wide hats and long-barrelled Winchesters thrust into the scabbards by their sides.

On the third night, with the wagons in a wide circle, the fires lit in the centre, the stock herded there for safety, with two look-outs moving slowly around the outer perimeter, Neil rolled himself into his blankets near one of the wagons, listening to the occasional crackle of the fire and the faint sound of the wind sighing over the prairie. In the distance he could just hear the low, mournful voices of the guards as they sang the songs of the Deep South, to keep up their spirits and to keep themselves awake until the others came to relieve them.

Another five days on the trail, he thought inwardly, and they would have reached their destination, and then his work would be done.

He would have finished what he had set out to do, would have fulfilled his promise to take this wagon train to California.

And then what of him, what of Neil Roberts, wanted in Idaho and Arkansas for murder, even though it had been the murder of a crooked sheriff?

He turned over Claire Vance's words in his mind, considering them seriously for the first time. Before he had merely allowed them to pass through his brain without really concentrating on them.

Now he held fast to them, turned them over and over in his thoughts. It was possible that, in California, he might be able to settle down and put the past behind him, never think of it again. Then, as he lay there, he found his thoughts slipping away to Claire Vance herself. The memory of her nearness that night, the feel of her slim hand on his arm, was still strong within him, and he doubted if he would ever forget that.

For a moment he pondered on the memory of the tall, golden-haired woman, then all thought of her, all thought of California and what might happen there, was driven from his mind. The sharp bark of gunfire came from the near distance, and close on its heels, he heard the drumming of running horses coming nearer.

Swiftly he was on his feet, the blanket thrown on one side,

the Colts whispering into his hands as he came upright and turned to face the sound.

The two guards were firing into the darkness, loosing off shot after shot. A few moments later they moved back out of the shadows, and came into the ring of the wagons.

'What is it?' demanded Jackson, running forward, his huge face alight.

'Gunhawks!' muttered one of the men.

His right arm hung limp by his side. He held the Winchester in the other, turned and pointed. More gunfire broke out and then Neil made out the horses as they came plunging forward out of the darkness.

Bullets hummed and droned through the air close to his body as he flung himself forward, hitting the ground behind one of the wheels of the nearest wagon. He fired swiftly at the fleeting shadows, saw a man topple from the saddle, one leg caught in the stirrup, his mount dragging him over the rough ground.

More vivid flashes in the starlit darkness, more riders converging on the wagon train. One of the riders put his horse to the shafts of a wagon, leapt over them into the centre of the ring.

Turning, without pausing to take a deliberate aim, Neil fired. The first shot missed its target. The second took the man in the shoulder, slamming him sideways in the saddle.

Rifles opened up from the wagons. The whole of the train was awake now. Everyone was a gunman now – a fighter. The women were firing and loading. Harsh voices yelled as the gunhawks were met by a hail of fire that poured into their ranks, thinning them savagely.

More yells from the darkness around the camp. Now there were more bullets flying through the air, hammering off the metal uprights of the wagons, shrieking thinly in distorted ricochet.

Neil felt something pluck at his left shoulder, winced involuntarily. How long could the firing last? Half an hour? An hour perhaps? It was impossible to tell, for when a man's life depended on killing his enemy first before he was killed himself, no one thought of time.

'They're turning away,' yelled Jessup, shouting the words at the top of his voice. Neil lifted his head, peering into the dimness, saw that what the other said was true. There were unmoving shadows on the ground around the perimeter of the camp now. It had been a grim and cold business. There had been no quarter asked and none given. California lay only a few miles distant, and nothing was going to stop these people from getting there. They had been through too much for that to happen.

For the rest of the night Neil remained awake, eyes watching the darkness, but there were no further attacks, and in the morning they bandaged up the wounds of the men who had been hit, ate a meal of jerked beef, washed down with weak coffee, and moved along the trail again.

Ten nights later they made camp beside a wide river that flowed sluggishly between low banks, the water muddy from the recent rains, but the current slow and leisurely.

With the sunrise, they crossed the river, the Conestoga wagons rumbling slowly on to the broad strip of ground that lay beyond, over into the State of California, into a bright and golden sunrise that sent light flooding over the whole stretch of territory around them. For the first time since they had left the East, even Neil felt that the danger was past for them. Slowly he reined his mount, and watched as the wagons rolled by, slowly, cumbersome and heavy. But they were bringing a new state into being. These were the pioneers, he thought, with a sudden sense of pride. These were the men and women who had not been daunted by the dangers which had faced them along the thousand miles they had crossed. They had brought with them some vital spark which was so necessary if this part of the continent was now going to live and become ready to take its place with the others in the years that were to come.

He sat tall and straight in the saddle, on a small knoll, shading his eyes against the sunlight. Was it his imagination, or was the air here really warmer and gentler than back east? He shrugged, then turned his head.

Already the wagon train was beginning to pull away from him. Slowly, he raked spurs over the flanks of the sorrel, turned his back on the mountains to the east, keeping the sunrise at his back, and rode to where a tall, golden-haired woman waved to him from one of the wagons.

SCIENCE IN EVERYDAY LIFE

William C. Vergara

BOOK CLUB ASSOCIATES
LONDON

To Patricia

PREFACE

This book tells how the many branches of science touch our lives in a thousand different ways. Science gives an insight into how things work, why things happen, and how things move, react, reproduce, and grow. It helps us understand where we came from, who we are, and—perhaps—where we are going. In countless ways, science answers the questions that each of us ponders at one time or another about our lives, our world, or our consciousness. So the question-and-answer format of this book seems a reasonable way to discuss the science in our lives.

It has become an article of faith that every effect has a cause, and every action a reaction. Even the most complex natural events—from the precise motions of the heavens to the ripening of a grain of wheat—seem to obey a system of rules imposed by nature. But when a new scientific principle is discovered we are astonished, more often than not, by its great beauty and simplicity. The most important scientific breakthroughs, in fact, have usually reduced a pre-existing condition of scientific chaos to one of symmetry and order. We can be thankful that nature seems to prefer the simple to the complex. That makes it possible to answer many questions without resorting to the complex interplay of many scientific concepts.

The information in this book is arranged in a random manner to encourage browsing and add to the general interest. There is a comprehensive index for the reader seeking specific information.

Because the book is for the general reader, I have omitted much scientific terminology that would tend to confuse the nonspecialist. Instead, I have tried to use everyday language to explain scientific concepts, at the same time omitting a great deal of relevant but overly intricate detail. I hope the book will stimulate further reading in the fascinating field of science, which reveals itself in marvelous ways to those who pursue it.

Finally, as we approach the twenty-first century, we cannot help but be aware that science has broadened into many varied fields. I have tried to emphasize this broad scope by the wide range of topics covered by the questions in the book. Answers have come from such diverse fields as physics, psychology, genetics, electronics, medicine, paleontology, astronomy, chemistry, and oceanography, to name just a few. There seems to be no limit to the kinds of knowledge being unearthed by dedicated scientists throughout the world. Here and there in the book the reader will find that close cooperation between scientists of different disciplines has led to important new knowledge of benefit to humanity.

One can hardly ignore all the available scientific knowledge while fascinating everyday questions beg to be answered. At least I cannot—and this book is the result.

WILLIAM C. VERGARA

Towson, Maryland
February 1, 1980

SCIENCE IN EVERYDAY LIFE

SCIENCE
IN EVERYDAY
LIFE

Why does bread get moldy?

Mold, such as that found in bread, is caused by the growth of fungi—one of the most prevalent and successful forms of life. Mycologists, who study fungi, tell us that of all the kinds of living things on earth, one kind in twenty is a fungus. At last count there were close to 100,000 fungus species! Most kinds are small and inconspicuous, and surround us in multitudes all the time.

Fungi, or molds, are plants without chlorophyll. So they cannot use the energy of sunlight to manufacture their own organic food, such as sugars, starches, proteins, and fats, as the green plants do. Instead, they must live on other plants and animals. Some fungi are parasites, attacking living organisms of one kind or another, but most fungi are scavengers that grow on the remains of plants and animals, causing them to decay and change into rich soil. Without fungi, in fact, most green plants could hardly survive, because they depend on the products of fungus decay in the soil.

Most fungi are not overly particular about the sorts of food they will accept. Practically all of the common materials around us furnish a satisfactory diet for many kinds of fungi. The fungus merely manufactures dozens of digestive enzymes and acids, which diffuse out of the fungus into the material in which it is growing. If it happens to be growing in bread, the digestive chemicals break down the bread into simple compounds, which diffuse back through the cell walls of the fungus to furnish food and energy for growth. The basic process of digestion is much the same in fungi as in human beings—except that we eat first and digest later while the mold does just the opposite. Given the right conditions of humidity and temperature, one can find a fungus that can digest just about anything but metal.

Many fungi are fast growers. A moderately speedy fungus grows a branch (or *mycelium)* at a rate of about eight-thousandths of an inch per hour. Each advancing branch puts out a new side branch about every half hour or so, and these grow at the same rate, producing new branches of their own. In twenty-four hours, a fungus colony of that kind can produce a total branch length of one-half mile. In forty-eight hours, the total length is hundreds of miles long! This explains why a fungus can grow through a loaf of bread in a few days.

Fungi reproduce by means of spores. A few of the higher plants, such as ferns, also reproduce by spores of a sort, but fungi produce spores on a big scale, making for rapid and wide dispersal. Almost no other form of life can equal them in that regard. Fungus spores fill the air in prodigious numbers. Within a few days, for example, a *penicillium* spore can grow into a mature but microscopic plant resulting in hundreds of millions of new spores. These spores are so small—about one five-thousandth of an inch in diameter—that the gentlest current of air can pick them up and whisk them away, ready to go out and make their moldy way in the world. Luckily for bread lovers, all fungus spores are killed by the heat of baking. But airborne spores still manage to contaminate the bread after it has cooled. In addition, particles of bread left in the breadbox can become an excellent growth medium for molds, which can contaminate any bread that is stored there.

Most fungi grow best between 70 and 90 degrees Fahrenheit. At 50 degrees, their growth slows down somewhat, and when the temperature is lowered to 30 to 40 degrees, they stop growing and become dormant. So storage of bread in the refrigerator or freezer is a good way to discourage mold without the use of chemical fungicides.

Why does the same side of the moon always face the earth?

This condition exists because the moon spins on its axis in precisely the same length of time that it takes to revolve once around the earth. If it were to spin (or revolve) a little faster or slower, the portion we see would change continually during the year. Instead, the two

2

motions have remained locked in step for as long as such matters have been recorded, and probably for millions of years longer. Scientists believe that this lunar peculiarity is an inevitable consequence of an effect similar to our tides.

The moon exerts a gravitational force of attraction on the earth, which generates two tidal bulges in the oceans. One bulge always faces toward the moon and the other bulge is on the side of the earth facing away from the moon. As the earth spins on its axis, these bulges remain locked in position with respect to the moon. To an observer on earth, therefore, they are seen to move from east to west, generating approximately two high tides per day. The motion of the tidal bulges generates friction, which converts energy of rotation to heat. Over a great period of time, as the earth's rotational energy is slowly consumed, the planet's rate of spin about its axis is reduced. The lunar tides act as a brake on the length of the day; as a result, the day grows one thousandth of a second longer each century.

Although we think of the tides as a strictly oceanic phenomenon, the same sort of effect occurs in the solid crust of the earth. The rocks also respond to the moon's attraction, but to a considerably lesser extent. Just as with ocean tides, two rock bulges circle the earth, generating friction as rock slides against rock. This friction also consumes part of the earth's energy of rotation, contributing to the braking action described above.

Although the moon has no water, its solid crust does respond to the gravitational force of the earth. Scientists assume that the moon once rotated on its axis at a much faster rate than at present. Millions, perhaps billions, of years ago the lunar rock tides began their braking action on the moon until the same hemisphere of the moon always faced the earth. At that instant, the lunar tidal bulges froze into position and no longer moved with respect to the moon. One bulge faces the earth and the other, on the opposite side of the moon, faces away from the earth. Because the tidal bulges no longer move, there is no longer any tidal friction tending to slow the moon's rotation. The moon will continue, therefore, to present the same face toward the earth indefinitely—all because of gravitation and friction.

How does antifreeze work?

Anyone who lives in a cold climate knows that the water in an automobile's cooling system will freeze sometime during the winter

3

unless antifreeze is added to the water. In the latter part of the nineteenth century, a French scientist, François Raoult, solved that problem for us by discovering that the freezing temperature of a liquid is always lowered when something else is dissolved in it. The substance added can be either solid or liquid. So adding salt, alcohol, or sugar to water reduces its freezing point below 32°F, the temperature at which pure water freezes.

Raoult also discovered that the lowering of the freezing point depends directly on the number of molecules dissolved in the liquid. For example, if one ounce of sugar lowers the freezing point of a certain quantity of water by 1°F, then 2 ounces (with twice as many molecules) will lower it by 2°F, and so on. The number of degrees by which the freezing point is reduced depends only on the number of molecules dissolved in the liquid and not on the kind of substance dissolved.

The so-called "depression of the freezing point" can be explained in the following way. As a liquid gets colder, the energy of motion (kinetic energy) of its molecules is reduced. This means that the force of attraction between the molecules becomes more effective in trying to solidify the liquid. When the freezing point is reached, the molecules stop moving around and join together to form a solid. The presence of "foreign" molecules, however, serves to keep the molecules of the liquid apart, reducing the effectiveness of the attractive forces. Only at some lower temperature will these forces be strong enough to bring the molecules together and form a solid.

It appears, then, that almost any substance can be used as an automobile antifreeze, as long as it dissolves in water. There are other important considerations, however. First of all, a good choice would be a liquid that mixes with water in any proportion. Some solids would be hard to dissolve and might tend to recrystallize at low temperatures. Second, we need a liquid that is inert and will not attack the elements of the cooling system. Third, the substance must be inexpensive, and fourth, it must have a relatively high boiling point so it will not boil off or cause excessively high pressures in the cooling system. The liquid substance used almost universally in antifreeze solutions is ethylene glycol, which has a boiling point of 387°F (197°C). A cooling system containing equal volumes of ethylene glycol and water has a freezing temperature of approximately -40°F (-40°C).

4

Why is alcohol a good antiseptic?

Ethyl alcohol, commonly called grain alcohol, has the ability to coagulate protein, thereby preventing it from functioning properly in living cells. Because of this property, it is effective as an antiseptic.

When used as an antiseptic, 70 percent alcohol is more effective than 100 percent alcohol. The accompanying diagram illustrates why this is true. The circle on the left represents a single-celled organism, such as a disease bacterium, before applying alcohol. The center circle shows the same bacterium after being covered with 100 percent alcohol. Pure alcohol coagulates protein on contact. It produces a hardened layer of protein just inside the cell wall, which prevents additional alcohol from entering the micro-organism. For that reason, no further coagulation can take place. This would render the micro-organism dormant but not dead. Given the proper conditions, it can later

(A)   (B)   (C)

Fig. 1.   The effect of alcohol on bacteria. A micro-organism is shown: A: Before treatment with alcohol. B: After using 100 percent alcohol. C: After using 70 percent alcohol. In B, a thin crust of hardened material protects the micro-organism from the alcohol. In C, the protein is completely coagulated.

begin to function again. If 70 percent alcohol is used on the micro-organism, the dilute alcohol also coagulates protein but at a slower rate. It is able to penetrate the entire cell before coagulation takes place. All the cell protein is coagulated, and the organism dies. This is illustrated on the right side of the diagram.

Beverages containing alcohol normally have a high tax rate. When alcohol is used for other purposes, the tax is eliminated, but the alcohol is made unfit for drinking. When treated in this way it is called denatured alcohol. Common denaturants are formaldehyde and gasoline.

Methyl alcohol, also known as methanol or wood alcohol, is a different compound from ethyl alcohol. It is widely used in industry as a solvent. Methyl alcohol should never be used medicinally. Even a small internal dose can cause blindness and paralysis, and larger amounts can be fatal.

Why are rainbows seen so rarely?

Some storms end on a delightful note when they die away to the pleasant spectacle of a rainbow. The appearance of a rainbow does not depend on the kind of rain or the size of the raindrops, but rather on whether the cloud cover opens up to admit the sun. If sunlight shines onto the rain, the raindrops reflect the sunlight like myriad tiny prisms, splitting it by optical refraction into an infinite assortment of colors. Rainbows usually form only several hundred feet from the observer, so the rainfall and the opening for the sun must not be too far apart. If the rainfall does not fill the air over a large enough area, only a partial rainbow will be created. The largest rainbows are seen when the sun is close to the horizon, so the best ones are usually seen in late afternoon, looking toward the east.

You can make your own artificial rainbow on a sunny day by squirting a water hose directly overhead with the sun at your back. You then have both ingredients needed for a rainbow: sunlight and "raindrops."

What causes an oasis in the desert?

Even the driest desert on earth gets occasional rain. Such rainfall may infiltrate permeable rock and eventually reach the groundwater table many hundreds of feet below. An oasis results when the groundwater table comes close enough to the surface for the roots of palms and other plants to reach it.

Some of the world's oases have been formed by the erosion of the wind. A famous example is the great oasis of Khârga in the Sahara, which is over 100 miles long and 12 to 50 miles wide. Wind has played a major part in developing this oasis. Ground water sets a lower limit to the erosion of land by the wind. Once the sand of the desert is removed down to the level of the water table, so that the ground is kept damp, the wind can no longer pick up loose material and carry it away. Thus, if conditions are favorable, wind erosion can scoop out a great deal of surface material, right down to the water level.

The sheer amount of material that can be transported by the wind is truly staggering. In an average dust storm, a cube of air 10 feet on a side carries one ounce of suspended dust. One ounce may seem a trifling amount, but if we increase the cube of air to 1 mile on a side, the cube of air can transport 4600 tons of solid material. Thus, a severe storm might well pick up and carry away 100 million tons of sand and dust. Wind, as it turns out, is the only method of erosion that can transport significant amounts of material out of a typical desert. Some dust from Africa, for example, has been detected as far away as the Caribbean Sea.

In the Khârga oasis, wind erosion removed sand and other material until springs appeared around the margins of a great depression. Such springs are the souce of water for Khârga and other true oases.

Why do salmon return to spawn in the stream of their birth?

It is now thought that salmon return to their home stream because of a phenomenon that biologists call *imprinting*. To illustrate, many kinds of birds treat the first moving object they see as their mother. Of course, the first moving object that a bird sees usually *is* the real mother, but during the first few critical hours a bird will imprint on almost anything, from boxes to balloons to match covers. Young birds will also accept foster mothers of the same species, or adults of another species, or various mechanical or inanimate objects. A scientist once induced young geese to imprint on himself, and the little goslings followed him around as if he were their mother.

Young birds experience a sensitive period of a few hours or days during which they are extremely responsive to nearby objects. Even color, shape, and motion do not appear to be essential. Young birds will imprint on any object that contrasts with the environment.

Although the study of birds has provided most of what is known about imprinting, the process is not limited to birds. Imprinting has, in fact, been extended beyond the original "mother figure." The return of salmon to the home stream after years in the ocean is believed to be the result of the imprinting of the stream odor on the newly hatched fish. They seek out this stream odor on their return to fresh water and rarely end up in the wrong stream.

Imprinting also occurs in mammals. Young dogs have a sensitive period between three and ten weeks of age when they become social animals—associating either with human beings or other dogs. We have all seen dogs that think they are people. Pups are not normal in this regard if they are deprived of such contacts during their early weeks of life.

Why don't brothers and sisters want to marry each other?

Many animals, including man, have a strong inhibition against mating with parents, children, brothers, or sisters. This so-called incest taboo seems to exist in whole or in part in such varied species as the graylag goose, the rhesus macaque, and the chimpanzee. The taboo seems to appear when members of a family live together for a long time. Scientists who study *ethology*, the biology of behavior in animals, believe that the incest taboo is a safeguard against detrimental inbreeding, which would tend to bring out undesirable traits in offspring. The taboo even seems to exist in certain plants, which have evolved complex mechanisms to prevent self-fertilization.

As a general rule, the incest taboo is practically universal in man. The inhibition against sexual activity with persons one has grown up with seems to occur without social or educational pressure. In the kibbutzim of Israel, for example, children are cared for from early childhood in small groups of the same age. When adolescence is reached, there develops in the group a strong brother-sister bond of affection. A study was made in 1971 of 2769 marriages of children raised in this way, and no marriages occurred between members that grew up in the same group, although no social pressure was exerted in that direction. The avoidance of marriage within the same group was entirely voluntary. Research has indicated that the critical period for the incest taboo is from birth to six years of age. People do not seem to fall in love with each other if they have spent the first six years of their lives in a closely knit group.

There is considerable argument as to whether the taboo has a biological basis in man, but no other explanation has received much support. Although scientists cannot explain the taboo, its existence is universally accepted.

Why does sound travel better "with the wind"?

Most of us have noticed that we hear a sound better if it travels with the wind rather than against it. On the surface, we might guess (incorrectly) that the wind "helps the sound along." Moving with the wind, a sound travels a shorter distance than when it moves in opposition to it. It's easy to show, however, that this effect is too small to account for the observed effect.

Sound travels at about 760 miles an hour. If the wind blows at 30 miles per hour, its velocity is only 4 percent of the speed of sound. So such a wind will increase or shorten the effective distance a sound must travel by only 4 percent. The resulting increase or decrease in sound level would be too small to be detected by the human ear. So the answer must lie somewhere else.

The actual explanation is connected with a property of liquids and gases, including air, that physicists call *viscosity*. A spoon drawn through molasses experiences a force that resists its motion. Much the same thing happens in air, but the effect is much smaller. This property of liquids and gases is called viscosity.

Because of viscosity, the wind is impeded somewhat near the surface and its velocity is lower there than it is at higher altitudes. This increase in wind velocity with increasing altitude is primarily responsible for the effect wind has on audibility. In still air at uniform temperature, sound waves spread out evenly in all directions from the source of sound. The sound waves have no tendency to favor one direction over any other. But when the wind blows, it blows faster at higher altitudes than it does near the ground. If a sound wave travels in the same direction as the wind, the "top" of the sound wave moves faster than the "bottom." This tips the sound wave downward so it can be heard easily at some distance from the source. Just the opposite sort of thing takes place when a sound wave tries to buck a head wind. The top moves more slowly than the bottom and the sound wave is curved upward so it passes over the head of a distant observer on the ground. This bending of sound waves, called *refraction,* is responsible for the effect of wind on the distance of audibility of sounds.

If an observer is high enough above the ground, by the way, sounds can be heard just as well upwind as downwind. Or, conversely, upwind audibility can be improved by raising the height of the sound source. In that arrangement, the sound waves start out in a downward direction and reach an observer on the ground despite having been bent upward in their travels against the wind.

When was the needle invented?
For countless thousands of years during the Old Stone Age, flint was the major raw material for the tools and weapons of mankind. Then, toward the latter part of that age, craftsmen began to work in bone and ivory. Perhaps the most wonderful invention of the time was the bone needle, which came into general use in northern and central Europe during the period from about 17,000 B.C. to 8,000

9

B.C. Bone was also used to make fishhooks, awls, belt fasteners, hooked rods for spear throwing, barbed points for harpoons, and many implements whose use is not clearly understood.

Before the invention of the needle, sewing had been done by boring a hole with a bone or stone awl, and then passing a sinew or fiber through the opening. The next step in the evolution of sewing was to carve a hook on the end of the bone awl so that the sinew could be pulled back through the hole. The awl performed both operations: first it pierced the hole, then—crochet-needle fashion—it pulled the sinew through. The final step was to cut a hole in the end of the needle so it could combine the operations of hole piercing and thread pulling.

Needles were made by cutting a splinter of bone from a reindeer antler. The splinter was then shaved to size and polished so it would not catch on the skins to be fastened together. Finally, the hole was bored to accept the thread. All of these operations were accomplished using specialized tools made of stone. As a final touch, hollow bones were fashioned into small carrying cases to protect the needles.

How do magicians do seemingly impossible card tricks?

First let's see how the human eye works. The function of the pupil is to maintain the correct intensity of light entering the eye. Too little light cannot adequately excite the light-sensitive cells on the retina, and too much light is annoying and even harmful. With low levels of illumination, the pupil is wide open. With higher levels, the pupil closes and reduces the amount of light reaching the retina.

It turns out, however, that the size of the pupil can also be influenced by other means. For instance, the pupil often dilates or constricts in response to the subject matter being observed. In fact, research has shown that the size of the pupil is a good indicator of a person's interest, emotion, attitudes, and thought processes.

Scientists have discovered that some magicians doing card tricks usually watch the subject's eyes because they know that the subject's pupils will dilate when the correct card turns up. Similarly, when a picture of a female pinup is shown to a man, his pupils usually dilate within a second or so. In other experiments, pictures of male pinups cause pupil dilation in female subjects. In general, pupils tend to dilate in response to pleasant or interesting pictures and to constrict for unpleasant or aversive pictures. Pictures of sharks, for example, tend

10

to cause pupil constriction in females and pupil dilation in males.

Research has shown that such pupil changes also apply to political preferences. Conservatives dilate their pupils when looking at a picture of a conservative politician but constrict to that of a liberal; the pupils of liberals reveal just the opposite pattern of political preferences.

Psychologists have discovered that the size of the pupil is affected by mental activity. When someone is given an arithmetic problem to solve, his pupils dilate and remain dilated until the problem is solved and the answer verbalized. Along with this change are increased heart rate and changes in electrical measurements made on the skin. For these reasons, scientists view pupil size as a good measure of arousal of the nervous system.

Experiments have shown that a negative response turns up when many subjects are shown examples of modern paintings, particularly abstract paintings. In fact, some people who claim to like modern art show strong pupil contraction in response to such art.

It has also been learned that a person's physiological state is a factor in pupil response. People who are hungry, for example, have much stronger positive responses to attractive pictures of food than people who are tested soon after a meal.

Interestingly enough, the pupils also seem to act in response to other senses, such as taste or smell. In one experiment, subjects were given five orange drinks to taste while their pupil sizes were recorded. One of the five drinks caused much greater average increases in pupil size than the others did. Later, the same drink also won out when the subjects expressed their preferences verbally. Scientists believe that the pupil response is so sensitive that it can detect taste differences too slight to be expressed verbally—a concept that has important marketing implications.

Experiments on pupil response seem to indicate that the pupil of the eye is an extension of the brain; a window through which the psychologist can observe the brain's very functioning. The pupil may make it possible eventually to observe mental behavior without the use of electrodes or other equipment that may affect the response being observed.

Scientists have found that the pupil-response method can be used as a kind of "lie detector" in areas of inquiry that involve social values or pressures. For instance, scientists do not get good agreement between

11

pupil response experiments and verbal responses when women are shown pictures of seminude men or women. The pupil responds much as one would expect to such pictures, but the verbal responses tend to hide the subject's true feelings. The pupil-response technique seems to be a much more reliable indicator of such attitudes.

The pupil-response technique is a new method of probing a subject's mind. It is being applied to study the development of sexual interest in young people and to explore their identification with parents. In other studies it is helping to explore changes in attitudes caused by hypnotic suggestion. In still others, it is being used to study responses to packaging, new products, and television advertising. Scientists are beginning to understand and exploit the information that is provided by the dilations and constrictions of the pupil.

Do birds engage in courtship?

When a male bird begins to sing in the spring, he is warning other males to steer clear of his particular territory. To an unattached female, however, that same song is an invitation from a prosperous landowner who is well able to support a family. When a female robin hears such a song, she is apt to fly over and investigate. Instead of welcoming her, however, a male robin is likely to threaten her and try to chase her away. And little wonder. In robins and many other species of birds, males and females are so similar that even the birds themselves have a problem telling one from the other. Female robins, it turns out, identify themselves by their *behavior,* and not by their appearance.

When another robin, male or female, flies into a male's territory, the male expects the worst and reacts aggressively. He sings wildly, puffs out his breast feathers, jerks his head, and makes assorted threatening motions. A second male meets the challenge either by retreat to other more peaceful areas or by threats of his own. A female, on the other hand, merely ignores the male's ungentlemanly behavior. After a while, she flies meekly after the puzzled male, refusing either to fight or flee.

In time the male accepts his new partner and shows off by preening and strutting, and by flying after the female. After two or three months of "engagement," the female begins to build a nest. The male brings food to her—even though she is capable of doing her own foraging—and she flutters and crouches down like a baby robin, as if begging for food. Scientists have discovered that a female will beg from her mate even if she is surrounded by available food. Courtship feeding of this kind is quite common among birds.

Many male birds carry out a variety of courtship rituals. The skylark, for example, goes through intricate flying maneuvers to impress his mate. Sparrows and other drab-looking males concentrate on their singing abilities. Peacocks and other brightly colored birds frequently strut and pose to show off their beautiful plumage. These activities intensify the mating drive in males and females by increasing the flow of sex hormones.

Some birds court by dancing. The lyrebird of Australia dances, sings, and does imitations in order to interest a female. Other birds gather in large groups before performing. The North American prairie chicken females watch as several dozen males dance and compete for attention. The sharp-tailed grouse not only dance in large groups but do so in unison! They lower their heads, open their wings, rattle their tail feathers, and stamp their feet as they coo and shuffle about. When one bird stamps, the others stamp; when one stops, the entire troop stops.

The ostrich of East Africa differs from most birds in that the females do the dancing. They collect in groups, fluff out their feathers, and go through a high-stepping dance before nearby males. Periodically, a female stops dancing and starts racing across the plain with a male in hot pursuit.

The rituals of courtship are also a means of identification between males and females of the same species. There are over three dozen species of ducks in North America, and some are quite similar in appearance. If a female of one species happens to meet a male of a similar but different species, his courtship signals are unrecognizable to her and she does not consider him a potential mate.

Scientists tell us that most of the characteristic acts of courtship are instinctive, not learned, behavior. If a male duck is raised in complete isolation from other birds, he will perform all the typical courtship displays of his species the first time the right conditions present themselves. Even if a duck is raised by foster parents of a different species, he will not use their displays, but will perform those of his own species without a single mistake. Experiments performed with insects, fish, and mammals indicate that courtship rituals are inherited just as surely as are the physical features of their bodies.

13

How are fabrics made rainproof?

Fabrics can be made rainproof in precisely the same way that insects can walk on water: all liquids possess a property called *surface tension*. A water surface acts much as a thinly stretched membrane. It takes a considerable force, relatively speaking, to break through that membrane.

The accompanying diagram shows a boat made of wire mesh floating on a surface of water. The wire mesh must be covered with a thin coating of wax, however, so that the water will not "wet" the wires. If this precaution is not taken, the wires will become wet and water will pass easily through the screen. As long as the wires are dry, the boat will float easily on the water.

Fabrics that are rainproof yet allow air to pass freely through use the same principle as the wire-mesh boat just discussed. The cloth fi-

Fig. 2.   A boat made of wire mesh can float on water.

bers are impregnated with a plastic-like substance that leaves a thin coating on each fiber. Raindrops falling on a garment made of such fibers cannot wet the fabric, and surface tension prevents them from passing through. Left with no other choice, they simply roll off.

Why is surfing better in California than on the east coast of the United States?

Water waves are generated by the action of the wind. To illustrate, imagine a calm surface of water just as a breeze starts to move the air. Tiny waves, or ripples—only a fraction of an inch high—begin to take shape as the breeze comes up. As the wind grows in intensity, the ripples grow into full-sized waves, their size depending on the wind's speed, the distance it blows over the water, and its duration. The energy of the wind's motion, therefore, is transferred to the water and shows up in the form of water waves.

14

Storms over the oceans generate large, irregular patterns of waves that radiate outward from the area of the storm. As they move outward, the waves become more regular and often travel hundreds or even thousands of miles before breaking against a distant shore. As the waves move along, they are also acted upon by the winds they encounter. If a system of waves—or ocean *swell,* as it is called—happens to move in the same direction as the wind, it is reinforced. If the wind blows in the opposite direction, the swell is diminished in size. The Pacific shore of North America is far better for surfers than the Atlantic shore because the waves from various Pacific storms are strengthened by prevailing westerly winds as they travel eastward. The Atlantic surf of North America is much smaller because the prevailing westerlies blow against the advancing waves and reduce their height. The Atlantic provides its best surfing on its European shore where the westerly winds have reinforced the waves.

Waves originating in different storms far out at sea arrive at a distant shore in an essentially parallel sequence of waves. But waves from two different storms have differing heights because of the variation in storm intensity. This explains why waves of varying heights often alternate as they break against the shore. Noting the sizes of waves and the time between crests (called the *period* of the wave pattern) can give a rough idea of the several storms near and far away that gave rise to the swell. Wave periods often vary from a few seconds between waves to as long as 20 seconds. A close inspection of wave periods often reveals more complex regularities, such as a few small waves with short periods alternating with larger waves with much longer periods. Experienced surfers study the particular sequence of waves on a given day in order to select the highest wave for a run toward shore.

How old are music and dance?

Music is a very important characteristic of culture, perhaps one of its supreme manifestations. So anthropologists were delighted, in 1974, when a scientific team of the U.S.S.R. announced the existence of a 20,000-year-old set of percussion instruments.

During the period from 1954 to 1962, Ukrainian archaeologists I. G. Pidoplichko and I. G. Shovkoplyas were carrying out excavations at the site of a Paleolithic settlement in the village of Mezin, in the Ukraine. Inside the remains of a house, they found a collection of large mammoth bones that were colored red and engraved with geo-

15

metric designs. Although they were set apart from other artifacts, and appeared to form a set, their purpose was not at all clear to the scientists. There were a shoulder blade, a thigh bone, two jaw bones, part of a pelvis, and a portion of a skull. Also found nearby were ivory rattles, a mallet fashioned from a reindeer's antler, and a bracelet made of five decorated pieces of mammoth-tusk ivory. Near the bones were heaps of pure yellow and red ocher.

It was eventually established, in 1974, that the mysterious bones were a set of percussion instruments. This conclusion was based on a number of clues: the way the bone surfaces are worn in certain localized places; the way the outer bone tissue is compacted as if by drumming; and the polished effect at certain places. There seems little doubt that this collection of bones comprises instruments from one of the world's oldest orchestras, dating back to the Stone Age. Prior to their discovery, such musical accomplishments were thought to date back only to civilizations of the ancient Orient, perhaps 5000 years.

The bracelet of ivory consists of five rings with carved openwork decoration. When rattled together, they make a harmonious sound much like castanets. It is believed the bracelet was used to accompany dances, which suggests that dancing—whether for ritual purposes or simply for pleasure—was practiced by Cro-Magnon man some 20,000 years ago. This dancing, of course, was done to the accompaniment of percussion instruments.

Scientists believe that further study of such instruments may lead to a better understanding of the musical culture of Paleolithic times. They hope to gain a deeper insight into Cro-Magnon man, his perception of the world, his emotional and behavioral makeup, and the way he thought.

How do birth control pills work?

Physicians have long known that ovulation, the production of egg cells by the ovary, ceases at the beginning of pregnancy because of hormonal changes. The same result can be achieved by taking birth control pills, which contain a variety of chemicals called *steroids*.

The active ingredients of the pill are the hormones estrogen and progesterone, or substances derived from them. They have the chemical ability to simulate the hormonal changes that occur during pregnancy and, in so doing, prevent ovulation.

Research is still going on concerning possible side effects of these drugs, but it is known that they are linked to a blood-clotting disease that is potentially lethal. Because of this very real danger, women taking birth control pills should have frequent medical checkups.

How do fossils get inside rocks?

Over much of the earth's surface there is a relatively thin blanket of sediment that has been transformed into rock through the relentless processes of nature. Perhaps the most distinctive characteristic of these *sedimentary rocks* is the great number and variety of fossils that they often contain. These are the remains of once-living plants or animals that were buried in sand, silt, or mud. Over great lengths of time, much of the living matter that they contained was replaced by minerals. For example, petrified wood was formed when the woody fibers and cellulose of the tree were replaced by minerals such as silica. Representatives of just about every kind of living thing have been preserved in that way as fossils. Even such fragile biological marvels as the compound eyes of flies or the delicate wings of butterflies have been preserved in rock. Most fossils, however, are the remains of shells or skeletons. But how do sedimentary rocks form around such things? How can sand, for example, which sifts gently through our fingers, change into a rock such as sandstone, which can be almost as strong as granite?

Scientists tell us that sedimentary rocks are formed at moderately elevated temperatures and pressures. As a sediment is buried by other sediments, it is subjected to increasingly high temperatures—on the average, 1°C for each 30 meters (100 feet) of depth near the earth's surface, and about 1 pound per square inch for each foot of depth. The increased pressure leads to a process called *compaction,* which is the squeezing together of the particles of a sediment. If, for example, enough pressure is applied to fine-grained mud, most of the water is squeezed out and the particles are forced closer together. Then, as minerals and the surrounding water in pore spaces are heated up, they tend to react chemically to form new minerals. This process—called *cementation*—involves the deposition from solution of minerals such as calcite, silica, and iron oxide, which build up as a layer or film on the particles of the sediment. Eventually, much or all of the pore space separating the particles is filled by the cementing minerals, and rock is the result. This is much the way that a limy scale forms on the inside of a kettle after long and repeated boiling of water.

The living organisms most commonly preserved as fossils are those that begin with durable elements such as shells, bones, and teeth. But in some instances, an entire rock may consist of organic matter. A layer of coal, for example, is made up of plant parts, and some limestones may consist of the remains of coral or seashells. In addition to the remains of living things, fossils may consist of footprints, tracks, trails, and burrows.

A great many fossils are the remains of micro-organisms. Visible only under the microscope, these *micro-fossils* are used as a guide by petroleum geologists in their search for oil. The tiny fossils are so small that they are not destroyed by the action of bits used in oil drills. So they are brought to the surface during oil-drilling operations in undamaged condition. There, scientists study them for possible clues to the location of oil-bearing rocks.

Why does aspirin sometimes cause upset stomach?

Each year some 30 million pounds of aspirin are manufactured in the United States alone and headache sufferers spend over a quarter of a billion dollars on them. Over 200 kinds of tablets and powders for the relief of headaches are on the market, and most of them use aspirin as the basic ingredient.

Taking an aspirin tablet, therefore, seems to be a simple act, yet scientists continue to search for a tablet that has fewer undesirable side effects for the user. One of the most severe problems with aspirin is that of stomach bleeding, which takes place when an undissolved tablet lies on the wall of the stomach. In passing through the stomach wall, aspirin molecules injure some of the cells, resulting in small hemorrhages. The bleeding experienced by most people taking two five-grain tablets amounts to about one-half a teaspoonful or less. Some people, however, are more susceptible to bleeding. Some tablets dissolve quite slowly, which greatly aggravates the problem of bleeding, with consequent discomfort. Aspirin tablets of high quality are designed to disintegrate quickly in water. These are least likely to cause stomach upset.

Where did the American Indians come from?

The vast majority of anthropologists believe that the Americas were populated through Alaska by small groups of Siberian hunters who crossed the Bering Strait. In fact, a land bridge about fifty-six miles long probably existed from Siberia to Alaska during the Ice Age.

18

This would have enabled the first American immigrants to walk from Asia to North America. At the very outside, this migration to the new world began somewhere between 50,000 and 70,000 years ago; perhaps even more recently than that.

A few scientists believe that the Americas may also have been peopled, in part, by Polynesians, either sailing across the Pacific to South America or island-hopping across the archipelago between Tasmania and Tierra del Fuego at the southern tip of South America. Indeed, Antarctica was free of glacial ice about ten or fifteen thousand years ago and actually had a temperate climate. There is, however, no archaeological proof to confirm these ideas. Scientists do agree, however, that the great majority of original American immigrants consisted of Mongoloid peoples arriving across the Bering Strait over a prolonged period of time.

Scientists have established that man was present in the United States as early as 40,000 years ago at a site near Lewisville, Texas. The oldest human settlement found in Mexico dates back 23,000 years. The oldest site in South America is about 16,000 years old. In general, as archaeologists go farther south, the human cultures are less ancient. This gives some confirmation to the theory that the settlers of America came by way of Alaska and moved slowly southward.

The early American immigrants were hunters and gatherers for many thousands of years before they learned to cultivate plants and domesticate animals. By the year 7500 B.C., agricultural sites existed in Mexico where hunter-gatherer tribes were simultaneously engaged in the growing of squash, chile beans, and, later, maize. In the United States, agriculture was engaged in over 5000 years ago.

About 3500 years ago, there was the beginning of what scientists call the high cultures, based on extensive farming, the manufacture of ceramics, the use of polished stone implements, and the beginnings of the textile industry. These advanced civilizations included the Toltec, Aztec, and Zapotec civilizations in Mexico and Central America, and similar great civilizations, including the Incas in South America. The "high cultures" continued to develop until the beginning of the sixteenth century, with the arrival of European immigrants.

Is an astronaut really weightless in space?

The weight of an object is the force that gravity exerts on that object. The weight of a stone, for example, is the force that gravity exerts on it. If we drop it, the stone falls to the ground. Yet we have all heard the comment that an astronaut in a space vehicle orbiting the earth or moon is "weightless." What does the term really mean?

To get a better understanding of weightlessness, imagine that an astronaut is in an orbiting space vehicle at an altitude of 4000 miles above the earth. If we were to calculate his weight, we would find it to be about one-quarter of his weight on the earth's surface. His weight is reduced because the pull of gravity drops off as one moves away from the center of the earth, but his weight is certainly not zero! How, then, can he float in apparent weightlessness in the space vehicle?

Suppose our astronaut tries to measure his weight by standing on a bathroom scale. The scale will read zero. To understand why, consider how you use such a scale. You step on it while it rests on the floor. Gravity pulls you downward, you press against the spring in the scale, and it registers your weight. Now suppose that you and the scale are in an elevator and the floor starts falling freely downward. You and the scale are now accelerating downward at the same rate under the pull of gravity. You can no longer press down on the scale because gravity pulls the scale toward the center of the earth just as rapidly as it pulls you toward the scale. For all practical purposes, you are "weightless" despite the fact that you have your normal weight! You, the scale, and the elevator are in a state of "free fall," as is an astronaut in an orbiting space vehicle. In both examples, the only force acting on the systems is the pull of gravity—and that is what is meant by free fall.

The only way that a body can become truly weightless is to move so far from a heavenly body that the gravitational pull is negligible. As long as gravity is not zero at a given place, any object will have a definite weight, even if it is in free fall. The term "weightlessness," as commonly used, means only that gravity cannot push a freely falling object against another freely falling object.

Why is the center of the earth hot?

The oldest rocks yet discovered are about 4 billion years old, so geologists have no direct evidence for events that happened earlier in the earth's history. Nevertheless, other evidence suggests that the earth began forming about 4½ billion years ago by the gathering up, or *accretion*, of rocky material near its present orbit. The new planet was probably a homogeneous accumulation of silicon, iron, and magnesium compounds, along with smaller amounts of all the other chemical elements. Although the original rocky materials were relatively cold, three effects soon began to heat the planet.

Each rock that fell into the earth during the process of accretion carried a great amount of *kinetic energy,* or energy of motion. This energy was converted to heat upon impact—much as the repeated blows of a hammer heat the head of a nail. Although much of the energy of accretion was radiated into space, some of it was "buried" by material that arrived later. The overlying material acted as an insulating layer, slowing the flow of heat to the surface and thus raising the temperature of the interior.

Compression is another effect that leads to a temperature rise in the earth. The heating of a bicycle tire pump is an everyday example of this effect. As the pump compresses air, heat is generated more quickly than it can diffuse away, and the barrel becomes warm. Similarly, as the earth grew in size, the inner regions of the planet were squeezed closer together under the ever-growing weight of the accumulating material. The gravitational energy used up in compressing the interior reappeared as heat, which was unable to escape completely. Heat flows very slowly through miles of rock, so it accumulated, and the inside of the earth grew hotter. Geophysicists have calculated the amount of heating that occurred, and most believe that accretion and compression generated an average internal temperature of about 1800°F (1000°C) for the new planet.

The third source of internal heat was provided by the elements uranium, thorium, and the small fraction of potassium atoms that are heavier than ordinary potassium. These elements are extremely rare on earth, yet they have had a profound effect on the planet's evolution because of their *radioactivity.* The atoms of these radioactive elements transform spontaneously into different chemical elements by emitting subatomic particles such as helium nuclei and electrons. The emitted particles are the key to the heating of the earth. As the swift particles are absorbed by the surrounding material, their energy of motion is changed into heat. By ordinary standards, the amount of heat generated may seem trivial: only about 330 calories generated by a cubic inch of granite over a period of one million years!

But here again, the flow of heat out of the interior was so slow that the earth's temperature grew continually higher. Over a few billion years of such radioactive decay, the temperature would rise to the melting point of granite—even sooner if the temperature rises due to accretion and compression are included. Geologists believe that these heating processes led to a considerable rise in temperature during the first billion years or so of the earth's history. At depths of about 250 to 500 miles (400 to 800 kilometers), the temperature would have reached the melting point of iron. At that temperature, the earth was changed forever by an event called the *iron catastrophe*.

Of all the common elements found on earth, iron is the heaviest. It amounts to about one-third of the earth's mass. When the iron began to melt, enormous "drops" of iron formed and fell toward the center. This displaced the lighter materials toward the surface. The melting and sinking of so much iron to form a *liquid core* was a catastrophic event. The "falling" of the iron transformed a huge amount of gravitational energy into heat. In physical terms, the process is basically the same as using the energy of a waterfall to turn turbines and generate electrical energy. The vast amount of heat released during formation of an iron core produced an additional temperature rise of 3600°F (2000°C), causing most of the earth to melt.

When the earth warmed to the temperature at which iron melts, it underwent a profound reorganization that geologists call *planetary differentiation*. Approximately one-third of the material sank to the center, and a large part of the planet was converted to a partly molten state. The lighter materials floated upward, where they cooled and formed a primitive crust. Before differentiation, the earth was presumably a homogeneous body, with roughly the same kind of material at all depths. After differentiation, it consisted of layers, or shells, with a dense *iron core,* a *superficial crust,* and between them the remaining *mantle.* Differentiation is probably the most significant event in the formation of our planet. It led to the formation of a crust and eventually the continents. It also probably led to the escape of gases from interior rocks, which eventually gave rise to the atmosphere and the oceans.

The earth has cooled considerably during the 4 billion years or so since the iron catastrophe. The crust and mantle have solidified, but much of the underlying core is still molten. The center of the earth is thought to consist of a solid iron core surrounded by a liquid iron zone on which the mantle floats.

Radioactivity is still important as a present-day heat-producing agent. Radioactive elements, such as uranium and thorium, became concentrated in granite during the early period of differentiation, so granite leads all rocks in radioactive heat production. The heat generated by the granite in the earth's crust is about 250,000 times greater than the energy in a one-megaton nuclear explosion. Much of the heat flowing out of the continents comes from the radioactivity of granite rocks in the outer 10 miles or so of the continents. Heat flow from the ocean floor, where there is no granite, comes from deep in the earth. Scientists believe that the temperature of the center of the earth is about 7700°F (4300 °C).

How do plants catch and eat insects?

Botanists tell us that the term "carnivorous plants" is really a misnomer, since no plant has ever been found capable of trapping even a small mammal such as a mouse. In addition, the so-called insectivorous plants—just like ordinary green plants—do manufacture their own food, and seem to partake of insects only as a kind of dietary supplement.

The pitcher plant has a watertight leaf formed in the shape of a tall, narrow-mouthed glass or funnel. Small insects crawl down the inside of the leaf and find a pool of water waiting for them. The inside of the leaf contains a great number of downward-pointing bristles, which prevent the insects from crawling back out. They eventually drown in the water. Digestive chemicals, called *enzymes,* are secreted by the leaf and break down the insect into nutrients that dissolve in the water. These dissolved substances are then absorbed by the plant.

The sundew plant uses an entirely different means of capturing insects. The leaves contain relatively long filaments that secrete a sticky material. A small insect, such as a fly, becomes entangled and stuck in place by these projections. Once again, the insect is digested by enzymes that the leaf secretes, and the plant absorbs the products of digestion.

Perhaps the trickiest of the insectivorous plants is the Venus's-fly-trap. The leaves are hinged along the center line, and the outer margins carry strong, long bristles. The top surface of the leaf carries tiny hairs that are sensitive to touch. When an insect lands on the leaf and strolls about, he inevitably touches one of the trigger hairs and the leaf snaps shut much like a clam. The bristles at the margin of the leaf imprison the insect and the process of enzyme secretion, digestion, and absorption begin to take place.

Perhaps the closest things to a carnivorous plant are a few fungi, and even they get most of their food from dead organic matter in the soil. One group of fungi manage to lasso nematodes—tiny wormlike animals in the soil. The fungus contains many circular, ringlike growths attached to its stems. Any nematode that tries to wriggle through one of the rings in his path finds that it suddenly clamps tight around his body. While the nematode is held fast by the ring, strands of the fungus grow into the body of the worm and the animal is soon digested.

How does air pollution damage plants?

Through the process of photosynthesis, green plants convert sunlight to chemical energy by combining the gases carbon dioxide and water vapor to form carbohydrates. In the process, oxygen is given off for man and animals to breathe. These gases enter and leave the plant through tiny pores called *stomata* located in leaves, stems, and other plant parts. Unfortunately, the stomata also provide entry for any pollutants carried by the air. Once through the stomata, toxic gases enter tiny open spaces within the plant and kill the cells of internal tissues.

Three major plant killers are sulfur dioxide, ozone, and automobile exhaust emissions. The symptoms of all three are similar. Leaf cells shrink, collapse, and acquire a water-soaked, dull, and spotty appearance. Mild pollution causes leaf damage and reduced growth; severe pollution causes eventual death of the plant. Exhaust emissions have become so severe in certain urban areas that dead trees along freeways have been replaced with plastic replicas.

Sulfur dioxide is given off from the furnaces of smelters, power plants, refineries, and other coal- and oil-burning industries. Coal and oil contain a small amount of sulfur, which combines with oxygen to form sulfur dioxide when the fuel burns. The gas then combines with additional oxygen in the air to form highly corrosive sulfur trioxide. In dry climates, sulfur trioxide is absorbed as a gas by the plant surfaces. In wet climates, sulfur trioxide combines with atmospheric moisture to form sulfuric acid, which later falls to earth as an acid rain.

Ozone has its origin in a number of sources, a prime one being the automobile engine. At high temperatures, nitrogen and oxygen combine to form nitrogen dioxide. Ultraviolet light in the upper atmosphere then disintegrates nitrogen dioxide to form nitrogen monoxide and atomic oxygen—a single atom of oxygen. Molecular oxygen in the air contains two atoms of oxygen joined together. The two kinds of oxygen then combine to form ozone, which consists of three atoms of oxygen. Ozone is extremely active chemically and succeeds in damaging any vegetation it comes in contact with.

Hydrocarbons, given off by engine exhaust, react with nitrogen oxides in the presence of sunlight to form complex toxic gases. One of these gases, peroxyacetyl nitrate (PAN), can damage plants in concentrations as low as 25 parts per billion in air. The plant turns silver or bronze with a glazed appearance.

Now that a great deal is known about air pollution and its effects on plants—not to mention human beings—many nations are beginning to fight the menace. Smoke stack "scrubbers" are being installed to reduce sulfur dioxide emissions. Automobile engines are being redesigned to reduce hydrocarbon emissions, and high-sulfur fuels are being used less as a source of energy.

Why does moving air feel cool in warm weather?

If our eyesight were sharp enough, we could see that the molecules in a liquid, such as water, are in a continuous, restless state of motion. Their direction of motion is entirely random and continually changing as molecules bounce off each other. Furthermore, if we could measure the molecular velocities, we would find that all possible speeds would be represented, with many distributed above and below an average or mean velocity. At any particular instant, a small proportion of the molecules just below the surface would have velocities considerably greater than the mean. Every so often, one of these high-velocity molecules would pass through the surface and enter the air above it. That is the mechanism behind the everyday occurrence that we call *evaporation.*

By its very nature, the process of evaporation involves the loss, by a liquid, of its faster-moving, more energetic molecules. Those left behind, therefore, are slower or less energetic on average. In physical terms, the average molecular velocity of a liquid is directly related to its temperature—so evaporation always lowers the temperature of the liquid that remains. Evaporation, in fact, is the major method used by the body to dispose of excess heat and maintain a normal body temperature.

Although evaporation causes body cooling, it may not be immediately apparent why the movement of air should hasten evaporation and increase the rate of cooling. To understand how this happens, imagine a quantity of water located in a sealed jar. The space above the surface soon becomes saturated with water vapor, which is to say that the space contains as many particles of water vapor as is possible under the prevailing conditions. As additional molecules pop free of the surface, an equal number are forced back into the water. A condition of equilibrium then exists, and evaporation ceases until some change is made in the system.

If the human body under discussion happens to be located in still air, the region of space just surrounding the skin soon becomes saturated with water vapor. Before evaporation can proceed further, some of the water vapor must move away from the skin by the relatively slow process of diffusion. This results in a slowing down of evaporation and a slower loss of body heat. But if an electric fan or a breeze is available, the vapor-laden air is quickly removed from the vicinity of the skin and replaced by air that is presumably "drier." No longer inhibited by a blanket of moist air, evaporation proceeds at a more rapid rate and cooling is speeded up.

There is, of course, a secondary cooling effect caused by the moving air itself. As air moves past the skin, it is heated directly and transports this heat away from the body. This effect is only important, however, if the air temperature is considerably cooler than the body temperature.

Evaporation also explains why many people are bothered less by high air temperatures in regions of low humidity. Evaporation tends to proceed at a higher rate in such places, thereby increasing the cooling rate of the body. In regions where both the temperature and humidity are high, air movement has little effect on the cooling rate; as the blanket of moist air is blown away from the skin, it is replaced by air that is almost as humid. The net result is little change in the evaporation rate and, therefore, very little cooling of the body.

Are many animals becoming extinct?

Various lists of rare and endangered animal species have given rise to considerable controversy in recent years. Some people believe that man has a right to use the resources of the earth for his own advantage, and the extinction of a few species of animals and plants is little to pay for the benefits received. Others regard the lists as a danger signal, indicating that human disregard for other life forms has exceeded the limits of compassion and sound ecology. Whatever one's point of view, the extinction of a species is a permanent loss that can never be recovered.

It should not be thought, however, that extinction of animal species is a rare event. Biologists tell us that the earth has seen 500 million species of animals and plants during the last 3 billion years or so. Of that number, only about 2 million are still alive. The loss of about 99.6 percent of all the species that ever lived shows that extinction has always been a typical fate for living things of the earth. Nevertheless, the rate at which species are lost has increased in recent centuries. The 3000 years of the Pleistocene Ice Age (when Stone Age man lived) saw the extinction of about twenty species of mammals and forty of birds, making a loss of about two species per century. Since the year 1600, however, some 130 species of birds and mammals have become extinct, a rate of about 35 per century. An additional 307 species are now in danger of extinction. We can argue about the accuracy of such figures, because they are obviously difficult to obtain. Nevertheless, estimates that differ so greatly cannot be dismissed lightly. Of the 130 species that died out since 1600, about 25 percent are thought to have met with a natural fate, not connected with man. The remaining 75 percent were lost as a result of excessive hunting, newly introduced pests or predators, and habitat disruption—all a result of man's activities.

The California condor is a large bird that was apparently headed for extinction before civilized man appeared on the scene. This bird is the largest North American vulture, with 9-foot wingspread and a weight of 22 pounds. It originally lived over the entire continent west of the Rockies from Canada to Mexico. It is now limited to a few nesting areas in the mountains north of Los Angeles. Its population has been steady at about sixty birds since 1943. Although the bird and its nesting sites are protected by law, the California condor shows no signs of increasing in number.

Although the condor may be on its way to natural extinction, other species have died out as a result of human activities. Commercial timber cutting, for example, is killing off the orangutan of Sumatra and Borneo, the only great ape outside Africa. Lumbering has forced them from the lowlands to the mountains, where their natural food, durian fruit, does not grow. There are only about 5000 of them left, and the orangutan may soon survive only in zoos.

The devastation brought on by excessive hunting can destroy species

27

in an incredibly short time. The Arabian oryx is an antelope with long, delicate horns. It once roamed the Arabian peninsula, but its last remnants now live in four zoos. The hunting of the animal in motorized vehicles sealed its fate. In the 1950s hunts with as many as 60 vehicles nearly obliterated all wildlife on the peninsula. In 1962 a special expedition was organized to capture three oryx for breeding purposes at the Arizona Zoo. The Phoenix herd now numbers about three dozen animals, and the estimated world population is less than 200.

The plight of the blue whale is another example of extermination being brought on by excessive hunting. At 90 feet in length and 160 tons in weight, the blue whale is three times the size of a large dinosaur. Its babies are larger than an adult elephant. Nevertheless, modern technology combined with human greed have reduced the population from about 10,000 or 15,000 in 1953 to perhaps 600 today.

Perhaps the blue whale and the oryx would have died out naturally in the course of time, but man has surely hastened the process. That human pressure is continuing today for hundreds of species that may soon cease to exist.

How do glaciers move?

In some of the colder places on earth, there is snow all year long. Only a portion of the snow melts during the warmer days of summer, so it is in such regions that glaciers are found. If the rate of snowfall exceeds the rate of melting, glaciers grow in size. If the rate of melting is greater, they shrink.

The weight of new snow packs down on the old. Over many years, the old snow changes to ice crystals and when the weight of ice is great enough, the glacier begins to flow.

Glaciers are great moving "rivers" of ice that have been present throughout much of the earth's history. Their effects are evident in many parts of the world where glaciers have gouged out depressions in the land that later filled with water to form lakes. Most of the world's lakes—including the Great Lakes—were formed in just that way. The movement of glaciers has also scooped out valleys and deposited glacial debris over enormous areas. This property of glaciers depends upon a peculiar property of ice and water.

The melting temperatures of all materials vary to a slight extent with pressure. For most materials, the melting temperature is increased as the pressure is increased. Ice, on the other hand, behaves in just the opposite way: the higher the pressure, the lower the melting point. Many scientists believe that this atypical behavior on the part of ice enables a glacier to flow, even though it is made of solid ice.

The effect of pressure on the melting temperature of ice is by no means a large one. In fact, it takes a pressure increase equal to that of 133 atmospheres to reduce the melting point by 1°C. Nevertheless, the weight of ice bearing down on the lower portions of a glacier melts the ice wherever a sufficient concentration of pressure builds up. When the melting occurs at such localized places, the stress is relieved and the water turns back into ice. In this way, the glacier creeps along its path in response to numerous melting and refreezing episodes.

You can demonstrate the effect of ice thickness on flow with a viscous fluid like honey. If you pour a thin layer of honey on a slightly tilted piece of bread, it will flow very slowly. But if more honey is poured on the bread to increase its thickness, it flows more rapidly. You can also increase the flow rate by increasing the tilt of the bread. Glacial ice behaves in much the same way: the greater the thickness of the ice, and the steeper its slope, the faster the movement of the glacier.

Like honey, ice tends to flow downhill—down the valleys between mountains. Glaciers flow outward from the center of an icecap thousands of feet thick. The ice continues to flow until it reaches the melt line, where it turns to water. Meanwhile, new ice forms and takes its place in the glacier.

Although ice seems solid enough, glaciers do not move as other solid materials do. A brick, for example, slides down an incline by slipping along its base, but a glacier also moves throughout its bulk by internal sliding or flowing movements.

The internal flow within the glacier accounts for a considerable part of its motion. Under the pressure of overlying ice, individual ice crystals slip tiny distances, measured in millionths of an inch, over short intervals of time. But the sum of those small movements of enormous numbers of ice crystals amounts to a measurable distance over longer periods of time. This kind of movement, however, is not the whole story.

A glacier also tends to slide along its base. The pressure is very great at the base of some glaciers and much movement takes place there as the ice melts and refreezes. The melting is caused by a combination of the pressure of overlying ice, as discussed earlier, and the flow of heat upward from the interior of the earth. If conditions are right, a layer of liquid water can be found at the bottom of the glacier. Such a layer was found at the bottom of the Antarctic ice sheet by drilling a hole more than a mile below the surface of the ice.

Measurements of the speed of glaciers are made by placing stakes in the ice and measuring their movements over a few years' time. Such measurements show that the center of the tongue of ice moves much faster than the edges, where friction of the ice against rock walls hinders the flow. A wide range of ice speeds have been measured in the past century, ranging from an inch or two to three feet per day. It has also been shown that the base of a glacier moves more slowly than the upper parts. This was accomplished by sinking a straight tube vertically into the ice and measuring its bending in the course of time.

Sudden rapid movements of glaciers, called *surges,* sometimes occur after long periods of little movement. Surges may last three years or more, and often travel at speeds of more than three miles per year. On occasion, glaciers have been known to move at truly remarkable speeds for several months at a time. In 1953, for example, the Kutiah Glacier in the Himalayas traveled seven miles in three months. Geologists are not sure why surges occur, or why many of them have been observed in recent years.

Glaciers give scientists valuable clues to weather conditions that existed hundreds of years in the past. Every summer the icecaps, such as the one in Greenland, begin to melt. At summer's end, the melted ice refreezes once again to form a thin crust of ice. Such yearly crusts provide telltale layers in the glacier much like the growth rings in a tree. Each layer marks a year's growth of the glacier.

In Greenland, scientists drilled a core of ice a quarter of a mile deep in the icecap. Counting the layers showed that the lowest layer had fallen as snow 800 years earlier! The layer thicknesses indicated the amount of snow that had fallen in each of those 800 years. They also contained samples of everything that had fallen with that snow—dust, ash from volcanoes, even fallout from modern atomic explosions. Information of this kind will help scientists learn much about the climate that existed during the past thousand years or so.

What causes a "rip tide"?

When waves approach a beach at an angle, the water is pushed along the beach in the form of a *longshore current,* as shown

RIP CURRENTS

Fig. 3.   Narrow, swift rip currents flow out from the beach at regularly spaced intervals. To get out of a rip current, merely swim several yards parallel to the shore.

in the accompanying diagram. This causes the water to pile up slightly along the shore. The increased water height, however, is too small to be noticed. At a certain place, a critical height is reached where the excess water breaks out to sea at right angles to the beach—through incoming waves—to form a fast-moving *rip current,* or "rip tide." (These currents have nothing to do with tides, so scientists prefer the term *rip current.*) The combination of incoming angular waves, longshore current, and rip current makes a closed loop of moving water. When conditions are right, a long beach normally has many such loops.

The occurrence of rip currents depends on many factors, so their location is difficult to predict. They are extremely dangerous to swimmers, however, and a knowledge of their behavior may help to save lives. Rip currents often reach a speed of three feet per second, too strong a current for many swimmers to fight against. The best way to overcome a rip current is to make use of the fact that they are very narrow. To avoid being carried out to sea, merely swim parallel to the shore and avoid fighting the current. In a short distance you will be out of the rip current and can swim to shore with little difficulty.

In order to avoid rip currents, avoid places on the beach that lack breaking waves. The rip current tends to erode a channel, which hinders the advancing waves. Also watch for rip currents at a bend or slight indentation of the beach where the water seems somewhat deeper than usual.

Why is sugar sweet?

The sense of taste is triggered when the tongue touches a wide range of chemical substances. Scientists are now quite sure that it is the geometrical shape of the molecule being tasted that results in the sensations of "pleasant," "unpleasant," "bitter," "sweet," and so on. Various receptors in the mouth are actuated by molecules with the appropriate shape, and the receptors send nerve impulses to the brain where the corresponding sensation is experienced.

A family of small carbohydrate molecules, called sugar, taste sweet. One of the sweetest of these is *sucrose,* which is sold in supermarkets as "sugar." All sugars have similar structural patterns, but other chemicals—quite unlike the sugars both chemically and structurally— also taste sweet. Saccharin is a well-known example.

In the 1960s it was discovered that a wide range of sweet-tasting chemicals all had one structural feature in common: two hydrogen atoms, spaced a short distance apart, which were available to form a chemical bond with receptors on the tongue. The distance of separation had to measure somewhere between 2.5 and 4 angstroms.* So the receptor molecule in the mouth must contain a matching two-pronged unit which permits the sweet molecule to combine with it by forming two chemical connections called *hydrogen bonds.* If a substance is to taste sweet, it must have two available hydrogen molecules just the right distance apart to fit into the receptor molecule in the mouth.

Later research on bitter-tasting compounds showed that they also had the two-prong-socket arrangement found in sweet substances. For bitter substances, however, the optimum separation of the two prongs

*An angstrom is a unit of length equal to one hundred-millionth of a centimeter.

was 1.5 angstroms apart—considerably less than for sweet molecules. This research has convinced most chemists that precise chemical geometry is involved in the triggering of taste sensations.

Physiologists recognize four basic taste sensations: sweet, bitter, salt and sour. Smell, on the other hand, seems to have about twice that number of basic odors—all of which seems to come down once again to a question of basic molecular geometry.

One theory of the sense of smell holds that each primary odor is related to the shape of a corresponding type of receptor. A complex odor results from a molecule fitting more than one receptor shape. Experiments show that molecules of different chemicals which happen to fit the same receptor site all have the same smell. Conversely, if two molecules fit only into different receptor sites, they always have a different smell.

Another theory holds that most odor receptors may not react solely to one type of odor. Instead, it is suggested that different receptors show different levels of sensitivity to different odors, so that the sensation of smell is a result of the pattern of response of a wide variety of receptors.

Research is still going on, of course, as scientists try to learn more about the methods we use to perceive the world around us. There seems little doubt, however, that taste and smell are closely related to the shapes of molecules that come in contact with our senses.

What was the first city in the United States?

The first city in the U.S.A. was not New York, or Boston, or Philadelphia, or any city founded by European settlers. The first city, known as Cahokia, began to take form nearly 1300 years ago in the heart of the Midwest, on the Illinois side of the great Mississippi River. The remains of this prehistoric city lie in a quiet suburb just half a dozen miles east of St. Louis. About half the site has already been destroyed in the construction of highways and buildings, but archaeologists have finally begun to catch glimpses of what happened as the first Americans built a remarkably advanced civilization in the heart of the continent.

Imagine that you are standing atop Cahokia's 10-story-high earthen mound about eight centuries ago when the city was in its prime. Atop the terraced mound is a platform overlooking the city's main square, and ramps and stairways lead to a large temple-like building at its

33

top. Down below are many buildings, a dozen smaller mounds, two smaller plazas, and a stockade of heavy logs a mile and a half in circumference that encloses and protects the inner city. Beyond the city walls are several square miles of prime farm land laced with waterways, farms, cornfields, thousands of thatched-roof houses, and a hundred more mounds. Canoes and barges ply the many waterways.

Beyond the city proper are its suburbs, spread across a fertile valley about 30 miles long, with more waterways and cornfields. These communities—about fifty towns and villages—have their own line of mounds extending to the banks of the Mississippi. More than 75,000 people live in Greater Cahokia, with perhaps a third in the city itself.

Within the city, archaeologists have found workshops for making pottery, shell beads, copper jewelry, stone tools, and arrowheads. The lifeblood of the city was undoubtedly trade. Archaeologists have found marine shells from the Gulf of Mexico, copper from Lake Superior mines, mica from the Carolinas, and flints from Oklahoma and Wisconsin.

Before the city's explosive growth began, people in the area had been living much as their ancestors had for thousands of years, on wild deer, fish, seeds, and nuts. Then, suddenly, farming of corn began on a vast scale to support the increased population. Similar developments of smaller scale took place at other places, but Cahokia's fertile farmlands gave it a considerable advantage. Furthermore, it had a unique location for trade, situated as it was, near the junction of the Mississippi, Missouri, and Illinois rivers.

Although scientists have literally scratched only the surface of Cahokia's archaeological secrets, they know that its leaders had constructed elementary astronomical observatories consisting of large poles laid out to form great circles. One of these New World "Stonehenges"—made of wood instead of stone—was a 410-foot-diameter circle with forty-eight logs placed around the circumference and an observer's post at the center. These observatories, perhaps as many as ten at different times, were calendars used to determine the seasons by sightings of the rising and setting sun. This information was needed to determine the times for planting crops and holding religious festivals.

Cahokia reached its peak of development and power about A.D. 1100, and its decline began about a century later. By the early fifteenth century its population had declined to perhaps 3000 to 5000 people. Three hundred years later, when French explorers entered the valley, the city had been abandoned.

Cahokia represents one of the most enormous and spectacular challenges facing New World archaeologists. Its very size is all the more striking when compared with other sites in the United States: no other prehistoric community supported more than a few thousand inhabitants and a mere two dozen mounds. There is enough work yet to be done at Cahokia and at other sites to keep a small army of archaeologists busy for many lifetimes of research. Let's hope that scientists can discover the origins and impact of these early people before the remaining sites are chewed up and destroyed by our advancing bulldozers.

How does LSD affect the mind?

Hallucinogenic drugs produce changes in human judgment, perception, thought, and mood. Typical hallucinogens include mescaline, LSD (lysergic acid diethylamide), cannabidiol (the active ingredient in marijuana), and at least fifty other chemicals. These substances disturb the normal functioning of the brain and generate bizarre experiences and distorted interpretations of the environment.

Mescaline is one of the natural hallucinogens, having been isolated from the peyote plant in 1896. At least by the sixteenth century, Mexican Indians were experiencing three-day periods of hallucinations by eating the plant or drinking its extracts. Today, there are many drugs that produce these experiences, and one of the most powerful is LSD.

Scores of scientists are doing research on LSD and other hallucinogens, both to understand them better and to see what light they can cast on the operation of the normal brain. They are investigating the effects of hallucinogens on genetics and heredity, nerve and brain function, body tissues, psychology, and physiology. Unfortunately, there is still a long way to go, and data are extremely difficult to obtain. Users of LSD, for example, are never sure of the purity, or concentration, of the drug they have taken, except in experiments. In addition, many have taken LSD in combination with other drugs, making it difficult to unravel the effects of LSD. Even the results of tests with animals show little correlation. Scientific debate over the specific toxic effects of LSD is continuing, and there is little expectation that it will be resolved soon.

35

There are, nevertheless, some dangers associated with LSD that all scientists agree on. For one thing, it destroys a user's judgment. A person under its influence sees no danger in height, heat, cold, or a fast-moving automobile. Prolonged use of LSD can cause permanent brain damage. After taking the drug, a user can experience a second "trip" at a later time, without taking another dose.

LSD is thought to operate by disrupting the normal signal pathways in the brain. Two chemicals—serotonin and norepinephrine—normally exist in the brain and carry messages from the end of one neuron, or brain cell, to the beginning of the next. Scientists now know that LSD blocks the action of serotonin and thereby interferes with normal signal processing in the brain. How this interference generates such a great variety of hallucinations is largely unknown. Psychiatry has produced many theories attempting to explain why LSD causes pleasant experiences in some people and frightening ones in others. There is no consensus at present, and scientists continue to seek answers.

What is meant by the Richter scale?

The amount of energy released by an earthquake can amount to a truly staggering figure. A great earthquake, for example, is thought to release an amount of energy equivalent to a thousand nuclear explosions, each with a strength of a million tons of TNT!

The equivalent energy of an earthquake is difficult to calculate precisely because of the many factors—mostly unknown—needed to compute it. So seismologists have developed the Richter magnitude scale, which is based on the strength of seismic shock waves recorded on instruments called seismographs. The Richter scale is arranged so that an increase in magnitude of one unit on the scale corresponds to a tenfold increase in the strength of an earthquake as measured by the magnitude of the recorded seismic waves. An earthquake of magnitude 8, for example, would be ten times larger than one of magnitude 7, or one million times larger than one of magnitude 2. Actually, the measurement of an earthquake also takes into account the weakening of seismic waves as they spread out from the origin of the disturbance. So seismologists all over the world can come up with nearly the same figure for the magnitude of an earthquake, regardless of its location. The accompanying chart shows the relationship between Richter scale magnitudes and the general effects caused by earthquakes on nearby settlements. The chart also gives the number of earthquakes that occur each year in each general range of magnitudes.

General Effects of Earthquakes in Nearby Areas	Approximate Magnitude	Number of Earthquakes per Year
Nearly total damage	8.0 or greater	0.1-0.2
Great damage	7.4-7.9	4
Serious damage	7.0-7.3	15
Considerable damage	6.2-6.9	100
Slight damage	5.5-6.1	500
Felt by all	4.9-5.4	1,400
Felt by many	4.3-4.8	4,800
Felt by some	3.5-4.2	30,000
Not felt but recorded	2.0-3.4	800,000

Fortunately, the great majority of all earthquakes are small. Great earthquakes, with magnitudes of 8 or more on the Richter scale, occur only once in five to ten years. Damage to buildings in nearby towns and cities begins at magnitude 5.5 and becomes nearly total for magnitudes of 8 or greater. The Los Angeles earthquake of 1971 was of magnitude 6.6, yet the resulting damage reached $1 billion. There are a hundred such earthquakes each year somewhere on the planet. Luckily, most of them occur in sparsely inhabited regions.

Why is it dangerous to fly a kite with a metal wire?

Measurements show that there is considerable electric charge in many clouds and in the clear air left behind when clouds evaporate. During the eighteenth century, Benjamin Franklin and others performed experiments with kites to show that an "electric fire" could be drawn out of the sky by such means. The great danger of electricity was not understood in those days, and many kite fliers received serious shocks and several were killed while experimenting with atmospheric electricity.

Kite flying is usually done on clear days with a dry string holding the kite. The string is then a good insulator of electricity, and little charge can move down to the operator. But if a wire is used, or if the string is wet, the charge can transfer readily to the operator's hand. If he happens to be standing on moist ground as well, he can receive a strong jolt of electric current. It is clear, therefore, that kites should never be flown in rainy weather or with a metal wire to the kite.

Most of the electricity in the sky is generated by thunderstorms. When conditions are favorable to a storm, humid air over a large area becomes heated, and a high-speed updraft is created. A thunderstorm often comes into being, and an enormous amount of electricity is generated. Although the theory of thunderstorms is not completely worked out, at least two mechanisms in thunderclouds are beginning to be understood.

Laboratory experiments have shown that when ice and water are in contact with each other, they assume opposite electric charges: one positive, the other negative. The impurities in the water determine which becomes positive and which negative. For the kinds of impurities usually found in clouds, the water becomes positively charged and the ice negatively charged. Physicists do not really understand why this happens; they just know it does. In a typical thundercloud, ice and water *are* in contact in the lower levels of the cloud—regions where it is not cold enough to freeze the two solidly. Here, the wet hailstones melt as they fall, and some of the water they carry is blown off and lifted high in the cloud in the form of a positively charged mist. The upper regions of the cloud, therefore, become positively charged. Meanwhile, the hailstones melt completely and fall to the ground as negatively charged raindrops. The net result is a cloud whose upper regions contain a great positive charge with respect to the bottom of the cloud and the ground.

Another effect has been discovered that can account for the charged conditions found in thunderclouds. Tiny droplets of water can exist in liquid form well below the normal freezing temperature. Called *supercooled droplets,* they change to ice when they strike an ice crystal or other substance that can trigger freezing. When a supercooled droplet freezes suddenly, it does so in two stages. First, a solid shell of ice forms around a liquid center. Then the core freezes and expands. This breaks the outer shell of ice, sending out a shower of microscopic ice splinters. The ice splinters carry away a positive charge, leaving the larger central part with a negative charge. The updraft lifts the tiny, positively charged splinters to the top of the cloud, while the negatively charged cores fall to the bottom. Once again, scientists are not sure why the charges are generated by the process of splintering. But calculations show that the effect is great enough to account for the charges found in thunderclouds.

Scientists believe that both of the processes mentioned above may be at work to generate electricity in a thundercloud—the former in the lower and warmer regions, the latter in the higher regions. In addition, other processes, as yet not clearly understood, may also be at work.

Practically all thunderstorms produce negatively charged rain. Obviously, this process cannot continue indefinitely. Some of the charge is neutralized by lightning discharges, which are really nothing more than king-sized electric sparks. The remainder is neutralized by electrically charged particles, or *ions*, which move through the air, positive ions to the earth, negative ions to the upper atmosphere. The ions are created in the atmosphere by cosmic rays and radioactivity.

Can human beings change the earth's climate?

After millions of years of existence on earth, we have acquired the power to affect our planet's climate. At least, many scientists think so. The theory has to do with the accumulation of dust and carbon dioxide that modern technology pours into the atmosphere in great quantities. The dust tends to reduce the amount of incoming solar radiation, thereby cooling the earth. The carbon dioxide tends to trap heat that would ordinarily escape to outer space, thereby warming the earth. If either effect is large enough, the earth's average temperature might change a degree or two, with catastrophic results. An increase in temperature might melt the icecaps and raise the level of the ocean as much as 300 feet. A reduction in temperature might start continental glaciers moving down from the north. All of this is hypothetical, of course. No one really knows what, if anything, is happening to the climate or how long such catastrophic events might take to occur.

Why doesn't food stick to Teflon?

Most inanimate things around us—air, water, metal, stone— are made up of relatively small molecules. Plastics, however, are an exception. Modern synthetic plastics, such as polyethylene and Teflon, are giant molecules called *polymers*. A polymer is made of great quantities of small molecules, often numbered in the hundreds of thousands, linked together in a repeating pattern. The process of forming polymers is called *polymerization*.

Polyethylene is an important synthetic polymer made of thousands of ethylene molecules. An ethylene molecule consists of four hydrogen atoms and two carbon atoms arranged as shown below:

The lines in the figure stand for pairs of electrons which are shared by the atoms they connect and which bond the two together. Of vital importance in forming a polymer is the fact that the carbon atoms are connected by two electron pairs. Now imagine that another molecule is added that tends to take electrons readily—a so-called strong oxidizing agent. Such a molecule would break one of the carbon-to-carbon bonds and remove one of its electrons. To that electron it would add an electron of its own to form an electron pair with one of the carbon atoms. The modified ethylene molecule now looks like this

where Q stands for the oxidizing agent. The lone electron left over from the broken bond pair is represented by the dot to the right of the molecule. That unpaired electron causes the new molecule to act as an oxidizing agent in its own right. Chemists call such a molecule a *free radical*. So this new free radical reacts with another ethylene molecule in exactly the way the molecule Q did earlier:

Notice that this new product is also a free radical.

The polymer grows almost endlessly until some other reaction happens to occur. For example, as two free radicals grow toward each other, they may join together, forming a very long molecule. A typical polyethylene molecule contains more than 2000 carbon atoms.

Polyethylene is widely used in making squeeze bottles and other containers of great variety. It is not useful for lining frying pans, however, because it melts at too low a temperature, and would stick to hot foods. Although Teflon is structurally similar to polyethylene, its properties are widely different.

If all of the hydrogen atoms in ethylene are replaced by fluorine, we have a molecule called tetrafluoroethylene, or Teflon. Fluorine behaves very differently from hydrogen in chemical compounds. Once it has become bonded to another atom, such as to carbon in this example, it steadfastly refuses to seek electrons from any other atom. In addition, the fluorine atoms are larger than hydrogen atoms. They surround the carbon atoms and shield them almost perfectly, refusing to be jogged loose by even the most violent chemical forces. For this reason, Teflon is more inert and stable than any other natural or manmade resin. The atoms in the Teflon polymer are so tightly bonded together that it is almost impossible to break them apart, so they cannot join up with the atoms of other substances. For that reason, Teflon does not burn, corrode, or damage any material it touches. That is what makes it so useful for nonstick cookware.

The problem in making Teflon-coated frypans, of course, is getting the polymer to stick to the pan. This has been accomplished by modifying the molecule slightly and suspending fine dispersions of Teflon in water. This makes it possible to spray the plastic on various surfaces. As most cooks know, this plastic is an ideal nonstick coating for cooking utensils and for steam irons as well.

Another version of the molecule makes it suitable as a water- and oil-repellent coating for fabrics. One end of the polymer is designed to react chemically with fiber molecules and stick to them. The other end has the typical nonstick properties of Teflon, so it refuses to combine with fabric, oil, or water. So the polymer has a sticky side that adheres to the material to be protected and a nonsticky side that wards off dirt, oil, and water. It is marketed under such trade names as Scotchgard and Zepel.

Finally, another modification of the basic polymer has produced fluorocarbon rubber, which is used to keep aircraft wings free of ice at high altitudes. Chemists created the rubber by altering the composition of the small tetrafluoroethylene molecule from which the polymer is made. Instead of replacing all the hydrogen atoms of ethylene with fluorine, only some of them are replaced. This produces a molecule consisting of carbon, hydrogen, and fluorine. When these molecules are polymerized, the rubber-like polymer is the result.

Why is it difficult to locate a high-speed aircraft from the direction of its sound?

When you locate a jet aircraft flying overhead, you find that the line of sight to the aircraft lies far ahead of the point from which the sound seems to come. This effect is a result of the fact that sound travels through air at a speed vastly slower than the speed of light—about a million times slower, in fact.

Fig. 4. The airplane emits sound waves at point *A*, but is located at point *B* when the sound reaches the ground. Because sound travels so much slower than light, the sound seems to come from a point far behind the aircraft's line of sight.

The accompanying diagram illustrates what happens when we observe a high-speed aircraft. An aircraft located at point *A* gives off sound waves that travel at a leisurely pace toward an observer at point *O*. Meanwhile, the jet plane moves to the right with a speed close to or even exceeding the speed of sound. By the time the sound reaches the observer, the plane is located at point *B*, and that is where the observer must look to see the aircraft. The observer's ears tell him that the plane is at point *A* (the direction of arrival of the sound), but his eyes pick it up at point *B*.

Sound travels at about 1100 feet per second (330 meters per second) at sea level and about 13 percent slower than that at an altitude of 40,000 feet, where jets usually fly. Because of this variability, aircraft speeds are often expressed in so-called *Mach numbers*. A speed of

Mach 1, for example, means that the airplane is flying at the speed of sound, whatever it happens to be at the altitude of flight. Mach 2 means twice the speed of sound, and so on. (This means that a plane flying at Mach 1 near the ground flies faster than a plane flying at Mach 1 at a high altitude.) In contrast to the speed of sound, light travels at about 186,000 miles per second (300,000,000 meters per second). For the question at hand, this provides essentially instantaneous transmission of light waves from plane to observer.

Referring once again to the diagram, the difference between the audible and visual directions to the jet aircraft can be quite significant. If the plane is flying at Mach 1, the visual direction to the plane is about 60 degrees ahead of the direction of arrival of the sound. This angle corresponds to the angle shown in the diagram for the two plane positions. The angle is approximately true, by the way, for any altitude of flight.

The speed of sound is relatively low in air and other gases because the molecules are quite far apart and must collide with one another in order to transfer the sound waves through the gas. The molecules of liquids and solids, on the other hand, are closer together and interact more quickly and strongly. The following table gives the approximate speed of sound in various everyday substances.

Approximate Speed of Sound

Material	Speed (feet per second)
Air	1,100
Ethyl alcohol	3,960
Water (pure)	4,915
Water (sea)	5,023
Copper	15,420
Glass	16,700
Iron	19,550
Aluminum	21,060

Can earthquakes be predicted or controlled?

Only a short time ago, no respectable scientists would have attempted to predict the occurrence of an earthquake. But today, seismologists of many nations are making considerable headway in this area and can point to important successes. In February 1975, scientists predicted an earthquake five hours in advance of its occurrence near Haicheng in northeast China. Millions of people had time to evacuate homes and factories before the earthquake struck. Despite the fact that many towns and villages were totally destroyed, only a few hundred lives were lost. Scientists from other countries estimate that tens of thousands of lives were saved by the timely warning.

Scientific earthquake prediction is based on several physical changes that take place in rock when it is deformed. When a rock is squeezed, and just before it breaks, it swells because of the opening and lengthening of tiny cracks. This swelling, called *dilatancy,* begins when the stress reaches about half the amount needed to break the rock. Other measurable changes also occur at that stress level, including changes in electrical resistance and the speed at which sound waves travel through the rock. The general idea is to monitor such changes in the earth's crust and issue a warning at the appropriate time. For great earthquakes, some of these changes occur several years before the shock, so long-term warnings can be given. Other physical events, such as a reduction in the frequency of occurrence of small tremors, followed by a rapid increase, can occur days or even hours before the earthquake. This can provide valuable time to evacuate structures, close down nuclear power plants, turn off gas lines, and make other necessary last-minute preparations.

Much more work must be done, however, before scientists will be able to predict major earthquakes with a reasonable degree of certainty. Another Chinese earthquake took place near T'ang-shan in August 1976. A long-term warning was given five years before the shock. Unfortunately, short-term predictions were not accurate enough to save the 700,000 people estimated to have lost their lives. On a happier note, smaller earthquakes have been predicted in the United States and the U.S.S.R., in connection with continuing research programs.

If the problems of earthquake prediction boggle the imagination, consider that the first tentative steps have been taken toward eventual control of earthquakes. In 1966 a chance discovery showed that the frequency of earthquakes near Denver, Colorado, had increased following the high-pressure injection of waste liquids into a deep well. Scientists concluded that the earthquakes were triggered by reduced friction between the rocks in the area. The injected liquids must have "unlocked" a fault, thereby releasing strains that had built up in the earth. The idea is to place earthquake-control wells every few miles along California's San Andreas fault. Fluid would then be injected into the earth so that the rocks would slip frequently along the fault line in small, controlled earthquakes. This would be preferable to allowing the strain to build up over a period of 50 to 100 years, to be released eventually in one great, devastating shock. There are, however, important political and legal implications involved with triggering man-made earthquakes of unknown strength. A great deal of research must be done before such an important (and, perhaps unattainable) procedure can be attempted.

What is radioactivity?

Before delving into radioactivity, it will be helpful to review a few scientific terms. An *atom*, of course, is the smallest part of a chemical element that exhibits all the characteristics of that element. It always consists of a *nucleus*, or dense central region, surrounded by one or more light *electrons*, located a great distance away. Most of an atom, in fact, is empty space. Current theory tells us that a nucleus contains *protons*. We can think of a proton as a spherical, positively charged particle of matter that is very heavy for its size. The nucleus of the hydrogen atom contains one proton, and all other nuclei have two or more protons, equal in number to the quantity of (negatively charged) electrons surrounding the nucleus.

In addition to protons, a nucleus almost always contains *neutrons*. A neutron is superficially much like a proton except that it has no electrical charge. The number of neutrons in a nucleus can vary, even for the same chemical element. Although most hydrogen nuclei contain no neutrons, a few contain one neutron, and a still fewer number contain two neutrons. All aluminum nuclei found in nature have 13 protons and 14 neutrons, but artificially made aluminum can have 13, 15, 16, or a greater number of neutrons to go with its 13 protons. All tin atoms have 50 protons in their nuclei, but the number of neutrons can vary from 62 to 74.

The three kinds of hydrogen atoms, containing zero, one, or two neutrons in their nuclei, are called *isotopes* of hydrogen. Aluminum has only one naturally occurring isotope, but tin has ten isotopes that occur in nature.

Some nuclei are stable and will last indefinitely. A stable oxygen atom, for example, has a nucleus with 8 protons and 8, 9, or 10 neutrons. Stable arsenic contains 33 protons and 42 neutrons in its nucleus. Gold is stable, with its nucleus of 79 protons and 118 neutrons. Any other isotopes of these three elements will have different numbers of neutrons in their nuclei and will be unstable.

The important point here is that all unstable nuclei tend to give off energy, and change eventually to a stable combination of protons and neutrons. An isotope may do this in one step or in many steps. The energy given off by the nucleus may appear in many forms: as energy of motion (a fast-moving particle that flies off); as a kind of light or electromagnetic energy (a gamma ray, or photon); or as both, in the form of a particle along with a photon or two. Whenever a nucleus changes in some way and gives off energy, it does so by losing total mass. For example, if you were to weigh an atom before the event, and weigh it again along with any particles that were given off, you would find that some of the matter had disappeared. The loss in mass in such nuclear events appears as energy.

If a nucleus is unstable because of an excess of neutrons, it gives off energy by a different method. A neutron changes into a proton, and a fast-moving electron, or *beta particle,* appears outside the atom.

For all such nuclear events, some of the energy shows up as one or more gamma rays. These are merely bundles of energy, called *quanta,* entirely similar to visible light except for their much greater level of energy.

We often hear the term *half-life* in connection with radioactive elements. Scientists cannot predict when any specific nucleus will experience *radioactive decay,* the term for what we have been discussing, but they do know that the process is random. That leads to the fact that if half of the nuclei decay in a known length of time, say ten years, then half of those that are left will decay in the next ten years, and so on into infinity.

Each unstable isotope has its own unique half-life. Bromine-82, for example, has a half-life of 34 hours. The "82" specifies the number of protons plus neutrons in the nucleus of the isotope. Bromine-80, on the other hand, has a half-life of 18 minutes. Radium-228 has a half-life of 6.7 years, while radium-226 has a half-life of 1620 years. Some half-lives are measured in billionths of a second, whereas the half-life of uranium-238 is 4.5 billion years, approximately the age of the earth.

Of the 100 or so chemical elements, each element has several isotopes. A few of them, however, such as gold and aluminum, have only one kind of nucleus as they are found in nature. All of the elements with 84 or more protons in their nuclei have only unstable, radioactive nuclei. Only a handful of the elements with fewer than 84 protons have unstable nuclei. One of these is potassium-40 which exists in extremely small quantities in table salt in the compound potassium chloride. This isotope has a half-life of 100 million years and emits beta particles, gamma rays, and an odd particle called a neutrino, which has no mass or electric charge. The salt on your breakfast eggs contained enough potassium-40 as a trace impurity to bombard your insides with an enormous quantity of beta particles all day long. We can think of a beta particle, a fast-moving electron, as a tiny projectile that bombards and damages living cells that it happens to strike. If a beta particle happens to strike a molecule in a cell, it may knock off an electron or two so that the molecule cannot function normally in the living cell. Each cell, however, has 10 billion molecules in it, so the disruption of one molecule would probably not be too important. Mankind has used salt for thousands of years, with little apparent effect, so the damage cannot be too serious. In any event, the body generates replacement cells as a normal procedure.

Before leaving the subject, we ought to discuss how radioactivity is related to the processes of *fission* and *fusion*. Nature has provided us with three isotopes of uranium, uranium-234, uranium-235, and uranium-238. Of the three, only the uranium-235 nucleus can be made to fission, or break in two. When fission takes place, the parts produced weigh considerably less than the original nucleus, and the lost mass shows up as a great deal of energy. During fission, the uranium-235 atom splits roughly in half, and two or three leftover neutrons are shot out of the nucleus. If there happen to be some other uranium-235 atoms nearby, the neutrons may strike some of them, causing more fission to take place. That produces more neutrons and energy, and the process may continue in an explosive chain reaction. All we need for a chain reaction—and, therefore, an atomic bomb—is about 5 pounds of uranium-235 atoms. The process can be slowed down in a nuclear reactor, of course, so that the energy is converted to heat and then electricity. A considerable amount of our electricity is now produced in just that way.

Nuclear fusion is also based on the conversion of mass to energy. To illustrate, two hydrogen-2 nuclei have a total of two protons and two neutrons, as does a helium-4 nucleus. The two hydrogen-2 nuclei, however, weigh more than one helium-4 nucleus. If we can somehow get the hydrogen nuclei to fuse together to form a helium nucleus, we will receive a large energy bonus because of the mass loss involved. That fusion process, in fact, is similar in principle to the fusion process going on right now in the sun and many stars.

The enormous difficulty with fusion is constructing a container capable of holding hydrogen at the extremely high temperature needed for fusion to take place. Up to the present time, no useful amount of fusion energy has ever been obtained in the laboratory despite much research by large teams of scientists. When that problem is solved in the laboratory, it will be an even greater task to scale up the equipment for the production of commercial quantities of power. When these problems are solved, scientists believe that fusion power will present an unlimited source of energy with few serious ecological problems.

How long will the universe last?

No one knows the answer to this question, of course, but scientists have made some interesting calculations on the absolute maximum life of the universe. Long ago, the Austrian physicist Ludwig Boltzman visualized the end of the universe in terms of energy. According to this conjecture, the end of the universe will occur when nothing is hotter or colder than anything else. Scientists describe this condition by stating that the universe will have attained a condition of maximum entropy.

Entropy is a term that was invented by scientists to give a quantitative measurement to the laws of heat flow. Heat, left to its own devices, always flows from a given place to another place that is colder. It always flows down a "temperature hill," so to speak. An ice cube melts in a glass of water because heat flows from the water into the colder ice. It is true, of course, that heat can be induced to flow in the opposite direction, but some additional amount of energy must be expended to take it up the hill. In a typical air conditioner, the room is kept cool because heat is transferred from the room to the warmer air outside the house, but electrical energy must be expended to run the motors and compressors that effect the transfer of heat.

Returning to the glass of ice water, we say that the system (ice plus water) has gained entropy when the ice melts. Initially, the water is warmer than the ice, and it is possible to use this temperature difference to perform some useful task. Every heat engine, for example, makes use of a temperature difference of some kind to make it run. But when the ice melts, the temperature difference disappears and the system is no longer capable of doing useful work. We say that the system has gained entropy.

The second law of thermodynamics tells us that in any system, some constituents (such as the ice) may gain entropy in the course of time; others (the water) may lose entropy; but the entropy of the entire system (ice plus water) *must increase with time,* if it changes at all.

In addition to heat, physicists have applied entropy and the second law of thermodynamics to all forms of energy. In fact, entropy is actually defined scientifically as a measure of the degree of disarrangement or randomness of a thing or system of things: the more random the arrangement, the higher the entropy. To illustrate, the atoms in an ice cube are arranged in a regular pattern called a crystal, whereas the atoms in a glass of water are moving about in a random manner. So water, with a higher degree of disarrangement, has the higher entropy.

We are now ready to see what energy and entropy have to do with the longevity of the universe. At some time in the future, every atom in the universe will be at the same temperature. Every radioactive element will have decayed into stable elements. Every star will have radiated away its energy. The earth and all the other planets will have slowed down by friction with interstellar dust and gas and will have fallen into the sun. All life will be extinct. In the burned-out universe there will be no changes taking place by which time can be reckoned. Scientifically speaking, the universe will have ended.

How long will all this take? The slowest physical process that we know of that involves the transfer of energy and, therefore, an increase of entropy, is the radioactive decay of lead-204. This substance has a half-life of 14 billion billion years, which means that half of it will be gone in that length of time. And if the halving process continues about 1000 times, it will be gone to the last atom. Multiplying the half-life of lead-204 by a thousand, therefore, gives an outside estimate for the life of the universe: about 14,000 billion billion years.

Many scientists suspect, however, that the universe will not last that long. According to the "big bang" theory of creation, the universe began expanding about 10 or 20 billion years ago from a tiny ball into its present enormous size. Scientists agree that it is still expanding.

But some suggest that the attractive force of gravity—feeble though it may be—will retard the expansion, cause it to stop and eventually reverse. Perhaps 25 or 30 billion years from now the universe will begin to contract. After another 40 billion years all the matter in the universe will be forced into a volume comparable to that of an atomic nucleus. The process may then begin all over again with another big bang.

On the other hand, many astronomers are inclined to the view that the universe will continue to expand forever. All of the calculations needed to decide the fate of the universe are subject to many errors and objections, so a clear-cut decision does not seem likely for some time. Until scientists reach a better understanding of the complicated physical processes at work in the cosmos, the nature of the catastrophe that lies in the future of the universe must remain open.

How did agriculture begin?

About 10,000 years ago, when agriculture began, there were about 5 million people in the world. They were divided into countless small tribes, all living by hunting or collecting food, usually by both. In general, these people had a great deal of knowledge about food, fibers, drugs, weapons, and boats. Many were craftsmen and tradesmen, especially in tools and ornaments. They were extremely well adapted to the world on which they depended for their living.

During this period, an important element of uncertainty entered people's lives—the climate. The last ice age was retreating rapidly at that time, and the climate was changing unusually fast. Snow was disappearing from what are now the temperate regions of the Northern Hemisphere, and mountain ranges were becoming passable. The ocean level was rising, and inland seas were drying up. Vast new regions were either opening or closing to human habitation.

Because of these climatic changes, there must have been great movements of people in search of more advantageous living space. The greatest mixing of people would naturally occur in those regions where the continents come together. And it turns out that agriculture did begin in the narrow necks of land in the New and Old Worlds where the continents join. In the Near East, this occurred at the so-called Crossroads of the Old World, extending roughly from the Balkans to the Persian Gulf. This region has come to be called the nuclear zone of early settled agriculture.

Agriculture did not expand outward from the nuclear zone until about 4000 B.C. Grain farmers then began a slow migration into the wild regions surrounding them. They moved into Europe, Africa, India, and China, and it took over a thousand years to settle these new lands. The reason for the long delay and slow migration has to do with the crops that were being cultivated.

The basic crop in the nuclear zone was wheat, and its two main forms exist even today. The first, known as emmer, grew wild as it does today. The second did not occur in the wild but probably evolved by the accidental crossing of emmer with a wild grass that also exists in that region in the wild. This second grain is bread wheat, still our most important food crop. Along with the two varieties of wheat, many other plants were cultivated, including peas, lentils, barley, linseed, and grapes.

When farmers began their movement into new regions, problems began to arise. In colder Europe, oats appeared beside the wheat. In India, cotton replaced flax. In China, buckwheat displaced wheat and barley. On the Upper Nile, sorghum displaced the other grains.

Many of these crop changes were not planned by the farmer. Whenever a crop is taken to a new region, it is apt to be invaded by strange, new weeds. When wheat moves to a colder area, for example, rye appears as a weed. As the crop moves further north, or higher in altitude, rye displaces wheat as the actual crop.

Scientists believe that such crop changes took place very slowly and limited the speed at which farming could expand to new territories. The farmer had to wait for the processes of natural selection to run their course—processes of which he was entirely unaware.

Another factor that delayed the spread of farming concerns evolutionary changes that occur when a plant passes from the wild state into the hands of a cultivator. For instance, wild emmer shatters into several parts when ripe, each containing one grain, which falls to the ground. Wild emmer distributes its ripened seeds in that way so it can survive in nature. But cultivated emmer—after thousands of years of cultivation—does not shatter when ripe. It can be cut and handled without breaking apart. Only when it is threshed does it yield its grain.

To understand why this is so, imagine what must have happened when an early farmer began to harvest a field of emmer. Many seeds would already have been lost because the grain had fallen prematurely to the ground. Because of genetic differences between individual plants, however, other grains would have been held more securely by the plants and would have been available for harvesting. Seed for the next year's planting would tend to consist of grains which had come from the more tenacious plants. These, in turn, would be more likely to produce new plants of the same kind—plants which hold their grain until after harvesting. This process, called *natural selection*, helps explain why the act of cultivation—over long periods of time— helped to develop a strain of emmer of the tenacious kind—a quality that reduces waste, increases yield, and enhances the plant's chance of survival in the hands of the farmer. The slowly improving yields eventually provided surplus seed for use in new, untried lands.

These changes in plant types and characteristics were not the result of intelligent plant breeding but rather of intelligent cultivation. They were a result of unconscious selection, because early farmers could not even know that such evolutionary changes were possible. Only after nature had completed each phase of its handwork could agriculture continue its slow advance over the face of the earth.

How does a solar battery work?

With the exception of nuclear energy, all our energy comes from the sun. Sunlight provides the energy for plant photosynthesis, which gives us food energy, wood to burn, and the materials from which coal and petroleum were formed. The sun also provides energy for the earth's water cycle, without which there would be no hydro-electric power plants.

Although the earth receives only three ten-millionths of the sun's energy output, the amount of solar energy reaching our upper atmosphere is truly staggering, about 2 quintillion calories per minute. This amounts to about 2 calories per minute falling on each square centimeter. Much of this energy is lost in the atmosphere, however, and only about half that amount reaches the surface of our planet. The actual amount depends on season, weather conditions, air pollution, and location. Under good conditions, the roof of an average-sized house receives about 100 million calories a day—an amount equal to the energy derived from burning 150 pounds of coal.

The *solar cell,* or *solar battery,* is one approach that has been used successfully to convert sunlight into electrical energy. At present it is capable of generating electricity at the rate of about 10 watts per

Fig. 5. A solar battery. When sunlight illuminates the boron-enriched layer, electrons flow through the external circuit.

square foot of illuminated surface. The solar battery is used in space vehicles and communication satellites, and in other applications where other energy sources are impractical.

A typical solar battery consists of two layers of almost pure silicon, a semiconductor. The thicker layer contains a tiny trace of arsenic, and the thinner layer contains a trace of boron. When sunlight strikes the boron layer, electrons are induced to flow through the external circuit, as shown in the diagram.

Pure silicon exhibits a regular crystalline structure, which is illustrated schematically in the second diagram. The atoms are bound together by sharing the four electrons contributed by each silicon atom. Arsenic, however, has five so-called valence electrons to contribute to the bonding process. When an atom of arsenic takes the place of a silicon atom, only four of its electrons are used for bonding, and the one leftover electron is free to roam throughout the crystal of silicon. Boron, on the other hand, has only three valence electrons. When a boron atom is substituted for one of the silicon atoms, there is a defi-

53

ciency of one electron in the bonding network. Physicists call this deficiency a "hole" in the boron layer. Like the free electrons, holes are also able to move throughout the crystal structure, although their mobility is not as great as that of the electrons.

When sunlight illuminates the boron-enriched layer, electrons flow from the arsenic layer, through the external circuit, and back into the boron layer. Theory tells us that electrons normally exist as pairs despite their negative charge. Sunlight unpairs the electrons in the boron layer, and the freed electrons are repelled into the arsenic layer and finally into the external circuit. They are then pulled into the boron layer, where the process is repeated.

The solar battery converts only about 10 percent of the energy received from sunlight into electrical energy. Although this conversion efficiency is small, a solar battery has no moving parts, uses no liquids or corrosive chemicals, and requires little care or maintenance. Its main drawbacks are high cost, large areas to generate moderate amounts of power, and the fact that it stops working at night or during cloudy weather.

Fig. 6. The atomic structure of silicon crystals in the pure state, and doped with small amounts of arsenic (As) and boron (B). A free electron and a positive hole are derived from impurity atoms in the crystal structure.

The low energy density of solar energy is, in fact, a drawback for all forms of solar energy conversion. The world's energy requirements amount to about one sextillion calories per year. To obtain that amount of energy from the sun would require an area some 500 miles square, assuming a conversion efficiency of 25 percent. Equivalent areas can be found in various deserts, but the cost of the installation and the problems of energy distribution are truly staggering. Science and technology are making progress in useful applications of solar energy, but sunlight is at present just a supplementary source of energy.

Which products are obtained from coal?

When coal is baked in an oven, or retort, a combustible gas is given off together with a liquid, called ammoniacal liquor, and a sticky, gummy substance known as coal tar. The liquor, which rises to the surface, is used to prepare ammonia, washing liquids, smelling salts, baking powder, fertilizers, and high explosives. The coal tar that is left is boiled, and the vapors given off condense to form "light oils," or coal naphtha. The temperature of the coal-tar "still" is then increased, and naphthaline, phenol, and carbolic acid are given off. The temperature is raised once more to yield creosote, which is useful in preserving wood. Following a fourth temperature increase, anthracene and "green oils" are separated, with a residue of pitch in the still.

These four "fractions"—light oils, middle oils, heavy oils, and anthracene oils—are the starting materials for a quarter of a million compounds that chemists have learned to produce from coal tar. Several thousand of these are important commercially and play vital roles in our lives. Each of the four groups of oils is distilled once again at accurately controlled temperatures, and various products are collected separately. In this way, a whole new series of substances is obtained, each substance with a different boiling point, and each with an important role in industry.

The light oils yield benzene, which is used in dry cleaning or is added to gasoline. They also produce aniline, the starting point for dyes of every conceivable color. Other products of the light oils are drugs, photographic film, wire insulation, TNT, food flavorings, perfumes for cosmetics, and many others. In 1907 the chemist Leo Baekeland made the first synthetic thermosetting plastic, Bakelite. This product was made of formaldehyde and phenol, the latter coming from benzene.

From the middle oils we get chemicals as diverse as aspirin and picric acid. One relieves headache pain and the other is an explosive. Other products include wood preservatives, tanning compounds, photographic chemicals, disinfectants, drugs, dyes, and nylon.

Creosote, or "heavy oil," finds many important uses without further chemical changes. A major application is in preserving timber, telephone poles, and railroad ties. In making these products, the wood is first placed in a vacuum chamber to remove air and moisture from the pores. Then creosote is admitted and allowed to cover the wood. Pressure is then applied and creosote enters the timber in considerable quantity.

The fourth group of oils—the anthracene oils—provides an enormous quantity of drugs: anesthetics, laxatives, purgatives, hypnotics, and many more. The brilliant, nonfading alizarin dyes, photographic chemicals, and still more disinfectants also have anthracene somewhere in their chemical makeup.

The coke that remains after the oils are removed from coal also has its uses. It is a fuel and a source of carbon, and is used to produce "water gas," from which methyl alcohol can be made. This liquid is the starting material for a host of other useful substances. There seems to be no limit to the variety and number of products that, directly or indirectly, owe their existence to coal-tar derivatives.

Incidentally, both coal tar and creosote can be combined with hydrogen to make motor fuel. German scientists were doing this as early as 1935. Coal tar itself is used for road surfaces. Pitch finds uses in making roofing materials, coal briquettes, and waterproof building paper.

Each ton of coal provides 10,000 cubic feet of gas for fuel, half a ton of coke, and 10 gallons of coal tar. The tar yields about 3½ pounds of benzene and toluene, 1¼ pounds of phenol, 6 pounds of naphthalene, and 2 ounces of anthracene. From these few basic materials chemists have built an industry that affects all aspects of life.

Today, chemists use a new and more efficient method of extracting useful substances from coal. Called *hydrogenation,* this process involves subjecting coal dust, water, and hydrogen to enormously high pressures—from 4000 to 6000 pounds per square inch—at a temperature of 550 degrees centigrade. The process breaks down the constituents of coal and causes them to recombine into hundreds of chemical compounds, including many new ones not obtained by the older process of distillation.

Where did the air come from?

Our atmosphere at sea level consists of 78 percent nitrogen, 21 percent oxygen, 0.9 percent argon, and traces of carbon dioxide and other gases. (A variable amount of water vapor is also present, depending on the relative humidity at various times and places.) Plants and animals depend directly on this mixture of gases for their life functions, so scientists have always wondered how it came into existence.

The earth itself was formed, scientists believe, out of clouds of dust and gas that are abundant throughout space. As these materials came together, the earth evolved as a rocky mixture of many elements held together by chemical forces. Various gases were also present, either trapped in spaces between the rocks or held in loose chemical union with them. Deep within the earth, excess metals sank through the rocky mass to form a hot, metallic core.

As the earth continued to grow in size, increasing pressure caused the gases to escape from the rocks and flow to the surface. The lighter gases, such as hydrogen, helium, and neon, were too light to be retained by the earth's gravity, and escaped to outer space. The gases that remained were mainly water vapor, or H_2O (hydrogen and oxygen), ammonia, or NH_3 (nitrogen and hydrogen), and methane, or CH_4 (carbon and hydrogen). Planets such as Jupiter and Saturn still have these gases in their atmospheres, although they are large enough to retain a number of lighter gases as well.

The atmospheres of the inner planets, such as the earth, then began to change chemically under the action of solar radiation. Ultraviolet light from the nearby sun separated water vapor into its constituent parts: oxygen and hydrogen. The hydrogen rapidly escaped to outer space, and the oxygen combined with ammonia (to form nitrogen and water) and with methane (to form carbon dioxide and water). Over a great span of time, therefore, the atmosphere came to consist mainly of nitrogen and carbon dioxide, with a small amount of water vapor. Mars and Venus have a nitrogen and carbon dioxide atmosphere today, much as the earth did a few billion years ago before life became established on the planet.

Once an atmosphere of nitrogen and carbon dioxide forms, it becomes quite stable. As ultraviolet light acts on oxygen, it changes it to a form called ozone, O_3, which has three oxygen atoms in its molecule. Ozone forms in great quantities in the upper atmosphere and removes ultraviolet light from the incoming sunlight. Therefore, little ultraviolet light can penetrate to the lower layers and break up water vapor molecules. The atmosphere stops changing and becomes stable, at least until a new effect takes over on a global scale.

On earth, that new effect was plant life. By a process called photosynthesis, plants use ordinary visible light (which *does* penetrate the ozone layer) to consume carbon dioxide from the air and give off oxygen. The carbon dioxide supply was thereby depleted and the oxygen supply increased. In that way, many hundreds of millions of years ago, the atmosphere was finally converted into the life-giving air we breathe today.

Can food production be increased greatly in the open ocean?

As our population increases, mankind continually searches for new sources of food. Scientists tell us, however, that we should not expect the open ocean to be a great untapped reserve of food waiting to be harvested. This somewhat pessimistic view is based on a study of the food chain in the ocean.

The upper layers of ocean water are teeming with microscopic algae, called *phytoplankton,* which play the same role as grasses and other plants on land. That function is *photosynthesis,* a process that uses the sun's energy to build organic matter upon which larger organisms depend for food. Plant-eating animals of the sea graze on the algae, or phytoplankton, just as cows and sheep crop grasses on land. Algae production is the first link in the food chain. It is limited to the upper 120 feet of water because light is completely absent below that depth and photosynthesis cannot take place.

The abundance and size of algae depends on the amount of mineral nutrients in the water, especially phosphorus. Water tends to be rich in nutrients in coastal regions where rivers discharge their enriched water into the sea. Algae grow very well in these coastal zones. Regions of even richer algae growth occur where deep water moves to the surface of the ocean carrying a high phosphorus content from the bottom. The major upwelling areas, as they are called, occur off the coasts of Peru, California, northwest and southwest Africa, Somalia, the Arabian coast, and Antarctica. These regions are the most productive in the ocean; their production rate is three times that of the coastal zones, and six times that of the open ocean.

Another factor tends to reduce fish production in the open ocean: phytoplankton organisms become smaller in size as one travels from the coast to the open ocean. Because of this small size, the food chain is longer in the open ocean than on the coast. The open ocean has five links from phytoplankton to fish, while the coastal zones and upwelling areas have two or three at most. In the open ocean the small phytoplankton are eaten by slightly larger organisms and the process is repeated through the five-step food chain before arriving at fish. By contrast, the coast and upwelling areas develop large phytoplankton, some of which are eaten directly by anchovies and sardines, the greatest present source of food from the seas.

It turns out that food energy is lost every time food passes from one link in the chain to another. As a result, the open-ocean food chain suffers a much greater food-energy loss than either of the other types of fish-producing areas. The ocean, in fact, is a biological desert of fish production when compared with the coastal and upwelling areas. Fish production in the open ocean is about 1.6 million tons per year, while the other two regions yield 120 million tons each. A great deal of algae that grows in the open ocean is reduced by the food chain to a small amount of useful fish.

The fishing industry already exploits most of the species of interest to man. Any future growth must be developed from different species or from the few remaining underdeveloped fishing waters. According to current opinion, the world's fish catch can probably be doubled, a feat well within the reach of current technology.

What causes hay fever and other allergies?

About one person in ten is allergic to something: pollen, cosmetics, mold, certain foods, penicillin, and even cold, heat, and ultraviolet light. Each year in the United States alone, 5000 people die from bronchial asthma, about 300 die from ordinary injections of penicillin, and about 30 die from the stings of bees, wasps, hornets, and other insects. More than 16 million people suffer the familiar symptoms of hay fever: headaches, sneezing, congested sinuses, inflamed eyes, and a running nose. All of this suffering and illness is caused by chemical reactions called allergies.

An allergy is an adverse reaction to a foreign substance—called an *allergen*—which produces little or no ill effects in most other people. Most allergens are complex chemical substances, usually proteins or combinations of proteins and sugar molecules. Allergens usually consist of many thousands of atoms that often weigh at least ten thousand times as much as a hydrogen atom. The molecular weight, therefore, is said to be 10,000 or more.

For a sufferer of pollen allergy, such as hay fever, a grain of pollen enters the nasal passage and becomes attached to the mucous membrane. The allergens contained in the pollen are then dissolved by the nasal secretions and penetrate the outer layer of the mucous membrane. The major allergy producer in ragweed has been named ragweed antigen E, a protein molecule with a molecular weight of 38,000. It represents less than 1 percent of the ragweed pollen, but produces about 90 percent of its allergic activities. The allergen is so destructive that an injection of a trillionth of a grain is enough to cause an allergic reaction in an allergic person. Scientists do not know why the ragweed allergen is so unusually reactive.

Each of us has a number of molecules, called *antibodies,* in our cells and blood which react with and protect us from harmful bacteria, viruses, and the like. These antibodies are large proteins which inhabit our bodies in extremely minute quantities. One of these antibodies, called *IgE* (Ig stands for immunoglobulin), is formed in the nose and bronchial tubes and attaches itself to specific cells in these regions, called *mast cells.* An allergic person has at least 100 times as many IgE antibodies as a nonallergic person. The ragweed allergen reacts chemically with the IgE antibodies to form antigen-antibody complexes, which remain attached to the mast cells.

In a way that is still imperfectly understood, the antigen-antibody complexes cause the mast cell to release a potent chemical called histamine. This chemical is responsible for most of the symptoms of hay fever, bronchial asthma, and other allergies. Histamine causes dilation of blood capillaries and reduces their ability to contain the blood fluids. These fluids, therefore, are able to leak out and cause tissue and skin to swell. In addition, histamine can cause spasms in certain muscles, which leads to the problem of asthma. Histamine can also produce hives, and it often stimulates the glands to secrete watery nasal fluids, mucus, and tears.

Allergies are usually treated in one of three ways: avoidance, desensitization, and drug therapy. Avoidance, of course, means minimizing contact with a particular allergen. People who are allergic to lobster or strawberries should not eat lobster or strawberries. If you are extremely allergic to pollen, avoid the eastern half of the United States where pollen counts are high, and consider moving to Seattle or Los Angeles where they are low.

The chemical idea behind desensitization is to break the chain of events leading to the release of histamine by the mast cells. This is done by injecting a special "blocking" antibody that reacts with the allergen. This prevents the allergen from combining with the IgE antibody so that little or no histamine is released. The treatment consists of many small injections spread over many days in order to build up a high level of the blocking antibody. Despite the cost and inconvenience of such treatment, the cure is rarely complete.

Drugs such as epinephrine (Adrenalin) and steroids are effective in treating bronchial asthma, while some 50 antihistamines compete with histamines by occupying the so-called receptor sites on cells that are normally sought out by histamines. This action blocks the toxic effects of histamines. A new drug, disodium cromoglycote, acts in a different way by preventing the release of histamine from the mast cells.

Scientists are searching for new drugs that can neutralize the effects of histamine while avoiding unpleasant side effects such as drowsiness, headache, nausea, depression, and blurred vision. Unfortunately, no drug is now available that will relieve an allergy while completely avoiding all unpleasant side effects.

How did civilization begin?

It was during the Old Stone Age that mankind evolved into *Homo sapiens* and began to make some sense out of the world in which he lived. The Old Stone Age lasted a long time indeed, at least 2 million years; we emerged from it fairly recently, archaeologically speaking, no more than about 10,000 years ago. During the Old Stone Age, early man used trial and error to learn how to communicate verbally, to cooperate in hunting and warfare, to discover the secret of fire, and to develop a wide assortment of tools and implements of value in everyday life.

From what we know today, man took his first halting step toward civilizing himself near Lake Rudolph in North Kenya when he shaped a piece of lava into a sharp chopping tool. The layer in which these choppers were found has been determined, through the use of radioactive dating methods, to be approximately 2.6 million years of age. This is by no means the final word on when the Stone Age began. As older artifacts are discovered, the Old Stone Age, or Paleolithic period, as it is also known, may well be pushed further back into prehistory.

It may seem that little was accomplished during the Paleolithic, considering its vast length. We should keep in mind, however, the low level of man's intellect and ability during much of the period. In addition to a small brain, his hands were probably clumsy compared with our own, and the early diet of primitive hunters and gatherers was undoubtedly a constant brake on mental and physical development.

Despite these disadvantages, man's tool-making ability enabled him to rise in intellect from an animal-like creature to a status higher than that of any animal. His hunting weapons and methods improved slowly but continually. He learned to build shelter, to control and later build fire, to make clothing, and to exchange ideas by speech. Toward the latter part of the Paleolithic, he buried his dead, cared for the handicapped with compassion, and created decorative art and orchestral music. These latter accomplishments demonstrate how far civilization had advanced through the use of conceptual thought. By the end of the period, man had evolved—both physically and culturally—into a human being.

How are temperatures converted from the Fahrenheit scale to the Celsius scale?

The Fahrenheit thermometer, commonly used in the United States, was developed in 1710 by the German scientist Gabriel Fahrenheit. The scale is set up with +32° representing the melting point of ice, and +212° representing the boiling point of water. These two points of reference are separated by 180 divisions, or degrees.

In 1742, the Fahrenheit scale was given competition by the Celsius scale (also called the centigrade scale). The new scale was developed by the Swedish scientist Anders Celsius and is now the most widely used temperature scale in the world. Even in the United States, it is used universally for scientific purposes. The Celsius scale sets the melting point of ice at 0° and the boiling point of water at +100°. On the Celsius scale, there are 100 divisions, or degrees, between the reference points. Comparing the two scales, 180 Fahrenheit degrees correspond to 100 Celsius degrees, so each Fahrenheit degree is only five-ninths of a Celsius degree.

Changing from one temperature scale to the other can be accomplished by using the following conversion formulas:

$$C = \frac{5}{9} (F - 32)$$

$$F = \frac{9}{5} C + 32$$

To illustrate their use, suppose you want to convert 68°F to degrees Celsius. Substitute 68 for *F*, and the number in the parentheses becomes (68 − 32) = 36. Multiplying 36 times ⁵⁄₉ yields 20. So the corresponding temperature is 20°C.

$$C = \frac{5}{9} (68 - 32) = 20$$

Similarly, the temperature 25°C can be converted to Fahrenheit by substituting 25 for *C* in the second equation.

$$F = \frac{9}{5} \times 25 + 32 = 77$$

The equivalent temperature is 77°F.

Neither the Fahrenheit nor the Celsius scale is quite right for all scientific purposes, so a third scale is often used in scientific work. This scale, called the *absolute* or *Kelvin* scale, sets its zero at the temperature at which all molecular motion ceases. Theory tells us that this is the temperature at which there is no heat. The zero temperature on the Kelvin scale is equivalent to −273°C. The melting of ice occurs at 273° Kelvin (273°K), and the boiling of water occurs at 373°K. The degree divisions for the Kelvin scale are equal to those of the Celsius scale, since both have 100 degrees between these two reference temperatures.

Temperatures can be converted between the Kelvin and the Celsius scales with the help of the following formulas:

$$K = C + 273$$

$$C = K - 273$$

Do birds hibernate?

Ornithologists discovered early that birds migrate, and they also thought that some of them hibernated. It was believed at one time, for example, that swallows hibernate in the mud of ponds. Such beliefs were slow to die.

There is one bird, however, that *is* known to hibernate: the North American poorwill, which nests in the western and central parts of North America from British Columbia to Mexico. Other hibernating birds may turn up in the future, but this is the only one so far discovered. During the winter of 1946–47, scientists found poorwills hibernating in rocky crevices in the mountains of the Colorado Desert.

The poorwills were completely dormant and unable to move. Their eyes did not react to light. Their body temperature was measured in the range of 64°F to 68°F, well below their normal temperature of 106°F. Subsequent studies showed that many poorwills solve the problem of winter food shortages by hibernating. When the warm spring sun begins to shine, they awaken and fly about in search of food.

How are truffles grown?

If you have ever eaten truffles, you know that they have a tantalizing, mouth-watering, all-permeating flavor that promises all that is noble and good. If you have ever bought them, you know that they are undoubtedly the most expensive vegetable at the market! Many landowners in southern France or northern Italy have used truffles as a cultivated cash crop year in and year out for decades. In the wild form, they have been gathered for many hundreds of years. History tells us that they tickled the palates of upper-crust Romans two thousand years ago.

The fruit bodies of truffles, a rather special kind of fungus, resemble a puffball that grows somewhere between an inch and six inches below the soil in a forest. They cannot be seen, of course, but they can be smelled and so are tracked down by scent. Dogs and wild goats have been used for the purpose, but French professionals vouch for the skill of domesticated pigs. First of all, pigs have an enormous craving for truffles and seem to enjoy them as much as we do. Second, a pig has a keen sense of smell, well attuned to the delicate smell of any truffle within range of its nose. Pigs, in fact, have relished truffles ever since there were both pigs and truffles! Once a pig locates a truffle, the animal begins to root it up and must be forcibly restrained from eating it up on the spot.

The cultivation of truffles, although profitable, is far from routine. Truffles grow only in association with the roots of certain species of trees. Oak or beech trees are planted and allowed to become established. Then pieces of truffle are scattered on the soil and covered. The first pig-assisted harvest comes only six to ten years later, and a yearly crop can then be expected for two or more decades. What happens under the ground is a kind of partnership, called a *mycorhiza,* between the truffle fungus and the roots of the tree. Mycorhiza means *fungus root,* an apt name as it turns out, because that is just what it is—the combination of a fungus with the small, food-collecting roots of a tree or other higher plant. Neither fungus nor root alone, the mycorhiza is the combination of the two, which form a working unit.

The food-collecting portion of a root consists of innumerable tiny root hairs that absorb water, dissolved minerals, and other vital things from the soil. A growing radish plant has a million of them or more. A young mustard plant can have a branched root system that laid end to end would be a couple of miles long, covered with vast numbers of these tiny absorbing roots. Remove too many of these vital but microscopically small hairs—by rough handling, for example—and the plant may die. That is the reason, by the way, that certain kinds of plants are devilishly hard to transplant.

Many plant varieties, including most orchids and many of our trees and shrubs, have few or no root hairs. In their absence, the prosaic task of absorbing food and water from the soil is performed by a suitable fungus partner. Truffles willingly perform this drudgery for the trees with which they are associated. The fungus also contributes vital growth-promoting substances to the tree. In payment for its services, it gets several substances manufactured by the tree that are essential to its own growth and well-being. The partnership, therefore, is a mutually agreeable arrangement.

In 1978 a French agronomist named Jean Grente announced the accomplishment of what farmers and scientists have been trying unsuccessfully to do for hundreds of years—he had learned how to seed, plant, and harvest truffles. Grente had managed to isolate the fungus involved *(Tuber melanosporum)* and had inoculated oak seedlings with the fungus in his greenhouses at the French National Institute for Agronomic Research, at Clermont, France. Needless to say, the world was startled at his success in cultivating and harvesting the wild truffle. But Grente's seedlings are now growing splendidly on test farms in France and have yielded their first crops of those gastronomical treasures.

Most forest trees seem to derive a great deal of their nourishment from fungi of various sorts located on their absorbing roots. About 90 percent of the absorbing roots of a conifer tree, for example, is likely to be mycorhizal, without root hairs, and surrounded by a fungus. This kind of partnership, it seems, goes back at least 350 million years to the Carboniferous age, which indicates that mycorhizas are of considerable antiquity.

Before we leave the subject, it is worth noting that most orchids depend for life and food on a fungus partner at their roots. When orchids were first cultivated, it was found necessary to plant seeds in soil taken from around growing orchids of the same kind. Or even better, bits of root from established plants were placed in soil where seeds of the same kind were planted. Many orchid growers still follow this procedure because it works. But it is now possible to isolate the desired fungus and inoculate it into sterile soil so it is the only organism present. This assures the proper establishment of the seedlings.

How was the geologic time scale developed?

It was in 1815 that an eminently practical canal builder named William Smith announced to the world that a relationship existed between various layers of rocks and the fossils they contained. Prior to that time, it was generally believed that fossils were either the artifacts of Satan or chance arrangements of minerals that bore no relationship to living things.

Fortunately for geology, Smith lived in England during a period of active canal building. In constructing canals, it was important to understand the physical properties of rocks: their hardness, porosity, and strength. All told, he observed and studied rocks up and down the English countryside for twenty-four years. He well knew that a careless canal builder, after all, would soon go broke. When he was finished, he had made two fundamental discoveries: (1) the rock strata in southeastern England always occur in the same order—chalk beds, for example, were always found above coal layers, and (2) certain kinds of rock layers always contained assemblages of specific and distinctive fossils. As a result, he could always pinpoint a layer from which a given fossil had come. Smith's discovery was the key by which rock layers could be correlated with one another, not only in southern England, but in places half a world apart.

Correlation of rock layers is no simple matter. During the great span of geologic time, various kinds of animals and plants slowly evolved into more complex forms while others remained more or less unchanged. Still other species—such as dinosaurs—became extinct. Paleontology, the study of ancient life, has shown through fossil records in thousands of feet of layered rocks that many creatures have evolved from relatively simple forms. As geologists learned more about strata in different parts of the world, they were able to match up rock layers with one another based on the fossils they contained. They knew that the older layers would underlie more recent layers, so it was possible to establish a chronologic order on the basis of fossils in the rock. In that way, it was possible to construct a relative geologic time scale for the different layers of rock. The same time scale, of course, would apply to the fossils contained within the rocks.

Geologists have divided the time scale into *eras, periods,* and *epochs.* Eras represent the large divisions of time. The most ancient era is the *Precambrian,* which shows meager evidence of life. Then comes the *Paleozoic* (ancient life), *Mesozoic* (middle life), and *Cenozoic* (modern life).

The eras are divided into smaller units of time called *periods.* Most of the periods—such as the Pennsylvanian—are named for regions where fossils of that particular time segment were found. The Devonian period was named for Devonshire in southwestern England, and Permian for the ancient kingdom of Permia in Russia. The Cretaceous period, an exception, is derived from the Latin word *creta,* chalk, and describes the chalky cliffs on England's southern coast. Most of the world's chalk, in fact, is of Cretaceous age.

The *epochs* are given specific names only for the Cenozoic Era. In the Pleistocene (from Greek words that mean most and recent), over 90 percent of the fossil shells represent species that are alive today. In the Eocene (from the Greek for dawn and recent), only about 1 to 5 percent of the species are still alive. The Pleistocene epoch is thought to coincide with the ice age and probably lasted about 2 million years.

With the discovery of radioactivity in rocks, scientists were able to add an absolute time scale to the geologic calendar we have just discussed. Scientists know the rate at which a radioactive element, such as uranium or thorium, disintegrates to form the end product lead. By measuring the relative amounts of the radioactive element and lead, it is possible to calculate how long the process has been going on in a rock sample. In this way, dates have been attached to each of the eras, periods, and epochs of geologic time.

GEOLOGIC TIME SCALE* (Millions of Years)

Era	Period		Epoch	Absolute Time Scale	Life Forms
	GEOLOGIC TIME				
Cenozoic	Quaternary		Holocene		Mammals
			Pleistocene		
	Tertiary		Pliocene	2	
			Miocene	12	
			Oligocene	26	
			Eocene	38	
			Paleocene	54	
				65	
Mesozoic	Cretaceous				Reptiles and dinosaurs
	Jurassic			136	
	Triassic			195	
Paleozoic	Permian			225	
	Carbon- iferous	Pennsylvanian		280	First reptiles
		Mississippian			
	Devonian			345	First land animals
	Silurian			395	
	Ordovician			440	First fish
	Cambrian			500	
Precambrian				570	Primitive life forms
				3800	

*The relative geologic time scale with traditional names for various eras, periods, and epochs. The time scale gives the approximate dates for boundaries in millions of years before the present based on radioactive dating of rock samples.

What does a digital computer do?

During the past century man's new knowledge, technology, and business methods have generated an information explosion, and the world is becoming more complex every day. To help ease this burden, scientists have developed the electronic computer. The computer can count and "remember" millions of bits of information. It can compare facts and solve complex mathematical equations. It is a powerful and versatile information-handling machine.

Computers do their job by counting and calculating. So whatever the job to be done may be, it must be stated in mathematical terms. Let us illustrate with a simple example. Suppose you buy six shirts from a mail order firm and have them charged to your account. The problem is to calculate how much you owe. A computer might solve the problem with the following formula: the number of shirts × unit cost + tax + shipping charges + previous unpaid balance − credits for returned goods = amount due. This sort of calculation would be done at lightning speed for literally millions of transactions. But how?

All computers, no matter how complicated, do four basic operations: *input, storage, processing,* and *output.* These are very much like the steps to be followed in calculating a student's final average. The pupil's grades on homework, recitations, and examinations are the input. The teacher's records are the storage. The teacher herself is the processor, because she does the calculations. And the pupil's report card is the output. A computer carries out each of these steps at enormous speed.

The first step in using a computer is to gather all the information it needs—the numbers or data it must deal with. Next, we develop a set of instructions—called a program—which tells the computer exactly what to do with the data. Then we enter all the data and instructions into the computer through an input unit.

One kind of input unit uses punched cards. Different patterns of holes in the cards represent different numbers and letters. Metal brushes in a "card reader" can then make electrical contact through the holes. This tells the computer the information that was coded on the cards. Other types of input units use punched paper tape, typewriter-like keyboards, or magnetic tape much like that of a tape recorder. You may have noticed the strange-looking numbers at the bottom of a bank check. They are printed with magnetic ink, and each number generates its own characteristic magnetic pattern, which an input unit can read and send to the computer circuits. Some credit cards, such as VISA and Master Charge, have magnetic strips that enable the input unit of an automatic teller to read the charge account number and verify the transaction.

The information and instructions proceed from the input unit to the computer's memory, or storage unit, in the form of electronic pulses. In one type of storage unit the information is stored in tiny iron doughnuts—called cores—which are strung on wire grids. Other types of storage units use magnetic material in the form of tape, drums, or disks. In all such storage systems, the information pulses produce magnetic patterns that represent numbers and letters. To find a given piece of information, the computer quickly searches for and finds the desired record.

The computer has now stored the numerical data and program instructions. The program tells the computer where to find the data, how to arrange them, what calculations to perform, how to determine the final answer, and what to do with it. All these steps are performed by the processor unit.

The electronic circuits used in storage and processing are based on a simple principle. They have only two possible conditions or states, just as an ordinary light bulb has two states—on and off. In computer circuits, "on" represents "1" and "off" represents "0." Various combinations of 1's and 0's represent numbers or letters. The number 37, for example, is represented by the following combination of 1's and 0's: 100101. This is called a binary number because it is based only on ones and zeros. All digital computers store and process information in a similar code made up of binary numbers.

When the computer's processing is finished, it presents the answer in a usable form by means of an output unit. On some machines, the output is a high-speed printer—working at speeds greater than 1000 lines per minute. It can print reports, lists of data, bank checks, invoices, purchase orders, even report cards. Computer results can also be recorded on punched cards or on magnetic disks or tapes, or in the form of graphs or drawings. Results can be displayed on a device much like a television tube, or they can be transmitted to any place in the world by telephone or radio. We can even talk to some computers, and some of them can talk back, too. For example, a businessman can use a telephone and dial the number of a customer's account. The computer immediately replies with the customer's account balance, what he has purchased, and when. The information is given in the form of spoken words put together from sounds recorded on a magnetic drum.

The computer has become a part of just about every area of human activity. Its applications seem to be limited only by the imagination and ingenuity of man.

Why are there two sexes instead of one?

If a human being received all his genetic endowment from one parent, he would be much the same as his parent, and people in general would be much more alike than they are now. Under the present dual arrangement, the offspring is more likely to differ in many ways from his parents. This difference, as we shall see, is good for the species.

The information that determines the hereditary characteristics of a person is contained in complex molecules called DNA (deoxyribonucleic acid). Each parent contributes to the offspring a half-set of DNA molecules, and there is a very high probability that each half-set will be different from any other half-set of that parent's reproductive cells. So the complete set will not only be different from that of either parent, but is very highly likely to be different from the complete set of a sibling. The new set of DNA molecules is contained in the cells of the offspring and constitutes a "blueprint" from which the new human being is developed.

The wide variety in human characteristics provided by a system of two sexes makes it easier for the species to adapt to changing environmental conditions. From time to time, the environment changes and the old established sets of DNA might not be well suited to the new conditions. On the other hand, some of the new DNA combinations that occur naturally may produce better-adapted individuals. Other combinations, of course, may be less well adapted. The better-adapted individuals are more likely to succeed in the new environment and pass on some of their DNA. A species having two sexes, therefore, would be more likely to avoid extinction than a species based on one sex.

How does a Xerox copier work?

At one time or another, most of us have found that we can attract small bits of paper, dust, or powder with an electrically charged plastic or glass rod. To try such an experiment, cut a long, narrow strip of paper and hold it vertically from one end. Then rub a plastic rod—such as a ball point pen or ruler—against your clothing and bring it close to the free end of the paper strip. If the humidity is not too high, you will see the strip of paper move toward the plastic rod and adhere to it. The same sort of attraction takes place with other rubbed materials, such as sealing wax, glass, resin, and hard rubber. The effect you observe is a result of the force of attraction between dissimilar electric charges—that is, between positive charge on one body and negative charge on the other. We will go into this matter in greater detail a little later on.

As for the Xerox machine, its principle of operation is also based on the force of attraction between positive and negative electric charge. What happens is something like this. Suppose the page of a book is to be copied. An optical system "reads" the dark areas on the page and transfers electrical charges to the copy paper in those regions where darkening is desired. Electrified carbon particles are then attracted to the copy paper and subjected to rapid heating. This fuses the carbon dust to the paper, making a permanent copy of the original.

In the experiment described earlier, the rod became electrically charged by friction. In the normal state, all objects contain an equal number of positive and negative charges, so they are electrically neutral. They neither attract nor repel other electrically neutral objects. However, if a rod of polystyrene is rubbed against a flannel cloth, a great many electrons are transferred from the flannel to the polystyrene. Because electrons carry a negative charge, the rod ends up with an excess of negative charge over positive charge and is said to be negatively charged. By a similar process, the flannel becomes positively charged.

A rod charged by friction can be used to induce a charge in another object. The accompanying diagram helps to show how an *induced charge* comes about. Part A of the diagram shows a positively charged rod next to a metal body that is insulated by a plastic handle. The proximity of the positive charge attracts some of the electrons in the metal, and they move to the end closest to the rod. This leaves a net positive charge at the opposite end. (Electrons are free to move about in a metal, but positive charges are fixed in the atomic nucleus and do not move.) In part B, the metal conductor is momentarily connected to ground. This can be done by touching it for a short time with a finger. In this way, the metal body, the experimenter, and the whole earth become one conducting object. Negative electricity flows from the metal object to the earth, leaving a net positive charge on the metal body. After removing the finger, the polystyrene rod is also removed, leaving a positively charged metal body, as in part C. If a negatively charged object is now brought near the metal body, there will be a force of attraction between the two. Conversely, if the second body has a positive

Fig. 7. Induced electric charge. A: Equal positive and negative charges are induced in the metal body by the charged polystyrene rod. B: A momentary earth connection allows negative charge to flow from the metal body to ground. C: The metal body retains a net positive charge after the rod is removed.

charge, there will be a force of repulsion between the two. Scientists have long known that unlike charges attract and like charges repel one another.

You may wonder why a charged rod attracts small particles and bits of paper even though we take no particular pains to induce a charge in them. The generation of an induced charge is a result of the paper being a sufficiently good conductor of electricity for some charge to leak off to ground or other large objects. The possibility of observing the effect of the induced charge (attraction to the rod) is due to the conductivity not being great enough for the induced charge to leak away before it can be observed.

The fact that the kind of electric charge associated with electrons is called "negative" instead of positive is purely an accident of history. By the early eighteenth century, scientists knew that there are two kinds of electricity. One kind, originally called *resinous electricity,* is obtained on a rod of resin or sealing wax when rubbed with flannel. The other kind, called *vitreous electricity,* is produced on glass when it is rubbed with silk. Scientists knew they were not the same because two rods charged with the same kind of electricity always repelled one another, while a rod charged with resinous electricity always attracted one with vitreous electricity. It occurred to Benjamin Franklin, the American statesman, publisher, and scientist, that it would be useful mathematically to label the two kinds of charges "positive" and "negative," instead of vitreous and resinous. The choice concerning which label to attach to each kind of charge was purely arbitrary, because no one could find an argument favoring either alternative. As it happened, resinous electricity became negative, and it was later discovered that electrons have that kind of charge. Protons, which usually abide in the nuclei of atoms, carry a vitreous, or positive, charge.

How do archaeologists date the artifacts they find?

The artifacts and materials uncovered by archaeologists provide an insight into how peoples lived in prehistoric times. They help us understand how and why such ways of life evolved from the earliest days of the Old Stone Age to the present. Because writing was invented only about 5000 years ago, archaeological methods provide the only clues we have to 99 percent of the human past. From a few fragments of tools and weaponry, a grave site or two, or the faint remains of ancient earthworks or structures, the archaeologist attempts to draw an accurate picture of a people's culture, religion, politics, economic system, and social structure. But even that difficult task is only part of the job. The complete problem is to learn how a culture changes in response to inventiveness, environmental pressures, contact with other cultures, and movement from place to place. One of the most important aspects of such studies involves the dating of artifacts discovered in archaeological sites.

Like history, archaeology depends on a sound chronological framework: historical events must be arranged in time if we are ever to unravel cause and effect in the affairs of mankind. A principle called *stratification* enables scientists to set up a system of relative dating in which object A is known to be older than object B. The method gives no hint of when such objects were used in terms of absolute dates. In an archaeological dig, stratification exists if one layer of soil overlies another. The lower layer is then known to be older than the upper. In practice, of course, the layers are often disturbed by ditches, pits, buildings, banks, and mounds. The archaeologist observes soil changes accurately and digs only one layer at a time, noting all its contents. In that way, all of the layers and artifacts can be arranged in a relative time scale.

Another method of relative dating is called *typology,* which simply means the study of types. Typology involves the study of the material, form, and purpose of artifacts so they can be arranged in an evolutionary sequence. Weapons and tools evolve as new materials and improved methods become available, as the objects become more complex, and as fashions change. A group of prehistoric cutting tools or modern automobiles, for example, can be arranged in convincing chronological sequence from the primitive to the most sophisticated, based on their construction and appearance.

Although stratification and typology provide important information about the relative age of artifacts, archaeologists always try to obtain absolute dates for their finds. A traditional method, called *cross-dating,* is to establish a connection between an object and a civilization dated by written records. Egyptian documents exist back to 3000 B.C. and written records from Mesopotamia have survived from about 2600 B.C. This makes it possible to date artifacts by their association with records that mention actual dates or rulers of known periods. Quite often, objects of known age from a literate civilization are found with other objects of nonliterate peoples. This makes it possible to date many otherwise undatable artifacts. Ancient trade, looting, and conquest caused objects to travel hundreds, even thousands of miles, so a cross-referenced network makes it possible to transfer absolute dates over great distances. Obviously, cross-dating is not possible for dates prior to about 3000 B.C.

Using modern scientific methods, archaeologists have obtained new ways of dating their discoveries. Paleobotanists, for example, have worked out the successive phases of climatic and vegetational changes from ancient deposits of pollen and other plant remains. Key absolute dates have been obtained using a method called carbon-14 dating. Organic material such as wood is analyzed to measure the amount of radioactive decay that has occurred since the substance was alive. This information can be converted directly to the object's age.* Another method, called *dendrochronology,* is used to calculate the age of timber by counting tree rings and correlating the tree-ring pattern with known climatic conditions. Another method involves the counting of sediment layers that were deposited in a yearly cycle. Still another method, called *thermoluminescence,* permits the dating of pottery by studying the light emitted by heated fragments of the object.

The new absolute dates have certain inaccuracies built into them because of the difficulty of making absolutely accurate measurements of physical quantities. To illustrate, if a carbon-14 date is given as 2000 ± 200 B.C., it means that there is a two-to-one probability that the true date falls between 1800 and 2200 B.C.

Using these new methods, archaeologists are pegging the older relative dates to a more accurate chronological framework and making unexpected discoveries. To illustrate, as recently as 1954 it was believed that British agriculture began about 2500 B.C. With the invention of carbon-14 dating, evidence began to pile up that there were farming communities in existence by 3000 B.C. and perhaps as early as 3400 B.C. Later tests have pushed the date back to about 4000 B.C. This one example illustrates how important results can be achieved when several branches of science are brought to bear on a particular problem.

What are cosmetics made of?

Although modern chemistry plays a great part in the manufacture of cosmetics, the basic ingredients of many of these products have

---

*A more detailed discussion of carbon-14 dating is given on pages 143–45.

been in use for thousands of years. Face creams, for example, are generally made from an emulsion of olive oil or mineral oil, lanolin or beeswax, water, and borax. Perfume, of course, is added to make the product more attractive.

Vanishing creams are usually made of a soft potassium soap, and lipsticks consist of waxy face creams. Nail polish is nothing more than a quick drying cellulose lacquer—cellulose being the basic cell material of wood. Creamy colored or opaque nail polish can be made by adding titanium oxide. Nail polish remover consists of acetone, amyl acetate, or a mixture of these cellulose solvents.

Most toothpaste is basically chalk. Manufacturers usually add a little soap or soaplike material, and a good-tasting flavoring such as peppermint. Some toothpastes also contain fluoride to reduce tooth decay.

The chemistry behind "permanent" waving of hair is based on a chemical called thioglycolic acid. This substance breaks up the protein material in hair by removing a sulfide molecule that links the protein together. When used in high concentrations it actually loosens hair roots and is used in tanneries to remove hair from hides. In low concentrations, under controlled conditions, it partly decomposes hair. While in that state hair can be set into waves and curls. These are then "fixed" into position—or "set"—by applying dilute hydrogen peroxide or some other mild oxidizing agent to restore the damaged protein in the hair.

How does a nuclear breeder reactor work?

There are three kinds of uranium, called isotopes, found in the earth. Of the three, only uranium-235, or U-235 for short, can undergo fission and generate energy. Unfortunately, less than 1 percent of our uranium is of this fissionable isotope. Over 99 percent consists of U-238, which is useless for generating nuclear power.

The numbers 235 and 238 refer to the total number of protons and neutrons contained in the nucleus of the isotope. Uranium always contains 92 protons, so the two isotopes differ by 3 neutrons in their nuclei. This difference makes U-235 fissionable while U-238 is not. If enough U-235 is assembled in one place, an atom that fissions, or breaks apart spontaneously, can set off a chain reaction that produces energy in the form of heat. When the atom splits, a few unwanted neutrons are given off, which may strike other U-235 atoms, and these split apart to release more neutrons, and so on. The whole process can be nicely controlled to produce just the amount of energy that is wanted from time to time—within the capability of the reactor, of course. The products, or "ash," left over consist of lighter elements, which must be carefully controlled and shielded because these, too, are very radioactive and dangerous to health. Although we are using great amounts of nuclear energy, no completely satisfactory method has yet been devised to dispose safely of these waste products.

There seems to be enough U-235 around to last a few centuries, even at greatly increased rates of use. However, if we could somehow manage to use U-238 in generating power, the supply would last many tens of thousands of years. The function of a breeder reactor is to convert the "useless" U-238 into a different element, Pu-239 (plutonium-239), which *can* undergo fission.

Making Pu-239 is really a simple matter for nuclear physicists. All they need do is put a load of U-238 in a nuclear reactor where there are plenty of available neutrons because of the nuclear fission going on. Some of the neutrons will be "captured" by U-238, thereby producing—or breeding—Pu-239.

The reaction proceeds in stages. The first reaction that takes place produces U-239, another isotope of uranium.

$$1 \text{ neutron} + \text{U-238} \rightarrow \text{U-239}$$

This isotope has a very short life and rapidly emits an electron, to become neptunium-239.

$$\text{U-239} \rightarrow \text{Np-239} + 1 \text{ electron}$$

Even neptunium is unstable; it quickly gives off another electron to become the desired isotope, Pu-239.

$$\text{Np-239} \rightarrow \text{Pu-239} + 1 \text{ electron}$$

After a few weeks, the entire process of converting U-238 to Pu-239 is complete and there is on hand a new supply of fissionable material. Pu-239 is relatively long-lived, so it can be stored for future use.

Another variety of breeder reactor can be built beginning with thorium-232. The end product of the reactions involved is the fissionable isotope of uranium, U-233, which does not occur in nature.

Of the two materials, uranium and plutonium, the latter is far more poisonous. Inhaling two dust-size particle of plutonium oxide, a likely product of a nuclear accident, would probably cause cancer in one person in a thousand. If there were a massive nuclear accident or terrorist attack, the effect on human life would be enormous.

The uranium fuel used in a reactor is not easily processed or purified into a form suitable for making an atomic bomb. The difficulty lies in the fact that all isotopes of uranium are the same chemical element and cannot be separated by chemical means. The process is so complex and costly, in fact, that only a high degree of technical expertise and costly equipment would make the separation possible. Plutonium is another matter. Plutonium would be mixed with uranium in a breeder reactor, and the two can be separated chemically because they are different chemical elements. It would not be a difficult feat for a knowledgeable group to purify plutonium for a bomb. For these reasons, many scientists feel it would be a serious mistake to depend on breeder reactors as the source of energy for the world.

Does lightning travel upward or downward?

The answer to this question is that, in a sense, it does both. To understand how this can be so, suppose we follow the formation and discharge of a typical lightning stroke. A flash between cloud and ground usually begins at the base of a cloud. The initial discharge is a traveling spark, called a *stepped leader,* which moves from the cloud toward the ground in rapid steps about 50 yards long. The steps are not very bright at this stage of the process. Each step takes less than a millionth of a second, and the interval between steps lasts about fifty-millionths of a second. Although the stepped leader is not visible to the eye, it can be photographed with special cameras. The average speed of the stepped leader in its trip to the ground is about 75 miles per second, and the trip takes about twenty-thousandths of a second.

When the stepped leader gets close to the ground, its great negative electrical charge induces large amounts of positive charge on the earth beneath it—especially on elevated objects on the surface. Since unlike charges attract each other, the large positive charge on the ground tries to join the negative charge on the stepped leader. This produces upward-moving discharges. One of these eventually reaches the stepped leader and completes a path from cloud to ground. Negative charges in the cloud then produce large currents from cloud to ground, and the channel near the ground becomes very bright. This brightness of the channel—called the *return stroke*—moves quickly up the channel at speeds approaching 60,000 miles per second. The entire trip from ground to cloud takes only about 100 millionths of a second. It is the return stroke that generates the bright channel of light that we see. The stepped leader and return stroke occur so quickly that the eye cannot resolve any of the individual steps involved. The entire channel seems to light up simultaneously.

The usual cloud-to-ground lightning flash has a branched channel, with the branched end reaching toward the ground. It is one of these branches that eventually makes contact with an upward-moving discharge from the ground. Scientists have discovered, however, that this process is usually reversed when a very tall structure, such as the Empire State Building, is involved. Most flashes to such structures are initiated by the structure itself. These lightning strokes are quite different from the usual cloud-to-ground flash. Strokes to tall buildings are started by an upward-moving leader, and the branches of the stroke are pointed toward the sky instead of toward the ground.

Are our water wells running dry?

The amount of fresh water in the ground staggers the imagination. Recent estimates indicate that ground water amounts to more than 90 percent of all of the earth's fresh water in liquid form. (Glacial ice amounts to several times the ground water supply.) Yet in spite of the great supply, shortages are beginning to develop in certain regions because of excessive drawing from water wells.

Water enters the ground from rainfall and melting snow. Some soils are like porous sand in soaking up rain water, whereas others have dense clay layers—or "hardpans"—that obstruct the absorption of water. In rocky areas, little water can enter the ground except through joints and cracks.

Water leaves the ground in various ways. Here and there, a bubbling spring shows where some of the water reaches the surface. In other places the ground water feeds rivers and lakes.

There must be an underground connection, of course, between the rainfall that sinks into the ground and the springs, rivers, and wells where it leaves. The usual path of underground water is through soil and rock. Except for rare underground openings in limestone and volcanic regions, there are no open spaces under the ground through which underground rivers can flow. Instead, water moves slowly through the small pore spaces in sand and rock. The smaller the pore spaces, the slower the movement of water. The porous layers that permit the flow of ground water are called *aquifers*. The level below the surface at which water is found is called the *ground water table,* or just the *water table*.

Scientists have learned that the rate of movement of ground water in an aquifer is fairly slow. In most aquifers, ground water rarely moves faster than 40 inches, or slower than a quarter of an inch, per day. An average figure is approximately 2 or 3 inches per day.

Tied in with the slow velocity of ground water is the long distance it often must travel. Typically, the rainfall, or recharge, area of an aquifer is in an upland region, so that the water can run "downhill" under the ground. Many areas in the great plains and central midwest of the United States are fed by aquifers that extend for hundreds of miles. Hence, the water takes a long time to move from the recharge area to the lower reaches of an aquifer. If extensive water-well pumping removes water faster than the slow recharge rate can replace it, the underground reservoir becomes depleted and the water table begins to drop.

An example of the so-called mining of water is taking place in the Ogallala aquifer, a formation of underground sands and gravels in western Texas and New Mexico. The aquifer has provided water for irrigation for the past century and is the water support for half a million people. During that time, the water table has dropped as much as 100 feet because of extensive pumping. At present rates of water use and recharge, it will take thousands of years to build the water table up to its original level. Other aquifers in the high plains tell much the same story. Water from such aquifers is in a real sense being mined, because of the extreme slowness of recharge and the slow rates of ground water movement. As pumping continues, the amount left in the ground steadily diminishes, much as coal, or oil, or gold does. Ground water, when pumped faster than the recharge rate, is an exhaustible resource that cannot be replenished in our time. So, to that extent, many of our wells are indeed running dry.

Why are salt and sugar used to preserve food?

If red blood cells are placed in water, they gradually swell and eventually burst. This is caused by the diffusion of water through the cell's outer wall, or membrane, into the cell. Just the opposite effect takes place if the red blood cells are placed in a strong or concentrated solution of salt water. Water diffuses out of the cell and the red blood cell shrivels up and dies. The cells can only be maintained in their normal state if they are placed in a salt solution that approximates the concentration of salt found in the blood. Water passes through membranes in this way because of a physical principle called *osmosis*.

To understand how osmosis operates, imagine a beaker fitted with a membrane as shown in the top of the accompanying diagram. The membrane is attached to the walls of the beaker in such a manner that no liquid can leak around its edge from one side to the other. One side of the beaker contains water, and the other side is initially filled to the same height with a solution of heavy sugar syrup. The pore spaces, or openings, in the membrane are sized in such a way that the small water molecules can readily pass through. The much larger sugar molecules, however, are too big to pass through the membrane and are confined to their own side. In the course of time, many of the randomly moving water molecules pass through the membrane in *both* directions. The greater number, however, move from left to right—from the pure water side to the solution side—and that difference in rate of diffusion is the key to osmosis. Initially, there are more water molecules on the left than on the right side of the membrane. So the probability is greater that a water molecule will strike an opening on the left side. In scientific terms, the concentration of water is greater on the left side than on the right, and water diffuses through the membrane toward the region of lower water concentration.

The lower part of the diagram shows that the water, after a time, has indeed invaded the sugar solution and raised its level. The process of osmosis continues until a sufficient pressure is achieved to equalize the diffusion rates of water in the two directions. That pressure is called the *osmotic pressure*. When equilibrium is reached, the osmotic pressure is just sufficient to prevent a net flow of water through the membrane.

Returning to the example of red blood cells given earlier, water can be induced to leave the cells if they are placed in a strong salt solution. Because of osmosis, water diffuses from a region of relatively high concentration of water (in the cell) to a region of lower water concentration in the salt solution. Just the opposite happens when red blood cells are placed in pure water. Water then diffuses from the region of

Fig. 8. Osmosis. A: When water and a sugar solution are separated by a semi-permeable membrane, water diffuses into the sugar solution and raises its level. B: The pressure caused by the difference in height of the two liquids is called the osmotic pressure.

83

higher water concentration (outside the cell) to a region of lower water concentration (in the cell).

Osmosis enables us to understand why salt and sugar solutions can be used to preserve food. The major cause of food spoilage is the presence of micro-organisms. Any process that kills micro-organisms is an effective process for preserving food. Perhaps the oldest method is the drying of grains, fruits, fish, and meat. Without water, the growth and metabolism of micro-organisms cannot take place, so they become dehydrated and die. Fruit preserved in a sugar syrup and meat preserved in a salt solution are protected in much the same way. Because of osmosis, water diffuses out of the micro-organisms into the surrounding solutions. The salt and sugar have the same effect on the micro-organisms as does the process of drying. Both methods, osmosis and drying, dehydrate the micro-organisms and destroy their ability to reproduce and give off dangerous poisons to the food.

How are metals polished?

The modern theory of friction has led physicists to a better understanding of what goes on at the surface of metals and many non-metals when they are polished. From an atomic point of view, the smoothest surfaces that can be prepared are extremely rough. Such surfaces contain myriad tiny "mountains" and "valleys" too small to be noticeable. When two smooth, flat surfaces are placed in contact, they actually touch over an extremely minute fraction of their surface area. For flat steel surfaces, for example, the real area of contact is often less than one ten-thousandth of the apparent area. The contact takes place where high peaks on one piece happen to engage high peaks on the other.

When two objects are pressed together, the force involved must be supported by the relatively few places that actually touch. This means that the pressure at such places can be enormous because the force is exerted on a tiny area. When two objects are rubbed against each other, the pressure is high enough to cause a hard metal, such as steel, to become deformed; the summits are crushed down, which increases the contact areas. As the contact areas increase, the pressure decreases, because the force is now spread over a greater area. The process of deformation continues until the pressure drops below the point that causes deformation of the metal. In many cases, the pressure between two sliding parts is so intense that it brings about actual melting of some of the peaks, causing the two parts to be welded together for an instant at a few of the points of contact.

Even if welding does not take place, there is a great deal of interlocking between two flat surfaces that are molecularly rough. This is a major factor in producing friction between surfaces. When the surfaces are made to slide over each other, there is a kind of plowing of some of the peaks through others, causing abrasion of the surfaces.

The local hot spots caused by sliding friction can reach temperatures well over 1000°C, even though the temperature of the piece as a whole is hardly affected by the sliding. This local, temporary heating plays an important role in polishing. The process of polishing depends primarily on the melting, by localized frictional heating, of the metal being polished. To illustrate, an experiment was performed by rubbing an alloy known as Wood's metal (with a melting point of 72°C) against camphor (melting point 178°C). Although Wood's metal is considerably harder than camphor, it is the Wood's metal, not the camphor, that gets polished by the rubbing. Scientists believe that this is a result of the lower melting temperature of Wood's metal. Camphor, in fact, will not polish metals such as tin, lead, and zinc, which have higher melting temperatures than camphor.

Scientists have found that similar results are obtained in the polishing of nonmetals. The mineral calcite, for example, with a melting point of 1333°C, is polished by zinc oxide (melting point 1850°C) but not by cuprous oxide (melting point 1233°C). Once again, the material being polished must have a lower melting temperature than the substance doing the polishing.

How is steel made?

Unlike gold, silver, copper, and platinum, nuggets of pure iron are rarely found in nature. Nevertheless, in today's world, iron and steel find important uses in every walk of life. Without iron, our civilization would slip back thousands of years.

In ancient times, iron ore—which consists of iron oxide, a compound of iron and oxygen—was heated in a charcoal fire to produce a spongy lump of iron that could be hammered while hot into sturdy tools and weapons. With minor variations, the same process is still in use today. Carbon, from the charcoal, "robs" the molten iron ore of its oxygen, producing iron that contains various impurities. Later, a primitive forced-air furnace evolved, much like those still in use in parts of Asia and Africa. Today iron is made in a blast furnace loaded with limestone, coke, and iron ore. Hot air is forced upward through the heated mixture so that the coke will combine with oxygen to form carbon monoxide—a compound consisting of one atom of carbon and one of oxygen. The carbon monoxide abstracts oxygen from the ore to form metallic iron and carbon dioxide (one atom of carbon and two of oxygen). Lime from the limestone combines with stone or rock substances in the ore to form slag. Molten iron and slag fall to the bottom of the furnace, where they form two layers, the heavier, denser iron being the lower. Tapping holes at the bottom are used to withdraw both iron and slag as liquids.

Iron from the blast furnace is known as pig iron and is only about 90 percent pure, containing perhaps 6 percent carbon and quantities of silicon, manganese, phosphorus, and sulfur. When pig iron is cooled quickly, a brittle white cast iron is formed. Slower cooling results in gray cast iron, which is softer and tougher than the white kind.

When pig iron is remelted with additional iron oxide, some of the impurities are removed. Rolling or hammering then produces a soft, tough, corrosion-resistant material called wrought iron, which is used to make bolts, chains, pipe, and anchors.

Iron is converted to steel by removing most of the impurities present in cast iron. Steel is basically an alloy of iron and carbon, with less than 1.5 percent carbon. The Bessemer process of steelmaking was invented in 1855 by Henry Bessemer. A tilting, silica-lined container, called a converter, is loaded with several tons of molten pig iron. Air is then blasted through the molten mass, and the temperature rises to 1300°C or more. During this "blow," silicon, manganese, and most of the carbon are eliminated. The desired amount of carbon and manganese are then added to produce a steel of the desired qualities. After a short time, the converter is tilted and the steel runs off into molds for further use. Bessemer steel contains sulfur and phosphorus as impurities and is used where the steel will not be subject to shock or corrosion.

Higher-quality open-hearth steel is further purified by mixing pig iron, iron oxide, limestone, and scrap iron in a furnace lined with dolomite rock. Gas is burned over the surface of the mixture. The iron oxide provides the oxygen needed to combine with and remove metallic impurities. Sulfur and phosphorus are removed by combining with the dolomite (magnesium calcium carbonate) lining of the furnace.

After ten hours or so, steel of the desired specification can be drawn from the furnace.

Still higher-quality steel is made in an electric furnace. Large carbon electrodes dip into the molten mixture of iron and slag, and an electric current produces the required heat. The slag is designed to remove the impurities, and the composition of the steel is then adjusted by adding the desired ingredients. This method produces excellent steels of superb quality, because no burning fuels are present to contaminate the melt. In recent years oxygen has been used to replace air in steel manufacture, and improved kinds of steel have been produced as a result.

Steel furnaces are essentially large containers in which carefully controlled chemical reactions take place. They produce an almost endless variety of steels, each with particular properties that are desired for a specific application. It is hard to visualize an industrial society without this versatile and useful metal.

Can volcanic eruptions be predicted?

The Hawaiian Islands, undoubtedly one of the most beautiful archipelagos on earth, owe their very existence to volcanic activity. The islands are part of a chain of volcanoes—active, dormant, and extinct—which have been built up from the ocean floor in a 1600-mile arc across the Pacific Ocean. The islands grow progressively older from the southeast to the northwest, which means that Hawaii—the only island with active volcanoes—is the youngest of the group. Kauai, the northwesternmost of the chain, is about 5.3 million years old, whereas Hawaii was born about 750,000 years ago.

There are five major volcanic centers on the island of Hawaii. Two of them are enormous volcanoes: Mauna Kea, 13,792 feet above sea level, and Mauna Loa, just 14 feet lower. To calculate the total height of these mountains, we must consider that their bases rest on the ocean floor, about 15,088 feet below the water surface. That makes them about as tall as Mount Everest, but of much greater bulk because of the enormous circumference (about 200 miles) at the base. They are the largest, by far, of the world's volcanoes. Mauna Kea is dormant now, but Mauna Loa is still quite active, generating lava flows that break out of its flanks and flow down toward the sea.

Kilauea is a smaller and partially buried volcano located far down the gently sloping sides of Mauna Loa. Kilauea has had more than fifty eruptions in historic time. With a road leading directly to its rim, it has been visited by streams of tourists for more than a century. Its crater measures 2 miles by 3 miles, with walls that drop vertically to a nearly level crater floor. Volcanic activity today is limited to a volcanic throat, or fire pit, on the floor of the crater. Called Halemaumau, the fire pit is filled with lava that periodically rises and falls hundreds of feet, sometimes spilling over onto the crater floor. Lava boils and seethes within Halemaumau in response to volcanic pressures deep within the earth. When the volcano is ready for an eruption, molten lava may find a new channel to the side of the cone, from where it flows out onto the land. During the eruption of 1960, 3.5 billion cubic feet of lava poured out of a long fissure, destroying the village of Kapoho before the lava flowed down to the sea.

The island of Hawaii has been the subject of intensive research on the occurrence of earthquakes. The U.S. Geological Survey operates the Hawaiian Volcano Observatory on the very edge of the Halemaumau fire pit. Scientists at the observatory study the nature of lava and gases that are emitted during an eruption; they monitor minute changes in dimensions of the volcano; and they record earthquakes that occur beneath the island. From earthquake data they have learned that the molten rock, or *magma,* originates about 31 miles or more beneath the surface and moves up periodically to fill normally empty chambers just below the surface of the volcanic cone. As magma fills the upper chambers, the cone just above them becomes "inflated"—that is, it expands upward and outward—which generates a measurable stretching or tilting of the surface of the volcano. This "ballooning" of the volcano continues until an eruption of hot gases and solid material reduces the pressure and permits the volcano to return to its static condition. Using such data, scientists can now predict when an eruption is likely to begin, how long it will probably last, and whether the eruption has ended or is merely resting temporarily.

Volcanoes like Kilauea, whose style of eruption is the release of molten lava flows, offer the best chance of successful prediction. But volcanoes that tend to explode with great violence offer a greater problem, because it is still not possible to predict the instant of explosion. In such cases, it is only possible to predict the onset of a general period of dangerous activity. Unfortunately, this is more like a long-range weather forecast than a weather report for the next day.

Although it will not be easy, scientists expect to learn how to predict future eruptions of active or temporarily dormant volcanoes. But long-extinct volcanoes also present a difficult problem. Will they come to life suddenly—as Vesuvius did in A.D. 79, when it destroyed Pompeii, Herculaneum, and Stabiae? Other currently inactive but potentially dangerous volcanoes are Mount Baker and Mount St. Helens in Washington, Mount Hood in Oregon, and Mount Shasta in California. Even more difficult is the problem of predicting the eruption of new volcanoes, such as Paricutín, which rose up out of a farmer's field in Mexico. Learning to predict the movements of deep lava in relation to new outlets to the surface is a major challenge for earth scientists.

Is the Grand Canyon the earth's deepest gorge?

Anyone who has seen the Grand Canyon of the Colorado River in Arizona will find it difficult to imagine a greater chasm tucked away in some out-of-the-way corner of the world. Yet such a yawning chasm does exist—at the bottom of the ocean. Studies of the ocean floor show that it is slashed by deep canyons and trenches that dwarf even the mighty Grand Canyon. Off the coast of the Philippine Islands, for example, the Mindanao Deep plunges to a depth greater than 37,700 feet—about seven times deeper than the Grand Canyon!

The bottom of the sea also contains the world's greatest mountain ranges. The Mid-Atlantic Ridge, for example, is a huge pile of rocks that rises 5000 feet or more from the ocean floor and extends in a great chain of mountains for over 10,000 miles. Between such mountains and canyons can be found plains, plateaus, and other features of every conceivable size and shape. Submarine scenery clearly rivals anything found on land.

For obvious reasons, mariners have always had a great desire to chart the ocean floor. For centuries, sailors used weighted lines to sound the bottom in order to locate underwater reefs and other obstacles that might be hazardous to navigation. Such methods, although time-consuming and far from accurate, did provide information about a small part of the ocean. With such limited information, it is little wonder that scientists of the past visualized the ocean floor as a somewhat flat, featureless plain.

With the help of modern electronics, today's mariners take soundings of the bottom quickly and accurately, using instruments called *echo sounders,* or *fathometers.* These devices measure the greatest depths or the shallowest channel by transmitting a sound signal that is

89

echoed, or reflected back, from the ocean bottom to a receiving device on the ship. The returning sound signal is picked up by an underwater detector called a *hydrophone*. The echo sounder measures the elapsed time for the two-way trip of the sound signal to the bottom and back and converts the time interval to the corresponding distance in feet, meters, or fathoms. The echo sounder can then mark the depth on a recording chart called an *echogram*. Echo sounding is possible because sound travels through sea water at a known speed of about 4800 feet per second. If the elapsed time of the sound signal's trip is known, the water's depth can be computed quickly and easily by electronic means.

Sophisticated echo-sounding equipment can draw a continuous profile of the bottom as the ship sails along. The profile shows the variation in depth of the bottom and is used to prepare hydrographic charts of the sea floor. Using these instruments, marine geologists can determine such submarine features as exposed bedrock, old shorelines, mountains, and trenches.

Even though a good deal is known about the ocean floor, scientists are puzzled about the many V-shaped underwater canyons that cut into the continental shelves. These spectacular gorges measure many thousands of feet in depth, and up to 10 miles in width. Two well-known examples are the Hudson Canyon off the New York coast and the Monterey Canyon off the California coast.

Scientists originally thought of the V-canyons as drowned, seaward extensions of river-cut valleys. Now they are not sure. Many geologists believe that the canyons have been carved out by streams of water flowing along the ocean floor. These underwater flows carry much sand and mud and are very effective as tools of erosion. It is thought that these dense currents carve out the sea floor and scour out their canyons as the flows move toward deeper water.

Why is activity difficult at high altitude?

A lowlander who visits the mountains at 7000 feet usually finds himself huffing and puffing during relatively mild exercise. The breathing difficulty is due to the reduced air pressure at such altitudes. The lower pressure reduces the efficiency with which oxygen is transferred from the air to the blood in the lungs. The visitor must breathe harder and the heart must beat faster to compensate for the reduced efficiency of oxygen transfer.

How does the memory work?

When we retrieve a past event from our memory, we have the impression of "seeing" or "hearing" that event—as if it were filed in the brain as a kind of silent or talking picture. The memory, of course, does not store information that way. The brain consists of nerve cells, or neurons, the only material available for storing information and enabling us to search for it and retrieve it.

Scientists suspect that memories are made using some kind of code, analogous to the Morse code. A telegraph operator is able to change a rapid series of dots and dashes into words, and then into ideas. Some sort of electrochemical code must do the same thing in the storage portion of our memory. All of that, of course, is speculation, because we know very little about the memory despite many years of research on the subject.

One theory involves the *synapse,* or junction between two neurons, in the brain. An electrical impulse moves down one neuron to the synapse. Here, it is transferred to another neuron by a chemical substance between the two neurons. Once across the gap, it repeats the process along the second neuron until it arrives at a second synapse, and so on. The brain consists of billions of neurons that are so small that some parts of the brain contain 100 million of them in a cubic inch. Any one of them can communicate with up to 270,000 of its neighbors. There are estimated to be at least 250 trillion (250,000,000,000,000) interconnections within the brain. So the brain can be thought of as an enormously complex network of possible pathways for electrical signals. The theory of memory that we are discussing holds that learning influences the chemical substances at the synapses so that a given electrical signal is guided down a specific pathway. In simpler terms, it is as if a certain group of railroad switches have been activated. These switches direct the train over a given route depending on how the switches are set. In the brain, the synapses represent the switches and direct the electrical impulses over a certain series of neurons. This pathway represents a specific memory. Each time that specific memory is triggered, it will follow the same route of neurons.

To illustrate how this memory system might work, imagine that you are learning a date in history. With each mental recitation of that date, the appropriate set of synapses would produce more and more of the "enabling" chemical substance at the synapses. After a time, you could simply "fire" the sequence and retrieve the date from memory.

91

The "right" neurons have been connected to provide a path for the memory.

A competing theory tells us that memories are stored in protein molecules. These molecules are responsible for the structure of the living cell as well as the chemical reactions going on within the cell. Protein molecules are made up of highly complex building blocks, long twisted chains called *amino acids*. Amino acids have the ability to link together to form extremely complex molecules of protein, and the structure of the protein can contain an enormous amount of chemical information. Scientists assume that this coded information can somehow be translated into the process we call memory. We do know that one protein molecule, in the form of DNA (deoxyribonucleic acid), contains all the information to construct a human being. So it is not too far-fetched to speculate that protein molecules might also contain memorized information. The structure and complexity of DNA is such that one molecule is capable of holding, in a kind of chemical code, enough information to fill one thousand large volumes of printed material.

The protein theory and the synapse theory do not have to exclude each other. It is possible that they operate side by side, since protein molecules are located in neurons. The firing of various neurons might trigger the memory by electrically actuating the protein molecules.

Research has shown that memory exists in two forms: long-term memory (LTM) and short-term memory (STM). This has been illustrated by tests conducted on amnesia victims. Amnesia can be produced by a sharp blow to the head. Many people with amnesia can recall events of the distant past but cannot recall recent events. When memory finally returns, it starts with the oldest memories and moves toward the present. Apparently, the longer we have a memory, the more firmly it is fixed in our brain. Newer memories can be temporarily lost by blows or electrical shocks. Very recent memories are often permanently lost.

Short-term memory seems to be a temporary process probably used to retain the information until we evaluate its importance. From there, if the brain gives a go-ahead, it is placed in a more permanent form. STM may be a continuous firing of a series of synapses to hold the memory temporarily, and LTM may involve the actual formation of a protein molecule for that memory.

Is the universe infinite in extent?

In response to this question, scientists can only give us a tentative "maybe." The basic problem in finding the answer has to do with a phenomenon called the "red shift." To illustrate, imagine an auto moving toward you at constant speed with its horn blowing. You hear a definite pitch. As soon as the car passes by, however, and starts moving away, the pitch lowers. This *Doppler effect,* as it is called, was first explained by Christian Doppler in 1842. It applies with equal effect to all kinds of wave motion, including sound, water waves, x rays, and light.

To understand how the Doppler principle works, suppose that a stone is dropped into a calm lake. Waves travel out from the center of the disturbance at a fixed rate, and a cork on the surface bobs up and down. Now suppose that the cork is made to move toward the center of the wave circles. It will encounter more waves per minute than when it was stationary. Just the opposite happens when it is moving away from the center: it encounters fewer waves per minute than when it was stationary. Similarly, the horn of an auto sends out a fixed number of sound waves per second. If the auto is approaching an observer, the observer hears an increased number of sound waves in one second. Consequently, the pitch is higher than when the auto is at rest. When the auto is moving away, the observer hears fewer waves in one second and the pitch is reduced.

The same sort of thing happens to light waves coming from distant stars. When scientists observe such light through a telescope, they find that it is redder than it was when the star emitted it. This red shift corresponds to fewer waves per second reaching the earth than there "ought" to be. The greater the distance to the star, the greater the red shift. Scientists interpret this red shift as a Doppler shift caused by an expansion of the universe. In essence, every star is receding from every other star as though they were born in a gigantic explosion from one great ball of matter.

The really important point, as far as this question is concerned, is this: the farther apart two objects may be, the greater the red shift and, hence, the greater the velocity at which they move apart. As an astronomer on earth looks deeper and deeper into space, he finds galaxies that are moving ever faster away from him. If this sort of thing keeps up at greater distances, and there is no reason to suspect that it won't, there will eventually be a distance at which star light cannot reach us at all. That is, the red shift will be so great that we will not be able to observe such distant galaxies. Thus, electromagnetic waves—such as light—arrive on earth from only a finite part of the possibly infinite universe. Using our present scientific theories, we may not be able to determine just how big the universe really is.

How is soap made?

Man has used soap for two thousand years or more. Pliny, the Roman historian, mentions it as an invention of the Gauls, and it seems to have been used in ancient Rome. Prior to the sixteenth century, when soap manufacture began, householders had to make their own soap. Waste kitchen fats and wood ashes were saved as the raw materials. The wood ashes were soaked in water and strained, to produce a solution of potassium carbonate. Boiling this solution with the fat produced a soft soap that considerably improved the cleansing power of plain water.

In manufacturing ordinary soap, or sodium stearate, steam is passed through a mixture of fat and lye (caustic soda or sodium hydroxide). After several hours, a reaction known as *saponification* takes place. Soap forms into a large floating curd, which is made to coagulate by adding common table salt.

Soap can be given varied properties by using different raw materials, or by adding various substances to it. Coconut oil, for example, produces a soap that will lather in salt water as well as fresh. Olive oil produces a greenish soap that is attractive for the bath. Similarly, perfumes or antiseptics are often added, and resin can be used in laundry soaps to make them lather easily. If tiny air bubbles are trapped in the soap, it floats. Transparent soap can be made by dissolving the raw materials in alcohol instead of water. Soap powder is made by spraying a mixture of melted soap and sodium carbonate into a heated chamber. The soap particles, held together by the carbonate, collect as a powder on the floor of the chamber.

What is the Coriolis effect?

For most practical matters, we can neglect the fact that the earth rotates on its axis at surface speeds close to 1000 miles per hour at the equator. Although the speed diminishes to zero at the poles, it represents a rather significant velocity over most of the earth's surface.

The whirling of the earth does not usually concern us, because we and everything else on the surface go around with it. When a person jumps straight up, for example, he lands in about the same spot from which he jumped. This happens in spite of the fact that the earth moves as much as 150 feet to the east during one-tenth of a second! The jumper takes off with the earth's rotational velocity and merely moves to the east in synchronism with the earth's motion. Upon landing, both the jumper and the earth are in the same relative position as before—despite the fact that both have moved perhaps several hundred feet to the east.

Things get a little trickier, however, when such things as projectiles, rockets, and airplanes travel long distances without physical contact with the earth. In 1844 a French scientist named Gaspard Gustave de Coriolis discovered a phenomenon that comes into play for such motion. Simply stated, the Coriolis effect tells us that an object moving in any direction over the earth's surface is deflected to the right in the northern hemisphere and to the left in the southern hemisphere. It was originally referred to as the Coriolis force, but no real force is involved; the deflection is merely an apparent change in the path of an object as seen by an observer on the rotating earth.

An example may help make all of this clear. Suppose you are flying an airplane from Seattle to San Francisco. Since San Francisco is essentially due south of Seattle, you might well set your airplane on a southerly course in the confident expectation of landing near San Francisco. Unfortunately for logic, you would end up somewhere in the Pacific Ocean, to the west of San Francisco. In response to the Coriolis effect, the plane is deflected to the right. This deflection takes place because the earth's surface speed becomes greater as one moves south. Like the jumper mentioned earlier, the plane acquires the earth's speed on takeoff in Seattle. In its path to the south it flies over land that gradually speeds up in its movement toward the east. This is because the earth is a sphere, and its rotational velocity changes from zero at the poles to 1000 miles per hour at the equator. So the plane drifts to the right with respect to the land over which it flies. This explanation omits such factors as air resistance, winds, and the like, but it does describe the basic cause of the Coriolis effect.

Much the same effect takes place on the return trip from San Francisco to Seattle. The plane acquires the relatively high rotational velocity of San Francisco on takeoff and flies toward Seattle, which rotates more slowly. Therefore, the plane's high initial velocity to the east carries it to the right of Seattle, rather closer to Spokane than Seattle. To counteract the Coriolis effect, the pilot must veer slightly to the left in the northern hemisphere. Similar compensation is required when shooting projectiles, missiles, and rockets.

According to the Coriolis principle, the deflection takes effect for motion in any direction, even east or west. The effect is zero at the equator and increases toward the poles.

The Coriolis effect has an important influence on large-scale currents in the ocean. All of the major currents in the northern hemisphere travel clockwise (to the right), and those in the southern hemisphere travel counterclockwise. It is not true, by the way, that the Coriolis effect causes water in sinks and tubs to drain in the prescribed direction. The effect is noticed only on large scale motions such as ocean currents and winds. If the earth were to reverse its direction of rotation, the Gulf Stream would undoubtedly be replaced by an Atlantic current flowing in the opposite (counterclockwise) direction. That would have a profound influence on the climate of Northern Europe and Eastern Canada.

The Coriolis effect also explains why winds flow clockwise around high-pressure areas and counterclockwise around low-pressure areas. The accompanying diagram shows a pressure map containing a high- and a low-pressure area. Each line connects points having the same barometric air pressure. (The air pressure increases as one moves from a low to a high.) The lines are called *isobars* (from the Greek *iso*—meaning equal). To understand what happens, consider any small volume of air on the pressure map. The high-pressure side will experience a higher force than the side facing the low-pressure area. Consequently, there will be a net push sending the volume of air from the high toward the low. As soon as the volume of air begins to move, however, the Coriolis effect enters the picture, deflecting the volume of air to the right. The final result is to send each volume of air in the direction of the isobars. When that happens, the pressure force just balances the Coriolis effect and the winds flow around the high and low in the prescribed directions. The clockwise circulation around a high is called an anticyclone, and the counterclockwise flow around a low is called a cyclone. (In the southern hemisphere, these directions of flow are reversed.) In practice, the winds deviate slightly from exact coincidence with the isobars, because of friction between the air and the earth.

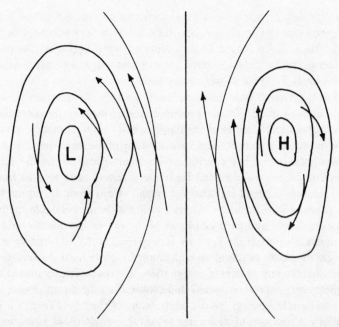

Fig. 9. Winds tend to follow lines of constant pressure in the atmosphere because of the Coriolis effect. In the northern hemisphere they flow clockwise around a high pressure system *(H)*, and counterclockwise around a low *(L)*. This effect is caused by the rotation of the earth.

What is dry ice?

Dry ice is frozen carbon dioxide, the gas that animals exhale in the process of breathing. Dry ice is particularly useful as a coolant, because it is quite cold ($-109.3°F$) and changes directly from solid to gas under normal conditions without going through a messy liquid phase. Dry ice is used widely because it is harmless to life in normal concentrations and is quite easy to convert into the frozen form.

Scientists often have need of a small quantity of dry ice, and they make it easily in their own laboratory. If a tank of liquid carbon dioxide is handy, they need only open the valve and a mixture of dry ice and carbon dioxide is blown out. The dry ice is collected in a cloth bag tied to the outlet pipe. This simple method is the most convenient way to obtain small amounts of dry ice for occasional use in the laboratory.

The first step in making dry ice on a larger scale is to compress car-

97

bon dioxide gas until it liquefies. During this process, the carbon dioxide heats up, just as the air in a bicycle pump does when the air is compressed. If the excess heat is removed, keeping the gas at room temperature, the carbon dioxide begins to liquefy at a pressure of approximately 870 pounds per square inch.

To understand what happens next, imagine a tank partly filled with liquid carbon dioxide produced in the manner just described. The individual molecules of the liquid are in continual motion in random directions and at random speeds. Many of the faster-moving molecules break through the surface for a short distance into the space above the liquid and then fall back into it. Every so often a molecule does manage to break free completely and escape from the liquid, but the pressure in the chamber forces another molecule back into the liquid. The liquid and gaseous phases of the carbon dioxide are said to be in equilibrium. If the pressure is now reduced, by allowing some of the gas to escape, evaporation will proceed rapidly from the surface of the liquid. In any process of evaporation, it is the molecules having the highest energy (greatest speed) that escape from the liquid. Those left behind have less energy, so the temperature of the liquid (which is essentially a measure of molecular velocity) goes down as evaporation proceeds. That, of course, is the important point: evaporation abstracts heat from the liquid because only the swiftest—and, therefore, most energetic—molecules leave the body of the liquid.

As the pressure is reduced over the liquid carbon dioxide, the temperature drops until freezing begins at $-71°F$. With further evaporation, the entire volume freezes. When atmospheric pressure is reached, the temperature drops to $-109.3°F$, the temperature of dry ice.

Not all gases can be liquefied as easily as carbon dioxide. Each gas has a *critical temperature,* above which it cannot be liquefied, no matter how much pressure is applied. The critical temperature of carbon dioxide is a relatively high 88°F, which means that it can be liquefied at normal room temperature. Sulfur dioxide and ammonia are also easy to liquefy. Gases such as oxygen, nitrogen, hydrogen, and helium are very difficult to liquefy because their critical temperatures are extremely low, ranging from -180.4 to $-450.4°F$.

Household and industrial cooling also depend on evaporative cooling. In a refrigerator, the working liquid is evaporated at low temperature within the chamber to be cooled. This abstracts heat from the surroundings. Once outside the cooling compartment, the gas is changed back into a liquid by applying considerable pressure. The liquid is quite hot at this point, and excess heat is removed from the liquid by passing it through a cooling device similar to an automobile radiator. The rejected heat, for the most part, represents the heat taken up by the gas in the cold part of the refrigerator. Once the liquid is returned to room temperature, it is ready for another evaporative cooling cycle in the cold chamber. The working substance used most widely in air conditioning and refrigeration is dichlorodifluoromethane, better known as Freon.

Do fish navigate by the sun?

It is a well-known fact that fish migrate in the open ocean. Unfortunately, it is not the easiest task to study their movements over thousands of miles of open water. Studies have been made, however, in lakes and ponds, where it is not too difficult to keep track of the moving fish.

Scientists have found that an American species of perch selects specific places on lake bottoms to lay its eggs. In order to study their means of navigation, fish were caught in the spawning area, marked, and released about 1.5 miles away. Almost all of them returned very quickly to the spawning area.

Some of the perch were tracked by attaching small radio transmitters or brightly colored floats to their bodies. The transmitters sent out radio signals that could be followed, and the floats made direct visual tracking possible. Scientists found that the fish swam a straight line to the spawning ground when the sun was out. On overcast days, however, the perch swam in all directions, as though they had lost their way.

Experiments of this kind with perch and other species of fish seem to show that they use the sun as a compass over short distances much as many of the insects do.

Is Yellowstone National Park a dormant volcano getting ready to erupt?

As spectacular as modern volcanic eruptions may be, they shrink to insignificance before those that occurred on three separate occasions in the Yellowstone National Park region at the eastern edge of the Snake River Plain, in Idaho. After careful mapping of the region, geologists have discovered three enormous depressions, called *calderas,* which represent the final stages in the lives of three different volcanoes. The largest of these depressions measures approximately 45 miles in diameter.

A caldera is a large crater-like depression that is formed when the cone of a volcano collapses following a particularly violent eruption. Crater Lake, Oregon, for example, is a circular caldera about 6 miles across that was formed in prehistoric times when Mount Mazama erupted and collapsed into its hollow interior. The lake is nearly 2000 feet deep, and the rim reaches up another 2000 feet above the level of the lake. Wizard Island, in Crater Lake, is the tip of another volcano that erupted at a later date from the floor of the caldera.

The great Yellowstone caldera is apparently the largest yet discovered by geologists. The formation of each of the three calderas at Yellowstone resulted from the cataclysmic eruption of hundreds of cubic miles of material from the volcanic chambers. The temperature of the material must have reached 1450°F. The volcanoes erupted with sufficient force to hurl volcanic material as far as 50 miles from the center of eruption. Fine-grained ash, carried eastward by the prevailing winds, has been discovered in deposits as far away as Kansas. Rivers, such as the Yellowstone, have cut canyons in the deposits of the eruptions, showing that each of the three deposits is over 200 feet thick.

A sobering aspect of the Yellowstone eruptions is their timing. Using radioactive dating techniques, scientists have determined that the first eruption took place 2 million years ago, the second 1.2 million years ago, and the third 0.6 million years ago. Thus, there was a lull of about 800,000 years between the first and second eruptions but only 600,000 years between the second and third. Furthermore, 600,000 years have elapsed since the last eruption. One wonders whether the geysers and bubbling hot springs so common in the Yellowstone area may be the harbingers of a forthcoming eruption. Such an eruption would bring with it enormous loss of life and property. Because of that possibility—as well as for the potential of geothermal energy—the area has been studied extensively in recent years. The results seem to indicate the presence of a large body of hot and possibly molten rock just below the surface, measuring 40 miles in diameter and 30 miles deep. Most earth scientists believe that the calderas and volcanic eruptions of the past 2 million years are merely the surface manifestations of that hot body of rock just below the surface. The remaining unanswered questions are: how much of that rock is still molten, and is it building up pressure for another eruption?

We ought to keep in mind, however, that a few tens of thousands of years are merely an instant in the geologic scale of time. I would not cancel a trip to Yellowstone National Park even if I were certain it would erupt again someday!

What is meant by the "green revolution"?

Until about 12,000 years ago, man obtained most of his food by hunting and fishing. Berries, nuts, roots, and other foods derived from plants were merely incidental additions to his main diet of meat and fish. During the past few thousand years, however, the proportion of food derived from plants has grown dramatically. Today, wheat and rice are mankind's chief dietary staples. Wheat is the more widely cultivated of the two and is the main nutrient source in most industrialized countries. Rice is the basic food for most poor people throughout the world. Along with potatoes, cassava, sugar, and various grains, wheat and rice make up 70 percent of the food energy of mankind. Fruits, vegetables, fats, oils, and nuts provide another 18 percent. Meat and fish make up the remaining 12 percent, although this percentage is considerably higher in wealthy nations such as the United States.

Farmers now use 10 percent of the earth's land area to produce food. Ten percent may seem a small figure, but it represents just about all the land suitable for farming. There are no more hidden paradises awaiting exploitation. Sub-Saharan Africa and the Amazon River Basin are the only two large areas of the world left for agricultural use, and little is known about farming in such areas. Most attempts to cultivate new land areas since mid-century have been too inefficient or too costly to maintain.

Because little new land is available for agriculture, farmers have managed to increase the production of food in recent decades by raising crop yields on land already under cultivation. Since 1950 most of the world's increase in grain production has come about through greater yields per acre. Most of this improvement is a result of scientific advances in two major areas: plant genetics and the use of synthetic fertilizers. These two advances gave birth to an agricultural breakthrough, called the green revolution, which has reduced food

101

costs and helped feed the poor nations of the world.

Beginning in the mid-1940s, plant breeders developed new strains of wheat that gave substantially higher yields per acre. With the assistance of the Rockefeller Foundation and the Mexican government, Norman E. Borlaug developed new strains that tripled wheat production in Mexico between 1944 and 1964. For this achievement, Borlaug received the 1970 Nobel Peace Prize.

Encouraged by this success with wheat, the Rockefeller and Ford foundations established the International Rice Research Institute in the Philippines in 1962. Using scientific methods developed earlier for wheat, scientists were able to create a high-yielding strain of "miracle rice" called IR-8. Later, even better strains of rice were developed and planted throughout Asia.

Unlike traditional varieties of wheat and rice, the flowering of most of the new strains does not depend on the *photoperiod*—the length of time during which they are illuminated each day. Rice, for example, will normally flower only if illuminated for less than a certain number of hours each day. Conversely, traditional wheat varieties will flower only if the daily photoperiod is greater than a certain number of hours. Thus, the traditional varieties of wheat and rice must be planted at certain specific times of the year if they are to flower and produce grain. Most new varieties not only flower under a wider range of photoperiods but also produce grain more quickly. This means that the new varieties can be planted and harvested repeatedly throughout the growing season. Using these new varieties of plants, Pakistan increased its wheat production by 60 percent between 1967 and 1969; India did the same between 1967 and 1971; and the Philippines has ended a half century of dependence on rice imports.

The achievement of such high yields requires much irrigation, fertilizer, herbicide, and labor. The use of fertilizer, for example, has increased enormously, reminding us that land cannot sustain high yields unless we replenish the minerals removed by the plants. Indian farmers use ten times the fertilizer and five times the irrigation water on high-yield wheat as on local strains.

A problem associated with high-yield varieties has been their susceptibility to disease. Plants bred for one major characteristic—such as high yield—tend to have other weaknesses. The wheat from Mexico and the rice from the Philippines are attacked by new strains of fungus when planted in Asia. Thus, research must continue on herbicides

102

to protect the new plants. Failing that, still newer varieties of wheat and rice must be developed that are less susceptible to disease.

Why do insects become less active in cold weather?

The manufacture of organic compounds in the cells of living things is controlled by special protein molecules called *enzymes*. They are essential to every chemical reaction in the living organism, and today, well over 700 have been discovered. Enzymes speed up a chemical reaction without taking part in it themselves. For example, the enzyme *pepsin* changes food proteins into less complex substances called polypeptides, but pepsin itself remains unchanged.

The importance of enzymes to activity in a living cell lies in their ability to generate chemical reactions that would otherwise occur only at excessively high temperatures. Chemical reactions within the cell—upon which life and activity depend—are restricted to a rather narrow temperature range, because cells are destroyed at temperatures much below freezing or much higher than 100°F.

Each enzyme has a temperature at which it is most effective, and its activity decreases as the temperature rises or falls from that point. It is the decrease in activity of enzymes at low temperature that accounts for the torpid nature of insects in late autumn when temperatures begin to fall.

Is speed reading an aid to comprehension?

You may have seen coverage on television or in newspapers of individuals who can read tens of thousands of words a minute. Such performances, of course, are impossible and involve some sort of trick. Scientists who have studied the matter tell us that it is not physically possible to read faster than about 1000 words a minute. Even this figure is several times the normal rate for college students, 150 to 250 words per minute. The problem with speed reading, however, is the effect it has on comprehension. For most people, if their reading speed is doubled, their comprehension score for the material drops to about one-half of the original score.

As your eye moves along this line of type, it takes in only 1 to 2.7 words for each eye fixation. We have been told that this figure can be increased with training, but it just is not true. To prove this to yourself, concentrate for a split second on a random word on this page. If you keep your eye from cheating and peeking at words farther out, you will see how narrow your field of view really is. You can probably feel your eye pulling one way or the other. In fact, a major scientific criticism of speed reading is that at 800 words a minute one becomes so conscious of eye movements that little attention is paid to the reading matter.

There really seems to be no such thing as speed reading when difficult textbook material is involved. A more appropriate term is *speed skimming.* That is really what you learn to do when you study speed reading. You can skim along at a few thousand words a minute, picking out a few phrases here and there to get the general idea of a passage, but you cannot understand much of it at such speed. Skimming is useful if you have a large amount of material to read and merely want to get a general idea of what it is about, or if you want to locate a certain section. It will not work well for school texts, however, unless you are willing to settle for a low comprehension percentage.

If you are about average in your reading speed, be cautious about increasing it; the faster you go, the less you will remember.

How was pottery-making discovered?

For at least a quarter of a million years man has practiced the art of firemaking. It is not unreasonable to suppose that early man—or, more probably, early woman—would have noticed the hardening effect that a bonfire has on damp clay. Then, when the need arose, it would be a natural step to shape lumps of wet clay into useful objects before placing them in the fire. In any event, pottery made its appearance early in the Neolithic Age and became one of mankind's most important discoveries.

The potter's art grew and spread when mankind adopted the agricultural way of life. The use of ceramics may have sprung in part from the need to store and protect grain from the incursions of rodents and moisture. In addition, the sedentary life of the farmer would have made it practical to maintain a household of heavy and bulky luxuries, which would have been out of the question for earlier nomadic peoples.

The making of true pottery involves a chemical reaction that can only be carried out by baking the clay at a temperature of at least 400 to 500°C (750 to 930°F). The intense heat drives out the water that is bonded chemically to the aluminum silicate in the clay. Once that is done, the fired vessel no longer reverts to loose clay when wet and can survive in the ground for centuries. That, by the way, is why pottery is so important to archaeologists. It holds up against the elements much better than most other substances and often tells tales of the past when other clues fail.

The earliest pots were made without the potter's wheel, probably much the way that the Kikuyu of Kenya have worked in recent times. The Kikuyu ready the moist clay by pulling it into small pieces, removing stones, and drying it in the sun. It is then mixed with water until it is plastic. An equal amount of fine sand is then kneaded in, and the finished clay is formed into long rolls. One or two of the rolls are shaped to form the top of the pot, one hand working inside and the other outside the pot. More clay is added as needed until the top half of the pot is finished. The half-finished pot is allowed to dry in the sun, except for the lower edge, which will later be joined to the bottom section. The edge is protected by leaves. The next stage is accomplished by turning the pot upside down on its finished mouth and adding additional clay as before. Once again, the bottom is formed by both hands, one inside and the other outside, until the pot is complete. After a few hours in the sun for hardening, the pots are placed upside down on the ground and a large bonfire of brushwood is made all around them. When the fire is out, and the pots cool, they are ready for use.

It is the women of the Kikuyu who make pottery, and it may well be that neolithic women also did this work, while the men hunted and tended the herd.

With the coming of ceramic pottery, the first step was taken toward the evolution of the modern saucepan. Before ceramics, food could only be roasted over a fire or baked in a cooking pit. The availability of a sturdy, heat-resistant earthen pot made it possible to cook the neolithic equivalent of stew or soup. Ceramics made it possible to heat water, store milk and grain, and ferment fruit juices.

Although pottery can be hardened in an open campfire, the results are never as good as in a kiln. Some ingenious early potter must have discovered that she could concentrate and conserve heat by covering the fire—perhaps building it in a pit. The next logical step would be a kiln containing a lower chamber for the fire and an upper one for the pottery. Really thorough firing of pottery requires temperatures up to 900°C, which can most readily be attained in such a kiln.

How does a battery work?

What do the action of an electric battery, the rusting of iron, and the bleaching of clothes have in common? On the surface, very little. Yet these and many other everyday processes are a result of certain chemical reactions called *oxidation-reduction* reactions. *Oxidation* reactions, such as the corrosion of certain metals, the bleaching of hair, and the burning of coal, are defined by chemists as the loss of electrons by the chemical substance involved. Thus, iron rusts and coal burns only when iron and carbon are induced to lose electrons. The opposite reaction, such as the conversion of iron ore to metallic iron, is called *reduction*. In general, reduction is defined as the gain of electrons by a chemical substance, and can be thought of as the opposite of oxidation. Nature has a way of balancing its supply of electrons, so oxidation and reduction always occur simultaneously. The gain of electrons by one substance always occurs at the expense of another that loses electrons.

Because an electron is a tiny, negatively charged particle of matter, chemical reactions always involve electrical considerations. A simple example will help to introduce some needed definitions. Take a fireworks display, for example, with its shower of sparks splashing forth from a rocket high in the sky. The sparks we see are often the metal sodium, which is burning, or being oxidized, by oxygen. In this reaction, the sodium atoms have lost electrons and are said to be *oxidized*. Oxygen has gained electrons and is said to be *reduced*. By gaining electrons (and being reduced), oxygen enables sodium to lose electrons (and be oxidized). Sodium is called a *reducing agent* because it gives up electrons and causes reduction; oxygen is called an *oxidizing agent* because it gains electrons and causes oxidation. The term *oxidation* was derived from the name of the element because oxygen was the first oxidizing agent to be studied in detail. It was later found that many other elements, such as fluorine, chlorine, and bromine, also gain electrons from metals, so all such elements are called oxidizing agents. The term *reduction* comes from the field of metallurgy where it has long been used to describe the conversion of an ore, such as iron oxide, to a metal, such as iron. When the ore loses its oxygen atoms, it is reduced in weight—hence the term *reduction*. In this example, charcoal acts as the reducing agent.

A simple experiment will help to demonstrate the nature of an oxidation-reduction reaction. You will need a clean, large iron nail and a clean silver-plated or sterling-silver spoon. They must be clean because you are going to put them in your mouth. Put the nail on one side of your tongue near the back of your mouth. One end of the nail must extend out of your mouth. Put the spoon along the other side of your tongue, also near the back, with the large end sticking out of your mouth. Next, with the nail and spoon in place, touch the two firmly together outside the mouth. If everything has been done correctly, you will taste an oxidation-reduction reaction.

What happens is this. Near the end of the nail that is in your mouth, iron atoms are oxidized, by giving up electrons, and dissolve in your mouth. Atoms (also molecules, which consist of two or more atoms) that have gained or lost electrons are called *ions*. The taste you perceive near the nail is that of iron ions dissolved in your saliva.

The electrons that have left the iron atoms travel through the nail, into the spoon, and toward the back of your mouth near the spoon. There, they reduce some of the water in your mouth to form some hydrogen gas and a substance called a hydroxide ion. Unlike water molecules, which contain two atoms of hydrogen and one of oxygen, the hydroxide ion contains only one of each. In addition, being an ion, it carries an electric charge. So, near the spoon, you taste the hydroxide ion.

The iron atom, like all atoms, carries no net electrical charge to begin with. Its negatively charged electrons are balanced exactly by an equal positive charge in its nucleus, or center. When it loses electrons, to become an ion, it acquires a net positive charge, because the charge balance is disrupted. Similarly, the hydroxide ion carries a net negative charge, because it has an excess of negatively charged electrons.

If you are wondering what all this has to do with batteries, we should note that the experiment you have just performed—at least mentally—is an example of an electric *voltaic cell,* or battery. All batteries, in fact, operate on just those principles, even though the materials used and the mechanical arrangement may be different. To begin with, we should notice an important fact. There was no taste of iron or hydroxide ions until you touched the spoon and nail together. Only then could the electrons flow and allow the chemical reactions to take place. Touching the two together was like closing the switch on a flashlight. No electricity could flow until a continuous electrical path was made to exist between the two electrodes, the nail and spoon. The three essential items—nail, spoon, and mouth—constitute a small electric cell, or battery, based on an oxidation-reduction reaction that was separated into two halves: an oxidation half near the nail and a reduction half near the spoon.

107

LAMP

POSITIVE TERMINAL

COPPER WIRE

PLASTIC SEAL

+

ZINC CAN

MAGNESIUM DIOXIDE POWDER

NEGATIVE TERMINAL

ELECTRICAL CONDUCTING MEDIUM (ELECTROLYTE)

−

Fig. 10. A dry cell. Electrons are forced out of the negative terminal through an external circuit to the positive terminal.

An ordinary dry-cell battery used in transistor radios or flashlights is also based on an oxidation reaction taking place near a metal, using zinc, and a reduction reaction near a carbon electrode surrounded by manganese dioxide. As shown in the diagram, the zinc electrode constitutes the outer casing of the dry cell, and the carbon electrode is located in the center. Electrons are given off by the ionizing zinc metal (oxidation) and flow through the external circuit to the carbon electrode. Near the carbon electrode, the manganese dioxide gains electrons (reduction) to form hydroxide ions and a new compound called basic manganese oxide.

The oxidation reaction pushes electrons out of the negative terminal of the cell, and the reduction reaction takes them in at the positive terminal. The electric force or voltage produced by such a cell is 1.5 volts. If 9 volts are required, six such cells must be connected in tandem, or series, to make the total voltage equal to 9.

The chemical reactions described above apply to dry-cell batteries normally used in flashlights, transistor radios, and the like. Different oxidation-reduction reactions are used in automobile storage batteries, in "ni-cad" (nickel-cadmium) batteries used in some electronic calculators, or in tiny "mercury cells" used in electric watches or automatic cameras.

How do meat tenderizers work?

The cooking of food involves the breaking up of large protein or carbohydrate molecules—called *polymers*—into smaller molecules to aid in digestion. The polymers involved are the carbohydrate cellular walls in vegetables and the connective tissues in meats. In the presence of heat, both types of polymers combine with water to form smaller molecules that our digestive systems can handle. In addition, cooking makes foods more tender by reducing the number of chemical bonds holding the food together.

Meat tenderizers, which have become popular in recent years, are chemicals called *enzymes*, which can perform at room temperature some of the functions normally done by cooking. An enzyme is a substance that enhances or speeds up a particular chemical process. Meat tenderizers cause the breaking of certain chemical bonds in meat protein molecules at room temperature. As a consequence, meat that is quite tough can be made tender prior to cooking. Meat tenderizers include plant substances such as papain, a protein-splitting enzyme from the fruit of the papaya tree. Other useful enzymes are derived from bacteria or fungi.

Why does "heat lightning" have no thunder?

Heat lightning is the everyday name we give to the intermittent illumination of distant clouds near the horizon. This illumination is not accompanied by thunder, and we usually fail to see individual lightning strokes. Heat lightning probably gets its name because it occurs on hot, humid nights—conditions that are just right for thunderstorms to form. If we were closer to the storm, we would see the lightning strokes and hear the thunder. We fail to hear the thunder because the lightning flashes are more than about 15 miles away. Beyond that distance, thunder cannot generally be heard.

Thunder is rarely heard beyond 15 miles because temperature and wind vary at different heights in the region around a thunderstorm.

109

The sound of thunder curves upward and passes over the head of an observer who is more that 15 miles from the lightning.

Before we leave the subject, perhaps we should mention how thunder comes about. Scientists now believe that thunder is caused by the rapid expansion of air that is heated by a lightning stroke. The enormous energy of lightning heats a narrow channel of air above 50,000°C. This is done so quickly—in a few millionths of a second for each short section of the stroke—that the channel of heated air has no time to expand while it is being heated. This produces a high pressure in the channel, which may be in excess of 1500 pounds per square inch. The pressure then generates a sound disturbance, which we hear as thunder.

Why is much of the Alaskan oil pipeline located above ground?

In polar regions, or at high altitudes in warmer latitudes, the ground is frozen solid just beneath the surface. Ground that remains frozen from one year to the next is called *permafrost*. Permafrost merely means, however, that the ground remains below 0°C (32°F); it does not imply that the ground is necessarily saturated with frozen water. So the content of ice in permafrost can vary from a small amount to a very large amount. A knowledge of how much ice is located in permafrost is important to builders and engineers who must work in cold regions.

Permafrost underlies almost 20 percent of the land area of the earth, including some 85 percent of Canada and the U.S.S.R. It reaches its maximum thickness along the coast of the Arctic Ocean in Alaska, Canada, and Siberia. Permafrost reaches a depth of almost a mile in the Soviet Arctic and half that figure in parts of Alaska and Canada. Most of the permafrost in Alaska is discontinuous—it occurs only in patches.

Above the permafrost is a thin layer of soil in which the ice thaws in spring and freezes in the fall, remaining frozen throughout the winter. This so-called *active layer* varies in thickness from about 3 feet to 9 feet. The upper surface of the permafrost is called the *permafrost table,* and below that level the pore spaces can be filled with ice that never thaws. The permafrost, therefore, can act as a barrier that prevents water in the active layer from sinking underground. This explains why much of the Arctic tundra consists of bogs and water-soaked land during the summer.

110

Many buildings were built in the interior of Alaska before the effects of permafrost on construction were clearly understood. In and around Fairbanks, for example, visitors cannot fail to notice many warped houses and tilted trees that have been forced out of line by the changing permafrost level. Heated buildings tend to thaw out the underlying ground and melt their way unevenly into the soggy soil beneath them. Floors tilt, walls tip, and doorjambs twist out of line. One solution is to build houses on stilts, so that heat from the building cannot enter the ground significantly and melt the permafrost.

The insulation provided by vegetation is also of great importance in preserving the delicate thermal balance in regions of permafrost. Even a slight change in the plant cover can have amazing results. Driving a truck over the tundra can leave a scar that will be visible for generations. During the winter of 1967–68, a trail was bulldozed on Alaska's North Slope (the area between the Brooks Range and the Arctic Sea), near the Canning River. When warmer weather arrived, the trail filled with water, producing a narrow lake over much of the trail's length.

When oil was discovered on the North Slope of Alaska, a heated controversy arose over the construction of the Alaska pipeline. Conservationists feared, among other things, that melting and refreezing of the permafrost would lead to breaks in the pipeline and numerous oil spills. The 3-foot-diameter pipeline extends from the oil fields to the ice-free port of Valdez, a distance of 808 miles. In order to keep the viscous petroleum moving at reasonable speed in cold weather, it is heated to a temperature between 158° and 176°F. If the pipeline were buried, it was feared, the permafrost would melt, allowing the pipeline to sink lower and rupture. It was calculated, for example, that after ten years the melting would reach 30 feet around the pipeline—well into the permafrost region in most places.

The most important factor in such construction turns out to be the amount of frozen water in the permafrost. If the permafrost is dry, thawing has no serious effect. In permafrost containing a great deal of ice, thawing produces a soupy mixture into which a heated pipe can sink. If the pipeline is on a hill, the wet soil can flow downhill allowing the pipeline to sink even deeper. Eventually the pipe would break, leading to disastrous oil spills.

After much study, engineers decided that about half of the pipeline had to be built above ground so cold air could circulate underneath it.

The platforms are about 60 feet apart. The vegetation that was disturbed by the construction was replaced so it could again insulate the ground and prevent melting.

After some initial start-up problems, the pipeline seems to be operating as expected. Only time can tell, however, how well the engineers have done their job in this land of unpredictable problems.

Can gold be extracted from sea water?

Oceanographers tell us that there are upwards of 25 tons of gold in each cubic mile of sea water. That is an impressive figure, but so is a cubic mile of ocean. Although the gold is really there, it is present in such minute concentrations that no method has yet been devised to extract it profitably. To illustrate, imagine a room 10 feet long, 10 feet wide, and 10 feet high. That represents a volume of one thousand cubic feet. The amount of gold present in one thousand cubic feet of sea water is only about five-thousandths of an ounce. Put another way, only 5 ounces of gold can be found in a billion ounces of water. There have been many attempts to recover the tiny flecks of gold contained in sea water, but all have thus far failed.

**Approximate Mineral Content in
One Cubic Mile of Ocean Water**

Sodium chloride (common salt)	128,000,000 tons
Magnesium chloride	17,900,000 tons
Magnesium sulphate	7,800,000 tons
Calcium sulphate	5,900,000 tons
Potassium sulphate	4,000,000 tons
Calcium carbonate (lime)	578,832 tons
Magnesium bromide	350,000 tons
Bromine	300,000 tons
Strontium	60,000 tons
Boron	21,000 tons
Fluorine	6,400 tons
Iodine	up to 1,200 tons
Barium	900 tons
Arsenic	up to 350 tons
Rubidium	200 tons
Silver	up to 45 tons
Copper, Lead, Manganese, Zinc	up to 30 tons
Gold	up to 25 tons
Uranium	7 tons

Despite their failure with gold, chemists continue to look with interest at the minerals contained in the oceans. The accompanying table shows the approximate weights of some of the minerals contained in a cubic mile of ocean water. We can see that enormous quantities of valuable minerals are available for the taking, if efficient means of extraction can be developed.

The most abundant mineral derived from the sea is sodium chloride, common salt. In some places, it is still recovered from sea water by evaporation, just as the Chinese did as early as 1000 B.C. The amount of salt contained in one cubic mile of sea water is enough to supply the world's needs for several years! Most of today's salt is mined, however, from brine wells and salt domes. Even this salt, it turns out, came originally from the ocean—it was left behind from ocean water that evaporated many millions of years ago.

The only metal that has ever been recovered from sea water in commercial quantities is magnesium. There is about one pound of magnesium in 1000 pounds of sea water, and chemists have developed a way to extract much of it efficiently and economically. They mix sea water with lime in large tanks, setting up a chemical reaction that produces magnesium hydroxide. The latter substance is not soluble in water, so it settles to the bottom of the tank and is eventually removed. It is then a simple matter for chemists to recover the magnesium. Magnesium is almost five times lighter than steel, so it is widely used in space vehicles and aircraft, where weight is at a premium. Most of the magnesium used in the United States comes from sea water.

Bromine, used in medicines, dyes, photography, and leaded gasoline, is also obtained from the ocean. About 70 pounds of bromine are contained in a million pounds of sea water. It is recovered by treating the water with sulfuric acid and chlorine gas, which free the bromine for removal. Air is then blown through the water, carrying off the bromine as a vapor. About half the bromine used in the United States is extracted from the sea.

Chemists will no doubt continue to seek processes that can recover the wealth of chemical elements available in ocean water. These minerals represent a resource that is seemingly inexhaustible and to a large extent automatically renewable.

What makes water boil?

The answer to this question is not as simple as it would seem at first glance. We learned in school, for example, that water always

113

boils at 100°C (or 212°F). The centigrade, or Celsius, scale is defined, in fact, by setting 100° equal to the boiling temperature of water, and 0° to its freezing temperature. Yet scientists, in very specialized experiments, have succeeded in heating water as high as 178°C (or 352°F) before it would boil!

To understand the major factors that affect boiling, imagine that a pan of water is being heated and that small bubbles have begun to form on the bottom. In order to produce boiling, these tiny bubbles must grow rapidly in size and rush to the surface. Initially, however, the bubbles hardly seem to grow at all. What happens is this. In order to increase in size, the pressure of the water vapor inside the bubble must exceed the pressure exerted on it by the liquid.

A large part of the pressure opposing a bubble's growth is a result of an effect called *surface tension*. Surface tension can be thought of as a kind of skin on the surface of a liquid that acts as a stretched membrane. It is surface tension that allows insects to walk on water. With care, you can even float a steel needle on the surface of water because of surface tension. With respect to our bubble, surface tension acts to contract the surface of the bubble, thereby tending to make it smaller in size. Furthermore, this effect of surface tension is progressively greater as the bubble is smaller. In other words, tiny bubbles must overcome a greater surface tension effect than do larger bubbles. In order to overcome this effect, the bubble's temperature must be raised higher than the "normal" boiling temperature of water. In fact, there is a critical, or threshold, bubble temperature that must be reached, which depends on the initial size of the bubble: the smaller the bubble, the higher the temperature.* Once this temperature is reached, the bubble begins to grow in size, and the effect is cumulative: not only does the pressure in the bubble increase, but also the effect of surface tension decreases. An increase in size leads to further growth, and the bubble expansion becomes explosive.

The rising bubbles cause considerable turbulence and mixing, which causes the "bumping" we often notice when water is boiled. The average water temperature then settles down to its normal boiling temperature.

In order for bubbles to form below the surface, the temperature must be higher there than at the surface, because pressure increases

---

* The temperature must produce a pressure difference between bubble and water greater than $4A/B$, where A is the surface tension and B is the bubble diameter.

with depth. This condition normally exists in cooking, because heat is applied at the bottom of a pan. But if a pan of water is mixed by stirring, it will tend to lose heat and vaporize only at the surface, without boiling. This happens because heat is transferred rapidly to the surface, and tiny bubbles do not have an opportunity to reach the temperature required for growth. This explains why a vigorously boiling pot of food can usually be prevented from boiling over by stirring.

How was fire made in prehistoric times?

Archaeologists remind us that man was merely the discoverer, not the inventor, of fire. Long before man took to experimenting with flints, great fires had raged on this planet. Molten lava had flowed from volcanoes, lightning had kindled dead trees and dry grass, and winds had rubbed dead branches together until they burst into flame. There are clues to such ancient fires, occurring long before the time of man, in prehistoric fossil beds that lie deep below the surface of the earth.

Although man did not invent fire, he did learn long ago how to use it and then how to make it. Precisely when that happened, however, is still unknown. Neanderthal man of 50,000 years ago was certainly adept at firemaking. Clues to a fire that was used 250,000 years ago have turned up in a cave of Peking man—that primitive human being whose brain was only two-thirds the size of our own. Whether the use of fire was discovered once or many times we have no way of knowing. We do know that it was in worldwide use at the dawn of civilized history, so we can infer that it is a truly ancient art of human culture—probably one of the oldest. Furthermore, it is very likely that man used fire long before he mastered the tricks needed to produce it himself.

Of all the materials that early man learned to use, flint is one of the most important. Since it can be made as sharp as a razor, it served as the knives of the day. The very term *Stone Age* comes from the use of this rocky material for prehistoric implements. In practice, the stone is held in one hand, and flakes of flint are knocked off by another stone held in the other hand. If a piece is struck against steel, tiny fragments fly off, heated to incandescent sparks by the blow. Prehistoric man may have produced fire in this way, substituting marcasite, an iron sulfide often found with flint, for steel. The sparks, when aimed at dry moss, can be blown into flame.

Another ancient method of making fire uses friction. One piece of wood is rubbed rapidly up and down in a groove in another piece until the wood dust ignites.

The native Australians used another method of lighting fires by friction. A slender wood rod is held vertically between the palms of the hands and rotated in a hole in a second piece of wood until the dust is ignited. A variation of this method involves a flexible stick about 18 inches long with one end pressed against the chest (suitably protected, of course) and the other end pointed into a hole in a piece of wood. The curved part is then turned rapidly like a carpenter's drill. The Eskimos had an even more efficient tool for firemaking. It consisted of a bow, much like that used to shoot arrows. One turn of the bow string is passed around a round stick and the stick is placed vertically into a hole in a piece of wood. The top of the stick is supported by a hole in a second piece of wood. The stick can be made to rotate very rapidly by moving the bow back and forth until the particles of wood ignite.

Many scientists believe that fire was the magic that led man to supremacy of the earth. It enabled him to cook his meat, which shortens the digestive process. It is suspected that he burned forests to extend his pastures for grazing herds. It is also possible that he set fire to grasslands to stampede herds of wild animals. Of the great herds of grazing animals that lived in America during the last Ice Age, not a single animal remains: the American elephants, camels, and long-horned bison are all extinct. Scientists suspect that not all of them were killed by primitive weapons—that fire played its part in their extinction.

Fire also led to ceramic pottery and the refining of metals, all vital steps in human ascendency. One measure of civilization is the number of materials that man has learned to manipulate. Early man made do with a few. Today, man has stepped far up the temperature ladder and uses fire to extract, alter, or synthesize a great number of substances. It is hard to visualize a civilized culture without fire.

How does a sailboat move into the wind?

In the hands of a skilled helmsman, a sail can deflect the wind in such a way that the resulting force propels the boat partly into the wind. Before we look into this matter, however, it will be helpful to discuss a simpler problem.

Suppose we consider an airplane traveling due east at 100

116

miles an hour, as shown in the accompanying diagram. We can represent the plane's velocity as a line of a specific length drawn in a direction defined as easterly. The length of the line represents the speed of the plane, and the direction of the line represents the direction in which the plane is flying. Such a line is called a *vector* and is shown by the line *OA* in the diagram. Now suppose the plane encounters a cross wind moving northerly at 50 miles per hour. We can represent the wind's velocity as another vector, *OC,* with a length equal to half that of the plane's forward speed—because the cross wind's velocity is just half that of the plane. The direction of the cross-wind vector makes an angle of just 90 degrees to the plane's velocity vector, be-

Fig. 11.   Vector quantities. The plane's forward velocity is represented by an arrow, *OA,* whose length is proportional to the speed (100 mph) and whose direction corresponds to the direction of the velocity (east). The cross-wind vector (arrow), *OC,* represents that velocity in the same way. The so-called resultant vector, *OB,* gives the actual speed and direction of the plane's flight with respect to the earth.

cause the two directions, north and east, are 90 degrees apart. The two vectors *OA* and *OC* combine, as shown in the diagram, to produce the diagonal *OB,* which is called *resultant* of the two vectors. The resultant vector represents graphically the actual speed and direction of the plane's motion: 112 miles an hour at a direction 27 degrees north of due east.

Vectors, therefore, give scientists a way of solving problems that deal with quantities having direction as well as magnitude. Velocity and force are typical examples of such quantities. Whenever we use the term *force,* for example, a definite direction is always implied for that force. Weight is a force that always acts toward the center of the earth. When we push a stalled automobile, we are careful to push in the direction in which the wheels are aimed. By drawing vectors to scale on a piece of paper—being careful to maintain the correct angles—scientists can solve complex problems either graphically or mathematically.

Vectors can also help us understand why a sailboat can sail into the wind. The accompanying diagram shows a sailboat headed partly into the wind. The sail is placed so that the wind is deflected generally toward the stern of the boat. The force on the sail, represented by the vector *OA,* is always in a direction at right angles of the sail. This vector, *OA,* can be thought of as the resultant of two force

Fig. 12. Tacking of a sailboat. Through appropriate design, a sailboat can appear to circumvent the laws of motion by sailing partlv into the wind.

vectors—*OB* directed toward the bow of the boat, and *OC* at right angles to the boat. The vector *OB* tends to push the boat in its forward direction, while *OC* tends to make it slip sideways. The two vectors *OB* and *OC* work literally at cross purposes, and which one wins out depends on the design of the boat.

The forces tending to impede the motion of a sailboat are frictional. The friction in the forward direction is made as low as possible by streamlining the hull. The sideways friction, however, is made very high by adding a keel of large area to the bottom of the boat. The vector force *OC* must push against this large keel area, so motion in the sideways direction is relatively low. The forward vector, *OB,* encoun-

118

ters a very much lower frictional force, so forward speed is relatively high.

By positioning the sail and boat at appropriate angles to the wind, the boat can be made to sail partly into the wind. This process, called *tacking,* makes it possible for sailing vessels to navigate between any two seaports regardless of the direction of the wind.

Can a person reduce his or her blood pressure by mental means?

An exciting new field of psychology—called biofeedback—has begun to change some ideas about how the human body functions. It has always been assumed that certain body processes, such as blood pressure and heart rate, are not subject to voluntary human control. The term *autonomic nervous system* describes such activities of the body. *Autonomic* means "self-run," or "outside voluntary control." Although these processes are autonomic in everyday living, we now know that we can exert a measure of control over them with the help of biofeedback.

When a person hears words with a high emotional content, such as *sex, rape,* and *murder,* the heart rate speeds up—demonstrating that thought processes can indeed control the behavior of a body function that is supposed to operate automatically.

Biofeedback training is a technique in which a machine monitors a biological function, such as blood pressure or brain waves, and the subject observes or is told what the machine is indicating. In this way, data about blood pressure, for example, are fed back to the subject's mind. The subject then tries to control the body in order to reduce or change the reading. The subject comes to know what it feels like when the blood pressure is high and when it is low. After some practice, the subject learns to control blood pressure and heart rate. No one knows how this is done, but biofeedback experiments are showing considerable success in reducing blood pressure—sometimes by as much as 25 percent.

Another area of biofeedback research is associated with *alpha waves.* The brain generates electrical signals that can be measured on the scalp by a recording instrument called the *electroencephalograph* (EEG). When a person is awake but relaxed, the instrument often indicates an alpha wave, a slowly changing electrical signal. Studies show that yoga meditation produces alpha waves that grow stronger as

119

the degree of meditation grows deeper. If a subject is in a state of deep meditation, the alpha wave cannot be affected by outside stimulation. This is remarkable, because the wave ordinarily speeds up when we are surrounded by activity. Using this technique, therefore, we can truly escape from the world around us. With biofeedback, a person can learn when he is generating alpha waves and when he is not. With training, he can learn to generate them without assistance. Persons generating deep alpha waves are relaxed and calm and have a feeling of well-being.

Skeptical scientists performed an experiment to find out if there was really a connection between alpha waves and the subjective state of well-being. Using a control group of subjects in their study, they fed back incorrect information about their alpha waves. These subjects were never able to reach a state of well-being. So the whole business of meditation and alpha waves is more than hocus-pocus.

A great number of biofeedback courses and pieces of related equipment have been offered to the public in recent years. While such training seems to be useful, many commercial claims are not based on fact. One should exert the same prudence in using these new techniques that one would use in selecting a physician.

What is geothermal energy?

Early explorers of California discovered an awesome canyon that they described as "the gate of hell." About 90 miles north of San Francisco, this hill-rimmed valley is dotted with great plumes of hissing steam that escape from holes in the ground and shoot skyward. Californians call this valley "The Geysers," despite the fact that the steam vents are not really geysers. Nevertheless, the vents are of great importance in this era of energy shortages because they provide the United States with its only geothermal power plant.

The term *geothermal* literally means "earth heat," and geothermal areas are those areas where underground heat is great enough and sufficiently close to the surface to provide a usable source of energy. When water comes into a geothermal area, steam may escape to the surface from natural fractures or holes. Such steam vents are called *fumaroles*, from the Latin word *fumarolium*, which means "smokehole."

These geothermal "hot spots" are usually located in zones of volcanic activity—which is not too surprising, since volcanoes produce the most dramatic examples of natural heat and steam. Many earth scientists believe that much of the heat in a geothermal area comes from natural radioactivity in the earth's crust. In some areas the supply of heat is greater than normal, or the overlying rocks may serve as good insulators in preventing the heat's escape. In these subsurface "hot spots," temperatures are much higher than average.

Most geothermal areas fall into one of two classes: hot-spring systems or deep insulated reservoirs. Two famous hot-spring systems are located in Yellowstone National Park, Wyoming, and Wairakei, New Zealand. These areas contain an underground network of interconnected channels within the rock, and a supply of water from rain or snow seeping into the ground. When the water reaches a hot region, it expands and rises, being pushed along by the colder and heavier water that is entering the system. The hot water eventually shows up as hot springs or geysers.

Typical examples of deep insulated reservoirs are found in Larderello, Italy, and the Salton Sea area of California. These deep water reservoirs are capped with impermeable rock strata that prevent or greatly reduce the upward flow of water, steam, and heat. Both these reservoirs have only feeble hot springs at the surface.

Geothermal energy has been harnessed in a number of places. In Iceland, natural steam is used to heat buildings and agricultural fields by means of a system of steam pipes. Such steam was first used to generate electricity at Larderello in 1904, and Italy still leads the world in this application. New Zealand, Japan, and the U.S.S.R. also produce power from geothermal systems, and such applications are growing.

It is estimated that geothermal steam fields in the United States comprise over one million acres in California, New Mexico, Nevada, Montana, and Idaho. One field in California—the Imperial Valley—extends for some 2000 miles and contains water heated as high as 700°F. Scientists believe it could supply all of the electrical needs of southern California.

Most geothermal areas are not apparent at the surface unless they "leak" steam or hot water through various defects in the overlying rock. The most promising fields are thought to have their hot water locked tightly in the rocks and so are not easy to locate. Geologists are developing new techniques to find such geothermal areas because of the great importance attached to developing new energy sources.

Greater use has not been made of nature's geothermal energy because of the expense and difficulty of drilling steam wells. Another

121

problem is presented by the acidity of most natural steam, which tends to corrode pipelines and equipment. Steam also presents a disposal problem when the power plant is finished with it. Nevertheless, the world's geothermal areas are potential sites of enormous amounts of energy that can no longer be ignored. Future decades should see expanded use of this important energy resource.

Why does plastic furniture deteriorate when left outdoors?

Many plastics that are normally used in outside locations, such as those used in furniture, signs, tarpaulins, carpeting, and auto seat covers, must be protected from sunlight to avoid deterioration. Ultraviolet light has sufficient energy to break some of the chemical bonds holding the giant plastic molecules together. The polypropylene webbing of lawn chairs is particularly susceptible to such damage. The result is short life and high ultimate cost to the consumer.

There are other molecules, however, that absorb ultraviolet light and convert it to heat, thereby preventing the light from breaking bonds in the plastic. Such substances are added to high-quality plastic materials (about one-tenth of one percent by weight) to make them less sensitive to sunlight. Typical materials used for this purpose are 2-hydroxybenzophenone-type compounds. Unfortunately, few plastics intended for outdoor use contain sufficient quantities of such ultraviolet absorbers to prevent decay. The consumer would do well to purchase only those plastic items guaranteed for outdoor use. Failing that, the useful life of plastics can be extended by taking them out of direct sunlight when they are not in use.

Do suntan lotions prevent sunburn?

Suntan lotions do not provide complete protection against sunburn. They merely extend the length of time a person can remain in the sun before severe sunburn occurs.

The short-wavelength ultraviolet light from the sun is particularly harmful to white skin. In the past, various lotions were used to screen out as much of the ultraviolet light as possible. The modern theory is to exclude the shorter, more harmful wavelengths while letting enough of the long-wave ultraviolet through to permit gradual tanning. Some lotions, in fact, include ingredients that essentially dye the skin a tan color.

Tanning by the sun, as opposed to dyeing, takes place because sunlight stimulates the skin to produce the pigment *melanin*. This is the same brown-black pigment present in dark hair. While melanin is being produced in skin, the skin also becomes thicker and more resistant to sunburn.

The pain of sunburn is relieved somewhat by preparations containing a local anesthetic, such as benzocaine, and a skin softener such as lanolin. By softening the tissue, lanolin helps the flow of anesthetic and blood plasma to the sunburned regions.

Why are satellites placed in orbit by multistage rockets?

One reason is efficiency. Once a large fuel tank is empty, it can be left behind, so less fuel is then needed to place the reduced payload in orbit.

Fig. 13.   A projectile, fired at point *A*, cannot achieve an orbit around the earth.

A more fundamental reason for using multistage rockets has to do with the nature of orbits. A single-stage rocket that is not capable of subsequent maneuvers cannot go into an orbit around the earth. It is not possible, for example, to shoot a projectile into orbit no matter how powerful the gun. A glance at the accompanying diagram shows why that is so. If a rocket is fired at an angle to the earth, its path must be elliptical just as for any orbiting object. Because the rocket was launched from the surface of the earth, every possible elliptical orbit will always intersect the earth's surface. A rocket launched at *A* will rise to *B* and then fall back into the earth at *C*.

In order to avoid this rather unpleasant ending, the rocket's trajectory must be altered so that its elliptical orbit does not intersect the earth. The easiest way to do this is to wait until the rocket reaches the highest point in its orbit, *B,* and then fire a second rocket. The increased velocity at that point changes the trajectory and sends the rocket into a new elliptical orbit that will not intersect the earth. The precise orbit attained depends on the rocket's speed at point B, the duration of the second rocket firing, and other factors. If the orbit achieved is not precisely the one desired, subsequent brief firings of the rocket engine can make minor corrections in the orbit.

By the way, if you are wondering what happens if a rocket is shot straight up, there are just two possibilities: it may fall back to earth at the starting point; or—if its speed exceeds 25,300 miles per hour on takeoff—it will escape from the earth's gravitational field and wander forever in deep space.

How was writing discovered?

One of the greatest steps ever taken by the human mind was the invention of writing, a development that occurred in southern Mesopotamia just before 3000 B.C. Many scholars believe that this discovery was made by the Sumerians, who lived in the region where the Tigris and Euphrates rivers meet in what is now Iraq. Sumerians had a strong sense of private ownership of property, so they routinely identified their possessions—especially those given to the gods as offerings. It was this characteristic of Sumerian culture that led to writing.

Each Sumerian of means had a personal mark that was engraved on a cylindrical seal not unlike a very small rolling pin. The seals were rolled out on soft, moist clay and allowed to dry. The impression could then be attached to an object as a label of ownership. Similar identifying markers were used for cities and temples. In time, these markers became names that could be pronounced. From proper names, the symbols were extended to stand for important objects, to words in general, and finally to complete sentences.

An illustration may help to show just how this transformation took place. The symbols used were developed from *pictograms,* pictures of the object they stood for. After about two centuries of development, each symbol came to stand for the simple *sound value* of the word it represented, as well as for the original word itself. If the same method were used in English, the pictogram for the surname "Penn" could also be used for "pen" (a writing instrument), or "pen" (an enclosure), or for the syllable "pen" in *pen*cil. Once symbols came to stand for the sound value of syllables, writing was liberated from mere word painting and became a flexible way of recording speech and thought.

The use of separate pictograms for words or syllables is a complicated procedure that requires a key, or dictionary, to provide speed and precision. In Mesopotamia, the key consisted of lists of objects and beings that were arranged in a systematic way. These aids to reading and writing contained lists of fishes, birds, animals, plants, tools, weapons, and the like. In effect, these early Sumerian lists of objects were the first steps in a scientific approach to botany, zoology, mathematics, mineralogy, and so on. It turns out that many of our current botanical terms first appeared in Sumerian cuneiform lists. Cuneiform, by the way, comes from the Latin for wedge, *cuneus,* because of the wedge-shaped symbols impressed on clay tablets. Our words such as chicory, cumin, crocus, hyssop, and saffron all come to us from Mesopotamia.

The next great stride in writing took place sometime about 1600 B.C. with the change from syllables to an alphabet. This second invention occurred somewhere along the eastern shores of the Mediterranean Sea. The use of a single symbol to represent an isolated sound greatly reduces the number of characters required for writing and simplifies any system of reading and writing. One of the earlier alphabets, called the Ugaritic script, used only thirty-two signs. Its letter forms were borrowed from the earlier cuneiform writing. Another early alphabet is the Sinaitic, which developed its symbols from Egyptian hieroglyphics.

The Greeks, in adopting an alphabetic system, made a final important contribution: earlier alphabets only represented consonants, but the Greeks used additional signs to stand for vowels. This, of course, is a standard feature of all modern alphabets.

In Mesopotamia, as in all early literate cultures, writing was done by trained scribes, who made up an important professional group. They were trained in temple or palace schools, where the main method of learning was the copying of various texts. In fact, a good part of all the literature that survives consists of school exercises. And since scribes were often multilingual, an enormous number of two-language word lists have come down to us. Such lists are invaluable in deciphering other written languages.

What is cancer?

If a part of the liver in a man or animal is removed surgically, the liver cells begin to divide into new cells until the organ regains its normal size and shape. The liver possesses a kind of growth control; the generation of new cells comes to an end as soon as the normal dimensions of the organ are reached. Cancer cells, however, do not obey any laws of growth control; they continue to divide and produce new cancer cells until they replace the cells of vital organs of the body. Scientists do not know why the surgically altered liver stops growing when it does, or why cancer cells continue to divide without stopping.

Cancer is not just one disease affecting a single kind of cell in the body. It may, in fact, be as many as a hundred diseases if we consider the many kinds of tissues that can be affected. Scientists believe that cells become cancerous when body controls that normally restrain cell division become defective. The nature of these controls, unfortunately, is still a mystery. It is known, however, that four general kinds of factors often trigger conversion of normal cells to cancer cells. These are heredity, certain chemicals, radiation, and certain viruses. In most cases of heredity-induced cancer, the disease itself is not inherited. Instead, there exists a higher than normal tendency to develop certain types of cancer if certain trigger factors are encountered.

Cancer cells arise from normal cells in the body. In the early stages of the disease, the cells look much like those from which they originated. Gradually, their appearance changes and they lose their identity. Still later, they fail to respond to cell-to-cell contact and lose their orientation to one another. Whereas normal cells are usually arranged in orderly layers, or sheets, the cancer cells pile up helter-skelter, and chaos replaces the original orderly arrangement.

It is erroneously believed that cancer cells divide more rapidly than normal cells, but the two kinds of cell division require approximately the same length of time. This makes it possible for scientists to determine the number of cancer cells in an animal at any given time during an experiment. A single leukemia cell injected into a healthy mouse divides into two cells, and the two into four, and so on, about once a day or sooner. About fifteen days later, the cancer cells number about one billion and the mouse dies. To save the mouse, a method must be found that kills the cells faster than they can reproduce. This approach has had some success with mouse leukemia and a limited number of other cancer types. The treatment must meet two requirements. First, it must kill the cancer cells throughout the body without harming normal ones. Second, it must kill every cancer cell; even a single cancer cell left alive after treatment would permit the cancer to spread again.

Cancer cells are often moved from original sites to other parts of the body by the blood and lymph. Once they arrive in such new locations, they reproduce to form secondary cancerous growths called *metastases*. Each of these secondary sites can "seed" additional growths, and soon the body is riddled with cancer. Because of this uncontrolled reproduction and metastatic growth, cancer cells are often referred to as *malignant*.

Medical science now uses three general methods of treating cancer, often in combination. If cancer cells remain localized, it is often possible to remove all of them by surgery. Surgery is less effective, however, when the disease has progressed to a metastatic condition, because it is then extremely difficult to remove every single cancer cell.

Another form of treatment, *chemotherapy*, employs drugs that make use of the fact that cancer cells are continually undergoing cell division. Most of these drugs selectively kill cells that are reproducing without permanently affecting normal, nonreproducing cells. Unfortunately, none of the drugs yet discovered kills all types of cancer cells or discriminates perfectly between cancer cells and normal cells.

Cancer is also treated by *radiation therapy*. Cells undergoing reproduction are more sensitive to radiation-induced damage than are normal cells that are not reproducing. Radiation therapy is most effective when the cancer cells are localized. If they are distributed throughout the body, radiation therapy often cannot be used because of the many normal cells that would be destroyed by the treatment.

What is gravity?

In the seventeenth century, the great English scientist Sir Isaac Newton developed a mathematical equation that accounts for the motion of the moon around earth. Its great importance, however, is that the equation applies to any pair of objects. His universal theory of gravitation shows that every planet must follow an elliptical orbit. In recent years it has been used to predict the motions of artificial satellites both of the earth and of the moon. It has also been used to account for the motions of pairs of stars (binary stars) that revolve around one another. Scientists are convinced that every object in the universe obeys the gravitational law discovered by Newton.

It is clear that gravity is the force that maintains the earth and the planets in their orbits around the sun, but what is gravity, and how does it work? Scientists draw a fine distinction at this point. They are quite comfortable with the task of describing *how* nature behaves, but it is quite a different matter to wonder *why* it behaves in that particular way. A scientist can only ask how; a philosopher may ask *why*.

Newton's theory tells us that the force of gravity is proportional to the product of the two masses and inversely proportional to the square of the distance between them. The first part of the law tells us that the gravitational force increases as the masses increase. The second part indicates that the force falls off quite fast as the objects are moved farther apart. A doubling of the distance of separation, for example, reduces the force to one-quarter of its initial figure.

In the three centuries since Newton worked out his theory of gravitation, it has been modified only once—by Albert Einstein. That modification applies only when objects are moving at velocities close to the speed of light. For all everyday applications, Newton's law is still a correct description of how nature behaves. Science simply cannot answer, in any fundamental way, why gravity works the way it does. All it can hope to do is give a precise description of how it works.

From time to time you may find reference to a gravitational field in newspaper accounts of research on gravity. This concept was invented about a century ago as an aid in describing how gravity behaves. Scientists say that the earth, for example, sets up a condition in space (called a *gravitational field*) to which another object, such as the moon, responds by experiencing a force of attraction. The strength of the field is proportional to the mass of the object, and it decreases with distance in just the same way that Newton's force did. The field is strong near a large mass, such as the earth, and quite weak far out in space.

In a sense, the invention of the gravitational field has accomplished little: we have merely substituted a mysterious field for a mysterious force acting at a distance. The advantage to scientists is that the field concept handles complex problems with simpler mathematics than does the gravitational force directly. It is important to understand that the field concept takes us no closer to an understanding of what gravity is and why it behaves in a particular way.

Why are coral atolls always ring-shaped islands?

Coral atolls, those ring-shaped islands that surround a lagoon, are made up of the skeletons of innumerable marine animals. That much has been known almost as long as western European seafarers have made their way into distant tropical seas. But how did the islands form, and why do they surround a lagoon? Such questions have been the subject of intense discussion among geologists for almost a century and a half. Scientists now believe they have the answers.

In the early nineteenth century, Charles Darwin was assigned as a naturalist aboard the H.M.S. *Beagle*, a 98-foot-long brig carrying seventy-four people. The ship circumnavigated the earth, and the expedition is best known for the zoological observations that Darwin made on the trip. The knowledge gained contributed to the theory of evolution advanced in Darwin's *The Origin of Species*.

On the voyage of the *Beagle*, Darwin noticed that the coral reefs he encountered were of three kinds: fringing reefs, barrier reefs, and atolls. He further concluded that the three kinds were related to one another in a logical sequence, as shown in the accompanying diagram. He believed that a reef proceeds through a natural succession of forms from a fringing reef (adjacent to the shore of an island), to a barrier reef (surrounding an island but farther off shore), and finally to an

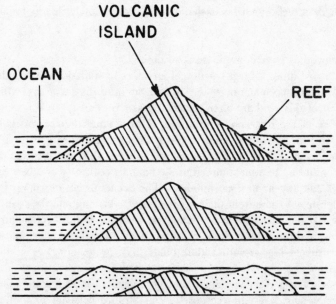

Fig. 14. The evolution of an atoll. Top: A fringing reef circles a volcanic island. Middle: The reef evolves into a barrier reef as the island begins to sink. Bottom: An atoll is left after the island disappears beneath the surface of the ocean.

atoll, in which the central island is missing. He further believed that the succession from one reef type to another could be explained if coral grows vertically from a sinking island. When the central island disappears completely, only a reef-enclosed lagoon, or atoll, would be left.

If Darwin's theory is correct, and the reef foundation sinks as the coral builds up, then atolls should rest upon many hundreds of feet of coral material, all of which grew in shallow waters. In 1881, Darwin suggested that drilling a vertical hole through a reef would be the best test of his theory. In 1951–52, deep holes were drilled on Eniwetok Atoll in the Pacific. The deepest measured 4556 feet, went through about 4000 feet of shallow-water reef coral, and bottomed in basalt rock, a typical Pacific volcanic rock. Scientists deduced from the age of the fossils taken from the hole that Eniwetok Atoll has been growing upward for the past 60 million years! The base of the atoll has been subsiding beneath the surface at a rate varying from about 50 to 167 feet per million years. There seems little doubt that many if not all atolls have been formed just as Darwin theorized, through the upgrowth of reef organisms in shallow water on a slowly sinking foundation.

Do animals ever commit mass suicide?

At times, a large fraction of an animal population may suddenly leave its normal range and spread out into distant areas. Movements of this kind are often referred to as *irruptions*.

One of the best-known examples of an animal that irrupts is the brown lemming of the Arctic regions. These small rodents fluctuate in numbers on a three- to four-year cycle. During this period their numbers build up to a maximum and the animals begin to leave their burrows and appear in great numbers. The Scandinavian lemmings then emigrate en masse from their home range, swarming into the countryside like an invading army. They cross roads, jostle through farmyards, and fall into ditches, and many drown in lakes, rivers, and the sea. An old Norwegian folktale holds that the lemmings leave their homes and swim out to sea in order to find the "lost continent of Atlantis!" There is no agreement among biologists concerning the matter of mass suicide or the reasons for this strange behavior of the lemming. Food may be abundant, but the lemmings cease to feed. Some biologists suspect the behavior is connected with stress produced by too great a population. Whatever the reason may be, some of the lemmings do not take part in the mass movement and survive to start the population cycle over again.

Irruptions such as those of the lemming are quite different from migrations. The term *migration* is usually reserved to cover movements of a regular or periodic kind in which the animals return to the site of their birth or hatching. It involves a round trip that is often of a seasonal nature but may require a lifetime to complete. Irruptions, on the other hand, are a kind of aimless wandering in which a return to the home site would be highly unlikely.

Perhaps the most spectacular irruptions on record have consisted of great swarms of locusts. In the northeast of Tanganyika, now Tanzania, on January 29, 1929, a swarm of the desert locust irrupted near the port of Ranga. The swarm was a mile wide and 100 feet deep and took nine hours to pass a given point. It was estimated that the swarm consisted of about 10 billion locusts.

Why does the freezing of water burst a water pipe?

The explanation of the bursting of water pipes in cold weather comes down in the end to the shape and nature of the water molecule. As we know, a molecule of water consists of two atoms of hydrogen and one atom of oxygen. Its chemical formula, H_2O, tells the same story: H stands for hydrogen and O for oxygen, and the subscript 2 indicates the number of hydrogen atoms in the water molecule.

A matter of crucial importance to the problem of frozen pipes is how the atoms of H_2O are arranged in space. There are four possibilities. Two are in a straight line:

$$H-H-O \text{ and } H-O-H$$

and two are at an angle:

All other arrangements are merely variations of these four structures. Chemists have determined that the angular arrangement best fits the experimental evidence and that the angle is about 105 degrees, slightly greater than a right angle, which is 90 degrees. They also know that oxygen must be located at the apex of the angle, like this:

The lines in the diagram between the hydrogen and oxygen atoms each represent a pair of electrons being shared by the atoms, and these electrons spend most of their time somewhere between the two atoms. It is this sharing of electrons, in fact, that holds the molecule together. The reasoning goes something like this:

An oxygen atom has eight electrons arranged in two layers or shells, with a positively charged center, or *nucleus*. Two of the eight electrons tend to stay relatively close to the nucleus and do not involve themselves with other atoms. The remaining six, however, move about in an outer shell looking for companionship. Because eight electrons is the number that will satisfy this need for "companionship," oxygen tries to find an additional pair of electrons somewhere. Each hydrogen atom has one electron, and this one also seeks to join with other electrons. So the six outer, or *valence,* electrons of the oxygen atom and two electrons of hydrogen atoms join up to form a group of eight. Naturally, they bring the rest of the three atoms along with them.

For reasons that are not really understood, electrons have a strong tendency to form pairs—and four pairs seem to provide a particularly favored condition. So the two electrons from the hydrogen atoms and the six from oxygen join forces to form four pairs of electrons. Chemical bonds that result from electron sharing of this kind are called *covalent bonds.*

Finally, to complete the picture of the water molecule, the oxygen atom has a stronger attraction for the shared electrons than do the hydrogen atoms. In other words, the negatively charged electrons are not distributed equally among the three atoms but tend to favor the oxygen end of the molecule. It turns out that the oxygen atom in a water molecule is a bit more negatively charged, and the hydrogen atoms a bit more positively charged, than would be the case if all atoms shared the negative charges equally. Molecules such as water, which have an uneven electrical charge distribution, are said to be *polar molecules.*

The polarized nature of the water molecule leads to several very important properties. Most other molecules that are similar in size and weight to the water molecule are gases at room temperature and normal atmospheric pressure. Water is a liquid under these conditions because the negative (oxygen) end of its molecule attracts the positive (hydrogen) end of a different water molecule, and the process is repeated many times over to build up a sort of network of large water

Fig. 15. Water molecules consist of one oxygen atom, O, and two hydrogen atoms, H, connected in the diagram by solid lines. Such molecules are joined together at low temperature by hydrogen bonds, symbolized by three dots. As water freezes, hydrogen bonding of water molecules causes them to move farther apart on the average, and the water expands on freezing.

molecules. Under ordinary conditions, this prevents water from being a gas like carbon dioxide or oxygen.

The attractive force between one water molecule and another is called a hydrogen bond. The hydrogen bond is a kind of "bridge" between two molecules (or between two places on the same molecule if it is big enough to fold back on itself). The strength of a hydrogen bond is about one-tenth to one-fifteenth that of an ordinary covalent bond involving shared electron pairs.

In order to get liquid water to evaporate, the hydrogen bonds between water molecules must be broken to obtain single H_2O molecules, which can then leave the surface as a gas. The bonds can be broken by adding energy to the liquid water. We can do this by heating a pan of water on a stove. This explains why washed clothing dries more quickly in warm sunlight than in shade.

Water is one of the few substances that expands upon freezing. As liquid water cools, the molecules have less energy and tend to slow down. When that happens, all the water molecules begin to attach themselves to their neighbors to form a very large interlocking network of molecules. This tends to open up the molecular structure to make the ice less dense than water. To illustrate how this can happen, imagine a room full of people that are milling about. Now imagine that they are told to hold hands, with their arms out at a 45-degree angle. Clearly, the crowd would have to become less dense because of its expanded structure, just as water does when it becomes hydrogen-bonded during freezing. The accompanying diagram illustrates how hydrogen bonding tends to spread the molecules apart.

The expansion of water on freezing also explains why ice floats. Since ice is less dense than water, it floats just as wood and cork do.

What are white dwarfs, pulsars, and black holes?

Astronomers use these terms to describe stars that are dying. Stars generate light by converting hydrogen to helium, a process that gives off enormous amounts of energy as a by-product. This energy shows up, in part, as light, which makes the stars visible. Each second, the sun converts about 5 million tons of hydrogen into energy. Obviously, such a process cannot go on forever. Sooner or later the hydrogen supply begins to run out and the star expands and becomes a *red giant*. Much later its luminosity decreases to perhaps one percent of the sun's luminosity, the star gets much smaller in size, and it is classified as a white dwarf, or a collapsed star.

Perhaps the most astonishing characteristic of white dwarfs is their small size and great mass. Sirius B, the first white dwarf found by astronomers, in 1862, has a mass about equal to that of the sun. But its diameter is more nearly equal to that of the earth. This means that Sirius B is made up of very dense material indeed—so dense, in fact, that a tablespoon of its matter would weigh thousands of tons on the earth!

What kind of matter can this be that has a density a million times greater than water? We have no such substance on earth. Scientists explain this paradox by reminding us that ordinary atoms consist mostly of empty space. A typical atom contains a nucleus surrounded by orbiting electrons, much as the planets orbit around the sun. Only a tiny portion of the atom's volume is occupied by solid particles. In the gases that make up the interior of a white dwarf, the atoms have been almost completely stripped of electrons. Under these conditions, the nuclei and free electrons can be packed into an incredibly small space compared with the volume occupied by a normal atom. Hence, the density—or weight per unit volume—of the material is enormously greater than anything we find on earth.

Not all stars, it turns out, end up as white dwarfs. Stars with a mass above a certain limit take a rather different evolutionary route. The limit, called the *Chandrasekhar limit* after Subrahmanyan Chandrasekhar, the scientist who calculated it, is approximately 1.2 times the mass of the sun.

If a collapsing star exceeds the Chandrasekhar mass limit, densities greater than 100 million times that of water can be achieved. Under these conditions, negatively charged electrons are forced onto positively charged protons, and neutrons are formed. These particles are only slightly more massive than protons but are electrically neutral. The matter in the star is now even more closely packed than in a white dwarf. A tablespoonful would weigh several billion tons on earth! The result is a *neutron star,* and in some cases a special type of neutron star called a *pulsar.* Although a neutron star's mass is not too different from that of the sun, it has a diameter of only 6 to 12 miles.

The term *pulsar* was devised to describe neutron stars whose electromagnetic radiation (such as radio signals) varies in intensity. The term was unfortunate, however, because such stars do not actually pulsate. The periodic variation of their signals is a result of their incredibly rapid periods of rotation, ranging from about one-third of a second to about 4 seconds. Discovery of the first pulsar was announced in 1968, and only a few score have been discovered to date.

Most neutron stars, including pulsars, reach a condition of stability when they stop collapsing in size. But if a neutron star's mass exceeds twice that of the sun, it continues to contract in size—with astonishing results. The star becomes so small (only several miles in diameter), and its gravitational attraction so strong, that even light is unable to escape. Such a star is called a *black hole.* Theory tells us that it has essentially zero volume and infinite density. It is black because no light can escape. Its enormous gravitational attraction swallows up any material that enters the space around it.

At this writing, black holes have been described mathematically but have not been shown conclusively to exist in space. In 1978, however, a team of British and American astronomers found what it believes to be the best evidence yet for the existence of a black hole. It is about five times as massive as the sun but smaller than the city of London. The black hole is orbiting about a visible star known as V-861 in the constellation Scorpius, some 6000 light-years from earth. X rays coming from the black hole have been studied in detail and timed accurately. Based on their findings, the scientists believe they have found a good candidate for a black hole.

Do jails prevent crime?

Psychologists tell us that there is no evidence that supports the idea that jails and prisons prevent crime; the evidence, in fact, indicates that they foster crime. Studies with animals suggest strongly that punishment brings little improvement in the animal's behavior. Instead, the animal keeps behaving in much the same way, despite punishment. Even children who are punished make few attempts to correct their behavior.

Laboratory studies with animals do show that punishment tends to discourage certain behavior, but it does not change the behavior permanently. Rather, as soon as the punishment wears off, the unwanted behavior pops up again as strong as ever. The fact that ex-convicts often return to criminal activities after serving a jail sentence (called *recidivism*) shows the parallel between animal and human behavior with regard to punishment. Regardless of the reasons for this recidivism, punishment alone is a poor deterrent.

Punishment can be effective in moderation when combined with a system of rewards. In other words, mild punishment of an unwanted behavior along with a reward for other desirable behavior can be effective in modifying behavior patterns. The rewarded action seems to take over and replace the punished one. From a practical point of view, reward seems to be more effective than punishment in changing behavior.

Why do we have day and night?

We were taught in school that day and night are a result of the earth spinning on its axis so that a given place on its surface passes through periods of sunlight and shadow during a twenty-four-hour period. A more fundamental question might be "Why does the earth spin on its axis?"

A clue to the earth's rotation is related to how the sun and other stars were formed. Astronomers believe that the sun and the planets began as a slowly rotating ball of gas about the size of the solar system. As it contracted, under the influence of gravitational attraction, it began to spin progressively faster—much as the spin of an ice skater speeds up when he draws in his arms. As the cloud of gas speeded up, a disk of material was ejected from the equatorial regions of the cloud, rather like droplets of water flying off a rotating bicycle wheel. The lighter elements, such as hydrogen, would have moved outward to the edges of the disk, while the heavier elements, such as iron, carbon, and nickel, remained closer to the center. It is from this spinning disk that the planets apparently formed. The large, light planets such as Jupiter and Saturn formed out of the large quantity of lighter elements near the edge of the disk, and the smaller denser planets, such as the earth and Mars, formed from the heavier elements nearer the sun. As the material in the spinning disk contracted to form the planets, a rotational motion was imparted to them, which gives rise to night and day on our planet.

Astronomers have calculated the age of the planets by measuring the degree to which radioactive substances, such as uranium, have decayed since the rocks formed. It turns out to be about 4½ billion years ago. So the earth is about half as old as the galaxy of stars that includes our sun, and about one-third the age of the universe.

How can a person protect himself in a thunderstorm?

No one is exactly sure of the number of lightning fatalities in the United States each year, but it has been estimated as high as 600 by some studies. In any event, more fatalities in a typical year are directly the result of lightning than of any other weather phenomenon. Most of these deaths occur outdoors.

If you are caught outdoors in a thunderstorm, there are a number of things you should *not* do. First of all, do not seek shelter under isolated trees. The greatest single cause of lightning deaths is standing under such a tree when it is struck by lightning. Many such victims are golfers. Also, do not stand above the surrounding landscape and make a lightning rod of yourself. Avoid open fields, beaches, and small boats on the water. Avoid small, isolated shelters such as those often found on golf courses. Do not stand under a lightning rod. Avoid all wire fences, rails, or other metallic paths that can carry lightning currents to you from a distant stroke. Stay out of the water, because a nearby stroke can send high currents through your body.

On the positive side, seek shelter in a large building, preferably one with a metal frame or lightning rod system. An automobile with a metal roof also provides good protection, but remember to roll up the windows. In open spaces, crouch in a ravine, valley, or low place in the terrain. In a forest, seek shelter in a thick growth of small trees.

If you are in a building without lightning rod protection, remember that lightning tends to follow water pipes and electrical wiring as it seeks a path to ground. Avoid using the telephone and stay away from fixtures connected to plumbing or appliances plugged into the house wiring system.

It is a good idea to have the mast of your TV antenna well connected to ground. If lightning is moving through such a conductor that is poorly grounded, it may leave the conductor and jump through the air to find a better path to ground. This trip through the air, or *side flash,* is responsible for many indoor lightning fatalities. The side flash is also one of the ways in which people are killed standing under trees. In a thunderstorm, it makes good sense to avoid sinks, appliances, bathtubs, or other objects that are connected in any way with the outside.

How does acupuncture relieve pain?

There seems to be little doubt, even in western medical circles, that the ancient practice of acupuncture can relieve pain under certain circumstances. Scientists are not sure, however, how this relief is achieved. Modern theories of acupuncture focus on both physiological and psychological factors. Acupuncture has been compared to hypnosis, or to pain relief produced by placebos—that is, to a patient's confidence in a medical procedure even though the procedure may be medically useless. Acupuncture has also been compared with direct electrical stimulation of certain places in the brain, which, when stimulated, prevent pain messages from reaching a patient's consciousness. These same places in the brain appear to be stimulated by certain narcotic drugs that also suppress pain.

Research performed at the National Institutes of Health and the Medical College of Virginia leads scientists to believe that acupuncture reduces pain by activating specific regions of the brain. An experiment was performed on thirty-five volunteers during a thirty-minute period. An electric current was gradually increased through the incisor teeth until pain was just recognized. Acupuncture was then performed in the web between the forefinger and thumb at the "Ho-Ku" point, which is believed to relieve toothaches. The electrical test was then repeated to determine if a stronger electric current was required to evoke pain. Scientists found that 27 percent more current was required after acupuncture to generate the same amount of pain. Thus, acupuncture produced a 27 percent increase in the threshold of pain.

The scientists then used a drug called naloxone to continue the experiment. Naloxone is known to counteract the effects of narcotic drugs such as morphine. Morphine, in turn, is thought to suppress pain by stimulating specific regions of the brain. In other words, a dose of naloxone will prevent morphine from performing its pain-killing function. Immediately after the acupuncture experiment described earlier, half the volunteers were given an injection of naloxone and the other half were given an injection of a salt solution, which would have no effect. Neither the doctors nor the patients knew who received which kind of injection. Subjects who received the saline had the same increased pain thresholds as before—acupuncture still acted as a pain suppressor. Subjects who received naloxone, on the other hand, were no longer benefited by acupuncture. This proved that naloxone counteracts the effects of acupuncture just as it does the effects of narcotic drugs. These results lead scientists to believe that both acupuncture and narcotics act on the same pain-inhibiting part of the brain, since naloxone counteracts both. Scientists suspect that acupuncture releases the newly discovered *enkephalin,* a pain-reducing morphine-like substance produced by the brain itself.

In contrast with acupuncture, related experiments show that hypnotism is more effective than acupuncture in reducing oral pain. Fourteen subjects were hypnotized and given the hypnotic suggestion that they would not feel pain. Tooth stimulation by electric current showed an average 85 percent improvement in pain threshold. Naloxone, however, did not reverse the pain-killing effect of hypnotic suggestion. So hypnotism must have a different mechanism than acupuncture, and is a more powerful method of relieving pain.

For which discovery did Albert Einstein receive the Nobel Prize?

The name of Albert Einstein has come to be synonymous with his theory of relativity in the minds of most scientists and laymen. And well it should, because relativity was a scientific breakthrough with few parallels in the history of science. His first paper on relativity was published in 1905, and in 1921 he received the greatest recognition a physicist can achieve, the Nobel Prize in physics. But the award was not for relativity—the subject was still too controversial and too little

Fig. 16. The photoelectric effect. Ultraviolet light (dotted lines) strikes a plate made of metal, such as zinc, and ejects electrons (solid lines) from the plate. Because it loses negatively charged electrons, the plate is left with a net positive charge.

appreciated. The prize was given instead for his explanation of the so-called photoelectric effect, which became the basis of our knowledge of the atom.

During the nineteenth century, scientists had become convinced that light travels in the form of waves, not unlike water waves. Then, toward the end of the century, certain experiments kept popping up that could not be explained by the wave theory of light. The accompanying diagram illustrates one such experiment. A plate of zinc metal is prepared by polishing it to remove the oxide layer that is normally found on its surface. The plate is now electrically neutral because the negative electrons just balance the positive charges contained in the

140

nuclei of the zinc atoms. It is then exposed to ultraviolet light, such as that contained in sunlight. Measurements then show that electrons are emitted by the zinc plate, which leaves it with a net positive charge. This phenomenon is called the *photoelectric effect*.

Scientists were troubled by the fact that ultraviolet light can eject electrons from zinc but ordinary visible light cannot. The only known difference between visible and ultraviolet light waves was the matter of its frequency (or wavelength). Frequency of light waves, like water waves, merely means the total number of waves that pass a fixed point in one second. Red light has the lowest frequency, and the other colors increase in frequency through orange, yellow, green, blue, and violet. Ultraviolet light is just outside the range of visibility and has a still higher frequency. Scientists could not explain why high-frequency ultraviolet light can eject electrons from zinc while low-frequency light cannot.

In addition to that mystery, physicists later found that different materials were sensitive to light of different frequencies. Cesium will eject electrons when illuminated by yellow light, but potassium and sodium require the higher frequency of green light. Zinc and most other metals require ultraviolet and even higher-frequency radiations. The reason behind these facts was completely unknown.

The final mystery had to do with the energy of the photoelectrons, the electrons given off by the photoelectric effect. It turns out that the energy contained by the electrons goes up directly with the frequency of the incident light. The higher the frequency, the higher the energy. And strangely enough, the energy of the photoelectrons depends *only* on the frequency and not at all on the intensity, or "brightness," of the radiation.

Try as they might, physicists could not tie all these observations together on the basis of the wave theory of light. Something new was needed, and it was supplied by Einstein.

Einstein's photoelectric theory tells us that light exists in the form of tiny oscillating bundles of electromagnetic energy. These light bundles are called *quanta,* or *photons.* When a multitude of photons act in concert, as they normally do, they join together and act as a wave. The frequency of oscillation of the photons becomes the frequency of the wave. On other occasions, an individual photon can revert to its bundle-of-energy status and act more or less as a particle. In the photoelectric effect, a photon interacts with an individual electron and not

141

with the whole piece of metal. The energy of the photon is transferred to the electron, and the electron is then able to break the bonds holding it to the metal and jump free. This ability of light to act both as a wave and as a particle is at the basis of modern physics.

Einstein went on to explain that the energy of a photon can be easily calculated by multiplying the frequency of the light by a number now known as *Planck's constant*—in honor of the German physicist Max Planck. In algebraic terms, (photon energy) = (photon frequency) × (Planck's constant). In order to eject an electron from a metal, the photon energy must exceed the binding energy that holds the electron captive. Different metals have different binding energies, which explains why each metal requires a certain minimum frequency of illumination before electrons can be knocked free. Now suppose the frequency of the radiation is increased still further. The photon energy now exceeds the amount needed to overcome the binding energy. Any excess is retained by the photoelectron. As the frequency is increased, therefore, the photoelectrons become more energetic.

Einstein's theory explained all the photoelectric observations that had long puzzled the scientific world. Even more important than that, the idea that light behaves as if it were discrete bundles of energy profoundly changed scientific thought and led to a new and comprehensive theory of atomic structure.

How do rivers form deltas?

Depending on their speed, river waters carry particles from the tiny size of clay particles up to pebbles and even cobbles. The faster streams wear away solid rock and carry along coarse particles at high speeds. Once in the stream, smaller particles are carried along in suspension. Larger particles move downstream at the bottom, where the force of the current pushes, rolls, and slides them along.

Eventually, all rivers stop when they empty into a large standing body of water. The mixing of water gradually transfers the energy of the river current to the surrounding water, and the current disappears. This is much like a billiard ball that loses its forward motion when shot into a cluster of balls on a pool table. Its motion is transferred to the more or less random movements of the other balls as they bounce off one another and the cushions, gradually coming to rest. The river current decays gradually, however, depending on its volume and speed. The world's largest river, the Amazon, was recently measured to discharge 4 billion gallons per minute. The current maintains its flow several miles out to sea. By way of contrast, small rivers may mix so rapidly with a turbulent coast that they stop flowing almost immediately.

The decay of river currents accounts for the formation of deltas. The dying current loses its ability to transport particles, and it deposits a series of sedimentary layers that make up the delta.The simplest deltas are formed where small streams enter fresh-water lakes. The current mixes in all directions in a conelike pattern and quickly slows to a halt. The largest particles are dropped first, followed by medium and fine particles farther out.

Deltas that form in the ocean are generally stretched out farther in the horizontal direction. This is because the fresh water of the river has a lower density than salt water—about 2 percent lower. The lighter river water tends to "float," or ride, above the sea water and consequently mixes with it horizontally but not vertically as in a fresh-water lake. The mixing rate, therefore, tends to be lower, so that coarse, medium, and fine particles spread out along a much longer path.

Great rivers, such as the Mississippi and the Nile, form large deltas thousands of square miles in area. The Mississippi delta has been growing in area and moving south for many millions of years. It started out around Cairo, Illinois, perhaps 100 million years ago and has advanced 1000 miles since then. The formation of the delta has helped shape the North American continent.

Many rivers, even some that carry large amounts of sediment, do not deposit deltas. Some enter the ocean at places where currents, waves, and tides combine to move the sediment away as rapidly as it is deposited by the river. Such processes move the river's sediment for great distances along the shore, sometimes for hundreds of miles. Some rivers form small deltas of coarse material; the finer material—most of the load—is carried away by currents and waves.

Whether or not rivers form deltas, they drop two kinds of load: the solid particles of soil and rock, and the dissolved salts from the land. The sediment load of the world's rivers adds up to a staggering 18 trillion tons per year. The salts carried in solution in river water add another 4 million tons per year.

What is the principle behind carbon-14 dating?

The principle of radiocarbon dating is the most important scientific technique to be applied to archaeological work in recent times. It was discovered by Professor Willard F. Libby at the University of

Chicago in the 1940s as a by-product of nuclear research. Professor Libby received the Nobel Prize in chemistry in 1960 for his discovery.

The value of radiocarbon dating lies in its ability to give absolute dates to organic substances, such as wood, charcoal, peat, bone, or antler, that are found in prehistoric graves and ruins. Its discovery made it possible for archaeologists to connect ancient artifacts with dates. Radiocarbon dating—or carbon-14 dating, as it is also known—is based on the principle that by measuring the radioactivity of a sample of organic matter, it is possible to estimate the number of elapsed years since the sample was alive.

Carbon-14 dating makes use of the fact that there are two kinds of carbon (called *isotopes*) in the carbon dioxide gas in our atmosphere. The "ordinary" kind is carbon-12, and the "heavy," or radioactive, kind is carbon-14. The radioactive isotope, carbon-14, is produced when neutrons bombard nitrogen in the air. The neutrons, in turn, are produced by cosmic rays in the upper atmosphere. The radioactive carbon (C-14) mixes with the ordinary isotope (C-12) in atmospheric carbon dioxide, and both behave in the same way thereafter.

Carbon dioxide is essential to all life. In the process of photosynthesis, all green plants absorb carbon dioxide gas in the manufacture of food. And because all life depends ultimately on plants for food, it is inevitable that both isotopes of carbon (C-12 and C-14) are incorporated into every living thing. During its life, all living matter contains a minute but constant level of radioactive carbon, which accurately reflects the proportion of C-14 to C-12 in the air. At the present time, there is about one atom of C-14 for every trillion atoms of C-12 in the atmosphere. The ratio of the two is exactly the same in all living things.

Once a plant or animal dies, however, it can no longer absorb carbon. In the course of time, the ordinary isotope, carbon-12, undergoes no change; its quantity remains fixed. But the radioactive isotope, carbon-14, begins a slow process of disintegration at an average rate of fourteen disintegrations per minute per gram of carbon. Because of this process of decay, scientists can measure the amount of radioactive carbon left in a sample under test, and determine how long it has been since the organism died. Carbon-14 dating is useful for objects up to about 40,000 years of age. For older samples, the amount of C-14 remaining is too small to permit accurate measurement.

The rate of decay is usually expressed in terms of the so-called *half-*

life of the radioactive isotope—the length of time it takes for half of it to decay. The half-life of carbon-14 is 5730 years, which means that the amount of C-14 contained in dead organic matter will drop to half its initial quantity in 5730 years. Similarly, matter containing one-quarter of the initial quantity will be 11,460 years old, and so on.

An underlying assumption to this technique is that the proportion of carbon-14 to carbon-12 in the air has always been the same. To find out if this is true, experiments were performed on a large number of objects taken from Egyptian tombs whose actual dates were known. These showed that carbon-14 dates were considerably more recent than true calendar-year dates. In general, radiocarbon dates are fairly accurate for the past 2000 years, but the errors become greater for older samples. This suggests that there was more carbon-14 in the air in the pre-Christian era than there is at present.

Scientists have been able to apply corrections to carbon-14 dates through a study of old tree rings. This procedure is based on the fact that trees grow by adding one growth ring to their trunks each year. The age of a tree, therefore, can be determined accurately by counting the number of tree rings it has developed. Furthermore, the size of each ring varies with the climate—in dry years they are thin and in wet years they are thick. These patterns are similar in all trees in a given area, so that the inner rings of a young tree will match the outer rings of an older tree and so on. This similarity makes it possible to fit the rings of timber found in archaeological sites into a master pattern of dates. A long series of tree-ring dates has been assembled from the bristlecone pine that grows in the White Mountains of California. It grows to an age of 5000 years. Dead parts of this kind of tree have been traced back to 6300 B.C., and work is being done on still older samples of wood.

Scientists have determined carbon-14 dates from the wood of this tree and compared them with known dates derived from counting tree rings. As a result, the discrepancy due to carbon-14 dating amounts to about 200 years at 1500 B.C. and 700 years at 3500 B.C.

All of this has had a profound effect on archaeological theories, since many dates must be set back several hundred years. It means, for example, that the prehistoric giant temples of Malta are older than the pyramids and could not have been inspired by them. Similarly, metallurgy was once thought to have been brought to Europe from the east. It now appears possible that it originated independently in Europe.

Can coal solve the world's energy problems?

Coal is by far the world's most abundant fossil fuel. A few facts will help to show why. Each year the world's population uses enough energy to boil one-quarter of the water in a lake the size of Lake Erie. On a per capita basis, this is equivalent to an average usage equal to operating twenty 100-watt light bulbs continuously for each inhabitant of the earth. For the United States, which accounts for about one third of the world's energy usage, each inhabitant accounts for one hundred 100-watt lamps. At the rate we are using oil and natural gas, most experts agree that supplies will run out in another generation or so. We have already experienced shortages and high prices as nations bid for the available supply.

Geologists estimate that there is enough recoverable coal in the ground to last a few centuries, even if it is used to supply all our energy needs at current rates of usage. The trouble with coal, however, is that it is high in pollution, largely because of the sulfur content of almost all our coal. About half the sulfur in coal exists in chemical union with metals such as iron. These metal sulfides can be removed by crushing the coal into a fine powder and removing the sulfides directly. The remaining sulfur is much more difficult to remove from coal.

One possible solution is to burn the coal and remove the sulfur dioxide, a gas that forms during the burning of coal. If it is not removed, the gas escapes from the smokestack to pollute the atmosphere. Chemists have proposed a number of chemical reactions that can perform this function, but they have not yet been put into practice on a large scale.

Another method of using coal for clean energy involves changing coal into a gas or liquid by chemical reactions. This solution would also solve the transportation problem, because suitable pipelines and tankers already exist. Once in liquid or gaseous form, the fuel can be cleaned of sulfur compounds by well-known chemical processes.

Many years ago, before the general availability of natural gas, every city had a "coal gasification" plant to convert coal and steam to hydrogen and carbon monoxide. Both these products are gases, and they burn in air to form water and carbon dioxide. The trouble with this fuel is the presence of poisonous carbon monoxide. The fuel can be further processed, however, with additional hydrogen, to produce methane, a gaseous fuel consisting of carbon and hydrogen. Any sulfur dioxide that happens to be present in the fuel can be removed by passing the gas through a solution of sodium hydroxide. The methane that is purified in that way is an excellent and clean fuel, much like natural gas.

Chemists also expect that coal will be converted to liquid fuels such as octane and nonane, two components of gasoline. Unfortunately, it is still too expensive to make this chemical conversion. As the cost of gasoline from petroleum increases, however, gasoline from coal may become economically feasible. Any chemist who can find an inexpensive way to convert coal to octane and similar components of gasoline will have made his fortune.

Why are we tricked by optical illusions?

Psychologists tell us that perception involves receiving information from the world around us and making sense of it. Most of the time, our visual perceptions of the environment are quite accurate—but occasionally we make big mistakes. Magicians, for example, make their living by inducing the audience to make faulty inferences about what the magician is doing. In making objects appear and disappear, magicians generate illusions: they provide the stimuli that induce the observer to make mistakes.

Ordinary photographs, paintings, and drawings can also be thought of as illusions. They mimic the real world and give us a perception of depth in a scene presented on the two dimensions of paper or canvas. In addition, we are induced to perceive movement in motion pictures, where no movement actually exists. Occasionally, the visual cues are so compelling that we are tempted to reach out to touch an object depicted on a plane surface.

Psychologists tell us that a principle called *size constancy* has a great deal to do with the generation of illusions about the size of objects and the length of lines. As an object is moved away from an observer, the image of the object on the retina of the eye gets smaller and smaller. Yet we know the object has not changed in size. For this reason, the brain corrects automatically for the reduction in size and we tend to "see" the object in its original size. This automatic size correction can lead to distorted perception (illusions) under proper conditions.

To illustrate, consider the accompanying diagram showing cylinders in a long hall. The cylinders are the same distance from the eye, but

Fig. 17. An optical illusion caused by cues of distance. The cylinders are the same size, although many people perceive the one on the right to be larger than the others.

the cues for depth in the drawing make the cylinder on the right seem much farther away. It appears larger to us because we compensate automatically for its supposed increased distance, even though the cylinders are actually of the same size.

In addition to illusions of size, there are also illusions of shape, movement, and orientation. An observer knows that a cube is a cube, for instance, even if it is seen from various angles (shape constancy), and the walls of a room are perceived as vertical even when an observer's head is tilted to the side (orientation constancy). The general theory that covers all such illusions is called *perceptual constancy*. It implies, in general, that we tend to make corrections automatically for changes that occur in the image formed on the retina of the eye. Ordinarily, the automatic corrections provide a true perception of the objects being viewed. But when the retinal image is kept unchanged—as in drawings that provide illusions—the automatic corrections cause misperceptions.

148

Fig. 18. Illusions of size and shape. A: The central circles are equal in diameter. B: All lines are equal in length. C: The horizontal lines are equal in length. D: The circles have the same diameter and shape despite the distorted appearance of the one on the right.

The automatic corrections made by the brain are so powerful that illusions occur even when natural features—such as trees, streets, and walls—are removed and only a geometrical drawing remains. The accompanying sketch shows several such illusions that occur because of perceptual constancy. In part A, the central circles are the same size, but the one on the right appears larger. The general rule is: the size of surrounding objects determines the perceived size of the object being viewed. The circle surrounded by small circles is perceived as large, while the circle surrounded by large circles is perceived as small. In (B), all the lines are equal in length although the vertical line on the left seems larger than the others. In (C)—known as the Müller-Lyer illusion—the line on the left seems larger. It is theorized that this illusion is a result of the perceptive cues that we learn in a modern environment. We live in a rectangular world of streets, buildings, rooms, and halls. If we lived in the forest, without such angular features, we would be less apt to be tricked by the Müller-Lyer illusion. In (D) the angular lines in the background lead to a distorted shape for the right-hand circle, even though it has the same shape and size as the one on the left.

Scientists who study illusions of various kinds believe that perceptual constancy may be a learned characteristic. Consider part B above, for example. The idea is that the presence in the environment of broad horizontal vistas (such as we see on the Great Plains of the United States) shapes the visual habit that leads to this particular illusion. Plains dwellers see large horizontal expanses and become subject to a shortening of the horizontal line. Experiments, in fact, have shown that plains dwellers are most subject to this so-called "horizontal-vertical" illusion, urban dwellers are moderately susceptible, and forest dwellers are least susceptible to it.

None of these theories is universally accepted, however, and the field of study is relatively new. More will be learned as scientists continue to study the factors that influence our perception of the world in which we live.

Do ants build roads?

Some kinds of ants actually build roads between their homes and their source of food. They select a narrow pathway and clear away all obstacles that might impede their mobility. Roads simplify their travels and speed up the task of provisioning the anthill.

Even on a smooth surface, like a large flat slab, ants lay out and follow a well-marked trail. Every ant takes precisely the same path, even if no other ant is in sight at the time. They find their way by following a scent laid down by the previous ants.

There seems to be some evidence that ant trails are marked by scent signposts in which the shape or pattern of the smell points in the desired direction. By examining the signpost, ants recognize its outline, as if its shape were an arrow telling it in which direction to go. Thus, some ants not only build roads but also appear to mark them with useful signposts.

Why do the bodies of animals tend to be softer than plants and trees?

Life as we know it is based on microscopic units of living matter called *cells*. Although cells vary considerably in their physical and biological properties, the cells in a chicken egg have the same basic features as those in the liver or in a flower petal. The common elements of most cells include an extremely thin *plasma membrane* surrounding the cell, a *nucleus,* containing genetic material, and a viscous, transparent material—called *cytoplasm*—that fills the space between the nucleus and the plasma membrane. It is in that sort of cellular arrangement that the processes of life take place.

Most plant cells differ from those of animals in having a rigid *cell wall,* which is absent in animal cells. This cell wall consists mainly of cellulose, a tough material that gives a specific shape to plant cells. Cells of animals, except for a few single-celled micro-organisms, assume a spherical shape if they are removed from surrounding cells, because they are contained only by a relatively soft plasma membrane. Lacking the rigid walls of plant cells, animal tissues are soft and pliable, whereas plants tend to retain their form and shape to a much greater degree.

Cellulose, the building block of plant cell walls, is one of the many substances known as carbohydrates. The "carbo" in carbohydrate refers to the fact that all such substances contain atoms of carbon— sometimes many thousands of them. The "hydrate" means that many water molecules, which consist of hydrogen and oxygen atoms, make up the rest of the carbohydrate. Thus, carbohydrates consist of a quantity of carbon atoms joined to a quantity of water molecules. If six carbon atoms and six water molecules are joined together in the proper atomic arrangement, the result is *glucose,* a common type of sugar. If precisely the same number and kinds of atoms are linked together in different patterns, the resulting substances may be *fructose* or *galactose,* different sugars but all with the same chemical formula, $C_6H_{12}O_6$ (six atoms of carbon, 12 of hydrogen, and 6 of oxygen). So all such sugars differ not in the kind and quantity of atoms present but in the patterns in which the atoms are bonded together.

Two or more sugar molecules of similar or identical type can become joined together end to end, forming a chainlike larger molecule. To illustrate, a combination of two glucose units forms *maltose,* or malt sugar; a combination of glucose and fructose forms *sucrose,* the familiar cane sugar used in cooking; and a combination of glucose and galactose forms *lactose,* milk sugar.

Molecules made up of two or more similar subunits are called *polymers.* A polymer composed of some hundreds of thousands of glucose units is called *glycogen,* which is the chief carbohydrate storage material in animals. *Starch,* a familiar food produced by plants, consists of 300 to 1000 joined glucose units. *Cellulose,* the material in plant cell walls, is a polymer of up to 2000 glucose units.

Cellulose is a tough material that can be digested only by certain bacteria and protozoa having special digestive enzymes. Cows, goats, and similar plant-eating animals depend on bacteria in their digestive tracts to break down the cellulose into a form they can use for nourishment. Termites can survive on a diet of cellulose from wood only because they harbor protozoa that perform the same function.

In addition to cellulose, woody plants contain *lignin,* a complex organic compound that provides additional strength and rigidity. Jute, hemp, and wood have long, tough fibers that contain considerable lignin, while cotton fibers—with no lignin and a high percentage of cellulose—are more suitable for use in clothing.

Is another ice age coming?

Scientists tell us that ice ages seem to recur on a cycle of about 300 million years. But there is also another kind of periodicity within an ice age—the alternation between glacial and interglacial phases. These changes can be measured in thousands rather than millions of years. During the last ice age, for example, the glaciers advanced several times to cover vast land areas, only to recede during warmer interglacial periods. The most recent retreat of the glaciers took place between 8000 and 15,000 years ago. Scientists have determined that at least four major periods of advance and retreat have taken place during the current ice age.

For decades, geologists have calculated, theorized, and speculated, but no general agreement yet exists as to the causes of ice ages. The theories have sought to explain both parts of the ice-age puzzle: the gradual cooling that led to the glacial epoch of 2 million years ago; and the advance and retreat of ice during the glaciations and interglacial periods.

Most theories have tried to explain why the earth would cool, causing the onset of glaciation. Some suggest that there may be periodic changes in the rate at which the sun burns its nuclear fuel, but no supporting evidence has been found. Another theory suggests that great quantities of volcanic ash may have been injected into the atmosphere to block a portion of the sun's rays and so cool the earth. But a measurement of deep-sea sediment shows no pronounced change in volcanic ash when the ice ages were believed to have occurred.

A more satisfying theory for general cooling of the earth relates to the positions of the continents relative to the north and south poles. Today, there are large land masses near the poles. In past ages, one or the other pole was in the middle of the ocean, where ocean currents allowed good exchange of heat across the globe. This would make the distribution of temperature more uniform from the poles to the equator. Once the land areas shifted toward the poles, the temperature became less evenly distributed and the polar regions became very cold. When conditions became right to restrict the flow of heat, the glaciers began to grow and the ice age began. Such ideas are now being studied by historical geologists, glaciologists, physical oceanographers, and meteorologists.

The alternate cycles of glaciation and interglacial periods within an ice age might be explained on the basis of astronomical cycles. The earth's orbit around the sun changes periodically, placing us sometimes closer to and sometimes farther from the sun. In addition, the earth wobbles slightly as it rotates on its axis. Both these variations have a slight effect on the heat received by the earth from the sun. These motions were worked out by the Yugoslavian geophysicist Milutin Milankovitch in the 1930s and seem to fit the cycle of glacial and interglacial periods reasonably well. Milankovitch's theory must be added to some other theory of general earth cooling, however, in order to explain why the ice ages have taken place in the first place.

Scientists are still not certain why glacial periods have occurred every so often in the history of the earth. But if another ice age does take place, it will come on a time scale of thousands of years. Our first warnings would be the slow advance of mountain glaciers in Alaska, Norway, and elsewhere. But we could not be sure that such an advance was not merely a temporary period of slight cooling that might give way in a few decades to another warm period.

How does a cucumber change into a pickle?

Consider two salt solutions, one rather weak and the other strong. The solutions are separated by a semipermeable membrane that tends to let the water through but not the salt. With such an arrangement, the weaker solution tends to become stronger and the stronger one tends to become weaker. This change takes place because the water flows from the weaker solution to the stronger one through the membrane, a process called *osmosis.**

Osmosis also takes place when a cucumber is placed in a strong salt solution. The cucumber skin acts as a semipermeable membrane. The liquid inside the cucumber is quite weak, or *dilute,* compared with the salt solution, which is strong, or *concentrated.* Water flows from the dilute solution to the concentrated solution through the skin of the cucumber. The cucumber shrinks, therefore, and becomes a pickle through the process of osmosis. The salt also passes through the membrane, but at a vastly slower rate. This process is called *diffusion,* and it gives the pickle a somewhat salty taste.

The process of osmosis also takes place when a dried prune is placed in water. The skin acts as a semipermeable membrane separating the rather concentrated juices inside the prune from the dilute solution (water) surrounding it. Once again, the water flows into the more concentrated solution inside the prune, causing it to swell.

How does galvanized iron prevent rust?

The rusting of iron or steel is essentially an electrical process. To illustrate, consider the steel body of an automobile. If a bit of paint is chipped off, corrosion begins as soon as a drop of water lands on the unprotected metal. What happens runs something like this. Iron atoms

---

* For a more detailed discussion of osmosis, see pages 82–83.

give up electrons, which are immediately gobbled up by the oxygen atoms that are usually dissolved in the water. This results in a new kind of molecule—iron oxide, or rust. Of course, if there are no oxygen atoms available in the drop of water, the rusting process stops even before it gets started. After a few iron atoms have released their electrons (which have a negative electric charge) to the metal, the resulting negative charge forces some of the electrons back where they came from, and rust cannot form. On the other hand, if the free elec-

ELECTRONS

MAGNESIUM

BURIED TANK

Fig. 19. If magnesium is connected electrically to a buried steel tank, the magnesium is more easily oxidized than the iron in the tank. The magnesium is slowly corroded away while the tank is being protected. When the magnesium is used up, it can be replaced by another block.

trons are used up, say by the oxygen molecules dissolved in the water, the rusting can continue. Oxygen, in fact, is dissolved in all natural water, so it is always available to help rusting along. The rusting process is nature's way of transforming iron metal back into a compound much like iron ore, thereby undoing all of man's work in refining the metal. The cost of rusting runs to several billion dollars each year in the United States alone.

Rusting is clearly a serious problem, and it has interested scientists for many years. There are four major ways of preventing such corrosion. The first is to protect the metal with paint. The second is to rely on the metal's own impervious oxide coating, if it happens to have one. Aluminum has such a hard, impervious coating, which effectively protects the metal from corrosion. Gold and platinum, of course, are even better at resisting corrosion. The third method of preventing corrosion is to coat or plate the metal with another that is not easily oxidized, such as tin on steel in "tin" cans. Of course, if the protective layer becomes damaged so as to uncover the iron, rusting will proceed quickly.

The fourth method is perhaps the most unexpected. In practice, iron can be protected by coating it with a *more* easily oxidized metal. Typically, zinc is used, and the process is called *galvanizing*. Even if all the iron is not covered, the iron will not rust. In such a system, the zinc-coated iron still gives up electrons to oxygen, but the zinc (not iron) is the source of the electrons. As a result, the zinc is corroded instead of the iron. As shown in the accompanying diagram, this method—called *cathodic protection*—is often used to protect iron or steel objects buried in the ground. These include pipelines, tanks, and bridge supports. Protection ends only when the more reactive metal, often magnesium, is used up.

Stainless steels are alloys of iron that contain nickel, chromium, and other elements. They are produced by melting the metals together in an electric furnace. Stainless steel alloys resist corrosion because their surface forms a tough, impervious, and adherent layer of chromium oxide. This oxide protects the alloy from further contact with oxygen, and it becomes extremely resistant to corrosion under most conditions.

Is it possible to produce a human clone?

A clone is an organism that has been produced from a genetically identical parent. Every gardener that has divided an African violet plant into several new plants has produced a clone. The organisms that result from that kind of reproduction are genetically identical to each other and to the original parent. Although many organisms reproduce by cloning, the process does not occur naturally among the higher animals. Nevertheless, scientists believe that human cloning is possible in principle, and there seems no reason to believe that it cannot be achieved in practice.

For natural human reproduction, the offspring consists initially of a single cell. The tiny nucleus of that cell contains all the genetic material necessary for the development of a new human being. Half the genetic material comes from each parent. In nature, this procedure provides the variation among individuals upon which evolution depends. As the single cell divides and the new human being develops, the genetic material in the nucleus is duplicated over and over again for all the other cells in the individual. This nucleus, with its genetic information, is the "blueprint" that causes a fertilized egg cell to develop into a specific human being rather than into a horse or dog.

Is it possible, then, for scientists to remove the nucleus from an egg cell and substitute a different nucleus of their own choice? It is indeed, and scientists have already tested the idea in frogs and mice.

Cloning experiments have been performed in which the nuclei of frog eggs were removed and replaced with nuclei transplanted from intestinal cells of a single donor tadpole. The reconstituted egg cells developed normally into a clone of genetically identical frogs.

Some biologists believe that several practical applications of cloning may well become commonplace in the next decade or two. Cloning may replace selective breeding in the reproduction of certain "select" cows, horses, chickens, and other animals. The winner of horse racing's triple crown, for example, could generate a clone consisting of scores of horses genetically identical to the parent.

The same cloning procedure is possible, in principle, with human reproduction. It would be accomplished, as with animals, by removing the nucleus of an egg cell and replacing it with one taken from a cell of an appropriate parent. The new individual would be a genetic copy of the person who donated the nucleus. This type of asexual reproduction is biologically feasible for the future and might be used to reduce genetic disorders in human offspring. Suppose, for example, that both prospective parents have the characteristics of a genetic disease. They might well decide against having a child in the natural way because of the high probability that the child will be abnormal. If cloning were a practical alternative, the woman could have a nucleus transplanted from one of her cells (or from one of her husband's cells) to an egg cell. The resulting cell could then be implanted in her uterus. A child produced in this way would be identical to the parent who supplied the nucleus.

Although human cloning seems entirely feasible, the procedures involved are far from simple. The small size of the human nucleus would require procedures of extreme delicacy and precision for implantation. Nevertheless, the technological know-how could be made available if human cloning ever became an important item of priority.

Such possibilities raise a host of legal, moral, and ethical questions that must be answered before the cloning idea is fully explored.

Another aspect of reproduction has caused a great deal of soul searching in biological circles. Until a few years ago, the growth of the egg of a mammal *in vitro* (outside the body) was considered an extraordinary biological accomplishment. Normally, such an egg depends upon the mother's tissues for its nourishment. Today, mouse eggs are fertilized *in vitro* and grown to the stage where heartbeats are visible. This suggests to biologists that we may soon be able to raise a mammalian embryo to adulthood outside the mother's body. Human embryos have been grown in that way up to the six-day-old stage. The rearing of human embryos in an assembly line of flasks may not be just around the corner, but scientists are beginning to think about such a possibility along with its consequences.

The prospects of raising a "test-tube baby" are so real that ethical questions have already been raised on the subject. Some scientists consider the *in vitro* culture of human embryos to be dehumanizing. The control thus obtained over embryo fertilization and development, they maintain, would be gained at the expense of important human values—dignity, love, and family. Nevertheless, the time is not too distant when the possible advantages of biological engineering may have to be weighed against the importance of traditional social and ethical values.

Before leaving the subject, we should point out that a so-called "test-tube baby" was born in England on July 25, 1978, at London's Oldham Hospital. Doctors had fertilized an egg cell from the mother with sperm from the father, reimplanting the fertilized egg in the mother's body. Although quite an accomplishment, this is a far simpler procedure than raising a human embryo entirely *in vitro*.

How long will the continents last?

The turbulent flow of water in streams and rivers performs an enormous amount of work that continually changes the shape of the land. The average height of the continents is about 2720 feet above sea level. The average streamflow downhill is about 8860 cubic miles of water per year. Geologists have calculated that this annual runoff from the land generates over 12 billion horsepower. Assuming that all this power is used to erode the continents, it would be comparable to having one horse-drawn plow or scraper at work on each acre of land, eight hours per day, year in, year out. You can imagine how much downhill erosion of land such a collection of scrapers could generate! Of course, some of the energy of runoff is wasted as frictional heat by the turbulent splashing of water. But the process is quite efficient and does transport rock debris down to the oceans almost as fast as if all those horses were really at work on their one-acre plots.

The amount of erosion can be understood by studying the Mississippi River, which every day carries over a million tons of sediment to the Gulf of Mexico. That enormous amount of soil amounts to about 2 inches of land removed from the central part of the United States each thousand years. Over the past million years the river has built up a 12,000-square-mile platform of sand, silt, and clay to a central height of one mile or so.

In the United States as a whole, the rate of erosion—before European settlers arrived—was about 1.2 inches per thousand years. The settlers, through their use of large-scale agricultural and building practices, have doubled that figure on the average. On a worldwide basis, the rate of erosion amounts to about 2.5 inches per thousand years. At that rate, water-caused erosion would level the continents in about 100 million years.

Geologists doubt, however, that the continents will ever be reduced to sea level. First of all, the geologic history of the earth shows that it has never happened before. Although highlands are surely eroded away, other lands—originally low—are forced up to produce new highlands. This helps to explain, by the way, how marine sediments can be found high on Mount Everest.

Erosion, therefore, may not do away with the continents, but it will surely change them. A hypothetical space traveler, returning to earth after several tens of millions of years, would not recognize the continental features. Mountain ranges, rivers, lakes—even continental shapes—would be very different from those he remembered from his youth. The continents will continue to change dramatically as long as the earth retains its supply of air and water.

Are airplanes in flight ever hit by lightning?

The average commercial airplane is struck by lightning once in every 5000 to 10,000 hours of flying time. During the two-year period including 1965 and 1966, the Federal Aviation Administration received reports of about 1000 such lightning strikes. In 1964 a Boeing

727 in a holding pattern at Chicago was hit by five separate lightning strokes within a 20-minute period. In 1969 four airliners were struck by separate lightning strokes near Los Angeles.

Aircraft almost always continue to fly after being hit by lightning. Because the outer surface of an airplane is made almost entirely of metal, the lightning currents seldom penetrate the interior or affect passengers. As a general rule, lightning produces burn marks or holes on the metallic skin. The holes commonly measure about one-half inch in diameter, but holes up to 4 inches in diameter have been reported. The major danger of lightning to aircraft is the possibility of igniting the fuel supply. This was the cause of two known commercial disasters related to lightning. In both cases, the fuel tanks exploded in flight. It is believed that sparks from the lightning ignited an explosive air-fuel mixture in a fuel tank or near a fuel leak.

Scientists believe that the two explosions would have been prevented had the fuel tanks not contained oxygen from the air. If oxygen is excluded from the space above the fuel in the tanks, the fuel can neither burn nor explode. It is believed that replacing the air in such tanks with nitrogen will make aircraft immune from most explosions caused by lightning. Leaky tanks, of course, would still present the possibility of explosion.

When an airplane is hit by lightning, its metallic skin substitutes for part of the lightning stroke's air path. In a typical incident, lightning enters at one of the wing tips and leaves by the tail.

Thunderstorms are involved in about half the reported cases of lightning strikes to commercial aircraft. The remainder occur in conditions of ordinary precipitation in which no lightning is present before the stroke hits the plane.

Commercial pilots use airborne radar sets to help avoid thunderstorms. Without this guidance, thunderstorm-related lightning strikes would undoubtedly represent a much greater percentage of the total number of strikes.

Does the study of mathematics help train the mind?

Educators and psychologists make valuable use of a learning process called *transfer of training*. The idea is quite simple: learning in one field can sometimes be an aid to learning in another field. For instance, many French, Italian, and Spanish words are similar, so learning one language makes learning either of the other two somewhat easier.

A more complicated example of transfer of learning is involved with the training of airline pilots. Replicas of aircraft cockpits are computer-controlled to simulate what happens in an airplane during a real emergency. The corrective actions taken by the pilot are interpreted by the computer so that the simulated aircraft behaves just as the pilot tells it to. This learning technique transfers a great deal of learning from the simulator to the real-life situation. During a real emergency in the sky, the learned behavior will help the pilot deal effectively with unexpected problems.

It was once an article of faith that certain courses, the very hardest ones—mathematics, logic, and Latin—were valuable as "mind trainers." Such courses were thought to provide a kind of generalized transfer, in the sense that they would exercise the mind. This would equip the student to handle better *any* difficult academic or life problem.

Such theories were found wanting in the 1920s when psychological studies showed that students majoring in sewing and cooking did just about as well in reasoning tests as those who had concentrated on Latin and math. Such studies showed that transfer of information takes place only if the new material is similar in some way to the material that was originally learned. Latin, for example, is helpful in learning Spanish because of the similarity in grammar and vocabulary. However, there does not seem to be any such thing as mind exercise or training—despite the feeling we may have to the contrary.

In some situations, a transfer of knowledge can actually impede the solution of problems. Suppose a group of people are given ten mazes to solve, all in a row, all with left-hand turns. Then they are given traditional mazes requiring both left-hand and right-hand turns. We would find that they have difficulty with the traditional mazes because of a mind set induced by the earlier left-hand mazes. As long as we stay with the same kind of maze, the general method of solving the problem works well, but when the type of maze is switched, the wrong method of problem solving is transferred to the new problem. What happens is a kind of negative transfer in which the original information interferes with learning.

Why is there only one queen bee in a beehive?

Human beings usually communicate through speech and hearing or by means of the written word. Although the sense of smell can provide us with important signals, it is not nearly as useful as hearing.

161

When we study animal communication, however, we find that odor is often substituted for sound as a main form of language. A dog that wets every tree around his house is merely announcing his sovereignty over the region to all would-be trespassers. The roe deer that rubs a secretion from a forehead gland on tree branches does so to mark the boundary of his territory. Many animals use odors for identification, territorial marking, sexual attraction, alarm, and a variety of other purposes.

Animals often communicate with the help of chemical substances, called *pheromones,* which are secreted in order to influence the behavior of other animals of the same species. For example, bees that have discovered a food-rich area secrete pheromones to attract other bees. A wounded minnow secretes pheromones from the skin that cause other minnows to attempt escape. Similarly, many ants in distress broadcast alarm substances that cause fellow ants to become aggressive. Although pheromones have been detected in all groups of vertebrates from mammals to fish, they are most developed in the social insects— ants, bees, and termites. Pheromone signals bind these insects into well-organized colonies.

Scientists now know that pheromones are responsible for the caste system in bees and termites. To illustrate, all female bees have the capacity to reproduce, but only one becomes the queen. The queen bee controls reproduction in the colony by a glandular secretion of 9-keto-decanoic acid, which prevents ovarian development in other females. As a result, the latter all become worker bees. The same pheromone attracts the male when a queen leaves the colony on a nuptial flight.

Pheromones are widely used as sex attractants by insects. The female cabbage looper moth gives off a pheromone that a male can detect a considerable distance away. Using his antennae as "sniffers," he follows the chemical trail in the air until he reaches his mate. He then goes through a well-documented, complex mating procedure. The whole sequence of events, in fact, can be triggered without the presence of a female moth; all that is needed is a drop of pheromone on a piece of paper. The male acts as if it were a computerized robot with a complex behavior pattern programmed into its nervous system. Just as a punched IBM card actuates a computer, the pheromone sets in motion a sequence of actions that continues until the appropriate behavior is completed.

Biologists foresee the practical application of synthetic pheromones in the control of insect pests. In fact, they have already used artificial pheromones to attract specific species of insects to locations where they can be killed selectively. Used on a large scale, this method would do away with insecticides that kill many species of insects indiscriminately—the beneficial with the bad.

Pheromones show considerable promise because they are easy to identify and synthesize in the laboratory. In addition, they are effective in infinitesimally small concentrations. The gypsy moth, for example, has only one-millionth of a gram of the sex-attractant pheromone gyplure. Yet that tiny amount is enough to set off the ritual mating dance of a billion males! It takes only a few hundred molecules per cubic centimeter to excite a male gypsy moth.

One example of success with the pheromone method shows the possibilities of the technique. The Oriental fruit fly was eliminated completely from a Pacific island through its use. Small pieces of cane fiber containing a sex attractant for males and a fast-acting insecticide were dropped from airplanes. Only the males were killed, but of course without any males the fruit fly was completely eradicated in several months. In this instance, the targeted insect was the only species killed; wildlife and desirable insects were not affected, and dangerous insecticides were not spread throughout the environment needlessly.

Where does gold dust come from?

A modern way to locate gold deposits is to "track" the metal to its source. Because of erosion, some tiny particles of the metal will be chipped away from a deposit and carried downstream by the flowing water. If gold exists anywhere within a river's watershed, it is likely that some of it—in the form of gold dust—will show up in the riverbed.

It is now possible, with the help of sensitive scientific instruments and chemical tests, to detect the presence of even minute amounts of gold or minerals that contain gold. Once the presence of gold is established, testing can proceed upstream until a point is reached at which the gold disappears. The scientific search can then proceed up the riverbanks until the source of the gold is located. This method has been used to discover extensive gold deposits in Nevada as well as zinc and lead in New Brunswick, Canada.

Does light always travel at the same speed?

The speed of light varies considerably, depending on the medium through which it is moving. The speed of light is at a maximum when measured in a vacuum and drops to less than half that speed in a diamond. We do not notice this variability because light travels so fast, about 186,000 miles per second (300,000 kilometers per second) in a vacuum. The following table gives the approximate speed of light in various substances.

Velocity of Light in Various Media

Medium	Velocity (miles/second)	Velocity (kilometers/second)
Vacuum	186,280	299,790
Air	186,240	299,720
Ice	142,000	229,000
Glass (flint)	109,000	175,000
Diamond	77,000	124,000

Perhaps the strangest behavior of light is the variability of its speed of transmission through different substances. If a bullet is fired through a wooden board, it slows down as it encounters the particles of wood in its path. When it emerges from the other side, its speed is considerably slower than when it entered the wood. Light behaves quite differently. When light passes from air into a second medium, such as glass, it slows down—just as the bullet did. But when it emerges from the glass, it speeds up again and resumes its normal speed in air.

This odd behavior on the part of light can best be understood if we view light as tiny *photons,* or bundles of energy, rather than waves. When a photon enters a medium, it strikes or interacts with the particles of the medium—such as atoms and their orbital electrons. The photon is absorbed by the atom and causes one or more of its orbital electrons to vibrate. This vibration, in turn, causes the emission of a second photon identical to the incident photon. The second photon then moves a short distance in the medium and is absorbed by another atom, which leads to the emission of a third photon. The process of photon absorption and emission is repeated many times until a photon finally reaches the air surface, where it moves away at its normal high velocity. All of the photon-atom interactions and photon emissions within the glass require time to occur, which explains why light travels more slowly in solid or liquid media than in a vacuum (or air, for practical purposes). The photon that leaves a pane of glass is not the same one that entered the glass, but one that was emitted within the glass.

What causes the earth to move at the San Andreas Fault?

At approximately 5:00 A.M. on April 18, 1906, the sleeping residents of San Francisco were awakened abruptly by a violent shaking of the earth, accompanied by the thunder of collapsing buildings. This jarring event was the start of one of modern history's most famous earthquakes. Before it was over, the quake had caused about 700 deaths, destroyed the homes of a quarter of a million people, and laid waste about 3000 acres of the city. As with many earthquakes, much of the property damage was a result of fires that raged out of control because water mains had been broken in many places by the violent movements of the ground.

The cause of the San Francisco earthquake was a sudden slippage of the earth along the San Andreas Fault, one of the world's more renowned sources of earthquakes. The fault parallels the Pacific Coast of California, beginning at the coast north of San Francisco and ending about 600 miles to the south, where its several branches disappear beneath the waters of the Gulf of California.

During the 1906 earthquake, the western side of the fault moved horizontally northward with respect to the eastern side. Slippage occurred over about 268 miles of the fault, from Point Arena, north of San Francisco, to San Juan Bautista to the south. The maximum amount of slippage was 21 feet north of the city. In San Francisco, it amounted to about 15 feet. Over the entire length of the earthquake region, there was a continuous trail of furrowed ground, displaced fences, fractured buildings, and other evidence of lateral slippage of the ground.

Many geologists believe that the energy responsible for earthquakes, volcanism, mountain building, and other processes that have changed the earth's features down through the ages exists in the form of heat in the earth's interior. Some of the heat may have been trapped far below the surface during the early stages of the earth's formation. Additional heat is probably provided by the decay of the radioactive elements occurring naturally in the interior. It is this internal energy that is thought to power the geological changes that take place on the earth's

165

surface. Scientists believe that activity within the earth is about as vigorous today as at any time in its 4.7-billion-year history.

Geologists have developed a theory, or model, that seems to explain satisfactorily many of the changes that take place on the earth. It is called *plate tectonics,* from the Greek word *tektonikos,* meaning carpenter or builder. According to this model, the earth has a rigid outer shell, about 60 miles thick, which is made up of a number of plates or segments—somewhat like a set of irregularly shaped tiles on a floor. These plates are not fixed, but can move very slowly with respect to one another. At some boundaries the plates converge, at some they move apart, and at others they slide laterally with respect to one another. These motions are believed to cause earthquakes and other changes in surface features that occur on the earth. The plate boundaries include most of the world's earthquake belts, volcanic regions, deep-sea trenches, island arcs, and mountain ranges.

In accordance with the plate tectonic model, the San Andreas Fault lies at the boundary of the North American Plate and the Pacific Plate. Recent measurements along the fault show a steady slip of about eight-tenths of an inch per year. The leisurely drift of continents across the earth's surface takes place at about the same speed.

As long as the rocks on either side of a fault are free to slide, slippage is smooth and continuous. If, on the other hand, the rocks on opposite sides of the fault become locked together because of irregularities in the rock walls, slippage proceeds in fits and starts. If little or no movement occurs for a long period of time, slippage is greater and more violent when it finally does occur. During periods when the rocks are locked together, they become bent and strained much as a diving board is bent when a diver stands near its end. When the rocks break, as illustrated in the diagram, there is rapid movement when the rocks snap back—much as the springboard does when the diver jumps off. This so-called *elastic-rebound* theory is the accepted explanation for the generation of earthquakes.

Earthquakes can also be accompanied by a vertical movement of the ground. On May 21, 1960, a devastating series of earth tremors shook Chile near a fault between the South American Plate and the Nazca Plate in the Pacific Ocean. The major shock, which occurred at 3:15 P.M. on the following day, rocked the entire region. Witnesses in the city of Concepción said that the motion of the earth was as if one were in a small boat at sea in a heavy swell. The ground rose and fell with a slow, smooth, rolling motion. Parked cars rocked to and fro as they bobbed on the rolling ground. Treetops swayed and tossed as if in a violent storm. Although buildings fell, the earthquake itself was silent. The motion lasted for several minutes and was followed by other shocks for the next hour. Although the earthquake area was 100 miles wide and 1000 miles long, no evidence was found of any large-scale horizontal offset of the earth along a fault. Surveys were conducted later, however, which indicated that two strips of land parallel to the

FENCE
OR ROAD

FAULT
LINE

(A)

ROCKS BEND
NEAR FAULT

(B)

(C)

Fig. 20. Three stages in the elastic rebound theory of earthquakes. A: Before any movement occurs along the fault line, a road (dotted line) is a straight line. B: The two blocks of earth move as shown by the arrows, but the fault is locked and rocks bend near the fault line. C: The rocks finally yield to the stress and slip along the fault line, causing an earthquake. The road is straight again but offset at the fault line.

coast, each about 1000 miles long, had changed in elevation; one went up about 3 feet and the other went down about 5 feet.

Geologists know that tectonic plates have been in motion for great lengths of time. They estimate that the movement along the San Andreas Fault has amounted to 119 miles during the last 60 million years, and possibly 350 miles during the past 120 million years. For that reason, scientists are certain that it is only a matter of time before another extensive slip along the San Andreas Fault will generate a violent earthquake somewhere along its length.

What is meant by the wind-chill factor?

Aside from the temperature of the air, the wind is the greatest culprit in making us uncomfortable in cold weather. It cools us down by removing heat from the skin and by blowing away the warm air that tends to accumulate between our skin and clothing, between layers of clothing, within the clothing itself. It is this loss of heat that we feel so keenly on cold, windy days. We can notice this cooling effect even on a calm winter day when we walk briskly through the air or ski rapidly down a hill.

Scientists have combined the effects of air temperature and wind speed to arrive at an approximate idea of the cooling effect of moving air. This is expressed as a number, called the wind-chill index, or wind-chill factor. It indicates in a general way how many calories of heat are carried away from the surface of the body. To illustrate, a wind speed of only 2 miles per hour removes almost twice as much heat as does calm air at the same temperature; at 20 miles per hour the cooling effect is about three times as great as in still air.

In order to make the wind-chill factor more useful, scientists have devised an equivalent temperature scale, which makes the concept more meaningful. In effect, it reduces everything to still air. An example will show how the system works. Experiments have shown that the body loses a certain amount of heat at 0°F in still air, and it loses about the same amount of heat at 30°F in a wind blowing at 25 miles per hour. So the wind-chill factor for the latter conditions (30°F and 25 miles per hour) is said to be 0°F.

The accompanying wind-chill chart can be used to determine the wind-chill factors for various combinations of temperature and wind velocity. To use the chart, find the wind speed in the column on the left and find the temperature reading in the horizontal row at the top.

168

Wind Chill Chart

Wind Speed (mph)	Temperature Reading (°F)											
	50	40	30	20	10	0	−10	−20	−30	−40	−50	−60
	Wind-Chill Factor (°F)											
0	50	40	30	20	10	0	−10	−20	−30	−40	−50	−60
5	48	37	27	16	6	−5	−15	−26	−36	−47	−57	−68
10	40	28	16	4	−9	−21	−33	−46	−58	−70	−83	−95
15	36	22	9	−5	−18	−36	−45	−58	−72	−85	−99	−112
20	32	18	4	−10	−25	−39	−53	−67	−82	−96	−110	−124
25	50	16	0	−15	−29	−44	−59	−74	−88	−104	−118	−133
30	28	13	−2	−18	−33	−48	−63	−79	−94	−109	−125	−140
35	27	11	−4	−20	−35	−49	−67	−82	−98	−113	−129	−145
40	26	10	−6	−21	−37	−53	−69	−85	−100	−116	−132	−148

Little Danger	Danger	Most Dangerous

The intersection of these two points gives the corresponding wind-chill factor.

For example, a temperature of −20°F along with a wind speed of 30 miles per hour corresponds to a wind-chill factor of −79°F. This is in the "most dangerous" region of the chart, which means that an individual should avoid exposure to such conditions whenever possible. In general, wind-chill factors above about −25°F pose little danger to a person in suitable clothing. When the factor falls to about −80°F, however, there is extreme danger to survival. Such conditions prevail in the Antarctic, on the Greenland icecap, on high mountain peaks, and even in parts of Siberia and Alaska. Wind-chill factors between about −25°F and −80°F represent considerable danger, even to properly clothed persons.

Are stars being formed at the present time?

Astrophysicists have come to realize that the stars were not all made at one time but are continually forming, evolving, and changing. Although these changes take place over enormous periods of time, astronomers can study star formation as a continuing process by observing individual stars in different phases of the process.

A star begins life as a large ball of slowly rotating gas that contracts slowly under its own weight. It heats up gradually as it contracts until the interior reaches several million degrees, a process that takes about

100 million years. When the temperature is high enough, nuclear reactions begin to take place and the contraction stops. A typical star then settles down to a constant size and generates a steady energy output based on nuclear fusion of hydrogen to form helium.

On a clear winter night, you can observe a star being born in our own galaxy in the constellation of Orion. Orion, the "hunter," dominates the southern sky of the northern hemisphere in winter. To find the constellation, look for four widely spaced stars, as shown in the accompanying diagram. These form the outline of the hunter. Then find a line of three stars inclined somewhat to the horizontal, forming a

Fig. 21. Three successive positions of Orion as seen on a December night.

"belt." Just below the belt is Orion's "sword," a nearly vertical row of three fainter stars. A closer examination through binoculars shows that the middle member of the sword is not a star at all, but a hazy patch of light. This object is called the Great Nebula in Orion, a fan-shaped cloud of gas that is considered by many to be the most beautiful object in the sky. It surrounds a star called Orionis, which was described by Tennyson as

A single misty star which
is the second in a line of stars that
seem a sword beneath a belt of three.

This nebula is a star being born inside our own galaxy of stars: an enormous cloud of luminous gas that measures 17 light-years (100 million million miles) across and 1500 light-years away. It is much more distant than the stars in Orion, which are all relatively close to the earth.

Astronomers now believe that our Milky Way, and other similar spiral galaxies, contain stars of varying ages. The older stars formed soon after our galaxy began to take shape, perhaps 10 billion years ago. They are distributed in a more or less spherical arrangement, with a high concentration near the galactic center. A second part of such galaxies contains spiral arms and gas clouds with most of the younger, second-generation stars, along with the material for future generations. It is here that the process of star formation can be most easily observed in all its stages.

How does hair spray work?

Hair sprays are solutions of a plastic in a quick-drying solvent; they cover the hair with a plastic film strong enough to hold the hair in place. The first hair sprays often used shellac, but a wide variety of plastic resins and solvents are now used to provide easier application and better films.

A common plastic used in hair sprays is PVP (polyvinylpyrrolidone). It is often blended with a plasticizer, to make the plastic more pliable and "bouncy," and a solvent-propellent mixture. Silicone oils are sometimes added to give the hair a sheen. Since PVP tends to pick up moisture in damp weather, another plastic, vinyl acetate, is sometimes added to provide an "all-weather" hair spray.

How did primitive plants and animals evolve?

We have no trouble telling the difference between a horse and a tree. The horse walks about and notices our presence as it munches on grass. The tree stands still and shows no signs of perceiving our presence. This difference in behavior of plants and animals has to do with their basic difference in eating habits.

Plants make their own food from simple compounds found in air and soil. With the aid of green chlorophyll, the tree uses the energy of sunlight to combine carbon dioxide and water into food—a process called photosynthesis. The horse, on the other hand, must get its food by eating plants—a process that involves moving about to find a constant supply.

Not all animals move about, however. Sponges, for example, attach

171

themselves to the sea floor and use internal moving parts to circulate water and food toward themselves. Because of their lack of mobility, sponges were long classified as plants by early naturalists. There is no longer any doubt, however, that sponges and coral—although stationary—are animals.

As we consider simpler forms of life, the differences of behavior and feeding grow less obvious, until we find certain microscopic organisms that defy classification. Possessing characteristics of both kinds of life, these "animal-plants," the *flagellates,* swim about by wiggling long, narrow, tails called *flagella,* from the Latin word for "whip." All flagellates swim about and exhibit the same sensitivity and speed of response that we associate with animals. Yet many kinds carry on photosynthesis just as plants do. Some flagellates, in fact, not only photosynthesize their food, as plants do, but also feed as animals do, thereby making themselves doubly sure of an adequate food supply. Still other flagellates have lost their chlorophyll and feed only as animals.

The existence of organisms that straddle the plant and animal kingdoms leads some biologists to think that there was no difference between plants and animals in the early days of life on earth. There is some evidence, in fact, that both plants and animals evolved from primitive flagellates. By losing their whiplike flagella, and assuming a round form, some types closely resemble algae—the simplest plants. Furthermore, many of the flagellates that contain green chlorophyll pass into an immobile alga-like state when they reproduce. Others lose their chlorophyll and become animals that capture and ingest their food.

Taking a rather long evolutionary step backward from the flagellates, we find the viruses. Of the many hypotheses that try to account for the origin of life, one states that it all began with virus-like molecules. The theory points out that primeval ponds must have contained, as they do now, the simple compounds that add together in a complex way to form the living substance, protoplasm. Energy from the sun, from warm springs, or perhaps from lightning may have formed various combinations. Some, like viruses, had the ability to reproduce themselves. Viruses, of course, are hardly alive in the ordinary sense. They can be prepared in pure form by distillation, a process that involves boiling. Even after such an ordeal, they proceed to multiply when returned to favorable conditions. The major drawback to the theory is the fact that nobody has been able to grow them in the absence of living matter.

Some biologists believe that the earliest self-propagating substances were something like viruses. This might have led to aggregations of such proteins into larger bacteria-like organisms, which may have created their own food using energy from the sun. Present-day organisms like the *independent bacteria* conduct photosynthesis without chlorophyll. Others form carbohydrates by oxidizing ammonia or hydrogen sulfide. From such forms to the flagellates is a relatively short evolutionary jump in complexity, as such jumps go. Nevertheless, the main gap in the theory still remains to be bridged: no virus has ever been known to reproduce in the absence of a living host.

Is it wrong to study lying down?

For a variety of reasons, many children equate education with an unhappy, unpleasant chore. It is a rare child who finds learning to be fun despite all the hard work. Study is supposed to be unpleasant, and so generations of students have been taught to make themselves physically uncomfortable while studying. They have been admonished to sit in a straight-backed chair to avoid feeling relaxed. It was taken for granted that the learning environment must be unpleasant in order to be effective.

When the matter was studied experimentally, psychologists found that grade averages were just about the same whether students studied on a bed or in a straight-backed chair. In fact, when groups of honor students were studied, the number that lie down was the same as the number who sit up while studying. It seems reasonable to suppose, therefore, that a relaxed, pleasant study environment is no deterrent to effective learning.

How was Egyptian hieroglyphic writing deciphered?

Ancient Egypt has been described as a culture of graffiti. No other people seem to have been so devoted to writing on walls or so proficient in raising the practice to a fine art. Each succeeding generation strove to perpetuate its deeds and its leaders' names by carving written characters of matchless beauty and clarity on all their buildings from top to bottom. No other culture has given archaeologists a more abundant mass of physical remains, including temples, tombs, public works, furniture, tools, jewels, clothing, and even their own

173

bodies. Most of this material is inscribed with ancient Egyptian text in the form of beautifully carved hieroglyphs, but for hundreds of years nobody knew how to read them.

When Napoleon Bonaparte invaded Egypt in 1798, the war news brought Egyptian antiquities into the forefront of fashion. He had a shrewd grasp of the importance of international prestige and took with him a group of over a hundred distinguished French scholars. It was their task to follow in the wake of the army, studying, measuring, drawing, describing, and removing to France all manner of antiquities and artifacts. In August of 1799, a French officer named Pierre Bouchard (or Boussard—the records are not precise on the spelling) was in charge of a detachment of troops working on fortifications in a place called Rosetta (Rashid) on the western side of the Nile Delta. Bouchard noticed a slab of old black basalt rock that had been built into the wall of an Arab fort that was being demolished. The stone slab—now called the Rosetta Stone—was completely covered with inscriptions of three different kinds. The stone measured about 45 x 28 inches and was divided into three sections, each of which carried an inscription in a different script. The lower section was in Greek. The other two were in Egyptian, one in the form of hieroglyphics and the other in a form of cursive writing known as demotic. Its importance, therefore, was obvious to all: it could provide a key to understanding the long-elusive hieroglyphs (literally, sacred carved signs).

Copies of the Rosetta Stone texts were circulated among scholars throughout Europe. The stone itself, originally destined for the Louvre in Paris, became a trophy of war and ended up in the British Museum instead. The scholars who tried to translate the Rosetta Stone had one important advantage: one of the languages was Greek, so they knew precisely what the inscription meant. It was a relatively unimportant decree of Ptolemy V in 196 B.C.

One of the scholars who undertook the translation of the hieroglyphics was a brilliant young Frenchman named Jean-François Champollion. By the time he was eighteen he had taught himself Arabic, Syriac, Hebrew, Latin, Greek, and a medieval form of ancient Egyptian called Coptic. Champollion received an important clue to hieroglyphics from Thomas Young, a Cambridge physicist with a deep interest in ancient Egypt. Young noticed that some of the hieroglyphs were enclosed in oval frames, called *cartouches,* as if to emphasize a name of special importance. Although he succeeded in identifying and translating only a few words and letters, he did show that the hiero-glyphs were in part alphabetic.

Champollion went on from there. He selected as a beginning the names of Ptolemy (in Greek Ptolemaios) and Cleopatra—each in a cartouche. He also knew that hieroglyphs could be written either from left to right or right to left, depending on which way the pictorial signs faced. He then compared the two names:

Ptolemy

Cleopatra

and deduced that the first letter of Cleopatra (C) should not occur in Ptolemy. It did not. The second letter (l) should correspond to the fourth of Ptolemy, and it did. In this way, a full alphabet emerged. The Greek script told him roughly what each word should mean, and Coptic—which is very similar to the Rosetta Stone language—gave him the sound value. In this way he was able to translate the entire text.

Actually, Champollion discovered that the hieroglyphic script was not quite that simple. After thousands of years, it had acquired a number of complications. A given word, for example, can be used or written in at least three ways. The English-language word *man* can help to illustrate the point. A picture of a man can stand for the word itself—an ideogram standing for "man." Secondly, the sound of the pictogram can be separated from its meaning to form part of another word, as in the first syllable of *mandate*. In that case only the sound value of the sign is used. Lastly, a word can be spelled out alphabeti-cally using the individual letters *m, a,* and *n*. The ancient Egyptians had evidently discovered that alphabetic signs were necessary to write foreign names or concepts for which there were no Egyptian counter-parts.

In its final form, Egyptian writing included ideograms (which gave a word in picture form), phonograms (which represented the sounds of words), alphabetic letters, and determinatives (which gave a clue to a word spelled by phonograms). For instance, a picture of writing mate-rials might mean the activity of writing, the equipment used in writ-ing, or the person doing the writing. A determinative sign that shows a man kneeling in the scribe's attitude indicates that the scribe himself is being referred to.

Champollion announced his success in 1822 in a letter to the Academy of Inscriptions in Paris entitled "Letter to Monsieur Dacier in Regard to the Alphabet of the Phonetic Hieroglyphs." Unfortunately, Champollion died in 1832, the subject of criticism and resentment from the academic world. He was vindicated some thirty years later when another bilingual stone was discovered in Egypt (the Decree of Canopus) and successfully translated using Champollion's methods.

How old is the universe?

The concept of a definite time of creation is an old and well-established part of western culture. In 1642 John Lightfoot of Cambridge University announced that the creation had taken place on September 17, 3928 B.C. at 9:00 A.M. Several years later, Archbishop James Ussher modified the date to October 3, 4004 B.C., a date that was accepted for the creation for over a century. Today, as a result of scientific studies of the radioactive composition of rocks, we know that the early estimates were too low by at least a few billion years.

Astronomers have determined that the entire universe is expanding, which is to say that every galaxy is receding from every other galaxy in the universe. Furthermore, the recession is not taking place in a haphazard manner. There is a definite connection between the distance between two galaxies and their mutual speed of recession. In mathematical terms, these quantities are in direct proportion: galaxies twice as far apart recede at twice the speed, and so on. This relationship, known as Hubble's law, makes it possible to calculate the date of creation of the universe.

When Hubble discovered the expansion of the universe, it was clear that the galaxies, now moving apart, must have been closer together in the past. Furthermore, because gravity diminishes with increasing distance, the gravitational attraction between galaxies was also greater in the past than it is now. But gravity must act to slow down the recession of the galaxies, so their speed of recession in the past must have been greater than now. So the universe can never have been static. On the other hand, the expansion cannot have been taking place forever, because if that were true the galaxies would be completely dispersed by now and we would not be able to see them. The only possible conclusion to be reached is that the universe cannot have existed forever— there must have been a definite time of creation. Hubble calculated the age of the universe by measuring the present rate of expansion of the universe and working back into the past, allowing for the effects of gravity. The age works out to be between 10 and 20 billion years.

How are particles removed from smokestack gases?

Most industrial operations, including smelting, chemical processing, and the burning of fossil fuels for power generation, release huge quantities of particulate matter in the plant's exhaust gases. In the United States alone, this solid matter adds up to 40 million tons each year, or well over 300 pounds for every inhabitant of the country. At the present time, about half of this material is still released to the atmosphere, where it contributes significantly to air pollution.

A modern method of removing particles from smokestack gases is called *electrostatic precipitation;* it makes use of a phenomenon called *corona discharge.* To understand how the process works, consider a metal cylinder with a wire along its axis, as shown in cross section in

CENTRAL WIRE

METAL TUBE

Fig. 22. Corona discharge. A high voltage between the wall of a metal tube and a central wire generates a luminous corona discharge near the center of the tube.

the accompanying diagram. A very high voltage is connected between the cylinder and the central wire so that the wire is charged negatively and the cylinder positively. If the voltage is raised sufficiently, a kind of continuous sparking or luminous glow takes place around the central wire. This glow is called corona discharge, in which electrons are knocked free of gas molecules, resulting in free electrons and positively charged molecules called *ions.* The negatively charged electrons are attracted by the positive cylinder wall and move outward at great speed. Many of the electrons strike dust particles and become imbedded in the particles. The particles, now negatively charged, are attracted to the cylinder wall.

In a practical application, the cylinder becomes the inner wall of a smokestack. If the smokestack gases contain liquid droplets, they collect on the cylinder wall and run down into a collecting hopper at the bottom. If the gases contain solid particles, they build up on the smokestack wall, which is vibrated periodically to let them fall into the hopper.

Electrostatic precipitators are extremely effective in reducing the amount of particulate matter released into the air. Properly designed and maintained, they remove as much as 99 percent of all particulate matter contained in exhaust gases.

How many human senses are there?

The popular concept is that man has five senses: touch, taste, smell, sight, and hearing. Many dictionaries, in fact, define the senses in terms of those five faculties. But scientists tell us that there are at least eight more to add to the list: pressure, pain, heat, cold, thirst, hunger, kinesthesis, and equilibrium—which brings the total to thirteen.

Sense organs are like biological sentries. They send information to the central nervous system concerning changing environmental conditions such as contact, temperature, and radiations. They perform this task by triggering nerve impulses when they are activated by some external stimulus. It turns out, however, that each kind of sense organ responds only to certain specific kinds of stimuli. To illustrate, some respond to light waves, some to chemicals, some to sound waves, and some to pressure. The work of our sense organs is the first step in the complex chain of events that makes us aware of the world we live in.

The nerve endings that give rise to the sense of pain are widespread in the skin and also in other parts of the body. It is a very useful sense, because it usually triggers responses that tend to protect the body from injury. A finger that touches a hot or sharp object may be jerked away, preventing more serious injury.

Various sense organs sometimes act in combination. If the sense organ cells of pain, pressure, and touch happen to be stimulated at the same time, the body may interpret the result as tickling. To take another example, temperature is sensed with the help of two kinds of nerve endings: one gives rise to the sensation of warmth, the other of coldness. A very hot object, such as a pot of boiling water, or a very cold object, such as dry ice, stimulates the nerve endings for warmth, cold, and pain. This combination gives rise to the sensation of burning.

The sensation of thirst is based on the concentration of salt in the

178

blood. Cells in a part of the brain called the *hypothalamus* are extremely sensitive to the blood's salt concentration. If there is too much salt (or too little water), we feel thirsty. After drinking some water, the salt concentration is reduced and the feeling of thirst is alleviated. There is also a sensitivity to dryness in the mouth which we interpret as thirst. When water eventually finds its way into the blood, more saliva is released and the mouth no longer feels dry.

Hunger is also sensed by the hypothalamus of the brain. Hunger depends on the blood's concentration of glucose, a kind of sugar. Several hours after the last meal, the glucose level in the blood tends to drop, and the hypothalamus tells us we are hungry. But soon after a meal, the glucose concentration rises again. This glucose is absorbed by the cells of the hypothalamus, and the sensation of hunger disappears.

Muscle sense is called *kinesthesis,* from the Greek, meaning sensation of movement. Nerve endings in muscles and other tissues are activated by tension and contraction. Impulses from these sense organs are interpreted by the brain to indicate the amount of relaxation or contraction of muscles. To illustrate, merely place your hand behind your back. The kinesthetic sense tells you whether the fingers are spread or clenched, straight or bent. Similarly, you can estimate the weight of an object by sensing the degree of contraction of certain muscles as they hold the object against the force of gravity.

The sense of equilibrium depends on sense organs in the inner ear called semicircular canals. The canals contain fine hairs that generate signals whenever the head accelerates. In addition, the vestibule of the inner ear contains small stones called *otoliths* (Greek: ear stones), which press against whichever nerve cells happen to be under them at the moment. If you lie down, for example, the otoliths stimulate a different set of cells from when you stand upright. The brain then interprets the impulses from these cells as indicating the new position of the head with respect to the gravitational pull of the earth.

What causes fog?

The blankets of fog that often cover coastlines and valleys are really ground-level stratus clouds. This is a layered, flattened type of cloud usually composed of minute water droplets or—if it is cold enough—tiny ice crystals. When seen at their normal altitudes, stratus clouds parallel the contours of the land and produce a threatening ap-

179

pearance across the entire sky. Fog is caused by the cooling of air until its water vapor condenses to form microscopic water droplets or ice crystals. These particles are so small that they remain suspended in the air for long periods of time, and a fog may last many hours or even days.

A ground fog often occurs when air near the ground loses heat at night to the rapidly cooling earth. This results in a cool layer of air nearest the ground with warmer air above it. When the air temperature falls below the dew-point temperature, air can no longer hold all its water vapor, and the excess condenses on suitable dust particles (called *condensation nuclei*) to form fog. If the air is still, little or no fog occurs, but if a gentle breeze is blowing, the fog builds up rapidly as the water-saturated air comes in contact with condensation nuclei. Strong winds, however, dissipate the fog by mixing it with warmer air aloft, where the droplets evaporate. Fogs of this kind usually form in the early evening and "burn off" in the morning as the air is warmed by the sun. Such a fog may form on the sides of a mountain. The cool, dense air "runs" downhill, generating a dense fog in valleys between the mountains. Fogs of this kind, called *ground,* or *radiation, fogs*, are most common in fall and winter because of the high humidity and longer night hours during those seasons.

A type of fog called an *advection fog* results when a mass of warm, moist air moves into a region whose temperature is cooler than the advancing air. As the warm air moves over the cool land or water, condensation occurs, forming a thick, low-lying fog bank. Fogs of this type can form during day or night. They are usually found along the seacoast or in areas partly covered with snow. In temperate regions, they often occur when warm southerly winds blow northward into cooler areas.

Advection fogs are common along the Atlantic coast of North America, where they are extremely hazardous to shipping. Most shipping lanes to Europe, in fact, move southward in winter, so ships can avoid the fog that forms off the coast of Newfoundland. Such fogs can persist for several weeks before dissipating.

Frontal fogs often form at the junction of warm and cold air masses. The transition regions between such air masses are called *fronts*. These fogs are relatively long-lasting and are usually accompanied by some sort of precipitation. They are quite common along the east coast of the United States.

180

What is the basis of the theory of relativity?

Before we discuss Einstein's theory of relativity, it will be helpful to discuss what is meant by acceleration. Suppose we drop a stone from a height of several feet and measure its velocity many times during its fall to the floor. The results of such an experiment tell us that the stone speeds up continously as it falls: its speed at any instant is faster than it was during the preceding instant. Motion of this kind, in which an object's velocity is always changing (either increasing or decreasing), is called accelerated motion. In contrast, motion at constant velocity is called uniform, or nonaccelerated, motion.

When Einstein began to think seriously about space and time, he came to the conclusion that there is no such thing as absolute motion or absolute rest. In the example above, for example, we spoke as though the floor were fixed in space and only the stone moved. But we know that the earth whirls on its axis at a prodigious rate, while it races around the sun. In our experiment with the stone we chose to use the earth as a convenient *frame of reference* within which to think about a moving stone. The point is this: the motion of an object can be described only with respect to some other object or frame of reference. All motion, therefore, is *relative*—which is precisely the reason that Einstein's theory is known as the *theory of relativity*.

Whenever we wish to describe a physical event, such as a falling stone, we must do so with respect to a frame of reference that we think of as being attached to some object or observer. The laws of motion are always the same in such reference frames that move uniformly—that is to say, without acceleration—with respect to each other.

To grasp fully the importance of this idea (which was well known before Einstein), imagine two people playing catch on the earth, while another pair plays catch in the aisle of a train moving in a straight line at a fixed velocity of 60 miles per hour. If you observe both games of catch you notice that the ball moves exactly the same way and obeys the same laws of motion in both situations. As long as such experiments are performed in a nonaccelerating reference frame, all nonaccelerating observers get exactly the same results.

Einstein extended the ideas given above to include all other physical effects, including light, and his theory, therefore, is based in part on the following two principles:

1. All physical laws are the same in all nonaccelerating frames of reference.

Einstein's second principle tells us that the speed of light is a constant number for all observers. In specific terms, it can be summarized as follows:

2. The speed of light (in a vacuum) is the same for all observers in nonaccelerating frames of reference regardless of any motion that may exist on the part of observer or light source.

Upon close examination, the second principle seems to contradict one of our firmest beliefs about motion. To illustrate, suppose a baseball pitcher can throw a baseball at a speed of 100 miles per hour. Now suppose the pitcher is located on a platform moving at a speed of 10 miles per hour toward the catcher. How fast is the ball moving when it reaches the catcher? Intuition tells us that we must add the two speeds to get the true speed of the ball: 100 + 10 = 110 miles per hour. In this example intuition is quite correct, as an experiment would show. Now suppose that we replace the pitcher with a source of light on the moving platform. In this experiment, we find that the speed of light as measured near the catcher is the same whether the platform is moving or fixed. Any observer in any frame of reference moving at uniform speed would measure the speed of light to be 186,000 miles per second (300 million meters per second). The same is true for any combination of motions of light source and observer, as long as the motion is uniform (nonaccelerating).

Albert Einstein used the two principles discussed above to develop his special theory of relativity—"special" because it deals only with nonaccelerating systems and observers. Prior to relativity theory, scientists had thought that space and time were entirely separate things—that events could be described as taking place at specific places in space and at precise times of occurrence, and furthermore that all observers—regardless of their motion—would measure the same distances and time intervals for the events. Einstein's theory of relativity showed that such ideas are not valid. Distances and time intervals are quite different for observers who are moving with respect to one another. Moreover, time and space are not independent but are linked together. It is not possible to specify an event in terms of its location in space, plus a separate designation for time. Space and time each have equal importance. That is why relativity is said to deal with a four-dimensional world—three for space and one for time.

Einstein's relativity is not evident in our lives because relativistic effects are insignificant at the everyday speeds at which we move. Only when speeds approach the speed of light do these effects become measurable. Thus, relativity is extremely important in the study of subatomic particles and the structure of matter and the universe.

As we have already seen, observers who are in uniform motion with respect to one another do not agree on time or distance measurements. Specifically, an observer will always find that a clock in motion with respect to the observer's frame of reference will run more slowly than an identical clock at rest. This behavior is called the *time dilation effect*. The closer the moving clock approaches the speed of light, the slower it runs. For example, when the clock's motion reaches about 87 percent of the speed of light (162,000 miles per hour), it runs slow by 50 percent—that is, a second on the moving clock is twice as long as a second on the clock at rest.

A similar effect takes place when an observer measures the length of an object that is in uniform motion. In such experiments the object in motion is always shorter in the direction of motion than it "ought" to be. This behavior is known as the *length contraction effect*. Once again, at a speed of 87 percent of the speed of light, the measured length is one-half the length measured with the object at rest.

Motion also has an effect on the mass of an object as its speed approaches the speed of light. In this case, the object's mass increases with its speed. A one-pound mass, for example, approximately doubles when its speed reaches 87 percent of the speed of light.

The question often arises as to whether the relativistic changes in time, distance, and mass are real or merely scientific "tricks" to assist in calculations. Time and again, measurements have demonstrated that relativistic effects are entirely real in rapidly moving systems. They are not illusions or hocus-pocus but a valid description of how nature behaves.

Einstein's first scientific paper on relativity was published in 1905 and dealt, as we have seen, with nonaccelerating systems and observers. Ten years later he enlarged the theory to include accelerating reference frames, and his theory became known as the general theory of relativity.

We know that all objects, including the heavenly bodies, have mass, which is associated with gravitational forces. Such forces generate accelerated motion rather than uniform motion. For that reason, gravitation could not be treated under special relativity. General relativity, however, is designed to deal specifically with mass, gravitation, and acceleration. It is, in fact, a theory of gravitation.

Einstein's space-time is really a four-dimensional world. It is not easy, of course, to make suitable analogies with which to describe such a world. But imagine that our four-dimensional space-time is curved here and there by the presence of mass. Similarly, a warping or curvature of space-time reveals itself as a mass. In Einstein's general theory of relativity, space and time are woven together into a single fabric, and mass distorts the space-time surface.

The general theory has provided scientists with a new way of viewing the behavior of nature and plays an important role in their attempts to understand the universe in which we live.

Can pleasure be produced electrically?

Using lower animals, scientists have located centers of pain and pleasure in a region of the brain near the hypothalamus, a region that regulates many needs, including those for food and water. Fine-wire electrodes can be implanted in these centers of the brain so that pressing a lever will send a minute electric current to the pleasure area. In one experiment, hungry rats were given the choice of two levers, one for pleasure and the other for food. They invariably ran faster to the pleasure lever than to the food lever. The pleasure involved seemed to be intense; some rats stimulated their pleasure electrode for hours or days on end if allowed to do so.

Similar experiments have been performed with some success on human beings. Patients press a lever to stimulate a pleasurable sensation when they feel pain coming on. In a few cases, cancer patients under heavy doses of morphine have been provided with "pleasure levers" for brain stimulation. With this help, some patients have been able to do without drugs for as long as three months. Such success is an exception, however, and not the rule.

Pleasure sensors or receptors outside the brain have been very difficult to find, if indeed there are any. However, we do have pain receptors, called *free nerve endings,* located just below the skin. Damage to these free nerve endings seems to trigger impulses that move toward the brain.

Although pain is a very real thing, to some extent it seems to be learned. In a few cases, children were reared in isolation with almost no love or stimulation. Some of these children showed little or no re-

184

sponse to a cut or minor injury. Similarly, when dogs are raised in complete isolation, they seem to have *no* ability to feel pain. They may place their noses in a candle flame repeatedly—with very little response. Scientists suspect that there is a critical period in the animal's life during which the pain receptors are formed. For a dog reared in isolation, that period seems to have been bypassed.

Why are tornadoes so destructive?

Of all weather phenomena, tornadoes are probably most feared because of their concentrated power of destruction. A tornado usually looks like a narrow vertical funnel, a cylinder, or a rope extending from the base of a thunderstorm to the ground.

Tornadoes, like other cyclonic wind systems, revolve counterclockwise in the northern hemisphere and clockwise in the southern. Inhabitants of the North American midwest call them "twisters," but the term hardly describes their violence.

Tornadoes are usually quite small in extent, less than a quarter mile in diameter, but some are much larger. The funnels often touch down for only a few minutes or so, although, here again, tornadoes vary widely. The path followed by a typical tornado covers an average of 16 miles, but this distance has been surpassed many times over. On May 26, 1917, a tornado crossed Illinois and Indiana leaving a path of destruction 293 miles long. This enormous twister lasted for 7 hours and 20 minutes. Yet in 1978 a small twister in Maryland affected an area no larger than an acre or two.

The energy in a tornado is enormous by any set of standards. In 1931 a tornado in Minnesota lifted an 83-ton railroad car, carried it a distance of 80 feet, and deposited it intact in a ditch. Luckily, all 117 passengers aboard survived the incident.

The winds around the vortex of a tornado often exceed 250 miles per hour. These winds alone can exert a force of several hundred pounds on one square foot of a building. In addition, the pressure within the eye is extremely low—as much as 1.5 pounds per square inch lower than the surrounding air pressure. The low pressure and strong winds account for the destructive power of a tornado.

When a tornado passes over a building, the pressure suddenly drops outside the building, while the inside pressure changes more slowly— particularly if the windows and doors are closed. The result is a great pressure differential that tends to make the building explode. The force tending to blow out the roof of a typical house can reach 400,000 pounds! As a result, the walls and roof blow outward and are pounded savagely by the destructive force of the wind. Tornadoes have scattered the remnants of demolished buildings over great distances.

Almost all tornadoes are associated with thunderstorms, but meteorologists do not agree on the relationship between the two. It seems likely, however, that a thunderstorm causes the funnel and supplies its energy.

Although tornadoes occur in many regions of the world, they are most prevalent, by far, in the United States. There may be perhaps 700 tornadoes sighted in an average year. Usually, a thunderstorm system will produce several tornadoes, although as many as forty separate funnels can be generated by one storm over a distance of a few hundred miles.

A tornado usually travels in a northeasterly direction, at a speed in the range of 35 to 45 miles per hour. Often, the tornado is preceded and followed by heavy rain, and the storm may appear and leave with little warning.

Tornadoes do not always move continuously along the surface but sometimes rise and fall a number of times along their paths. They skip some areas and suddenly drop down on others for no apparent reason. They often turn and move in unexpected directions. This makes it particularly difficult and dangerous to try to outrun a tornado.

Weather forecasters can outline areas, perhaps a hundred miles across, within which tornadoes are likely to occur. Unfortunately, it is not yet possible to pinpoint the specific places in which a tornado will strike. Once a tornado is sighted, however, radar sets can track a tornado-producing storm so that people in its path can seek cover or evacuate the region quickly.

How did life begin on earth?

Scientists do not know precisely how or when life first appeared on earth. Telltale traces of life have been found in rocks 3½ billion years old, so sometime during the previous billion years a form of living organism must have appeared that was capable of reproducing itself in the primeval ocean.

Astronomers have discovered recently that organic molecules exist in outer space. These are the basic molecular building blocks needed to construct living organisms. Radio telescopes have detected emissions that prove the existence of more than two dozen complex molecules of the kind found in living things. Even alcohol has been detected in outer space. No one knows how these chemicals formed, but their existence indicates that the chemical basis for living matter was probably available prior to the formation of the earth.

In 1953 Stanley Miller and Joseph Urey at the University of Chicago performed a remarkable experiment in a sealed glass flask. The flask contained pure water, and the gases methane, ammonia, and hydrogen, all of which were probably contained in the earth's primitive atmosphere. The mixture was boiled for a week in the presence of electrical discharges to simulate electric storms in the atmosphere. These electric discharges supplied the energy needed to combine the atmospheric ingredients into larger molecular units. The scientists did not expect to generate life with their simple experiment. What they did find, even after one week, was a deep red, soupy liquid instead of the pure water they had started with. In that soup were many of the basic organic molecules normally associated with living things.

Many biologists believe that—given enough time—the conditions prevailing on the primitive earth and in outer space would make the formation of living organisms highly probable. A number of energy sources were available to produce the required chemical changes: lightning, volcanic heat, ultraviolet light, and cosmic rays, for example. Complex molecules existed in the early oceans and in outer space. And there was plenty of time available for the complex series of molecular rearrangements to occur, ending in the first living, reproducing organism. The process might have taken many millions of years, for it is a long way from the formation of organic molecules in the Chicago flask to the first self-duplicating molecule. Yet that length of time is but an instant in the earth's 4½ billion years of existence.

When the first tiny living organism formed out of successive combinations of simpler molecules, it probably reproduced and spread over the entire planet, consuming the primeval soup. Later, a new kind of living thing evolved—the precursor of green plants—which produced oxygen by using sunlight to power a chemical reaction called photosynthesis. The oxygen in the atmosphere generated a layer of ozone, high above the air, which effectively blocked out the sun's ultraviolet rays. From that time on, conditions were favorable for organisms to develop toward the general pattern we know today. Plants use the energy of sunlight to release oxygen and manufacture organic substances, and animals consume oxygen and organic substances to capture the energy originally derived from sunlight.

Why do waves break against the shore?

Before waves reach the shore, they take the form of low, broad, regular, and rounded mounds or ridges, called *swell*. The swell becomes higher as it approaches the shore, builds up into the familiar sharp-crested wave shape, and breaks forward into foaming breakers, or surf, near the shore.

To understand how breakers take shape from ocean swell, consider the motion of a small piece of cork or wood floating on the water. As a wave crest approaches, the cork moves a little forward and then the same amount backward in the trough between waves. Although the wave moves steadily forward, the motion of the cork shows that the water moves back and forth slightly. Experiments in large laboratory tanks have been conducted on artificially generated waves, and these experiments show that the motion of the cork is approximately a circular vertical orbit. Further tests on small floats at different depths in the water show that all of them move with the same characteristic mo-

Fig. 23. Waves are produced by the motion of water particles in circular vertical orbits. As the lower orbits begin to strike the bottom of the shore, their vertical motion is impeded and the wave crest grows higher.

188

tion—approximately circular vertical orbits, as shown in the accompanying diagram. The orbits are greatest in size at the surface of the water and grow gradually smaller until they disappear at a depth equal to about one-half the wavelength—the horizontal distance between adjacent crests of the waves.

Now we can imagine what happens as waves approach the shore across a slowly rising bottom. When the wave reaches the point where the depth is equal to one-half the wavelength, the lowest orbits begin to "feel" the bottom. At that place, the presence of the bottom restricts

Fig. 24. As a wave approaches shore across a slowly rising bottom, the vertical orbits "feel" bottom and the wave crest grows higher and higher as its speed slows down. Eventually, the wave cannot support its height, and a breaker forms.

the vertical motion of the lowest orbit. As the wave moves into shallower water, successively higher orbits have their vertical motion restricted, and the whole wave begins to slow down. A further consequence of this effect is that the wave grows higher and steeper. The wave steepness increases until the water can no longer support itself, and the wave breaks with a crash into the splashing surf, as shown in the second diagram. The water's depth at this point is about 1.3 times as great as the height of the wave. Thus, the location of the surf zone—where the waves break—and the height of the waves combine to provide a good guide to the depth of the water.

189

What causes a chinook wind?

Chinooks are warm, dry winds that often cause a temperature rise of 20°F to 40°F in 15 minutes or less. On one occasion, a chinook at Havre, Montana, caused the temperature to increase from 11°F to 42°F in three minutes. In Europe these winds are called *foehns,* and an American Indian term for these winds is translated as "snow eaters."

Chinook winds are triggered by the movement over a mountain ridge of a low-pressure center aloft. Air is forced down the other side of the mountain and is warmed by compression much as a tire pump heats up when air is compressed. This causes a reduction in the relative humidity, and the wind is hot and dry.

To understand how a chinook forms, imagine a wind blowing across a mountain range. The air rises on the windward side of the mountains, cools, and forms clouds and rain. In addition, the condensation of water vapor to form rain releases a certain amount of heat, which is taken up by the air. This added heat retards the cooling effect as the air rises but does not stop the cooling entirely. The rising air loses approximately 2.8°F per 1000 feet of increased altitude.

Over the ridge, on the lee side of the mountain, most of the moisture has been lost. As the wind descends, it is warmed as its pressure increases. The increase in temperature amounts to about 5.5°F for each 1000 feet of descent. This wind, therefore, is warmer and drier than the windward air flow. Its relative humidity drops as the air descends, and the wind rapidly evaporates clouds, snow, or any moisture it finds on the lee slope. Mountain slopes on the lee side are said to be in the "rain shadow," a region of dry climate and sometimes desert-like conditions.

From the lee side of the mountains, the clouds raining on the weather side resemble a solid, dark wall, towering threateningly over the crest of the ridge. For this reason they are often called the chinook, or foehn, wall. In springtime, when temperatures are still rather cold, the chinook bursts suddenly into the valleys and melts the snow with its sudden and unaccustomed warmth.

The term *foehn* originated on the northern slopes of the Alps in Europe, but these winds are also common on the east slopes of the Rocky Mountains—particularly in Wyoming and Montana, where they are called chinooks. Minor examples are also found east of the Scottish Highlands, along the coast of the North Sea. Death Valley, in the

United States, is on the lee side of the Sierra Nevada range.

The human discomfort produced by chinook winds is sometimes referred to as "foehn sickness." The "sickness," however, does not seem to be medical in nature but is probably caused by stress associated with the sudden change in temperature.

Why does a human egg cell become a human being instead of a tree or another animal?

Every human being develops from a single fertilized egg cell. This tiny living organism divides and grows, developing gradually into a human being. How does the growing fetus "know" where the head should be, how many arms and legs there should be, that there should be hands instead of paws, skin instead of scales?

Scientists first came to the conclusion that the chromosomes are a kind of biological blueprint that somehow manage to convey information from one generation to the next. As more was learned about heredity, they added the theory that chromosomes contain genes, each gene being responsible for a specific characteristic. There would be genes for eye color, body size, hair color, and so on.

Latest research indicates that genes are made up of a chemical called deoxyribonucleic acid, or DNA for short. This substance consists of six kinds of smaller units arranged in the form of a long ladder that has been twisted to form a double helix. Before we discuss this structure and what it has to do with heredity and blueprints, let us look into the compounds called nucleic acids.

Nucleic acids, such as DNA, are built up of a great number of small units called nucleotides. These in turn consist of a kind of sugar molecule, a phosphate molecule, and a third kind of molecule containing nitrogen that is called an organic base. The DNA molecule contains four organic bases, one sugar, and one phosphate, repeated many times in a specific way to produce the double helix structure. The four organic bases (also called heterocyclic nitrogen compounds) are adenine, thymine, cytosine, and guanine.

If we imagine that the DNA double helix is untwisted and straightened out, a portion of it can be represented schematically as shown in the diagram, where the six structural compounds are represented by the letters P (phosphate), S (sugar), A (adenine), T (thymine), C (cytosine), and G (guanine). The solid lines represent ordinary chemical bonds holding the units together. The dotted lines indicate much

191

weaker bonds (called hydrogen bonds). As we shall see, the weak hydrogen bonds make it possible to separate the DNA molecule into two parts by dividing along the line of hydrogen bonds. It turns out that *A* (adenine) is always paired with *T* (thymine), and *C* (cytosine) is always paired with *G* (guanine) in forming rungs for the ladder.

All DNA molecules have the same sequence of sugar and phosphates in the long parts of the ladder. The difference between DNA molecules lies in the arrangement of the organic bases in the rungs, adenine, thymine, cytosine, and guanine. This sequence of *A, C, T,* and *G* molecules constitutes the genetic code—the blueprint for heredity—representing the four substances in the rungs of the ladder. These letters are arranged in groups of three (which will be discussed later)

Fig. 25.   The structure of part of a DNA molecule. The solid lines represent ordinary chemical bonds, and the dotted lines represent weaker hydrogen bonds. The letters stand for sugar, phosphate, adenine, thymine, cytosine, and guanine, the six constituents of DNA.

to form a specific code. Thus, the code might be *TAC, CCT, ATG,* or *AAA,* for instance.

The DNA molecule for a simple virus contains about 1800 pieces of information coded in groups of three letters. That amount of data is sufficient to describe that particular virus. If each such piece of information corresponded to one letter of our alphabet, it would take 1800 letters to genetically describe that virus. That amounts to somewhat less than a full page of this book. A human DNA molecule, on the other hand, has enough nucleotides to form about 1.7 billion coded pieces of information. Using the same analogy as above, it would take about 2000 volumes to hold all that information. A human being, it seems, is an extremely complex piece of apparatus.

Whenever a living cell divides, it produces two cells with precisely the same properties. This means that the DNA present in the original cell must duplicate itself exactly so that each new cell will contain the same coded information. What happens is this. The ladder "unzips" along the weak hydrogen bonds to form two half chains. Each of these then acts as a template on which nucleotide units can collect to complete the desired double helix structure. Recall that A and T attract only each other, and G and C attract only each other. This means that each half of the DNA chain is quite specific as to which nucleotides it will attract. Thus, the two new DNA molecules will be exactly the same as the original.

We have already mentioned that the DNA code consists of the four letters A, T, C, and G, arranged in groups of threes. Scientists believe that the DNA code groups specify individual chemical compounds called amino acids. Since there are twenty primary amino acids found in nature, there must be at least twenty different code groups in the DNA molecule—one for each amino acid type. It can be shown mathematically that each code group must consist of three letters to provide that many codes. It is known, for example, that the code group AAA specifies the amino acid phenylalanine, and TTT specifies lysine. The information coded in the DNA molecule can be used to assemble a specific sequence of amino acids to form a protein molecule. The procedure by which this is accomplished is complex, and beyond the scope of this book. Nevertheless, it is easy to see that human DNA contains an enormous amount of information, which is quite sufficient to describe the making of a human being.

Once in a while a DNA molecule can become changed in some unexpected way. Suppose, for example, that one of the code letters is changed to one of the other letters. The incorrect information would be used when the DNA is copied, and a mutation would occur. A mutation also takes place when a code letter is omitted, or added, or if the order of the letters is disturbed. The great majority of such mutations are undesirable; they occur as a result of exposure to radiation or certain chemicals.

What causes "damping off" of seedlings?

The seeds of most plants carry the microscopic spores of a great number of molds or fungi. Furthermore, the soil in which they are planted is likely to be teeming with fungi. Some of these fungi invade the germinating seeds and succulent seedlings of many kinds of plants and kill them. The fungal diseases of seeds and seedlings are most prevalent in moist soil and wet weather, from which comes the term "damping off."

Much of the loss caused by damping off can be eliminated by treating the seed or soil with fungicides that protect the young seedlings until they are strong and sturdy enough to fight off the effects of fungi. Unfortunately, no one fungicide is suitable for all crops and locations. One may work well for tomato seeds but not for corn. Another may protect soybeans in Illinois but not in Minnesota. Another may work in Maryland in one year but not the next. Nevertheless, fungicides have contributed mightily to the success and stabilization of modern agriculture.

On a small scale, damping off can be reduced by planting seeds in sand rather than garden soil. The fungi responsible for damping off are considerably more numerous in soil than in sand because soil provides a wealth of plant remains for them to feed on. Another small-scale solution to the problem is to heat garden soil in the oven for half an hour or so. The heat kills the fungi, so the soil, once it has cooled, can be safely used for planting seeds.

Can people do extraordinary feats under hypnosis?

The word *hypnotism* comes from the Greek word for sleep. In the early days of hypnotism there was little knowledge of the power of psychological influence, and hypnosis was thought to be a physical state—sleep—rather than a psychological process. Modern studies show that hypnosis and sleep are not the same thing at all. Brain waves under hypnosis are different from those of sleep, and reflexes are not the same. The resemblance between sleep and the hypnotic state is essentially superficial. Hypnotism is a form of suggestion in which outside interference is reduced and the subject is made to relax and place complete trust in the hypnotist. People under hypnosis do not lose consciousness but are aware of what is going on and can take control of themselves if they wish.

The easiest, or at least the most popular, way to put a person in a hypnotic "trance" is to require concentration on some object—perhaps a moving coin or other shiny object. Any rhythmic motion, however, seems to work, such as a voice speaking in measured patterns. A subject can even be hypnotized by listening to his own breathing. Some people can be hypnotized, in part, by monotony. Drivers of automobiles may become hypnotized by gazing steadily at the white line on the road.

The many varied ways in which hypnosis can be induced suggests to psychologists that it is not the mysterious thing it is often made to seem. Two factors that appear to be involved with hypnosis are a state of relaxation and a high susceptibility to the power of suggestion. To illustrate the latter, consider your left foot. You probably were not aware of it until I brought the subject up. Now you can feel it. Notice how tight your shoe feels, assuming you are wearing shoes. Why not wiggle your toes to help the circulation? All of this illustrates that suggestion can focus your attention and control your powers. This focusing of attention is extremely important to effective hypnosis. For hypnosis to work, the subject must be able to disregard information that contradicts the suggestions of the hypnotist.

In the entertainment field, even where trickery is not involved, hypnotists usually have their subjects perform unusual feats of one sort or another. For example, a person may be suspended rigidly between two chair backs, one under the ankles and the other under the neck. The hypnotist may then use a hammer to break a concrete slab resting on the subject's stomach. Such feats are entirely possible by a well-trained, relaxed, and trusting individual, even without hypnotism. The subject is not harmed because the trick is within the capability of the human body. The same argument holds for lying on a bed of nails. It has been shown that people can learn to lie on a bed of nails without harm if they are perfectly relaxed and the nails are not too sharp and are close enough together. Others can learn to walk on hot coals, if they have adequate timing and confidence, although I would surely not like to have to prove the point. Apparently many people have enough moisture to prevent burning, if they know how to do the trick. Scientists who have studied hypnosis tell us that people who are highly motivated and convinced of the possibility of doing the task can do just as well as those who have been hypnotized. Hypnosis does not endow the subject with any special qualities or abilities to perform extraordinary feats. All the hypnotist can do is bring out the subject's latent abilities.

One theory of hypnosis tells us that subjects behave as they believe they ought to when hypnotized. They accept the control of the hypnotist and really "live" the suggestions directed to them. Told to forget, they forget; told to recall, they recall. Most subjects probably do not realize that they actually have this power all along and that the hypnotist only acts as an aid in releasing it. It is much like the talented actress who becomes so involved in her part that she actually comes to feel like the person she is playing.

Another theory holds that the power of suggestion, once firmly established, enables the subject to suppress nerve impulses that might cause behavior contrary to the desires of the hypnotist. Scientists know, for example, that a relaxed person who is awake can control his or her brain waves, heart rate, and blood pressure—through concentration. It is not too far-fetched, then, to suggest that we may also be able to control nerve impulses that register on the brain. As a matter of fact, scientists have shown that hypnotized persons can create a kind of "hypnotic blindness." While in this state the brain blocks the brain-wave patterns that are usually present when a person receives visual stimulation.

All these ideas are still theories, however, and no one really has all the answers on hypnosis. The reader is cautioned, therefore, to avoid experimenting with hypnosis except under the guidance of a qualified individual.

Do insects engage in farming?

Many kinds of ants—of which there are thousands—have extremely complex and highly developed societies. Some groups, like the army ants, are primitive hunters that forage for food. The common garden ants are the "dairymen" of the ant world, who engage in the pastoral life. They "kidnap" aphid eggs, nourish the young, pasture them, and "milk" them for their honeydew secretion. Still others capture weaker species and employ them as slaves to do the drudgery while the masters go on picnics. All of which indicates that ants, considered to be the most successful of all insect groups, are anything but simple. The kinds we are interested in raise various types of fungi for food.

Fungi, of which the ordinary edible mushroom is a large and delectable example, are plants having no green chlorophyll, so they must depend on other plants or animals for food. This has led some fungi to strike up partnerships with various animals, to the advantage of both. And that is where the ants—or to be more specific, the leaf-cutting ants—come into the story.

How certain ants have come to cultivate fungi as their sole diet has been the subject of a good deal of speculation. Perhaps the most rea-

196

sonable explanation is as follows. Ants have a pouch in the bottom of the mouth called the *infrabuccal pocket*. Any solid food they eat goes into this pocket, where soluble substances are dissolved. The liquid solution is swallowed, but the solids are screened out and accumulate in the pouch. Being fastidious animals, much of the ants' leisure time is spent in combing bits of dirt and debris off their bodies. This grooming is accomplished by means of fine combs on the forelegs. The combs, in turn, are cleaned by passing them neatly through the mouth. So the particles of dust, dirt, and other solid matter so acquired end up in the infrabuccal pocket. In time the pouch becomes filled, and the contents are thrown out, much as a baseball player or cowboy may dispose of a spent chew of tobacco.

Before such disposal, the pouch is moist and warm. And it is highly likely that among its contents would be a great variety of microscopic fungus spores, or seeds. Although most of the spores perish in the pouch, others thrive. When the waste material is deposited in the nest, fungi grow and cover the material. Since certain kinds of fungi are high in food value, and since the ants can subsist on them, it is not surprising that some of the more clever kinds of ants should have learned to cultivate them.

Each of the hundred or so species of leaf-cutting ants prefers the leaves of certain particular plants for its compost pile. Their preference presumably depends on the kind of compost that their particular fungus variety grows best on. They go out in hordes to gnaw out pieces of leaves as large as they are able to carry and march home with them, only to repeat the process over and over. Other specialists of the community chew up the leaves and pack them neatly in growing beds for the fungus. To the beds they add the rich contents of their infrabuccal pockets, their own dung, and the remains of their deceased brethren. This serves not only to tidy up the living quarters of the nest but also to enrich the compost with nitrogen and other good things on which the fungus may thrive. Some may consider the ants' use of night soil as fertilizer to be a primitive and disease-inducing procedure, but ants have been doing it since ancient times and appear to have few problems with intestinal upset.

Perhaps the most amazing aspect of ant farms is the purity of the crop. Leaf-cutting ants—or parasol ants, as they are also called—do not cultivate just any fungus, willy-nilly, but only certain specific ones. The leaves and other matter carried into the nest for composting must contain hundreds, perhaps thousands of different varieties of fungus. Scientists cannot help wondering why some of these "weed" fungi do not take over and ruin the ant farms, just as weeds often ruin our gardens. If ant farmers do experience crop failures of that sort, scientists are not aware of them. Ants are able to maintain for decades on end an essentially pure culture of fungus for their food crop. This is not a simple task even in a modern laboratory or commercial mushroom-growing operation.

Ant gardens vary greatly in size—from a half-inch or so in diameter in arid regions to garden chambers as large as a house in tropical regions. The larger ones feed upwards of a half million ants.

When a young queen is ready to go forth and found a new colony, she packs up her infrabuccal pocket with the fungus that has nourished her ancestors for millions of years. Her first task on her own is to grub out a small chamber and establish the traditional garden. Only then does she concentrate on the urgent task of raising ants.

Ants, by the way, are not the only animals that have taken so well to farming. Some of the termites also cultivate fungi for food. Ambrosia beetles, which inhabit dead trees, also subsist entirely on a fungus they cultivate. The fungus is planted in the wooden wall of a chamber, where it forms enormous quantities of pear-shaped spores much like the food cells raised by the leaf-cutting ants. The more spores the beetles eat, the more are formed. So the beetles have hit upon a marvelous arrangement. In order to assure themselves of a plentiful supply of food, all they have to do is eat.

Why are some dogs shy and unfriendly?

Animals, as well as human beings, seem to be born with certain built-in behavior patterns. These patterns might be compared with those of a flower that follows an orderly sequence of events to blossom at a preset time. So, too, do animals and man develop certain characteristics only at specific times during their growth cycle. Like the flower, they follow a certain sequence of events over which they have little control. To illustrate, a human child seems to be preprogrammed for the ability to walk, a natural process that begins between nine and fifteen months of age. Experiments have shown that children will walk at about the same age whether or not they are "taught" to walk by their parents.

Psychologists tell us that many animals are programmed from birth to recognize someone or something as their mother. In psychology, this programming is called *imprinting*. In general, the animal's brain is embossed or imprinted with a mother image—or what it considers to be its mother—at a certain age. When an object, whether its real mother or not, is shown to the baby animal at the correct time in its development, the object is labeled "mother" somewhere in the brain. This label is usually extremely difficult to erase.

Psychological studies have covered another kind of imprinting that occurs in the lives of dogs. Apparently, dogs have a critical period— about six to nine weeks long—for forming social bonds or attachments to human beings. If a dog is kept isolated from human companionship during this period, it will tend to remain undomesticated, shy, and unfriendly. The critical period ends at about twelve weeks of age, so a person would not want to buy a puppy older than twelve weeks that has been isolated in a kennel. This is particularly true if the dog is large and potentially dangerous.

Psychologists believe that human beings have similar critical periods. The wagging of a puppy's tail, for example, is similar to the baby's smile that appears about a month and a half after birth. Both serve to elicit love from others.

Learning to speak a foreign language with a natural accent also involves a critical period. Such linguistic skill is rarely possible for people over twelve years of age. Beyond that age, some change seems to occur that prevents full development of foreign-language speech sounds, except with extraordinary coaching and practice.

How are icebergs formed?

Glaciers are vast flowing rivers of ice that move downhill at relatively slow rates of speed. When glaciers terminate on land, streams of meltwater combine to form a single stream or river, such as the Rhone. Glaciers that end at the water's edge form great cliffs of ice, many of them standing 200 feet or more above the level of the lake or ocean. Because ice floats, its buoyancy, combined with tidal movements and melting, breaks off enormous icebergs from the edge of the glacier. The icebergs then drift with ocean currents and end up in warmer waters, where they melt.

Many icebergs are as large as small islands and become a menace to navigation. Such an iceberg sank the *Titanic* in 1912 with a loss of 1489 lives.

A physical law known as Archimedes' Principle explains why an object can float in water. The principle is based on the fact that a fluid—such as water or air—exerts an upward buoyant force on a body placed in it. The body is buoyed up by a force equal to the weight of the fluid displaced by the body. Ice has a *specific gravity* of about 0.9, which means that it weighs about nine-tenths as much as an equal volume of water. So an iceberg floats with about nine-tenths of its mass submerged. This underwater mass of ice is hidden from view and presents a great danger to nearby ships.

How do lightning rods work?

It was originally thought that a lightning rod protects a building by slowly discharging the electricity in a cloud harmlessly to earth. Scientists now know that lightning rods perform their function by diverting the stroke through electrical wires to ground instead of allowing it to pass destructively through the structure itself.

Lightning is essentially an enormous electric spark that seeks the path of least resistance to ground. A typical stroke can have a current peak of 10,000 to 20,000 amperes of current, and occasionally much higher. This compares with a conventional household light bulb that carries 1 ampere or less.

A lightning stroke reaches its peak current in a few millionths of a second. The current then usually falls off to a small amount in about a thousandth of a second. Flashes of that kind that fall off quickly are called *cold lightning,* because they do not cause fires. On some occasions, a continuing electric current of about 100 amperes flows for one or two tenths of a second following decay of the peak current. Such strokes are called *hot lightning,* because they are likely to set fires. The terms "hot" and "cold" are misleading, however, because both types reach the same temperature—between 15,000 and 60,000°F. Hot lightning sets fires because of its longer duration; the heat is in contact with wood for a longer period of time.

Experience has shown that no lightning rod, however tall, offers complete protection against lightning. Nevertheless, lightning rods are extremely effective if installed properly. The basic idea is that a single vertical rod will almost certainly protect a building that lies within its "cone of protection." As shown in the accompanying diagram, the cone of protection consists of all the imaginary lines drawn between the top of the rod and a circle on the ground. The diagram is drawn so

200

that the height of the rod, H, is equal to the radius of the circle on the ground. This corresponds to the British lightning code. In the United States, the code specifies a wider-based cone in which the ground circle has a radius of $2H$. The greater protection is provided by the smaller-based radius. For that reason, a building containing explosives or extremely flammable materials is often protected with a base radius as small as $H/2$.

A basic lightning rod system has three equally important parts: the rods on the roof, the grounding arrangement, and the wires that connect the rods to each other and to the grounding arrangement. The function of the wires is to carry the electric current of the lightning stroke from the rods to ground. They are usually made of copper or aluminum and measure between ¼ and ⅜ inch in diameter. Wires as small as ⅛ inch in diameter made of galvanized iron are sometimes used and will carry all but the most extreme lightning currents with-

Fig. 26. A: A house is protected by a single lightning rod with a 45-degree cone of protection. The height of the rod is equal to the radius of the circle on the ground that outlines the area of protection. B: A house is protected by three shorter lightning rods.

out damage. Wires of the lightning rod system must be well grounded or the lightning may jump to the building in search of a better ground. Grounding can be accomplished by driving long metal rods into moist ground.

Why do members of another race all "look alike"?

There are exceptions to the rule, of course, but many members of one race often have considerable difficulty in recognizing individuals of another race. Blacks, for example, have no difficulty identifying and differentiating the faces of other blacks, but whites, Japanese, and Chinese all tend to "look alike" to them.

Psychologists believe that the degree of familiarity we have with another race or ethnic group is an important factor in our ability to recognize and distinguish faces. That ability seems to depend on how much we perceive them to be similar to ourselves. Most of us can pick our own dog or cat out of a large group of similar animals, but we would have difficulty telling one unfamiliar Great Dane from another.

Suppose that some dark night, on a deserted street, you are mugged by a lion. When the police arrive and ask for a description of the attacker, what would you tell them? You would know whether it was a male or female by the fur around the head, but what other characteristics would come to mind? It was big, had large dark eyes, and large paws. That description fits quite a few lions. Would you be able to pick your attacker out of a lion line-up? Ridiculous, right? Wrong. There are people who could do that with no difficulty because they work with lions and are familiar with them. They pick up certain cues that help them distinguish one lion from another. Unlike most of us who are unfamiliar with lions, they notice such things as the length, shape, and color of teeth; the facial pattern, including eye separation and color; the different shades of fur coloration; the characteristic gait; the peculiar sounds the animal makes; and so on. The more familiar we are with the characteristics of a group of people, or animal species, the more likely we are to be able to distinguish between members of that group or species.

Some psychologists suspect that the problem of identification across racial or ethnic lines may result, in some instances, from prejudice. Because of prejudice, some people are thought to have emotional reactions to members of other races or ethnic groups that make it difficult to recognize individual differences. Recognizing individuals would tend to give them higher status, and that is ruled out by prejudice.

This is theory, of course, and certainly not proved.

The lack of interracial identification and recognition—or *perceptual blanking,* as it is called—has important implications in criminal law. Attorneys point out that witness identification is an important cause of wrongful conviction. Police are often frustrated by the great variation they get in witnesses' descriptions of criminals. Descriptions are distorted, to some extent, by the characteristic types that a witness does not like; instead of describing the actual criminal, the descriptions tend to fit the image of a "bad guy." Furthermore, a witness under stress tends to fill in details as he thinks they ought to be rather than as they were. By the time a trial comes up, the witness is more convinced than ever of his identification because he now sees the accused as being arrested, indicted, and under trial. Justice is endangered to the extent that perceptual blanking leads to incorrect identification of defendants. It is a trap that each of us must guard against, especially when we are involved in interracial identification.

Why are dyes not removed by washing?

Most commercial dyes are not removed from clothing by soaps or detergents because they are bonded tightly to the cloth. Effective bonding of dye to fabric is either chemical or mechanical in nature, and is accomplished in several ways.

A method called *ingrain dyeing* is used to dye cotton with such substances as para red. In this method, the para red molecule is formed directly on the cloth rather than synthesizing the dye first and then applying it to the cloth. When this technique is used, the small molecules that combine to make para red can penetrate tiny crevices in the fiber, which would be difficult for a large molecule to enter. The small molecules then combine chemically to form the larger molecules of the dye. After this synthesis, the large dye molecules are trapped in the fiber where they were formed. In addition to the mechanical entrapment of the dye molecule, cotton forms a kind of chemical union with para red by a method that chemists call hydrogen bonding.

A process called *direct dyeing* involves a chemical reaction in which a part of the dye molecule combines with the fiber itself. Wool and silk are easy to dye in this way because they are composed of protein molecules that combine readily with many dyes. With direct dyeing, the dye molecule becomes a part of the fiber and is very difficult to remove by washing.

When a fabric does not combine readily with a dye, it can often be colored by *vat dyeing*. The cloth is immersed in a solution of the water-soluble dye, and the dye penetrates into the crevices of the fiber. The dye is then caused to combine with oxygen, which renders it quite insoluble in water. In that form, the dye is not easily washed from the cloth, although the dyeing may not be completely permanent.

Many dyes do not adhere well to a fiber unless it is assisted by a *mordant*—the word comes from the Latin *mordere,* "to bite." Mordants do their job by interacting with both the dye and the fiber, forming a strong link between the two. Metal oxides make good mordants, and anyone who has tried to remove an iron oxide (rust) stain from an article of cotton clothing knows how stubbornly it adheres. Because mordants react chemically with a dye, they often change its color. The dye alizarin is a deep red, for example, but it produces violet colors with iron mordants and red colors with chromium mordants.

Why do we "see stars" when struck on the head?

When a person looks at an object—such as this book—light reflected from the object enters the eye. A lens at the front of the eye then forms an image on the retina at the back of the eyeball that is a miniature representation of the object reflecting the light. On the retina are more than 100 million sensitive nerve cells, which react to the light by sending nerve impulses to the brain. The act of seeing, therefore, really takes place in the brain, not in the eye. Seeing is the result of interactions of nerve impulses from the retina with other signals produced by the cells within the brain.

Scientists have shown that certain sharp blows to the head cause retinal nerve cells to generate nerve impulses just as they do when activated by light—and we "see stars." The random signals from the retina are interpreted by the brain as points of light. Scientists have also produced this effect in other ways, such as with electric shock and moving magnetic fields. These, too, induce the retina to generate signals that produce visual sensations when nothing is there to be observed.

How were the oceans formed?

Geologists believe that the young earth was so hot that it could hold neither atmosphere nor water vapor. A great deal of water was present, however, in loose combination with the rocks of the earth. As the earth's crust cooled and the rocks were packed more closely together by the force of gravity, the interior grew hotter. Water vapor and gases were released by the internal rocks and came explosively to the surface. For countless ages, water vapor escaped through fissures in the crust and condensed to form water. This water collected to form the oceans.

Scientists do not agree on whether the oceans formed early and have been the same size for billions of years, or formed slowly and are still forming today. Those in favor of early formation point out that the continents seem to have changed little in size over many millions of years. Others in favor of a longer period of formation maintain that volcanoes still pour large quantities of water vapor into the atmosphere. At present, there's little evidence upon which to base a choice between the two theories.

Why do "instant" potatoes and rice cook quickly?

A microscopic examination of raw starch shows that it consists of tiny grains with tough walls, which prevent the grains from absorbing cold water. Boiling the grains softens them so that they burst open and allow the contents to unite with water. Potatoes, rice, spaghetti, and other starchy foods are cooked in order to open the grains so that the starch can be more easily digested. "Instant" potatoes and rice are examples of foods that have already been cooked in order to open the grains of starch. It is then only necessary to add water and heat the product before serving.

Starch can also be cooked by dry heat. When starch is heated gently, it turns into a brown, slightly sweet substance that dissolves in water. This substance is called dextrin, which consists of molecules smaller than those of starch. Dextrin, in turn, can be broken apart into maltose molecules, and maltose can be divided into two glucose molecules. Maltose and glucose are kinds of sugar.

When a slice of bread is toasted, the brown outer surface consists of dextrin, which is easier to digest than starch. This explains why doctors sometimes recommend toast instead of bread for their sick patients.

There is a simple test that indicates the presence of starch or dextrin in a food sample. Merely add a few drops of iodine solution to a half glass of water. Dip a strip of toast or other food sample into the mixture. The starch in the sample will turn a blue-black color, and the dextrin will turn red.

205

Is it possible to learn while asleep?

Sleep learning has become an intriguing topic of study in recent years. The basic idea is to play a tape recorder while a person sleeps so that the material to be learned is somehow imprinted in the brain. The process is so effortless and attractive that everybody would be doing it if there were not a catch in it somewhere. Unfortunately, there is.

It turns out that we cannot learn anything at all when we are in a deep sleep, because the information is never recorded by the brain. As the depth of our sleep lessens during the night, we begin to learn a bit. When we are nearly awake, it works quite well. The catch, then, is that we learn pretty much in accordance with our degree of wakefulness. It works best, of course, when we are fully awake. In addition to not working too well, sleep learning has the added disadvantage of keeping us from having a good night's sleep. That means we wake up tired just when we might have done our most effective learning.

Recent research has tried to help people learn things when asleep that they seem to have trouble with when awake: giving up smoking, for example, or erasing excessive fears. In addition, brain activity seems freer when asleep, so attempts have been made to induce creativity or scientific problem solving at night. To date, however, little evidence exists to suggest that such ideas are workable. Perhaps when scientists get a better understanding of just what goes on during sleep, some of these exotic programs will prove to be feasible.

How does a thermometer work?

The first useful thermometer was invented in 1600 by the Italian scientist Galileo. As shown in the diagram, it consisted of a bulb at the top connected by a glass tube to a reservoir of liquid at the bottom. When the air in the bulb became warmer, it expanded and pushed the liquid to a lower point in the stem. Just the opposite effect took place on a cold day. The main problem with Galileo's thermometer was its sensitivity to changes in atmospheric pressure. Even if the air temperature did not change, variations in atmospheric pressure would affect the location of the liquid level in the glass tube.

The next step in the design of the thermometer was to place a liquid in a sealed glass system so that it would not be affected by changes in atmospheric pressure. The modern thermometer, as shown in part

Fig. 27. Principle of the thermometer. A: Galileo's air-bulb thermometer, invented in 1600. B: A modern sealed-tube thermometer.

B of the diagram, uses a liquid instead of air as the temperature-sensing substance. Liquids do not expand nearly as much as air in response to temperature changes, so the stem must have a very small bore.

Most important, however, is the need for a liquid that expands uniformly when the temperature increases. The second diagram shows how three liquids expand with increasing temperature. Mercury and alcohol are widely used in thermometers because their volume increases uniformly with temperature. This means that the graduation marks on the temperature scale can be equally spaced. If water were used, the scale markings near 100°C would have to be much farther apart than those near 0°C. In addition, water freezes at 0°C, so it is not useful in thermometers at or below that temperature.

The thermometers in use today were devised by the German physicist Gabriel Fahrenheit (1686–1736) and the Swedish astronomer Anders Celsius (1701–1744). Both men recognized the need for two fixed calibration temperatures on the scale of the thermometer. Fahrenheit marked the normal body temperature as 100° on his scale, and a mixture of salt and ice as 0°. (Since then, the reference points have been changed to 212° for the boiling temperature and 32° for the freezing temperature of water.)

Fig. 28. The relationship between temperature and volume for three liquids. Mercury and alcohol make good liquids for thermometers because their volume increases uniformly with increasing temperature.

Somewhat later, Sir Isaac Newton noticed that a mixture of ice and water always showed the same temperature on his thermometer. Similarly, the French physicist Guillaume Amontons noticed that his thermometer always showed the same boiling temperature for water. Celsius used these two points for a new thermometer that was marked 0° at the ice-water point and 100° for the boiling point of water. The distance between these two points was divided into 100 parts, or degrees, and the scale was called the *centigrade* scale. It is now known as the *Celsius* temperature scale and is used universally by scientists.

Who invented adobe brick?

The word *adobe* is thought to be derived from the Spanish word *adobar,* "to plaster"; but adobe brick was a common building material in ancient Egypt at least 5000 years before the Spanish landed in the New World.

The process of making Egyptian sun-dried mud bricks is much the same today as it was in prehistoric times. The mud used for making bricks in Egypt is the dark-gray sediment deposited by the Nile, mixed with sand or chopped barley straw and water to form a thick paste. The straw acts as a binder and drying agent, but sand is often used instead. If the mud happens to contain a large amount of clay, bricks can be made with no binder at all.

Adobe bricks are formed in a simple wooden mold, then allowed to dry on a flat mud surface under a scorching sun. In ancient Egypt, individual bricks measured 14 x 7 x 4½ inches.

For some 6000 years, sun-baked brick has been the major building material in Egypt. Stone was limited almost entirely to the construction of pyramids and religious monuments. Dwellings, city walls, forts, storehouses, and the like were made of adobe. Ancient Egyptians knew the secrets of the arch and vault, and were expert in laying and bonding brick. They constructed walls and embankments that are considered engineering marvels even today. Without the ramps, buttresses, and temporary scaffoldings made of brick, the great pyramids and temples of Egypt would probably never have been built. It is to the ancient Egyptians' skill in the use of humble adobe brick that we owe the existence of man's greatest stone monuments.

Why does soda pop fizz?

If we drop a spoonful of sugar into a glass of water and stir it, the sugar seems to disappear. A taste assures us, however, that the sugar is still there—it has merely dissolved in the water. Chemists describe this condition by saying that sugar is soluble in water. Water is called the *solvent,* and sugar is called the *solute.* If we keep adding sugar and stirring the solution, a point is reached at which no more sugar can be dissolved in the water (unless we heat the solution). The solution is then said to be *concentrated,* and the sugar at the bottom of the glass is in *equilibrium* with the dissolved sugar. This merely means that there is no net change in the status of the sugar: it is neither going into solution nor recrystallizing to form solid sugar.

It turns out that gases also dissolve in liquids and arrive at equilibrium in about the same way that solids do. The forces of attraction between the molecules of a gas are essentially zero, so they are free to move about without restriction. If a gas is in contact with the surface of a liquid, gas molecules encounter no difficulty in entering the liquid. As this process continues, a few of the dissolved gas molecules begin to escape from the liquid and reenter the gas above the surface. Eventually a condition of equilibrium is reached in which the rate at which gas molecules enter the liquid is just equal to the rate at which they escape. There is then no further change in the concentration of the gaseous solute in the liquid solvent.

Now suppose that the pressure of the gas is increased. This causes an increase in the number of gas molecules entering the liquid. The concentration of the dissolved gas increases, which causes gas molecules to pop out of the liquid at a faster rate than before. The process continues until a new equilibrium is reached, with a higher concentration of dissolved gas at the higher pressure. In general, the amount of gas dissolved in the liquid goes up directly as the pressure increases, a principle known as Henry's law. It is named for William Henry, an English chemist of the early nineteenth century.

Henry's law is responsible for the fizz we find so pleasant in beer, champagne, and soda pop. At a modern soda-bottling plant, carbon dioxide gas—which we breathe out all day—is forced into solution in flavored water under a pressure of 5 to 10 atmospheres (73.5 to 147 pounds per square inch). While under this pressure, the carbon dioxide solution is sealed in bottles or cans. The gas is not then evident in the liquid because the space above the soda is filled with carbon dioxide gas at high pressure. A condition of equilibrium exists between the gas in solution and the gas in the space above the liquid. When the cap is removed, however, the pressure above the liquid drops suddenly to one atmosphere and much of the carbon dioxide escapes from the solution in the form of gas bubbles. This "fizz," or rapid escape of a gas from a liquid in which it is dissolved, is called *effervescence*.

What are "pep pills" and "speed"?

Amphetamines, also known as pep pills and uppers, are synthetic drugs that stimulate the central nervous system. They are useful in the treatment of such diseases as narcolepsy (an overwhelming need to sleep) and mild depression. People likely to misuse the drugs are overtired truckdrivers and businesspeople, students cramming for examinations, and athletes who feel they need an extra edge for the game. Amphetamines tend to become concentrated in the brain and spinal fluid, so prolonged use or abuse leads to serious side effects. Users quickly develop a tolerance for the drug, and increasing doses lead to sleeplessness, weight loss, and paranoia.

Amphetamine (Benzedrine) was synthesized originally to simulate the action of the natural hormone epinephrine (adrenaline). Adrenaline elevates blood pressure and increases the level of blood sugar. Drug users refer to Benzedrine as "bennies" and dextroamphetamine as "dexies." When amphetamine and metamphetamine are taken intravenously, they are referred to as "speed."

The barbiturates are a different class of synthetic drugs that have sedative and sleep-inducing properties when used in therapeutic doses. Phenobarbital is a long-acting barbiturate (twelve hours), whereas secobarbital (Seconal) and pentobarbital (Nembutal) last about three or four hours.

Barbiturates, unlike amphetamines, act to depress the central nervous system. Prolonged use of the drugs develops a tolerance for them, and the user soon requires much stronger doses to produce the same effect. Large amounts of barbiturates cause confusion, blurred speech, mental sluggishness, loss of emotional control, and even coma. The drugs pose a great danger to the abuser, because the lethal dose does not change even though one's tolerance builds up with increased use. This reduces the addict's margin of safety.

Can tidal waves be predicted?

The *tsunami,* or *seismic sea wave,* is one of the most destructive of naturally occurring events. It was formerly called a tidal wave, but the term is no longer used by earth scientists because the wave is not related to the tides. Oceanographers use the term *tsunami* (Japanese for "harbor wave") or the descriptive term *seismic sea wave* to designate such waves. They are caused by disturbances on the ocean floor such as an earthquake or undersea landslide. To illustrate, imagine that the ocean floor in a given region suddenly drops 10 or 20 feet. This vertical movement of a relatively large area would produce a disturbance on the water surface immediately above it. The disturbance,

211

in turn, would generate a wave that proceeds across the ocean to distant shores.

The oddest fact about tsunamis is that they are not noticeable in the open ocean because they measure no more than a few feet in height and have wavelengths approaching 125 miles long. (The wavelength is the distance between one peak of the wave and the next.) This means that to an observer at sea, the ocean level would change so gradually in response to the tsunami as to be imperceptible. To place this fact in perspective, it takes about twenty minutes for a single seismic sea wave to pass a stationary object at sea.

On May 23, 1960, a tsunami hit Hilo, Hawaii, which is located about 2000 miles from the earthquake's epicenter. The captain of a ship standing off the port watched in amazement at a city being destroyed by waves that passed unnoticed and harmlessly past his ship. Tsunamis go unnoticed at sea despite their great velocity, which exceeds 375 miles per hour.

It is only when a tsunami approaches the shallow waters of a coastline that its true destructive nature is revealed. Although the speed of the wave decreases, the height of the wave increases. This enormous buildup of water can produce waves greater than 100 feet in height! Such enormous waves destroy everything in their path. Docks and buildings are demolished, trucks and locomotives are tumbled about like toys, and boats at anchor are swept thousands of feet inland.

Luckily, tsunamis can now be predicted and warnings issued to areas that might be damaged by the great waves. The system uses a network of seismographs to detect and locate earthquakes that might trigger tsunamis, as well as tide gauges to detect passing seismic sea waves. The latter are able to filter out normal tides and wind-generated waves. This makes it possible to record only the very long waves associated with tsunamis. In addition, a method was devised to calculate the probable travel time of tsunamis to various target areas. Once such a wave is detected, a vast communication network warns the entire Pacific Ocean area of an impending tsunami, giving the probable arrival times at various places. Thanks to seismological research, tsunamis should never again catch coastal residents unprepared.

Is it true that lightning never strikes twice in the same place?

No. Most of our knowledge about lightning has been gained precisely because lightning *does* strike the same tall structure over and over again. In order to study lightning systematically, scientists must know in advance where it is likely to occur. This makes it possible to position high-speed cameras and electronic measuring instruments close to many lightning strokes. New York's Empire State Building is struck by an average of twenty-three strokes per year, and twice that number is not uncommon. One thunderstorm alone caused eight strikes in less than half an hour. A tower atop Mount Lugano in Switzerland has been struck as often as 100 times in a single year. Scientists have used these locations to measure various properties of lightning current flowing into the structures and to obtain high-speed photographs of the formation of the lightning channel at the top of the building.

The chances of lightning striking a building depend on its height. The table below gives the expected number of strikes per year for buildings of various heights on moderately flat terrain in a region of moderate thunderstorm activity such as Pennsylvania or New York.

Building Height	Number of Expected Lightning Strikes
Ordinary house	One in 100 years
50 feet	One in 5 years
300 feet	One per year
600 feet	Three per year
800 feet	Five per year
1000 feet	Ten per year
1200 feet	Twenty per year

It is important to keep in mind that any structure, regardless of its past history with regard to lightning, can be struck by lightning. Over a period of 400 years, the famous bell tower of St. Mark's Church in Venice was either destroyed or severely damaged a total of twelve times by lightning. Since 1766, when a lightning rod was installed on the tower, no further lightning damage has taken place. Although the bell tower collapsed on July 14, 1902, its destruction was caused by natural decay over the centuries rather than by lightning.

Why is influenza a major health problem?

The term *influenza* (meaning influence) was first used in Italy in the fifteenth century to describe a highly contagious, acute disease of the respiratory system that has afflicted human beings throughout history. The word seemed appropriate at the time, because the disease was attributed to the influence of the stars. Three centuries later, the French selected the term *grippe* for the illness, and both words eventually worked their way into the English language.

An early influenza epidemic was described in 412 B.C. by Hippocrates, the father of medicine, and many others have been recorded down to present times. The first well-documented influenza pandemic took place in 1580 and spread from Asia to Europe and Africa. Many other serious outbreaks of the disease occurred during the succeeding centuries, with much loss of life. Not until the 1930s, however, did it become clear that the true "influence" causing the illness is a specific virus, occurring in many different strains. Only then did scientists begin to gain a better understanding of the disease.

The great influenza pandemic of 1918–19 was probably the most severe on record. Estimated deaths ranged from 20 to 40 million throughout the world. Over a half million died in the United States alone, and at least 25 percent of the U.S. population came down with the disease.

The influenza virus is a sphere approximately four-millionths of an inch in diameter, whose surface is closely packed with radial "spikes" or projections. These spikes are of two kinds: one called hemogglutinin (or H, for short), and the other called neuraminidase, (N). The H spike enables the virus to attach itself to a living cell, and the N spike assists the virus in getting out of infected cells and in moving from cell to cell. These spikes are protein molecules known as *antigens,* and the body eventually generates antibodies that neutralize them in order to provide immunity from their effects.

If there were just one kind of influenza virus, the disease would be much more manageable than it is. Once a person had contracted the illness, antibodies in his blood would provide long-term or perhaps permanent immunity. For other persons, vaccines could be developed to provide considerable protection against the particular virus involved. Unfortunately, the virus shows up from time to time in the form of many different strains, and no vaccine is effective against all of them. Many scientists suspect that there is a vast reservoir of these influenza strains in birds and domestic animals. As we shall see, this represents a continuing threat to mankind.

Of the three kinds of influenza virus, A, B, and C, only the A type produces widespread epidemics in man. For this reason, we will concern ourselves only with type A viruses, and their different strains that show up at various times.

Influenza viruses change in three ways that influence their effects on human beings:

1. The H and N spikes, or antigens, vary in molecular structure, so that antibodies existing in the human population cannot provide immunity against them.
2. The virus changes in its ability to pass easily from one human being to another.
3. The virus changes in its virulence, or its ability to cause severe illness.

Virologists keep track of major changes in the H and N spikes by designating different spikes as H0, H1, H2, H3, and so on and N0, N1, N2, N3, and so on. To illustrate, a virus strain isolated in 1933 was labeled H0N1. In 1947 a major change in the H spike was signified by calling the new strain H1N1. In 1957 a new pandemic strain (the first "Asian flu") appeared, with major shifts in both the H and N antigens. The new strain was named H2N2 to show that both spikes were completely unlike those of earlier strains. In 1968 the "Hong Kong flu" had a new H spike but the same N spike as the Asian strain. It was designated H3N2. For such major changes in spikes, especially the H spike, a new strain encounters little if any effects from past immunity in the human population. This means that major changes in the spikes are likely to encounter a large number of people who have no immunity against the new strain.

Even if a new strain of influenza virus shows up in the population, it may not necessarily cause an epidemic. The so-called "swine flu" strain showed up at Fort Dix, New Jersey, in January 1976. Because of its supposed similarity to the 1918 pandemic strain, a large part of the population was given a vaccine against it. Despite this great concern, the swine-flu strain apparently did not spread beyond Fort Dix. In addition to its inability to travel, the new strain did not develop the virulence of the 1918 strain. In order to produce a great pandemic, a virus must be able to travel widely and become highly virulent. Unfortunately, scientists do not yet know why some strains have these qualities whereas others do not.

Scientists have established that influenza viruses taken from man can cause the disease in animals. In addition, man can catch the disease from animals. In fact, a great number of wild birds seem to carry the virus without showing any evidence of illness. Some scientists conclude that a large family of influenza viruses may have evolved in the bird kingdom—a group that has been on earth 100 million years and is able to carry the virus without contracting the disease. There is even convincing evidence to show that virus strains are transmitted from place to place and from continent to continent by migrating birds.

It is known that two influenza viruses can recombine when both are present in an animal at the same time. The result of such recombinations is a great variety of strains containing different H and N spikes. This raises the possibility that a human influenza virus can recombine with an influenza virus from a lower animal to produce an entirely new spike. Research is under way to determine if that is the way that major new strains come into being. Another possibility is that two animal influenza strains may recombine in a pig, for example, to produce a new strain, which is then transmitted to man.

Our present knowledge indicates that new strains arise when new spikes show up on the virus. Even if this does occur, a pandemic will occur only if the new strain has the dual ability to move easily from person to person and to cause illness. Vaccines currently available offer only partial immunity from the disease and do not seem to restrict the spread of influenza over broad areas. In view of the vast reservoir of influenza strains in birds and domestic animals, there will always be a threat of disease in the human population. Pandemics will undoubtedly continue to occur as they have in the past, but our increasing knowledge of the disease should reduce the severity of these viral assaults on man.

Why don't we ever forget how to ride a bicycle?

Forgetting something does not necessarily mean that the information is completely erased from the memory. More often, forgetting merely means an inability to retrieve the material that is still stored somewhere in the memory. In that sense, forgetting can be thought of as an increase in errors made while trying to reproduce material that has previously been learned.

We tend to forget things very quickly. The first diagram is a curve that shows the percentage of material that is retained for various lengths of time after reciting it perfectly one time through. To illustrate, suppose a student studies a poem just well enough so that he can recite it one time with no mistakes. The graph shows that he will have retained only about 50 percent after one hour and only 20 percent after four hours. The only way to retain learned material permanently is to practice it over and over. The second diagram illustrates that point. After three learning episodes, for example, the student retains 50 percent of the material after 7 hours.

Fig. 29. The amount of learned material that is retained after one perfect recitation.

Most of us can recite, "I pledge allegiance to the flag . . ." most of the way if not all the way through. The first few words set in motion a sequence of words that is stamped indelibly somewhere in the brain. If you are like most people, you can perform the same feat with numerous proverbs and short poems.

Psychologists attribute permanent storage of that kind to a process called *overlearning*. When a teacher is dealing with material of less

Fig. 30. The amount of learned material that is retained after three separate learning periods.

than earth-shaking importance to the pupil, overlearning is often the only method that works. To understand overlearning, however, it is important to focus on the forgetting curve discussed earlier. If we continue to learn (and partially forget) the desired material, we will slowly increase the amount we retain until we are able to recite the material many times without an error. In essence, the material retained never falls below the 100 percent line and becomes a permanently stored memory.

Why is this process called *overlearning?* We have learned the material well beyond the initial one perfect recitation, so we have really overlearned the material. We must always learn something well beyond one perfect recitation to hold the 100 percent level indefinitely.

In a similar way, most adults can still ride a bicycle even though they may not have done so for many years. They do not retain this skill because physical activities are particularly easy to retain. Rather, it is because they have overlearned the procedure as a child. They

218

have ridden a bike so many times that they have little trouble achieving performance at a 100 percent level every time. The forgetting curve never falls below the level needed for perfect performance.

Can diamonds be mined from the ocean floor?

Perhaps the most unusual ship used by ocean scientists is the *Rockeater,* a small freighter that has been converted into a seagoing prospecting vessel by the Ocean Science and Engineering Company of the United States. Its drilling rig literally "chews up" the rocks on the ocean floor as it drills holes to a depth of 500 feet. It can also bring up loose gravels from depths of 500 feet by means of dredging equipment. The ship was designed to sample the sea floor for diamond-bearing gravels and rocks off the coast of Southwest Africa. Material brought up from the bottom is sorted and processed for diamonds. In its first year of operation, the *Rockeater* drilled more than 4000 holes and located diamond deposits estimated to contain millions of carats.

Oceanographers and marine geologists are searching vigorously for other valuable resources, in addition to diamonds, at the bottom of the oceans. One such discovery was made in the 1870s when the crew of the H.M.S. *Challenger* brought up potato-sized clumps of mineral matter from parts of the Atlantic, Pacific, and Indian oceans. Since that time, other oceanographic research vessels have located extensive deposits of these mineral nuggets. In some places, these lumps or nodules form a thick carpet on the ocean floor; in other locations they are widely spaced. They seem to be most abundant at depths between 1 and 4 miles.

Although the content of these mysterious nodules varies considerably from place to place, assays show that they are likely to contain from 20 to 50 percent manganese and about 15 percent iron. Some of them also contain as much as 3 percent copper, 2.5 percent nickel, and 2 percent cobalt. They typically vary in diameter from 1 to 9 inches, although one recovered nodule weighed close to a ton. When cut open, they are seen to consist of concentric layers, like an onion. Scientists believe that they form slowly as mineral particles build up around a nucleus such as a shark's tooth. Measurements suggest that they grow at rates ranging from about 1 millimeter per thousand years to 1 millimeter per million years. (There are about 25 millimeters in an inch.) Despite their slow rate of growth, so many are continuously forming that man could probably never use them all up. One location off the coast of Miami contains up to 80,000 tons of nodules per square mile.

Nodules have not yet been mined commercially because of the difficulty of bringing them to the surface. Nevertheless, the resource potential in manganese, nickel, and cobalt is important enough to spur continued research in ocean mining methods.

Another important mineral, *phosphorite*, has been discovered off the coast of San Diego, California, and in many other ocean locations around the world. Also called *phosphate rock*, the deposits contain about 28 percent phosphorous pentoxide. The deposits can be used in commercial fertilizers to enrich poor or overfarmed soil. Marine geologists estimate that the deposits off the California coast contain a billion tons of phosphorite, located in an area where recovery is economically feasible. Since California alone imports about 100,000 tons of phosphorite each year, the discovery seemed to be a real bonanza.

Unfortunately, the deposits will probably never be recovered. Why? The region was once used as a naval firing range and dumping ground for overage ammunition. Spread out among the phosphate deposits are thousands of live shells, mines, and other ammunition waiting to explode if they are disturbed. These devices make it highly improbable that the undersea riches will ever be harvested.

Do human beings have instincts?

An instinct is often defined as a quality that is not learned, but is universally held by a species. Many basic behaviors such as swimming ability, which most animals have, seem to exist in human beings as well, but contemporary psychologists are cautious about thinking of human behavior in terms of animal instincts because of the great variation they find in our species. Many of our animal needs, for example, may have been suppressed by social learning. A typical illustration is the sex drive, which has been overcome by people who are completely celibate for religious or other reasons. Furthermore, the suicidal kamikaze pilots of World War II proved that even the "instinct for survival" can be overcome. The important point is that human behavior cannot be explained in terms of instinct, even though parts of it may be. The term *instinct*, therefore, must be used with care.

If we analyze human and animal behavior, it seems clear that both groups come equipped with certain basic qualities—but to call them instincts, especially in people, is probably too vague. In addition, the term instinct leads to a kind of circular thought process that scientists are particularly wary of: a mother cares for her infant, so she has the maternal instinct; she has the maternal instinct, so she cares for her infant.

Scientists do try to avoid this kind of meaningless statement by sorting out inherited characteristics from learned behavior. The sorting process, however, poses extremely difficult problems because learning begins at birth, or perhaps even earlier. Can human beings be said to have instincts? No one really knows.

How old is the practice of mining?

Many hundreds of thousands of years before man learned to smelt metals, he used tools fashioned out of stone. The stone he preferred was flint—harder than steel and brittle enough to permit shaping by hammering and flaking. Nodules of flint are quite abundant in chalk layers that were deposited on the ocean floor some 80 million years ago. These layers, covered by other sediments, were uplifted in past geologic ages and are now found in Europe from England to Poland and southward to France. The flint used by Paleolithic, or Old Stone Age, hunters came from loose nodules of flint that nature had weathered out of uplifted chalk beds.

A few thousand years ago, as hunting and gathering of food gave way to farming, there was apparently a great increase in the demand for flint tools. The supply of loose flint on the earth's surface was not sufficient to meet the demand, and Neolithic, or New Stone Age, man began mining it.

One such mine has been discovered near Rijckholt in the southernmost part of the Netherlands. The mining complex covers an area of about 62 acres and is estimated to have yielded 54,000 cubic yards of flint nodules—enough to make 150 million ax heads! In the course of excavating a portion of the mining area, several charcoal remnants of prehistoric fires were found. Through radioactive carbon-14 dating methods (see page 143), these bits of charcoal showed that mining was in full progress at Rijckholt somewhat over 5000 years ago.

The mining area consisted of about 5000 vertical shafts, each from about 33 to 53 feet deep, from the surface down to the flint-bearing layer of chalk. The shafts were from 3 to 5 feet in diameter. At the bottom of each shaft were horizontal galleries about 2 feet high. The galleries associated with each shaft had an average area of about 270 square feet. The excavation of the galleries is similiar to the modern

221

"room-and-pillar" system in that pillars of chalk were left untouched here and there to support the roof of the gallery. Once a gallery was mined out, it was filled with waste chalk being dug from the next gallery.

The miners cut their way through the chalk with the help of flint ax heads with handles about 30 inches long. The heads were about 6½ inches long, 2 inches wide, and 1½ inches thick. Literally thousands of such discarded artifacts were found in the mines. Each shaft and gallery network used up 350 ax heads, which were considered irreparable and were abandoned in the galleries. It is estimated that the entire site was mined at a cost of 2.5 million ax heads, or somewhat under 2 percent of the total production.

While the miners were engaged in bringing flint to the surface, other workers were busily fashioning this valuable raw material into all manner of tools. In one area, archaeologists found a natural basin filled to a depth of 5 feet with flakes of waste flint. These are the parts that are chipped off of a piece of flint during manufacture of a stone tool. Excavations of the basin, later called the Grand Atelier (the Great Workshop), showed that the Neolithic artisans had divided the basin into several separate work areas. For example, ax heads were made in some areas, scrapers in others, and projectile points and knife blades in still others. Archaeologists were able to identify the specialized toolmaking areas by examining the shape of the waste flakes.

Beginning in 1964, a small portion of the Rijckholt mining area was excavated by a group of twenty dedicated amateur archaeologists who worked nine years on the project. The excavation took the form of a tunnel almost 500 feet long that intersected sixty-six vertical mineshafts, each with a system of radiating galleries. The tunnel followed the flint-bearing layer of chalk that had been mined by Neolithic man. Today, the tunnel depth has been increased so that visitors can walk upright through its entire length. Tourists can now see how early man mined the flint that was so vital to his economy over 5000 years ago.

Why does cement become a rock-hard solid?

Archaeologists tell us that the use of cement as a filler to bind stones and bricks together is an ancient art. The early Egyptians and Greeks made use of it, and the Romans raised its use to the highest levels of quality. "Roman cement," made by mixing lime (calcium oxide) with volcanic ash or crushed tiles, retained its popularity until the beginning of the nineteenth century. The large number of Roman structures still standing is probably the best evidence of the quality of the cement.

The invention of portland cement, which we use today, is usually credited to Joseph Aspdin, an English builder from Leeds. It is prepared by heating limestone or chalk (calcium carbonate) with clay (compounds of aluminum, silicon, and oxygen) in a high-temperature kiln. During the firing process, these materials combine to produce small lumps called clinkers. The clinkers are then ground up to form a dry, powdery cement. When mixed with water to form a thick paste, the cement and water combine to form the hard substance we know as cement. If sand and small stones are added to the mixture, it is called concrete.

Chemists tell us that portland cement is basically a mixture of *calcium silicates*—compounds consisting of calcium, silicon, and oxygen. In powdery form, they react chemically with water to form a paste that sets and eventually hardens. Only recently, however, have scientists come to understand why cement gets as strong as it does during this process of hardening. At first—within about two hours—the grains of cement become surrounded by a gelatinous coating, as shown in the accompanying diagram. This coating consists of calcium silicates combined chemically with water, a process called hydration. The particles of cement are joined together by these coatings to form a network of rather weak bonds. The true hardening of the cement begins after about four hours, when a large number of fibers "grow" out of the gelatinous coatings. They eventually grow into very thin, densely packed fibers that extend outward like the quills of porcupines or sea urchins from each particle of cement. These "quills" are the result of the chemical reaction between the cement silicates and water. As the fibers grow in length, they gradually lock together to produce an interwoven meshwork that holds the mass together.

Pictures taken with an electron microscope show that the fibers, which are so important to the strength of cement, consist of thin, hollow tubes. The second diagram illustrates how these tubes are thought to form. A particle of cement is surrounded by water *(A)*, and a shell of semipermeable material forms around the particle *(B)*. The coating is permeable to water, so the cement particle continues to dissolve as water enters the interior. This causes a pressure (called osmotic pres-

Fig. 31. Hardening of cement. A: Cement particles mixed with water. B: A coating forms around each particle. C: Fibers grow radially and lock the particles together.

sure) to build up inside the coating. Eventually, the coating ruptures *(C)*, and material is ejected in the form of hollow tubes, which solidify to give cement its strength.

Although initial hardening of portland cement takes place within the first few days or weeks, its strength continues to increase over extended periods of months or years. In fact, the process of hydration does not usually go to completion; that is to say, not all the cement reacts with available water. Typically, a considerable amount of unreacted cement can be found in hard cement even after several years of aging. Apparently, the coatings eventually become hard enough to prevent water from reaching the encased grains of cement. To prove the point, scientists have ground up hardened cement and have found that it will harden a second time if mixed with water. This helps explain why very fine cracks in cement can heal themselves. The cracks open up the hardened grains of cement, and these eventually grow new tubular fibers, which bind the broken parts together again.

Fig. 32.   Growth of tubular fibers in portland cement. A: A particle of cement surrounded by water. B: A shell or membrane of semipermeable material forms around each cement particle. C: Water passes through the membrane and continues to react with the cement, building up the internal pressure. The membrane eventually ruptures in many places and material is ejected to form hollow fibers.

How do mosquito repellents work?

Mosquito repellents are not chemical substances that mosquitoes somehow find unpleasant or distasteful. They do not function by driving mosquitoes away. It is closer to the truth to say that repellents jam the mosquito's biological radar system. But before we discuss how mosquito repellents repel, it will be helpful to learn how the female mosquito senses and locates a prospective warm-blooded host.

If mosquitoes are left undisturbed in a cage, they will settle down quietly on the walls and do nothing. Occasionally, however, one will fly to another part of the cage. In experiments it was discovered that about half the mosquitoes move in about one hour. This characteristic rate of movement reminds scientists very much of radioactive decay, where half of the radioactive atoms of a particular element always decay randomly in a fixed length of time. This period of time is called the *half-life* of the radioactive substance. By analogy, we can speak of the "rest half-life" of a mosquito population, meaning the time it takes for half the group to move spontaneously from its position of rest. The mosquito population, therefore, has a resting half-life of about an hour. This suggests to scientists that the process, like radioactive decay, is random. Nerve cells in the mosquitoes' brains fire randomly and every so often one of the insects takes to flight.

Scientists have discovered that raising the concentration of carbon dioxide in the air speeds up the random flights of the mosquitoes, so that the resting half-life is reduced to about five minutes. Since animals and human beings give off carbon dioxide, their presence causes nearby mosquitoes to take to flight in greater numbers than is normally the case. After a short period of time, however, the mosquitoes get used to the increased level of carbon dioxide and settle down again to the one-hour half-life. If the carbon dioxide level is raised still further, however, the mosquitoes become excited once again, followed by adaptation somewhat later to the new level.

Scientists who study mosquitoes have learned that low concentrations of common mosquito repellents affect mosquitoes in the same way: they produce an increased rate of random flights followed by return to the original slower rate. Also, as it turns out, such repellents cause mosquitoes to lose their sensitivity to carbon dioxide. In an enclosed area, mosquitoes can be tricked into not noticing the presence of carbon dioxide if a low concentration of a common repellent, such as dimethyl phthalate or diethyl toluamide, is maintained. Treating an area with such repellents is one way of suppressing the activity of mosquitoes, because they seldom begin a search for food without being triggered by carbon dioxide.

Once a mosquito has taken to flight, it sets out to find a warm-blooded host. It was originally suggested that mosquitoes follow skin odors, but no such odor has ever been identified. It turns out, in fact, that no skin seems to be as attractive to a mosquito as a current of air having the right degree of warmth and humidity. An experiment was performed in which three cylinders were placed in a wind tunnel with a large number of mosquitoes. One cylinder was warm, one was wet, and one was warm and wet. The experimenter released some carbon dioxide gas into the moving air in order to "awaken" the mosquitoes and then counted the mosquitoes that had landed on each of the cylinders. The warm cylinder drew 7, the wet one drew 22, and the warm and wet cylinder drew 358. This demonstrates rather emphatically that mosquitoes follow warm, humid currents of air as they track down their next meal.

By careful study of mosquitoes, scientists have learned that a mosquito's flight is initially in a random direction. When the mosquito eventually comes across a wet, warm current of air, it moves straight ahead. If it happens to remain within the desired current, it maintains that direction. If it begins to move out of the current, it usually turns back into the current. If it happens to move out of the current into cooler and drier air, it changes direction. The new direction is not always the right one to keep the mosquito on target, but mosquitoes are tenacious, and the procedure works well enough most of the time to get most of the mosquitoes to the target.

Scientists have also shown that a repellent merely acts to turn a mosquito off course just before it lands. Here is how it accomplishes that feat. A mosquito senses humidity in an airstream by means of tiny pores in certain sensory hairs located on its antennae. These hairs send electrical impulses to the central nervous system whenever they encounter humidity in the air. When the humidity goes up, so does the electrical discharge rate. When the humidity drops, the discharge rate also drops. Scientists believe that repellents perform their function by "plugging," or blocking, the pores through which mosquitoes sense the presence of water vapor in the air. As a mosquito comes in for a landing on a moist, warm body, the presence of repellent plugs the mosquito's moisture sensors, leading it to "conclude" that it has lost the warm, moist current of air. Its instinctive reaction under such circumstances is to change course. For that reason, the mosquito does not land but goes into a new search pattern—only to be frustrated once again when it tries to land a second time.

We have no reason to suspect that a mosquito "thinks" very much about this problem. The mosquito's search-and-attack program is undoubtedly a specific series of quite automatic responses that occur in a definite sequence. The repellent merely interrupts that sequence, and the mosquito continues following the steps that are programmed into its very nature.

Various laboratories have tested tens of thousands of organic compounds for their usefulness as mosquito repellents. Nevertheless, scientists have found it difficult to identify the molecular characteristics that make for a good repellent. It is known, however, that spherical or

227

oval molecules tend to work better than flat ones, probably because they have a better chance of plugging the pores through which moisture is sensed. A specific repellent, by the way, will not work well against all species of mosquito. This is because the chemical nature of the pores in the sensory hairs is different in the various species.

To sum up, a repellent can work in two ways. If it is spread throughout the air in an enclosed area, the repellent suppresses the mosquito's response to carbon dioxide so it cannot detect the presence of a likely host. It also causes the mosquito to fly through warm, humid air currents without detecting them. If a repellent is applied to the skin, it turns a mosquito away just before it lands.

Why are we blinded temporarily when we move from a bright place into a dark room?

Each of us has been blinded temporarily after moving from bright sunshine into a fairly dark room or the dim interior of a movie theater. After a time, our eyes become adapted to the dark, and vague outlines gradually give way to objects and faces. This slow adaptation to the dark is a result of the way the eye is constructed and how it functions.

The retina of the eye, on which the image is focused, contains two kinds of light-sensitive cells: rod cells for high sensitivity to light, and the less-sensitive cone cells for acuity and color vision. As you would suppose, the cone cells are used during the day when light is plentiful, and the rod cells are used at night when there is little light. The rods are more sensitive to light for two reasons: first, each rod can be activated by a lower level of light than a cone cell; second, rod cells are usually arranged in such a way that several of them connect to the same nerve cell for transmission of information to the brain. This arrangement is illustrated in the accompanying diagram. When light falls on the several rods shown in the diagram, the signal is added up, or summed, at the single neuron to which they are connected. This pooling of impulses provides increased sensitivity so that the neuron can be triggered by a lower overall light level. This increased sensitivity is achieved, however, at the cost of sharpness of vision. The brain cannot "know" which of the several rods received the light that triggered the neuron.

Cones, as shown on the right of the diagram, are generally connected to their neurons in a one-to-one ratio so that they are less sensitive than rods. Each individual cone must receive enough light to trigger its associated neuron, because it can receive no help from its neighbors. Although they require higher light levels to fire, cones are better able to distinguish between adjacent portions of the image on the retina. This provides greater acuity, or resolving power, in transmitting picture information to the brain.

Under dim illumination, cones function poorly—because of their low sensitivity—and vision depends mainly on rods. In order for rod

Fig. 33.   Connection of rods (A) and cones (B) to neurons. Rods are more sensitive because light from several rod cells adds up to stimulate one neuron.

cells to adapt to the dark, chemical changes must take place within them. Specifically, a visual pigment, normally bleached out by bright light, must be regenerated in the rods. This chemical change requires about twenty minutes to occur—the length of time usually required for the human eye to adapt to the dark.

The relatively slow adaptation to darkness is a disadvantage only in man's technologically advanced culture. In nature, rapid changes from light to dark do not normally occur. The natural transition from light to dark—the period between dusk and the darkness of night—pretty well matches the twenty minutes required for dark adaptation of the eye.

What are rocks?

If someone is asked, "What is the earth's crust made of?" the answer would probably be "rocks," or maybe "rocks and a covering of soil." Either answer is essentially correct, because most of the earth's crust is indeed made up of rocks, and soil is mostly weathered rock with a bit of organic material mixed in. Rock, in fact, is probably the most common substance in the world, but what is rock?

Scientists define rock as a physical mixture of minerals—naturally occurring chemical compounds that have a specific chemical composition and exist in definite shapes called crystals. Some of these crystals are often quite large and pure, such as quartz, ruby, and diamond. Others are extremely small and mixed together in rock, so that it is hard to observe their crystalline nature. Minerals can contain both metals and nonmetals, and both kinds of substances are valuable and necessary to mankind.

Rocks vary enormously in color, size, shape, hardness, composition, and strength and in many other ways. Yet, despite this diversity, all of the rocks around us were formed in only one of three ways, and geologists classify them accordingly. The three broad classes of rocks are *igneous, sedimentary,* and *metamorphic.*

Igneous comes from the Latin word for "fire," and igneous rocks were formed by cooling and hardening from molten rock called *magma.* Many kinds of igneous rock (granite, for example) solidified deep below the earth's surface. They are called intrusive igneous rocks because they were intruded or injected into spaces between other buried rocks. Valuable minerals or ores, such as those containing gold, copper, and silver, are often found with certain intrusive igneous rocks. Other kinds of igneous rocks, such as lava from volcanic eruptions, are called extrusive igneous rocks, because they were extruded from the earth and then solidified on the surface. Although igneous rocks are not too abundant on the earth's surface, they become predominant at deeper levels. Igneous rocks make up 95 percent of the volume of the outermost 10 miles of the earth.

Sedimentary rocks began their existence as loose layers of rock fragments, such as sand, clay, and gravel. Over long periods of time, these fragments—called sediments—hardened into layers, or beds, of sedimentary rock. Most sediments are formed by the weathering or disintegration of earlier rocks and are moved from their original location by agents of erosion such as running water, wind, or glaciers. Other sedimentary rocks are formed by chemical means. Gypsum and rock salt (or halite) are two important minerals that are deposited from mineral-laden water. Other sedimentary rocks are made up of the remains of once-living organisms. Coal and many limestones were formed in that way.

Sedimentary rocks make up about 75 percent of the rocks we see on the earth's surface, and some of them contain valuable mineral resources. Water, coal, petroleum, salt, sulfur, and many other mineral products are usually found in sedimentary rock formations. Scientists are also interested in these rocks because they often contain fossils and other clues concerning the age of the rock and the conditions under which it formed.

Metamorphic rocks are clearly the most complex rocks. They get their name from Greek words that mean "change in form." Metamorphic rocks can be formed from either igneous or sedimentary rocks. To illustrate, an ordinary limestone can be changed into a much harder, crystalline, metamorphic rock called *marble*. Such changes take place when rocks are subjected to great heat and pressure. These conditions occur when the crust is deformed in the process of mountain building, or when hot intrusive igneous rocks are injected into the cooler rocks around them. When metamorphic rocks are formed, they are usually changed considerably both in form and chemical composition. This sometimes produces new minerals of great value in rocks that originally had no economic importance.

How is Roquefort cheese made?

Not all moldy food is unfit to eat. Moldy bread, fruit, or meat may be little more than garbage, yet some of the most delicious cheeses in the world owe their textures and flavors to the same molds or fungi that ruin other foods. Roquefort and other blue cheeses are perhaps the best known examples of this delectable quirk of nature.

Roquefort cheese is named for the region of France where it was first accidentally produced several hundred years ago. In those days, the farmers of Roquefort, France, like farmers everywhere, knew nothing of fungi, and were not noted for undue cleanliness. So there is every reason to suppose that the sheep's milk from which the cheese was made contained a goodly quota of molds, bacteria, debris, and assorted contamination of every conceivable kind. Cheese made from such milk was literally teeming with microorganisms, all fighting for

231

survival. This struggle continued during the months of aging that preceded sale or consumption of the cheese. The environmental conditions under which aging took place determined which of the many kinds of bacteria and fungi present would win out, and this had a decisive effect on the character, flavor, and quality of the finished cheese.

Centuries ago, in Roquefort, the new cheese was aged in cool limestone caves where a certain mold, now known as *Penicillium roquefortii* (a close relative of the penicillin producer *Penicillium notatum*), often became dominant. After a few months of growth of this fungus, the cheese had acquired a soft texture and tangy flavor. What had happened, of course, was that the mold had partly digested—or rotted—the milk curd and fat. It sounds much better, of course, to refer to the process euphemistically as *ripening* rather than rotting, but this is more a difference of words than fact. As the mold grows through the curd, it produces great amounts of blue-green spores arranged in irregular pockets throughout the cheese.

Today, Roquefort and other blue cheeses, are made throughout the world without the aid of limestone caves by careful control of temperature and humidity, hygienic conditions, and inoculation of the curd with a pure strain of the required fungus. Without this fungus, the cheese cannot develop into true Roquefort cheese. Roquefort cheese, once a rare and expensive imported product, is now made scientifically at reasonable cost and with a high probability that the product will be free of contamination and unwanted bacteria. Sadly, all of this has removed much of the romance from cheesemaking; on the positive side, it has also removed much of the dirt and risk of failure.

Camembert is another fungus-ripened cheese that, like Roquefort, is named for the part of France where it was first made. The fungi responsible for the savory flavor are *Penicillium camemberti* and *Oidium Lactis*.

What causes the weather conditions in the United States?

Weather conditions in the United States are determined by the movement of six large air masses, as shown in the accompanying diagram. The four air masses at the corners originate over the oceans (the *maritime air masses*), where they pick up a great deal of moisture. The centrally located masses (called *continental air masses*) originate over land and contain relatively little moisture. In addition to their moisture content, air masses are also designated according to their rel-

Fig. 34. The six air masses that control the weather over most of North America. The letter designations M, C, P, and T stand for maritime, continental, polar, and tropical.

ative temperature. The three northern air masses are referred to as *polar,* and the three southern air masses as *tropical.* Thus, a maritime tropical (*mT*) air mass moving up from the Caribbean Sea can be depended upon to bring warm, moist air to the southeastern states. Similarly, the flow of a continental polar (*cP*) air mass from Canada generally brings cold, dry air to the central and eastern part of the country. These several air masses meet over the United States in a meteorological tug of war that causes most of our weather.

The movement of the weather-controlling air masses is directed primarily by powerful high-altitude winds that blow continually from west to east in these latitudes. Called the *jet stream*, this high-speed river of air meanders north and south in an enormous, irregular path at altitudes between 30,000 and 40,000 feet. It normally reaches speeds of 220 to 280 miles per hour. Over the United States, the jet stream normally enters in the Pacific northwest, flows southeastward, and leaves over the middle Atlantic region. Its course may vary considerably, however, bringing great uncertainty to the science of weather prediction.

The jet stream drives polar air masses to the south and tropical air masses to the north, depending on its path at a particular time. This helps account for the variability of the weather in the region controlled by the prevailing westerlies. Weather satellites orbiting the earth take photographs of cloud conditions, which are relayed to meteorologists on earth. In this way, the cloud cover associated with various air masses can be tracked and measured to assist in weather prediction.

It is not unusual to have a single air mass cover most of the United States. The more common situation, however, is to find several air masses contesting for domination. The places where two different air masses meet is called a *front*—a narrow region usually containing rain, squalls, or thunderstorms. When a moving mass of warm, moist, maritime air meets cold polar air, the warm air moves up and over the cold air and we have a *warm front*. The moist air is driven to high altitudes, and clouds form in layers up to 20,000 or 30,000 feet. A region of rain and fog extends for about 200 miles in advance of a moving warm front.

A *cold front* develops when moving cold air pushes under warm air. Thunderstorm clouds often develop before an advancing cold front, with thunderheads reaching as high as 30,000 to 50,000 feet. Rainfall normally occurs in a region about 50 miles wide in advance of the cold front. A moving cold front can also generate smaller storms called *squalls*, which last only 15 to 30 minutes but can swamp small boats and blow trees down.

How does soap work?

Soap is able to wash grease and dirt away because of the nature of its molecular structure. The molecule of sodium palmitate, a typical soap, consists of two *ions*, or electrically charged particles. The positively charged sodium ion does not enter into the cleaning operations. The negatively charged palmitate ion has a unique property that makes it effective as a soap: one end dissolves in oil and grease, and the other end dissolves in water.

When you wash your hands with soap and water, the mixing action breaks up the oil and grease into many tiny particles. Each particle becomes coated with a layer of palmitate ions with their "heads" buried in the oil. But the other ends are not soluble in oil and attach themselves instead to water molecules. In effect, each globule of oil is then surrounded by a layer of palmitate ions with their "heads" in the oil and their "tails" in the water. This produces a spherical layer of water around the oil which prevents the oil globules from coming together again or touching your hands. The mixture of oil, water, and soap is easily washed away with clean water.

Oil and water are normally immiscible substances. Although they can be mixed temporarily by sufficient agitation, the mixture separates rapidly if allowed to stand. By adding soap, however, the mixture becomes much more stable. Such oil-water-soap mixtures are called *emulsions,* and soap is an emulsifying agent.

Strange as it seems, mayonnaise is also an emulsion of water and oil. In mayonnaise the emulsifying agent is egg yolk instead of soap, but the processes involved are precisely the same as for washing with soap.

Ordinary soap is one member of the broader class of cleansing agents called *detergents.* When scientists discovered how soap works, it became possible to make synthetic detergents out of petroleum. Many of these detergents have an advantage over soap in that they work better and do not form soap "curds" in hard water.

Can astrology foretell the future?

In ancient times, people believed that the heavenly bodies had a ruling influence over the physical and moral world. Astrology was then considered a science that could be used to judge these influences and foretell events by the location and different aspects of the heavenly bodies.

A true science, however, must do more than make observations and perform calculations. It must demonstrate a definite cause-and-effect relationship between events. Astrology cannot meet that requirement and so cannot be considered a science. True scientists place no credence at all in astrology.

How do psychologists use ink blots in testing?

Ink blot testing was invented by psychiatrist Hermann Rorschach as a tool to ferret out of a person's unconscious mind various bits and pieces of information. Using this information, a psychologist can gain an insight into the subject's self-image and overall thought processes. The idea is that by interpreting a person's responses to the ink blots, the psychologist can uncover facts about the subject that would be difficult or impossible to obtain in any other way.

To get in the spirit of ink blot testing, examine the accompanying diagram for a moment or two and decide what it looks like. A teacher or student might well see the letter M; a ski instructor might see

Fig. 35.   A stimulus that means different things to different people.

mountains; a carpenter might see the teeth of a saw; a camping enthusiast might see tents. Such answers, of course, have no deep meaning drawn from the subconscious, but they probably *are* influenced by a person's life experiences. The diagram does not really represent any one specific thing. There is no right or wrong answer. The assumption is that there is a connection between the person's life experience and what is seen in the diagram.

Now consider a random ink blot made by dropping some ink on a piece of paper and folding it in half to make a symmetrical design. Its shape has no real significance. What one sees in it is a product of one's imagination, a projection of one's own thoughts and ideas.

In the use of ink blots, the psychologist encourages the subject to

236

give many responses. This causes the subject to run out of ideas, so he has to dig deeper into his inner fantasy world. The deeper one goes, the more likely it is that the responses will touch the unconscious mind.

Psychologists consider not only the objects seen but also the context in which they are seen. To illustrate, seeing a pistol might be significant, but seeing a bullet leaving the gun can also have meaning. The blot, after all, is stationary. If you see two lions running away from each other, the tester might wonder why you attribute so much to the ink blot. Perhaps you are emotionally involved with what you are seeing. He might wonder if you are trying to escape from someone or something, a feeling that is revealed unconsciously by what you are saying. If you see eyes or faces staring at you, you might fear that people are trying to harm you. If you are depressed, the ink blots might look like stormy masses of dark clouds.

In theory, the ink blot approach suggests that a person's unconscious will attribute to the ambiguous dark patterns some of its own deepest feelings or desires. The person interprets the ink blot in terms of his or her own inner feelings and projects those feelings onto the pattern.

How much radiation can the body safely receive?

The near disaster in March 1979 at the Three Mile Island nuclear energy plant left many people confused concerning the units of measurement of nuclear radiation. Newspaper and television reports were replete with such units as roentgens, rads, rems, and curies. All apply to the measurement of radiation, and each is different from the others.

Scientists use several different units to measure radiation, depending on whether the measurement relates to physical substances, such as metal or plastic, or to living tissue in human beings.

Some elements, such as uranium and radium, are naturally radioactive. They disintegrate spontaneously and change into another element. Uranium, for example, goes through a series of such disintegrations and ends up as lead. Whenever such disintegrations take place, the radioactive substance emits radiation. The *curie* is the physical unit of radiation that measures the number of nuclear disintegrations occurring per second in a radioactive material. The curie is defined as the number of disintegrations per second in one gram of radium. In numerical terms, one curie equals 37 billion disintegrations per second. Smaller subunits are the millicurie (one-thousandth of a curie) and the microcurie (one-millionth of a curie). The smaller units are usually used to describe the potency of radioactive fallout from nuclear explosions and accidents. The curie and its smaller relatives are only useful in telling us what is going on in the radioactive material itself. It is not useful in biological work because it does not take into account the different kinds of radiation given off by the disintegrations or their effect on living tissue. This radiation can be in the form of particles of matter—such as electrons—or of electromagnetic energy, such as x rays and gamma rays. Each such form of radiation has a different effect on tissue.

The *roentgen* (abbreviated r) is a unit of radiation usually applied only to x rays and gamma rays. These rays produce ionization in air and any material through which they pass. This means, for example, that they are able to knock electrons out of atoms and change molecules of oxygen into charged particles, or *ions*. (The roentgen is defined as the radiation from x rays or gamma rays that produces one electrostatic unit of electrical charge from the ions in one cubic centimeter of air.) Once again, the effect of one roentgen is not the same for tissue as it is for air, so it is not a useful unit to indicate the effect of radiation on tissue.

The *rad* (radiation absorbed dosage) describes the amount of radiation energy absorbed by tissue that has been struck by radiation. One rad equals the absorption by one gram of tissue of 100 *ergs* of energy. An erg is an extremely small unit of energy: it takes over 40 million ergs to equal one calorie. Despite its small size, the rad is an important unit of measurement because it corresponds to a significant amount of ionization in living tissue.

The *rem* (rad equivalent to man) refers to the amount of radiation that is absorbed by a human being. This unit takes into consideration the nature of human tissue and the difference in energy of various radioactive sources. It is the unit most often used in relation to the human body. One rem is defined as the amount of radiation that, when absorbed by a human being, has an effect equal to the absorption of one roentgen. One millirem is equal to one-thousandth of a rem.

It is often desired to know the rate at which radiation is being absorbed by human beings in a given place. This is usually specified in terms of so many rems per hour, or millirems (mrem) per hour. If that figure is known, it is possible to calculate the total radiation absorbed by a person in a certain length of time. To illustrate, suppose a worker is exposed to a radiation rate of 1 mrem per hour for 100 hours. The total absorbed radiation would amount to $1 \times 100 = 100$ mrem.

The detection and measurement of radiation is important in the protection of people who might be exposed to radioactivity, either in their work or through nuclear accidents. One device that is often used for this purpose is the Geiger counter. This instrument contains a gas at low pressure in which is placed a pair of wires connected to a source of high voltage. When a ray enters the gas, there is an momentary surge of electricity from one wire to the other through the gas. A loudspeaker is usually placed in the circuit to produce a clicking sound to indicate the flow of current. Sometimes an electronic counter is used to indicate the amount of radiation.

Technicians who work around radiation are often required to wear badges containing photographic film. When developed, the darkening of the film indicates the accumulated amount of radiation to which the wearer has been exposed.

The biological effects of radiation depend on the kind of radiation, the dose received, and whether it is taken externally or internally. Received externally, alpha and beta rays are thought to be least harmful to man because of their relatively low depth of penetration. Taken internally, however, they can cause considerable damage because of their energy content. Gamma rays, and the less energetic x rays, have a powerful effect on tissue because of their great penetrating power and their considerable level of energy.

Radiation causes ionization of molecules contained in body cells, which can disrupt chemical processes within the cell. It can also alter the genetic material in a cell. Some of these cells can continue to grow and reproduce in changed form. Because of genetic changes, mutations can show up in future generations. Because rapidly dividing tissue is highly susceptible to radiation damage, pregnant women and young children should avoid all unnecessary radiation.

Large doses of radiation can cause "radiation sickness," cataracts, sterility, and leukemia. The symptoms of radiation sickness are gastrointestinal disturbances, a drop in blood count, loss of hair, skin damage, and sores. Extremely large doses are quickly fatal.

The National Council on Radiation Protection and Measurement, and the International Commission on Radiological Protection have established the following standards for radiation dosage for the whole body:

1. A dose not to exceed 500 mrem per year for individual members of the general population.
2. An average dose not to exceed 170 mrem per year for the general population.
3. A dose not to exceed 5 rem per year for radiation workers.

It should be emphasized, of course, that actual exposure to radiation should always be kept as low as possible. There is no "safe" level of radiation, because even a very small amount can cause damage in the human body if it happens to hit a cell the wrong way.

The general population receives radiation from three principal sources: natural radiation, medical radiation, and fallout from nuclear experiments and accidents. The natural background radiation in the United States amounts to about 150 mrem per year. The medical radiation received varies greatly, depending on the treatment received, but averages about 70 mrem per year. X rays are harmful to the body because of the effects they produce on tissue. Patients, therefore, should keep their physicians and dentists informed of recent x rays to avoid unnecessary duplication. Fluoroscopy produces more radiation than x ray photographs.

What is thermal pollution?

All nuclear and fossil-fuel plants generate electricity with steam that drives enormous turbine generators. The used steam is then condensed in a cooling system so that it can be used over and over again. The method of cooling can use water from a nearby lake, river, or bay, or it can use an evaporative cooling tower that releases heat to the atmosphere. For either method, each kilowatt-hour of electric energy produced by a fossil-fuel plant requires the release of one and a half times as much heat energy into the environment. For nuclear plants, the rejected heat is 50 percent greater. This discharge of heat into the environment is called thermal pollution.

If waste heat from a power plant is discharged into a flowing river, the water temperature in the vicinity of the plant is increased by a few degrees. If the heat is released into a lake, the effect can be greater. In either case, the increase in water temperature can affect the oxygen content of the water, as well as the biological processes of aquatic plants and animals.

The use of cooling towers also has disadvantages. Because cooling is accomplished by evaporation, large quantities of river or lake water are released to the atmosphere. This reduces the level of the body of water and leads to increased fog in the region.

Thus far we have talked only of the energy producer as a cause of thermal pollution. The user also contributes to the problem. Except for trivial amounts, just about all the energy we use ends up as heat. The heating of lamps and appliances, the friction in motors, even the light produced by a light bulb—all are eventually converted to heat, which contributes to atmospheric heating. This helps us understand why large cities, where energy use is concentrated, have air temperatures several degrees warmer than the surrounding rural areas. In Los Angeles County, for example, the heat generated by the use of electricity amounts to about 3 percent of that received from the sun. When heat derived from automobile combustion of gasoline is added in, the percentage is even higher. It has been estimated that by the year 2000 thermal pollution in the Boston-Washington corridor will reach about 16 percent of the solar energy in that region—a significant amount indeed. No one knows the long-term consequences of this subtle form of pollution.

When did human beings evolve?

The question of human origins has perplexed thinkers since ancient times, and the present is no exception. But archaeologists and paleontologists (biologists who study fossil remains of our ancestors) agree that the direct ancestors of human beings—called *hominids*—go back at least 5.5 million years and perhaps as far back as 20 million years. A great many issues are still in doubt, but the overall pattern of hominid evolution—the evolution of the human line—is now thought to be well understood.

Scientists believe they can almost point to man's first real ancestor, a creature that branched off about 20 million years ago from the group preceding our nearest relatives, the apes. The descendants of that creature, called *Ramapithecus,* evolved continuously by imperceptible degrees in a different direction from the apes from that time on. So we are not descended from the apes but rather have an ancestor in common with them.

After Darwin published his great book, *The Origin of Species,* the acceptance of evolution became inevitable. Soon thereafter, Thomas Huxley showed how similar we were to the great apes; they are, in fact, closer to us than they are to the monkeys. Just as we are believed to have descended from *Ramapithecus,* the apes are believed to have come down from *Dryopithecus.*

Scientists do not know what brought the split about. They know only that *Ramapithecus* resembled the ancestral apes far more than he resembled man. Like some of the present chimpanzee groups, he lived in an open wood and was still a tree user. He lived at least 8 million years ago.

Then there is a gap in knowledge until about 5 million years ago. By then, much more obvious human ancestors had appeared. They were bipeds, like man, capable of running on the open plains. They had left the trees and no longer used their arms (like the apes) to aid in walking. They walked with an upright gait, on arched feet, and with an upright body. Footprint fossils of upright-walking, human-like creatures have been discovered in Tanzania that date back 3.6 million years. The apes walk upright much more poorly—their feet are flat, their knees will not straighten, and their high pelvic bones make them top-heavy.

About a million years ago or earlier, *Homo erectus* appeared on the scene. When he first turned up in 1891 as the famous Java man, he was thought to be a large ape that lived in trees. Scientists now know that he was far from subhuman. He lived in Asia, Africa, and Europe for at least half a million years as the major ice ages were beginning. He made large stone hand axes that were increasingly well shaped in comparison with earlier rudimentary tools. During this period his brain grew larger and his skull and jaws became less massive.

There is a considerable gap in our knowledge of *Homo erectus* during the glacial periods because of a dearth of fossils. But it is known today that Neanderthal man occupied Europe from about 150,000 to 35,000 B.C. His skull was very long and low, with a protruding bony ridge across the forehead. His face was long, protruding forward from the top of the nose to the chin, and his brain was at least as large as our own. He made refined stone tools that were far advanced over those of his ancestors. He is known to have had compassion for his fellow man, caring for the wounded and burying the dead with dignity. Then, about 35,000 B.C., he gave way abruptly to men who were entirely modern in physique and who were in fact very like modern Europeans. There is a great controversy, at present, concerning whether Neanderthals simply evolved rapidly into modern man or were replaced by invaders with greater skills in tool and weaponmaking.

Scientists do not agree on the precise evolutionary path from *Rama-pithecus* to modern man. Indeed, it is frustrating to know so little about our closest ancestors. But much has been learned in the hundred years that have elapsed since it occurred to scientists that there might be origins of *Homo sapiens* to seek out. Our history contains many blank spaces, but they will probably be filled: the evidence has been in the earth for thousands and millions of years and scientists will continue to find it and sort it out.

How much energy does the sun generate?

Astronomers were greatly puzzled for a long time about the sun's enormous output of energy. The sun, as a typical star, radiates an amount of power equal to about a million billion billion kilowatts. Of this amount, only a tiny fraction—about two-billionths—falls on the earth. That quantity, however, amounts to more energy received in one second than is generated in a year by all the power stations on earth.

In earlier times, scientists believed that the sun consisted of a burning substance, perhaps coal or hydrogen. This idea turned out to be false, because such a sun would have burned itself out in a few thousand years.

About a hundred years ago, scientists theorized that the sun's power came from its own contraction. When a gas is compressed, it heats up. So if the sun began as a great ball of gas, it would contract under its own weight. This shrinkage would increase the temperature and pressure near the center by changing gravitational energy into heat. The sun would start to emit heat and light, which would gradually heat up the entire ball of gas, enabling heat and light to reach out into empty space. Calculations show that a contraction of only 100 miles per year would account for the sun's radiation of energy. The sun measures nearly a million miles in diameter, so the shrinkage would be barely noticeable. In this way, the sun could keep radiating for perhaps a few million years altogether. The theory of solar contraction fell apart, however, when geologists found fossil evidence that the earth is not just a few million but several *billion* years old. Some new physical mechanism had to be found to explain how the sun could shine for such a long period of time.

At the middle of this century, Einstein's theory of relativity suggested that matter and energy could be changed from one form to the other if conditions were right. The key point of the theory is that the tiniest amount of matter will generate an enormous amount of energy. One kilogram (2.2 pounds), for example, can be converted into 25 billion kilowatt-hours of energy: enough to supply an industrialized nation for many weeks.

Nuclear physics, therefore, has finally revealed the sun's source of energy. Each star, like our sun, is a gigantic nuclear reactor based on hydrogen fusion power—the same process that provides energy to the hydrogen bomb. The sun's energy source, in fact, is the equivalent of the controlled explosion of 10 billion large hydrogen bombs every second. Within this nuclear furnace, hydrogen atoms combine to form helium atoms, and in the process a bit of matter is converted into energy. Each second, 600 million tons of hydrogen are converted to helium, and 4 million tons of matter disappear in a dazzling display of radiation across the entire electromagnetic spectrum. This hydrogen loss, although large, can easily be supported for several billion years without exhausting the sun's enormous supply.

Whenever energy is released from any radiating object, such as the sun, a stove, or a hot kettle, the object ends up lighter by virtue of the fact that energy has mass. To illustrate, imagine a kilogram of coal inside a sealed, transparent container with enough oxygen inside to enable the coal to burn. If one should burn that lump of coal so that only energy could escape, the container would end up lighter by about three-millionths of a gram (about one ten-millionth of an ounce). The loss of mass is accounted for by the amount of energy that escaped through the walls of the container in the form of light and heat. Using this equivalence of mass and energy, it is possible to calculate that the sun loses about 4 million tons of mass each second. Although this is a considerable mass loss, it is insignificant when compared with the sun's total mass of about a billion, billion, billion tons.

Why does fire have to be started?

Coal, wood, and most other ordinary substances that burn in air contain carbon and hydrogen in chemical combination with other elements. Most of these so-called organic compounds were formed by the chlorophyll in green plants, using the energy of sunlight to bind the elements together. When they burn, the carbon and hydrogen combine with oxygen from the air to form two simpler compounds—carbon dioxide and water. And in the process of burning, the energy derived from sunlight over a long period of time is released very quickly in the form of the heat and light of the fire. The energy given off is called the energy of reaction. The products of combustion—carbon dioxide, water, and ash—contain less energy than the original material that burned.

Chemists know that chemical reactions, such as combustion, will not usually begin of their own accord. An *energy barrier,* which prevents the chemical reactions from starting, seems to stand between the original and the final materials. This energy barrier must be climbed by the system, and the energy that is required is called the *activation*

Fig. 36.   An "energy hump" consisting of the activation energy must be climbed before substances A and B can combine chemically to form substance C. The energy of reaction is the amount of energy given off after the chemical combination takes place.

energy. The energy conditions for combustion are illustrated in the accompanying diagram. Before the molecules of the starting substances, *A* and *B,* can combine chemically, they must pass through an intermediate state in which they have more energy than at the beginning or end of the reaction. This additional activation energy is used to break up the chemical bonds that bind the old substances together. They are then free to recombine in a different and preferred arrangement to form the bonds for the new substance, *C.* This is much like driving an auto from a valley to another lower valley by passing over an intervening mountain. The auto must generate considerable energy to reach the mountain peak, but once there it races easily down the other side of the mountain.

Once a fire is started, the process gives off the *energy of reaction* in the form of light and heat. This provides the energy needed to climb the activation-energy barrier. The process them becomes self-sustaining under ordinary conditions.

The activation-energy barrier to chemical reactions can often be surmounted more easily with the help of *catalysts:* substances that assist a reaction without permanently entering into it themselves. We can get a general view of how this is done by looking into a reaction that is used in scores of chemical plants to produce millions of tons of ammonia gas every year. As the basic raw material of artificial fertilizer, ammonia is extremely important for the feeding of the world's population. The chemical equation for the reaction is:

$$\text{Nitrogen} \quad \text{Hydrogen} \quad \text{Ammonia}$$
$$N_2 \quad + \quad 3H_2 \quad \rightarrow \quad 2NH_3$$

which means that one nitrogen molecule (N_2) plus 3 hydrogen molecules (H_2) yields 2 ammonia molecules (NH_3). The subscripts indicate the number of each kind of atom in each molecule; thus, there are two atoms of nitrogen in a nitrogen molecule, two atoms of hydrogen in a hydrogen molecule, and one atom of nitrogen plus three atoms of hydrogen in an ammonia molecule.

The activation energy of this reaction is very high, mainly because the nitrogen molecule, N_2, is one of the most stable of all molecules, being held together by an extremely strong bond. This bond structure must be broken down before ammonia can be formed. When heat is supplied, the reaction does indeed begin to take place, but the high temperature required causes another problem to arise: at several hundred degrees, the reaction starts to take place in the reverse direction. Ammonia molecules already formed begin to break down into nitrogen and hydrogen molecules. Using this method, the fraction of ammonia formed corresponds to less than one percent of the available material.

This problem is solved through the use of catalysts that speed up the reaction without themselves appearing on either side of the chemical equation. The essential point is that a catalyst lowers the activation energy of a chemical reaction so that the hump or barrier lying between the starting and end products of a reaction is partly or wholly removed. This point is illustrated in the accompanying diagram.

It is rather superficial, of course, to say that a catalyst lowers the

246

activation energy of a reaction. What really happens is that the desired end product of the reaction is reached by a diversionary route instead of directly. The catalyst, for example, might form an intermediate compound with one of the starting materials. This might react with the other starting material to form another intermediate compound. The latter might then decay into the desired end product, releasing the catalyst to perform its task over and over again. The desired reaction, therefore, is broken down into a series of steps. Each step has its own activation energy, but the greatest of these is smaller than that of the direct reaction.

Fig. 37. A catalyst assists the chemical reaction by lowering the "energy hump" of the activation energy. In the presence of a catalyst, much less energy is needed to push the system over the energy barrier.

The action of a catalyst is analogous to going from city A to city B by going around an intervening mountain, rather than up and over a pass. The catalyst used in the manufacture of ammonia is iron with the addition of small amounts of aluminum-oxygen compounds. This process makes it possible to use the inexhaustible reserves of nitrogen in the air to produce nitrogen-containing fertilizers for the benefit of humanity.

Do mosquitoes communicate with one another?

Many insects communicate with one another through the use of sound, often to locate members of the opposite sex. Insects in general can produce a wide variety of sounds, although any one species is usually limited to a very few. In the case of certain mosquitoes, it is the number of wing beats per second that is used for communication between individual insects.

Experiments have shown that mosquitoes are attracted by the sound of a tuning fork that emits a tone equal in pitch to that produced by the insects' wing beats. Additional study has shown that the mosquitoes "hear" the sound through sense organs located on their antennae. It was also learned that males of this species were unable to sense vibrations from immature females. The latter fly with a slower wing beat than mature females, and the pitch they produce is too low to be picked up by the males. This helps to ensure that only mature mosquitoes of the same species will mate.

Wing beat sounds, alas, can sometimes work to an insect's disadvantage. Eavesdropping birds and bats can hear the sounds made by insects and can even distinguish between desirable and undesirable species by the number of wing beats per second that each makes. The wasp with its 150 beats per second seems to warn would-be predators to stay away. The mosquito (500 beats) and the midge (1000 beats) seem to urge the predators on.

Why does the earth rotate around the sun?

Like all the other stars, the sun was formed by the contraction of a huge cloud of dust and gas that originally filled a large volume of space. Over several billion years, this material slowly condensed under the attraction of gravitational forces. Initially, the cloud of gas was rotating slowly, and that rotation had to increase as the cloud shrank in size. The effect is just like what happens when a spinning ice skater increases her rate of rotation by drawing her arms tightly to the side. The contraction and increasing rotation flattened the cloud into a narrow disk. The sun formed at the center where the density of material was greatest, and the planets formed farther out. This concept accounts for the fact that all the planets revolve around the sun in the same direction and in orbits that lie nearly in the same plane.

Is there any sure way to recognize poisonous mushrooms?

There are about 4000 known species of mushrooms, or gilled fungi. Of these, perhaps three or four dozen are known or suspected of being toxic to a greater or lesser degree. This lack of precision is unfortunate but is a direct result of the fact that there is no visible characteristic to indicate that a given kind of mushroom is poisonous when eaten. The only way to discover whether a given variety is poisonous is for someone to eat it and be poisoned by it. And that is precisely the way in which we have acquired our sketchy knowledge about the possible toxicity of mushrooms. Tests with animals are not definitive. Rabbits, for example, seem able to eat the mushroom *Amanita phalloides* without fatal consequences, but a child died after eating one-third of a small cap of the fungus.

There are a number of rules or tests, based on folklore, that are supposedly capable of distinguishing edible from poisonous wild mushrooms. Mycologists, who study such things, tell us that none of these rules or tests has any validity whatever. They may seem to work because the wild mushroom gatherer may be familiar by sight with a few of the most poisonous kinds and may avoid them. In addition, selecting mushroom types at random, the odds may be a hundred to one against a really bad variety. Nevertheless, such odds don't seem high enough to bet your life on.

How were the Rocky Mountains formed?

Nature builds mountains in a variety of ways. Volcanic activity can produce cone-shaped mountains such as those in Hawaii. Another process, called *faulting,* can produce mountains with sharp, straight ridges. In many parts of the world, however, mountain ranges are produced by a folding of the earth's crust accompanied by uplifting of the entire region. This process of *folding* and *uplifting* was responsible for the Rocky Mountains of the North American west.

When horizontal forces act to squeeze or compress a region of the earth's surface, the top layers of rock become crumpled and warped. This produces surface undulations that geologists call *folds,* similar to those in a rumpled bedspread or tablecloth. This wrinkling is often accompanied by vertical forces that lift the entire region to a higher elevation, thereby forming a series of parallel ridges. The accompanying diagram shows a cross section of the earth's crust before and after compressional forces have acted on the land.

Prior to the folding described above, there is always a period during which thick layers of sand and soil are deposited in large troughs, called *geosynclines.* The low region of a geosyncline can measure a few hundred miles or more in each direction. In some places, sediments accumulate to a depth of 50,000 feet and become converted to

249

various kinds of sedimentary rock before the folding begins. After folding has taken place, the high places are called *anticlines* and the low places *synclines*. In some places, erosion wears down the anticlines to such an extent that many different kinds of rock layers are exposed. Many such folded layers can often be seen in cuts made through mountains for superhighways.

The Appalachian Mountains in the eastern part of the United States were formed by folding much like that shown in Figure 38. The sedimentary layers involved were originally more than 40,000 feet deep. The Rockies and the Himalayas were also produced by such

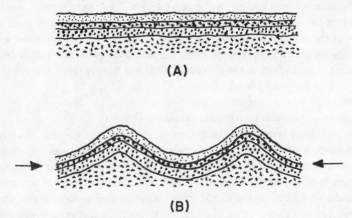

(A)

(B)

Fig. 38. How the Rocky Mountains were formed. A: A series of rock layers before being compressed by horizontal forces. B: Layers are deformed into *folds* by forces applied in the direction of the arrows.

folding and uplifting. The European Alps were formed by folds that were compressed much more closely together than those shown in the diagram. The squeezing forces were so intense that the folds merged together and overlay one another. The pressures responsible for the folding were so enormous that many of the rocks were changed physically and chemically in the process. Such rocks are called *metamorphosed rocks*.

Scientists are reasonably certain that folding and uplifting of sedimentary rock are responsible for the great mountain ranges of the world. Why these actions take place, however, is still largely a mystery.

250

An interesting sidelight to mountain building is the fact that many mountains are younger than the rivers that flow through them. If the flow of river water can erode away the rocks faster than the land rises, the river can maintain its channel while the mountains slowly rise on either side.

Why do plants flower at different times of the year?

Plants depend for their growth on the presence of sunlight. Using the energy of sunlight, plants convert carbon dioxide, minerals, and water into the carbohydrate, fat, and protein needed by the plants. As a by-product, they give off oxygen to the atmosphere. The intensity of this activity is determined by the length of the day, which varies with the season of the year. In the northern hemisphere, the longest day occurs on June 21, while the shortest day occurs on December 21. In the southern hemisphere these dates are reversed, and near the equator, the length of the day is nearly constant all year long.

The effect of the length of the day on the various activities in plants and trees is called *photoperiodism*. The day's length determines when a plant opens its blooms, when seeds sprout, when buds open and leaves unfold, and when plants grow or remain dormant. Perhaps the most dramatic effect of photoperiodism is its effect on the flowering dates for various species of plants. The so-called short-day plants— dahlias, chrysanthemums, salvia, cosmos, and poinsettias—flower in early spring or late summer when there is less than twelve hours of sunlight. In fact, many plants can be tricked into flowering earlier or later than normal by artificially adjusting the hours of illumination to which they are subjected. The so-called long-day plants—such as gladiolus, delphinium, and clover—produce flowers only when the photoperiod is close to fifteen hours. Others, called day-neutral plants, such as carnations and snapdragons, seem to be indifferent to the length of the day. Perhaps they evolved near the equator, where the seasons have little effect on the photoperiod.

Photoperiodism also has an effect on animals. Domestic hens tend to be short-night breeders, but a lamp in the henhouse cuts short their autumn and winter nights and induces them to lay eggs at the summer rate.

How is charcoal made?

Charcoal is made by heating wood in closed containers called *retorts* in which various substances in the wood are decomposed or distilled by heat. This process, called *destructive distillation* of wood, produces methanol (wood alcohol), acetic acid, combustible gases, and other volatile substances. The solid material, or charcoal, that remains consists mainly of carbon.

Charcoal is a black, brittle, and porous solid. It is odorless and tasteless and has the ability to adsorb a large quantity of gas. *Adsorption* is the concentration of a gas on the surface of a solid. Because of its great porosity, one cubic inch of charcoal can adsorb up to 90 cubic inches of ammonia gas.

Activated charcoal is processed in a way that greatly increases its internal surface area. This makes it particularly useful for the adsorption of liquid or gaseous substances. It is made by treating charcoal with steam or carbon dioxide at about 100°C. An ounce of charcoal prepared in that way can have an internal surface area as great as 70,000 square yards. Because of this property, it is particularly useful in gas masks or for the removal of odors from air circulated in offices, theaters, and restaurants. Activated charcoal is also used in the refining of sugar and syrup and in municipal water treatment plants to remove objectionable odors and tastes.

Where do meteors come from?

On a clear night it is not unusual to see bright streaks of light flash suddenly across the sky. Although we call them "shooting stars," they are nothing more than tiny bits of interplanetary matter that enter the earth's atmosphere. When these grains or pebbles strike the atmospheric molecules at high speed, they are heated to incandescence and become visible. Most of these tiny objects burn up in the atmosphere, but occasionally one is big enough so that a portion of its matter strikes the earth. When traveling in space, these objects are called *meteoroids*. When they are visible in our atmosphere, they are called *meteors*. The unconsumed remnants that reach the earth are called *meteorites*.

On extremely rare occasions, a very large meteorite does manage to hit the earth, where it can cause great destruction. Perhaps the best known example is the large circular-rimmed Barringer Crater (formerly known as Meteor Crater) near Winslow, Arizona. The crater's diameter is 4200 feet, its depth almost 600 feet, and its rim rises about 150 feet above the surrounding plateau surface. Rock fragments have been found scattered over a 6-mile radius from the center of impact.

The crater and surrounding region have so far yielded more than 30 tons of meteorite fragments.

In order to establish a date for the formation of the crater, scientists have taken into account such factors as the rate of erosion of the rim and the presence of sediments in the crater, which contain fossils dating from the latter part of the last ice age. Typical estimates of the crater's age vary from about 20,000 to 50,000 years, although the actual figure may fall somewhat beyond that range. Scientists cannot establish the crater's age with more precision because there is no physical evidence of the impact and subsequent explosion that can be dated with certainty.

In 1908 another meteorite is believed to have leveled a Siberian forest within a 20-mile radius of the point of impact. Each day, several tons of meteorites reach the earth. Luckily, most of them are very small.

Meteorites usually consist of iron, nickel, and rocklike silicon compounds. Most of them, however, consist of iron (85 to 95 percent) and nickel.

Using radioactive dating methods, scientists are able to determine when a meteorite was formed. All such measurements indicate that the maximum age of meteoric material is about 4.7 billion years—about the same as the age of the earth. This suggests that meteorites, meteors, and meteoroids were formed of the same material as the earth and other planets.

If you are interested in seeing a true meteor shower, it can be done on one of the following nights:

Shower Name	Date of Meteor Shower
Quadrantid	January 3
Lyrid	April 21
Eta Aquarid	May 4
Delta Aquarid	July 30
Perseid	August 11
Draconid	October 9
Orionid	October 20
Taurid	October 31
Andromedid	November 14
Leonid	November 16
Geminid	December 13

The showers are named for the stellar constellation from which the meteor trails appear to come.

Most meteoroids travel in great swarms in orbits around the sun. On certain dates, the earth's orbit intersects one of the meteoroids' orbits and the number of meteor trails increases from a few per hour to perhaps one per minute. Under favorable conditions as many as 100 per minute can be seen.

Modern technology has now made it possible to find meteorites of reasonable size that are first observed as meteor trails. The Lost City meteorite is a 22-pound meteorite that was photographed in its fall and then recovered near Lost City, Oklahoma, in 1970. It is the first meteorite ever recovered through the use of trajectory data computed from photographs. During its fall, the meteor was brighter than the full moon.

What is energy?

Petroleum shortages have brought the term *energy* into popular use in television, newspapers, and everyday speech. We find it used virtually as a synonym for such fuels as oil, gas, and coal. We read of the development of new energy sources as though energy could be dug, bottled, or shoveled. In actual fact, no one really knows what energy is. But scientists *do* know that energy is one of the fundamental quantities of the universe, and they have learned a great deal about how it behaves.

Physicists define energy as the *capacity for doing work*. *Work* as used in the scientific sense is different, of course, from our ordinary meaning of the word. Unfortunately, it is almost impossible to talk about energy without bringing up the matter of work, so that concept must be covered first.

In everyday speech, an employee might speak of doing work at the office, and a high school student might speak of playing tackle on the football team. To the physicist, the football player undoubtedly does more work than the office worker. To illustrate, imagine a woman drawing water from a well. She might measure the amount of work accomplished by the amount of water she has drawn from the well. But suppose another woman draws another similar quantity of water from a second well that is twice as deep. She can logically claim that she has done twice as much work as her neighbor, even though the end result (the quantity of water) is the same in both examples. It so happens that a physicist would agree with the second woman. Generalizing from these ideas, we can say that the work performed is a measurable quantity equal to the product of the weight of water drawn and the height through which it is raised. (For simplicity, I have neglected the weight of the pail and rope.) If 12 pounds of water is moved 20 feet vertically, the amount of work performed is 20 feet times 12 pounds, or 240 foot-pounds of work.

In lifting water out of a well, a person uses up a certain amount of energy, or capacity for doing work. The used-up energy existed previously in the form of chemical compounds in the body. This chemical energy disappears as part of the person is "consumed," combining with the oxygen breathed in to form carbon dioxide and water. In a similar way, coal is consumed in a steam locomotive by combining with oxygen to generate heat for the steam boiler. Once again chemical energy is used up only to reappear as work done in hauling the train. If the locomotive happens to run on electricity, the energy might have existed originally as chemical energy in oil or coal, or as nuclear energy in uranium. The energy is converted into an electric form in a generator and is transported through wires to the locomotive. Finally, the electrical energy disappears, as work is performed in pulling the train. In general, we can speak of energy in many forms: chemical energy in coal, oil, or in the tissues of man, heat energy, electrical energy, light energy, nuclear energy, mechanical energy, and so on. It is also clear that energy—the capacity for doing work—can be converted from one form to another.

Beginning in the year 1840, James Joule performed a long series of experiments to study the conversion of mechanical energy to heat. In one experiment he used a churn to heat water by rotating a paddle wheel inside the churn. He measured the work done in turning the wheel and the heat produced in the water, and found that a specific amount of work always produced the same amount of heat. Subsequent experiments showed that heat and mechanical energy are always converted back and forth in precisely the same ratio. We now know that the same rule is true for all forms of energy. In everyday terms, energy is never lost: when it disappears in one form, it always shows up in an equal amount in another form. This principle— *known as the law of conservation of energy*—is one of the fundamental laws of classical physics and is a very cornerstone of modern science and technology.

As a result of Einstein's theory of relativity, we now know that energy and mass are also convertible one to the other under special circumstances. But in ordinary situations of everyday life, we need not concern ourselves with mass-energy conversions, because they do not show up in our day-to-day activities.

Before leaving the subject of energy, we should understand why a nation like the United States cannot solve its energy problems by operating automobiles on electricity instead of gasoline. It should be clear by now that electrical energy is no easier to come by than the chemical energy in gasoline. Neglecting engine efficiency for the moment, it takes the same amount of energy to move an automobile a given distance regardless of the initial source of that energy. If all our autos ran on electricity, that energy could be supplied only by burning additional fossil or nuclear fuel at our electric generating plants. It is true, of course, that electric motors are more efficient than gasoline engines. But this advantage might be offset by the weight of batteries to be hauled about. From the point of view of energy use, it is certainly not clear that electric automobiles would provide any net savings in energy in providing for our overall transportation needs.

What is the most poisonous toxin known?

A microscopic rod-shaped bacterium called *Clostridium botulinum* is responsible for producing the most poisonous toxin known to science. Scientists estimate that one-quarter ounce of the toxin is enough to kill the entire population of the world! The toxin produces a kind of poisoning known as *botulism*.

The bacterium responsible for botulism poisoning does not act in the human body but grows and produces its toxin in nonacid foods in the absence of oxygen. These conditions exist typically in canned foods such as meats and beans. Toxin in the food is destroyed by boiling for 20 minutes. The bacteria can be killed during the canning process by extended cooking at elevated temperatures. Commercially canned foods are rarely found containing botulism toxin, but home canners sometimes fail to follow directions when preparing food for canning. As a result, people die each year from eating home-canned food that was not cooked for a long enough period of time. Botulism can also occur if canned foods are left open at room temperature for extended periods of time. This gives the bacteria an opportunity to infect the food and produce the toxin.

The botulism toxin enters the bloodstream and is carried to the nervous system, where it interferes with nerve signals. Speech, vision, pulse rate, muscle control, and other body functions are seriously impaired. The results of botulism poisoning are often fatal. If you suspect that you may have eaten the botulism toxin, seek medical treatment immediately.

Is the earth slowing down?

Geophysicists believe that the earth is indeed slowing down and has been doing so for most of its history. Their theory tells us that tidal currents in the oceans, which are impeded by the sea bottom in shallow water, are responsible for this effect.

Evidence for the gradual slowing down of the earth's spin is based on ancient records of eclipses. An eclipse can be seen by observers over only a small part of the earth's surface. The area of visibility can be calculated both for future eclipses and for eclipses that took place hundreds or even thousands of years in the past. Modern calculations of past eclipses, however, do not agree with ancient records of actual eclipses. In general, ancient eclipses seem to have been observed hundreds of miles to the east of where they "ought to" have appeared.

Eclipses run on orbital time, which means that their *time of occurrence* depends on the orbital locations of the sun, earth, and moon. But the *area of visibility* of the eclipse depends on which part of the earth's surface happens to be in the right position to see the eclipse, so the area of visibility depends on the earth's spin. Since the area of visibility of past eclipses was not where it ought to have been, it follows that the earth's rotation has not been constant back into history. Scientists express this idea by saying that rotational time has been out of step with orbital time. The discrepancies in eclipse data can be explained by assuming that the length of the day has been increasing over the centuries.

The average length of the day increases by slightly more than one-thousandth of a second during each century as a result of tidal friction in ocean shallows. That may seem too little to worry about, but over many millions of years the milliseconds add up. The earth once rotated much faster than it does today, though its time of revolution around the sun has not been affected. In addition, the moon's rate of revolution around the earth was faster in bygone years and it was located closer to earth. This means that the tides were once much higher, that the days were shorter, and that there were more days in the year.

Support for the last conclusion comes from the world of fossils. Corals, the tiny marine animals that build great coral reefs, lay down a microscopically thin layer of calcium carbonate each day. By carefully counting these layers in fossil corals of known age, paleontologists have determined that 400 million years ago, there were 400 days in a year.

Scientists have also determined that the earth spins a little faster at some times than at others. One cause of this variation is the wind. Wind speeds are higher in winter than in summer, and the pattern of wind flow changes from season to season. Through friction with the earth's surface, the wind can speed up or retard the earth's spin to a very slight degree.

Water, ice, and snow also play a role in affecting the earth's rotation. In winter, enormous quantities of water from the ocean are deposited as snow and ice on temperate and polar regions. This displaces the water to elevations many hundreds or thousands of feet above sea level. The transfer of this great mass outward from the center of the earth slows the earth's spin slightly—just as a spinning ice skater slows down by moving her arms outward. In theory, the winter increase in snow and ice in the northern hemisphere should be balanced by the simultaneous decrease in the southern hemisphere, which is experiencing summer. But there is a much greater land area in the northern hemisphere and so the effect there predominates. The net result is a seasonal variation of the earth's spin, which reaches a minimum velocity in the northern winter and a maximum velocity in the northern summer. These changes tend to balance out from one year to the next.

Can tides be used to generate electricity?

Historically, the first source of plentiful and continuous energy consisted of a water wheel run directly by moving water. Today, we no longer use water power directly but store the water behind a dam and use it to generate electricity. In practice, the water falls through a large pipe and drives a huge turbine whose shaft is connected to an electric generator. Electric energy can then be sent through wires to wherever the need may be.

A large hydroelectric power plant, such as the Grand Coulee dam on the Columbia River in Washington, can produce as much as 2000 megawatts of electricity. The total installed hydroelectric capacity in the United States amounts to about 60,000 megawatts, or about one-sixth of the electrical energy used in the nation. It would be possible, in principle, to increase that figure to perhaps 300,000 megawatts if all available water power were harnessed. It seems unlikely, however, that any such increase in hydroelectric power will ever be achieved because of the environmental impact of the huge number of dams that would be required.

It is possible, however, to abstract energy from the tides. In many parts of the earth, tides rise to astonishing heights. In parts of Nova Scotia, Alaska, and Brittany, in northern France, the tides rise 40 feet or more twice each day. In such places the water surges back and forth through narrow channels and provides a good opportunity to generate electric power. A tide-powered plant on the Rance River in France harnesses high tides that rise as much as 44 feet at that location. Gates are opened when the tide rises and closed again at high tide. This produces a lake behind the gates that measures 9 square miles in area. As the tide moves out, the impounded water is released through a battery of turbogenerators that generate up to 312 megawatts of electricity. Engineers believe that other tidal plants can generate as much as 1000 megawatts of average electric power.

Although tidal power is not a significant factor on a worldwide basis, it can be a valuable source of electricity in particular areas. Other potential sites for tidal power plants are in Maine, Argentina, and the U.S.S.R.

What would happen if all the ice on earth were to melt?

The glaciers of the world occupy about 6 million square miles of the earth's surface, or about 10 percent of the total land area. Most of this ice is contained in two great icecaps: Antarctica, which holds about 84 percent of the world's ice, and Greenland. The remainder is scattered here and there around the world, mostly in mountainous regions.

If all of this ice should melt, the sea level would rise about 330 feet above its present level. Most coastal cities and towns would lie under many feet of water, and many inland cities would become seaports. Much of the eastern seaboard of the United States would be submerged, including roughly half the area of the coastal states and all of Florida. An arm of the Gulf of Mexico would extend northward into

Illinois. California would contain a vast inland sea measuring half the length of the state.

There is no cause for alarm, however, because the icecaps are reasonably stable and any significant changes would take place over thousands of years. Glacial melting during the past century is thought to have raised the sea level only about 5 to 12 inches.

Why do the oceans moderate the temperature of nearby land masses?

It has long been known that the temperatures of oceans and large lakes vary over a narrower temperature range than do the temperatures of nearby land areas. Consequently, places just downwind from such bodies of water do not experience the wide extremes of hot and cold weather found in locations far downwind. Cities along the west coast of the United States, for example, are influenced by the prevailing westerlies off the Pacific Ocean and have smaller temperature ranges than cities in the midwest. The term *maritime climate* is used to describe the conditions of places such as San Francisco and Seattle, which are greatly influenced by the ocean. Places within large land masses are said to have a *continental climate,* and they usually experience relatively large temperature ranges from winter to summer.

The oceans accomplish this moderating affect on climate because their water is a huge reservoir of heat. In winter they add heat to the atmosphere, and in summer they remove heat from the atmosphere.

Several reasons account for the thermal properties of the ocean. First of all, water has one of the highest *specific heats* of all of the substances on earth. (Specific heat is defined as the number of calories needed to raise one gram of a substance by one degree Celsius.) This means that more heat is used in warming water 1°C than in warming an equal amount of rock or soil by 1°C. In addition, solar heat penetrates more deeply into water than it does into soil, and water mixes rapidly to distribute the heat vertically through a large mass of water. On land, heat is conducted downward very slowly and the heat that is absorbed is used to raise the temperature of a relatively small mass. As a result, the land heats up much more quickly, and to a higher temperature, than the ocean.

Whenever winds blow from the ocean toward the land, the ocean exerts a moderating effect on the temperature of the land. This is true even for regions that are normally influenced by continental winds. At times, oceanic air masses move from the ocean across the coastline, picking up heat in summer and providing heat in winter.

The energy stored in ocean water is also carried from warm to colder regions. Heat from latitudes near the equator, for example, moves toward the polar regions by the slow motion of the water. To illustrate, the energy received at the equator is three times that received at the north pole. Cold water in the north moves toward the equator and is replaced by warm water moving northward. Winds then transfer this heat to land areas in their paths.

How many comets are there?

Astronomers tell us that there are billions of comets that move in orbits around the sun. Most of these orbits are enormous in size, reaching out to distances thousands of times as far as the outermost planets. Only rarely is one of them visible from the earth.

The nucleus of a comet is a small collection of frozen gases and interstellar dust. When one of them has its orbit perturbed—perhaps by the gravitational attraction of a star—it may enter the inner part of the solar system and swing around the sun. If a comet gets close enough to the sun, its gases and dust are activated by radiation and by particles emitted by the sun and form a visible *coma*, or head and tail. Because of this solar pressure, the tail always points away from the sun—following the comet's head on solar approach and preceding it as the comet flies back into space.

Occasionally, a comet attains an orbit that periodically brings it close to the sun, where it becomes visible from earth. The most spectacular recurring comet to be seen in historic times is probably Halley's Comet, named after the English astronomer Edmund Halley, who discovered its periodicity in 1705. Halley successfully predicted its next appearance in 1759. It reached perihelion passage (the closest approach to the sun) in March of that year.

Astronomers subsequently calculated the date of every appearance of Halley's Comet back to 239 B.C. Historical research—mainly of European and Chinese records—indicates that a comet did appear in the right part of the sky and at the right time to match most of the calculated dates for Halley's Comet. The average period of the comet (the time for one revolution around the sun) is slightly less than seventy-seven years, but the actual period for any one orbit may vary as much as two and a half years from the average because of the gravitational effect of the planets, Jupiter in particular. Halley's Comet will next come into view during 1985, and perihelion will take place on February 9, 1986.

Halley's Comet seems to have been the inspiration for a number of artistic renderings of comets. Perhaps the best known is in *The Adoration of the Magi,* a scene in a fresco done by the Florentine master Giotto di Bondone. The fresco decorates the Arena Chapel, which was commissioned by Enrico Scrovegni, a businessman of Padua. It is sus-

Returns to Perihelion of Halley's Comet

	239 B.C.	March 30
	163	October 5
	86	August 2
	11	October 5
A.D.	66	January 26
	141	March 20
	218	May 17
	295	April 20
	374	February 16
	451	June 24
	530	September 25
	607	March 13
	684	September 28
	760	May 22
	837	February 27
	912	July 9
	989	September 9
	1066	March 23
	1145	April 22
	1222	October 1
	1301	October 23
	1378	November 9
	1456	June 9
	1531	August 25
	1607	October 27
	1682	September 15
	1759	March 13
	1835	November 16
	1910	April 20
Predicted	1986	February 9

262

pected that the chapel was built to make up for the sin of his father, who was described in Dante's *Inferno* as a usurer. In any event, the fresco was executed shortly after Halley's Comet appeared in 1301. In the fresco, Giotto depicts the star of Bethlehem as a radiant comet, much as it must have appeared to Giotto in the Italian sky.

The earliest portrait of Halley's Comet, in stylized form, appears in a scene of the Bayeux tapestry, which was made to illustrate the victory of William the Conqueror at the Battle of Hastings in 1066. In the scene, a group of Englishmen point to the comet and a legend reads: "They are in awe of the star." Nearby, King Harold foresees his defeat. The Battle of Hastings took place several months after the perihelion passage of Halley's Comet.

Why are temperature inversions often associated with smog?

Air pollution is always reduced when the lower levels of the atmosphere are able to mix with cleaner air aloft. Under certain conditions, however, this vertical mixing cannot readily take place. If there are sources of air pollution in the region, such as automobiles and smokestacks, the concentration of pollutants in the air can reach dangerous levels. A temperature inversion describes an atmospheric condition in which vertical mixing is virtually impossible, so smog is the result.

Vertical motions in the atmosphere can come about in a number of ways. Some are fairly obvious. Air rises, for example, when it is forced to move over a mountain or other rising terrain. Air also rises over weather fronts. When a large mass of cold air encounters a similar mass of warm air, they do not mix readily. Instead, the cold, heavier air intrudes in a wedgelike fashion under the warm, less dense air. The transition between the two air masses is called a *front*. As the cold air advances, it displaces some of the warm air and causes it to rise.

Air can also be induced to move vertically, depending on a condition of the lower atmosphere that meteorologists call *stability*. To illustrate, imagine a small parcel of air that happens to be pushed by the wind to a higher elevation by striking a building or hill. If, after reaching the higher altitude, it is warmer and less dense than the surrounding air, it will be subjected to an upward buoyant force and will "float" even higher. Consequently, the parcel of air will accelerate upward.

Under the conditions just described, the atmosphere is said to be *unstable*. When the air is unstable, vertical motions can take place both in the upward and downward directions. In scientific terms, the air is unstable when a volume of air, moved from one place to another and then released, continues to accelerate in the same direction.

Now imagine that we repeat the experiment under different atmospheric conditions. When the parcel of air arrives at the higher location, it is cooler and more dense than the surrounding air. Under these conditions, there is a downward force on the displaced volume of air, forcing it back toward the ground. The atmosphere is then said to be *stable*.

It is easy to see why meteorologists are so interested in knowing the stability of the atmosphere. If it is unstable, rising volumes of air move rapidly upward. Low-flying aircraft encounter turbulence generated by rapidly rising and falling columns of air. If the air happens to contain sufficient water vapor, large cumulus clouds may form, leading to thunderstorms.

Stable air, on the other hand, suppresses vertical movements of air. There is little vertical mixing of the air and little dilution of air pollutants.

The most important factor determining atmospheric stability is the rate at which air temperature drops with increasing altitude. Meteorologists call this figure the *lapse rate*. The average lapse rate in the lower atmosphere is about 3.5°F per 1000 feet. This means that the air temperature drops about 3.5°F, on the average, for each increase in altitude of 1000 feet. The lapse rate varies greatly from place to place and from time to time. On a hot summer day it would be much greater. On some occasions, the air temperature actually *increases* with height for several hundred feet before assuming the normal lapse rate. The air layer through which this occurs is called a *temperature inversion*. A typical temperature inversion is illustrated in the accompanying diagram. Temperature inversions are layers of great atmospheric stability, so they suppress vertical motions of the air.

Temperature inversions often occur when the earth's surface is cooled in late afternoon. As the ground cools, the lower levels of the atmosphere are cooled by the earth. This results in a temperature inversion, because the air temperature increases with altitude for some distance above the ground. The inversion usually persists until the ground begins to warm up late the next morning. In some cases the temperature inversion may continue for several days, leading to severe levels of air pollution in the lower atmosphere.

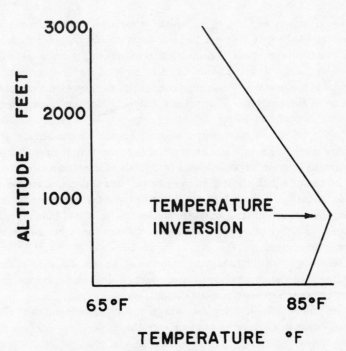

Fig. 39. A temperature inversion. Air near the ground increases in temperature with increasing altitude for several hundred feet. It then begins to get colder with increasing altitude.

How big is an atom?

The radius of a typical atom is approximately five-billionths (0.000,000,005) of an inch. Atoms of the different natural elements do not vary much in size, despite the fact that uranium, the heaviest, weighs about 236 times as much as hydrogen, the lightest. Atoms are tiny indeed! A drop of water contains about one sextillion atoms (a one followed by 21 zeros), and a page of this book contains something like one septillion atoms (a one followed by 24 zeros).

Scientists usually measure atomic radii in a unit of length called the angstrom unit, abbreviated Å. One angstrom unit is equal to one one-hundred-millionth of a centimeter, or about four-billionths of an inch. Hydrogen, the smallest element, has a radius of 0.32 Å and cesium, one of the largest, measures 2.35 Å.

265

The electrons and nuclei, of which atoms are composed, measure respectively about 10,000 and 100,000 times smaller than the atom itself. It would seem, then, that the atom is mostly empty space, since its diameter is tens of thousands of times larger than the diameters of its parts. Most of the atom's volume, however, is taken up by the complex motion of the electrons. They form a spherical electron cloud, which gives the atom its volume.

The "size" of an atom varies a small amount, depending on the method used to measure it. One method is to measure the distance of separation between adjacent nuclei in crystals of the element. The reported radius is half the measured distance, after a slight correction is made. Actually, the boundary of an atom is not a definite quantity, because the electron cloud around the nucleus is fuzzy and indefinite. It is distorted rather easily when the atom combines with other atoms. So the numbers given for radii are really the best estimates made by scientists. In spite of the fact that an atom's shape and radius is rather indefinite, the atom's volume resists change. Extremely great force must be used if an atom is to be compressed.

The following table gives the radii of various common atoms. The elements are listed in order of atomic weight.

Atomic Radii (Angstrom units)

Element	Radius	Element	Radius
Hydrogen	0.32	Nickel	1.15
Helium	0.31	Copper	1.17
Carbon	0.77	Zinc	1.25
Nitrogen	0.75	Silver	1.34
Oxygen	0.73	Tin	1.40
Sodium	1.54	Iodine	1.33
Aluminum	1.18	Platinum	1.30
Chlorine	0.99	Gold	1.34
Potassium	2.03	Lead	1.47
Calcium	1.74	Radium	2.20
Iron	1.17	Uranium	1.42

Atoms do not increase in size uniformly with atomic weight because of electrical forces within the atom. Nickel, for example, is smaller than calcium even though it has many more electrons in its cloud. Nickel also has a correspondingly greater positive charge in its nucleus, and the force of attraction between electrons and nucleus decreases the radius of the nickel atom. The various elements fall into several groups, or families. Within one family, the atomic sizes of successively heavier atoms tend to shrink because of electrical attraction. The average sizes in the next heavier family tend to be larger, as an additional layer or shell of electrons in added.

How are colored fireworks made?

Magnesium is a silver-white metal that is useful in applications where light weight is important. Like aluminum, it forms a tough surface coating that protects the underlying metal from tarnishing. When heated in air to the kindling temperature, it burns with a hot flame that gives off a dazzling white light. The burning produces magnesium oxide and magnesium nitride as the metal combines with oxygen and nitrogen in the air.

Because of the brilliant white light of burning magnesium, it is widely used in making flares and fireworks. Various other colors can be produced by adding certain substances to the flame. For instance, strontium compounds color the flame scarlet, and barium compounds produce a yellowish-green color.

Why is the ocean salty?

Ocean water is a complex solution of mineral salts that has been described as "a weak solution of everything." At least seventy-two chemical elements have been identified in sea water, although most are there in minute quantities. You may wonder where all this dissolved material came from.

Most of the dissolved salts in the ocean came from minerals contained in ancient rocks that were broken down by billions of years of erosion and weathering. During the earth's past history, mountains were thrust up, only to be worn away by rain as streams washed over the land. Minerals dissolved from the rocks were carried away by these streams and discharged into the ocean. Other salts were dissolved from rocks and sediments on the ocean floor. Still other salts probably came from gases and solids derived from volcanic activity.

Chemists estimate that the oceans contain as much as 50 quadrillion tons of dissolved solid material. If spread evenly over the surface of the earth, that amount of salt would form a layer some 500 feet thick. One cubic foot of ocean water contains about 2.2 pounds of salt. Of that amount, about three-quarters is ordinary table salt, sodium chloride.

The remainder consists of magnesium compounds (about 16 percent) and many other compounds in much smaller quantities.

Were the New World civilizations established by beings from outer space?

No serious scientist puts any credence in the sensational and popular accounts of extraterrestrial assistance or origins for civilizations in the New World. Anthropologists tell us that all the so-called mysterious remains that have been found in prehistoric New World archaeological sites can be explained and fully understood on the basis of the established capabilities of the peoples living during those times.

Does a slow learner forget more rapidly than a fast learner?

It is commonly thought that a slow learner forgets learned material more rapidly than a fast learner. But according to scientific research, that is a popular misconception. If a slow learner is given enough time to study the material so he can reproduce it as readily as a fast learner, the slow learner will score as high as a fast one in later tests of remembering the material.

Psychologists believe that a bright student does better on examinations than a less gifted student because he has learned the material better, not because his memory is better. It might take a slow student three hours to learn the material as well as a bright student does in one hour. The two are then likely to do equally well on an examination the next day. Many students of average learning ability do as well or better in school than bright students simply because they spend more time studying.

Another common misconception tells us that material that is easy to learn is also easy to remember. For instance, it should be easier to remember a list of meaningful words than a list of nonsense words, should it not? Surprisingly, experiments show there is no difference: the rate of forgetting is no different for the two kinds of words. If each is learned equally well to begin with, the scores of remembering, or forgetting, are essentially the same at some later time.

It is true, of course, that given the same length of time to study, the meaningful material will be remembered better in a subsequent test. To illustrate, if one group of subjects is given a list of words to learn and a second group is given a list of nonwords to learn, and the same time is allowed for each group, the first group will score higher on a test of recall the next day. This merely shows that it takes longer to learn the meaningless material than the real words. If we allow more time for learning the nonwords—so that each group reaches the same level of proficiency in the first place—then both groups will score about the same the next day. When it comes to remembering, what really counts is not the kind of material involved but the degree of initial learning.

How did ancient smiths make bronze and iron?

About 5000 years ago, Old World smiths began turning out a great variety of useful articles made of copper and its stronger alloy, bronze. Archaeologists, geologists, and metallurgists, combining their efforts, have now pieced together a reasonably accurate picture of the way this technology developed.

The oldest copper-producing sites yet discovered are located in Iran and Israel close to moderately abundant deposits of copper ores. Metalworkers of the eastern Mediterranean smelted copper by loading a stove furnace with alternating layers of charcoal, ore, and flux. The temperature of the fire was increased either by the natural draft of a chimney or by air forced into various parts of the furnace. The flux was added to remove the unwanted substances in the ore, called *gangue*. The flux often used in the eastern Mediterranean was hematite, a mineral consisting of iron oxide (which happens, by the way, to be an excellent iron ore).

When the temperature in such a furnace reaches about 1100°C, the charcoal combines with oxygen to form carbon monoxide gas, which reacts chemically with the ore and flux. As a result of this process, molten metallic copper is produced; it flows down to the bottom of the furnace, where it forms a pool. The gangue and flux, being lighter than copper, float on top of the copper.

If the copper ore happens to contain several percent of arsenic, the smelting process described above produces a puddle of natural bronze instead of copper. Being harder than copper, natural bronze was more suitable for producing durable articles and weapons. Smelters later discovered that tin could be added to copper to produce another strong metal, tin bronze, which was also hard but which did not have the toxicity of natural bronze. By 2000 B.C. the production of tin bronze had surpassed that of arsenic or natural bronze.

Several hundred years later a form of iron began to replace bronze for weapons, tools, and other articles. The strange fact about this substitution is that iron was not new. It had been known as a workable metal for almost 2000 years. Furthermore, it is not nearly as useful as bronze for most purposes: iron rusts quickly, while bronze is essentially indestructible, and bronze is stronger than iron, at least in the form available in those days. In addition, bronze could be melted and cast into useful articles any number of times, while prehistoric smelters could not attain temperatures high enough to melt iron. Iron, therefore, had to be hammered into shape. Some scientists suspect that unknown events—perhaps political instability, piracy, or worn-out mines—led to a scarcity of tin or copper ore. In any event, the change from bronze to the poorer material, iron, was relatively rapid.

Early metalworkers produced iron from ores such as hematite and magnetite, in stove furnaces much like those used for copper. They had one serious problem, however. Iron melts at a temperature of 1537°C, and the early furnaces could only reach a temperature of about 1200°C. So instead of a neat puddle of iron, the smelter produced a spongy mixture of iron, called a "bloom," and various minerals called slag.

The slag produced in iron-smelting remains viscous down to a temperature of 1177°C. The metalworker, therefore, reheated the iron-slag mixture in a forge and hammered the slag out of the iron bloom. Useful articles were then made by hammering the hot bloomery iron into the desired shape. Both iron and bronze could be strengthened by work-hardening—that is, by hammering the finished article—but bronze was still 20 percent stronger than iron.

About the year 1000 B.C., blacksmiths learned how to transform iron into an alloy that is far superior to bronze for tools and weapons. The treatment they used is called *steeling*, a process that was probably discovered by accident. The blacksmith's practice was to hammer the iron bloom over a charcoal fire in his forge. During this work the temperature of the iron had to reach about 1200°C. At that temperature the iron absorbed a small amount of carbon from the charcoal and from the carbon monoxide gas given off in the forge. This diffusion of carbon into iron follows well-known physical laws. At 1150°C, for example, the carbon content can reach 2 percent at a depth of penetration of one-sixteenth of an inch. Then, when the temperature falls below 727°C, the carburized iron becomes a form of steel called pearlite. By cold-hammering pearlite, the steeled iron could be made more than twice as strong as cold-worked bronze. By 900 or 800 B.C., blacksmiths had learned to control the amount and location of pearlite in their products. It was then possible to match the properties of a tool to its intended use.

After 900 B.C., the use of iron implements increased rapidly. Even though bronze was again available, steeled iron had demonstrated its superiority. Technology had left bronze behind, and iron was now the metal of choice for articles requiring high strength or hardness.

At least by the seventh century B.C., blacksmiths discovered that steeled iron could be improved even further by a process called *quenching:* cooling iron quickly by immersing it in water. Quenching of carburized iron produces a steel, called *martensite,* which is considerably harder than pearlite but much more brittle. Once again, blacksmiths had found a way to tailor steel to the particular needs at hand. For instance, hardness was important in such articles as arrowheads, which could tolerate a certain amount of brittleness.

By the fourth century B.C., blacksmiths had developed still another treatment of steel called *tempering.* It was undoubtedly clear to iron-workers that quenching made tools brittle. Tempering involves heating a previously quenched article to a temperature not above 727°C for a length of time to allow some of the brittle martensite to change in form to reduce hardness somewhat and increase ductility. In this way, tools and weapons could be made to provide precisely the desired characteristics.

Blacksmiths could not have understood why steeling, quenching, and tempering made such profound improvements in the characteristics of iron. Nevertheless, through trial and error they discovered the secrets of iron metallurgy over a period of perhaps a thousand years or less. It was through their tenacity and hard work that the Mediterranean peoples stepped from the Bronze Age into the Iron Age.

How effective is home insulation?

In 1789 Benjamin Thomson, later known as Count Rumford, made an important discovery while supervising the boring of a cannon in the military arsenal at Munich, Bavaria. He noticed that a blunt drill had created an enormous amount of heat during the boring operation. Count Rumford reasoned that the heat must have come from the mechanical energy provided by the horse-driven engine that ran the boring tool. This was the first time that anyone had noticed a rela-

271

tionship between heat and mechanical work. We now know that the two forms of energy are equivalent and can be converted one to the other.

Heat is defined in terms of the *British thermal unit,* or Btu for short. One Btu is the amount of heat needed to raise the temperature of one pound of water by one degree Fahrenheit. (In the metric system, one calorie will raise the temperature of one gram of water by one degree Celsius. The calorie used in nutrition is really a kilocalorie, or 1000 times as great as the physicist's calorie.)

The amount of mechanical work needed to heat water is really staggering. For example, to heat only 2 pounds of water—approximately a quart—from 32°F to boiling requires 360 Btu, or the same amount of energy as raising one ton to a height of 140 feet. If this work were done in a minute, it would require over 8 horsepower! To take another example, the Gulf Stream gives off heat equivalent to 360 billion horsepower as it cools 1°F in one hour.

When a gallon of fuel oil burns, it produces about 142,000 Btu—enough energy to raise one ton to a height of 10.5 miles! It is lucky for us that fossil fuels contain so much heat, because the heat is lost quite rapidly through walls and ceilings as we warm our homes. For instance, a one-square-foot area of ceiling constructed of wood and plaster with no insulation loses about 1200 Btu per day if the temperature outside is 50°F cooler than the temperature inside. If a 6-inch thickness of rock wool insulation is added, the heat loss is only 52 Btu per day under the same conditions. In other words, the heat loss in a ceiling can be reduced 23 times by adequate insulation.

If we scale up the area from one square foot to perhaps 1000 square feet for the ceiling of a small house, the figures become 1,200,000 Btu per day for the uninsulated ceiling and 52,000 Btu per day for the insulated ceiling. The fuel oil requirements for the two ceilings would be 8.5 and 0.37 gallons per day respectively. The example given above does not include heat loss through the walls of the building, but the same principles apply there. The fuel savings that can be accomplished by adequate home insulation are quite significant. Such savings are especially important in northern climates, where temperatures are quite low during the winter months. In hot weather, insulation reduces the heat flow from outside into a building, so it is just as effective in lowering the costs of air conditioning.

272

The table below gives the insulating effectiveness of various building materials in relation to one another.

Relative Insulating Effectiveness of Building Materials

Rock wool	1.0	Brick	0.06
Glass wool	0.9	Glass	0.05
Celotex	0.8	Limestone	0.04
Sawdust	0.6	Concrete	0.03
Wood	0.3	Sandstone	0.02
Building gypsum	0.1	Marble	0.02
Plaster	0.1	Granite	0.01

The data show that rock wool is roughly ten times as effective as plaster, for the same thickness, and about 100 times as effective as granite. Rock wool, like most good thermal insulators, owes its insulating effectiveness to countless tiny volumes of air trapped between its particles. It is manufactured from slag, a stony waste material produced in the smelting of iron.

Why does a rifle recoil when a bullet is fired?

Anyone who has ever used a firearm knows that it can exert a strong backward thrust when fired. Physicists explain this effect in terms of an ominous sounding principle called the *conservation of momentum*. As we shall see, the principle has many applications in the world around us and is not nearly as difficult as it sounds.

When a rifle is fired, the ejection of a bullet from the barrel is responsible for the push, or "kick," that the rifleman feels as the recoil. This effect is identical in principle to the action of a rocket in which the ejection of gases provides the push. You can observe the same effect when a balloon is blown up and then released without tying off the open end. The escaping air pushes the balloon in the opposite direction.

Carrying all this a step further, we can increase the recoil of a rifle by using a greater powder charge to fire an identical bullet at higher speed. Or we can achieve a greater recoil by increasing the mass of the bullet and maintaining the same speed of ejection. Clearly, the amount of recoil depends on two factors: the mass and speed of the fired bullet. Similarly, the push experienced by the rocket or balloon also depends on the mass and speed of the ejected gases.

Fig. 40. A: Equal masses are pushed apart by a spring at equal velocities. B: The large block moves away at a slower speed than the small block.

We can clarify the subject further with the help of the accompanying diagram. In part A we have two blocks with equal masses. A compressed spring is located between the blocks. Let's further assume that the blocks are on wheels, so we can forget friction. When the spring is released, it uncoils and pushes the blocks in opposite directions. If we measure the speeds of the blocks, we find that they are equal, as indicated by the two velocity arrows of equal length. There is really nothing unexpected about this result. The blocks are identical and they are pushed with the same force, so they end up with the same speed.

In part B of the diagram, the situation is quite different: one block is larger and more massive than the other. Now when the spring is released, the small block moves off at a higher velocity (large arrow) than the larger block. Suppose we were to carry out a large number of experiments using blocks of different masses. The results would show an important relationship: the mass multiplied by the speed of one block is always equal to the mass multiplied by the speed of the other block. In mathematical terms:

LEFT BLOCK		RIGHT BLOCK
(mass) × (speed)	=	(mass) × (speed)
M × V	=	m × v

The product (mass) × (speed) is such an important quantity that physicists have given it a special name, *momentum*.

$$\text{Momentum} = (\text{mass}) \times (\text{speed or velocity})$$

Referring again to the experiment in the diagram, we can say that the momentum of one block is always equal and opposite to the momentum of the other block, once they are set in motion by the spring.

This notion of direction of motion is important in physics. The velocities V and v, for example, have very specific directions with respect to each other. Since momentum is a product of velocity, it too has direction that it derives from the velocity. (We call such a quantity a *vector*.) A physicist, therefore, would say that the right-hand block has a momentum mv directed to the right, and the left-hand block has a momentum MV directed to the left.

From the ideas presented thus far, we know that MV and mv have the same magnitude. What happens if we add these two momenta together? The result of adding two such vectors of equal magnitude and *opposite directions* is zero! This really is not as absurd as it may seem. To illustrate, suppose a boy is running from bow to stern of a ship at 5 miles per hour. The ship is moving forward at the same speed, 5 miles per hour. What is the speed of the boy with respect to the earth? Since his speed is canceled exactly by the speed of the ship, the boy's speed with respect to the earth is zero. Once again we have two equal and opposite vectors (the velocities) that add up to zero. So physicists

275

state that the total momenta of the recoiling blocks must always be zero. But the initial momentum of the two-block-and-spring system was also zero. In other words, releasing the spring so that the blocks began to move had no effect on the total momentum of the system.

This conclusion is extremely important in the science of physics and holds true for the motion of all objects. The total momentum of a system of objects can never change unless that system of objects is acted upon by some outside agency. In our examples, the "system of objects" consisted of two blocks and a spring; or a rifle, a bullet, and a powder charge; or a balloon filled with air. In each example, the total momentum remained constant. This is known as the *law of conservation of momentum*.

We can illustrate the use of the law by calculating the velocity of recoil of a rifle. Suppose the bullet has a mass of 1 ounce and leaves the barrel at a velocity of 1200 feet per second. The bullet's momentum, mv, is $1 \times 1200 = 1200$. The momentum of the rifle, MV, after the shot must also equal 1200. If the rifle has a mass of 60 ounces, its velocity is $1200 \div 60 = 20$ feet per second.

The conservation of momentum helps to explain why a collision between a small automobile and a large truck can be so devastating. To start with, imagine a head-on collision between two identical cars moving at 30 miles per hour. Before impact, the total momentum of the two-car system is equal to zero because the momenta are equal and opposite in direction. Upon collision, the cars come immediately to rest. The total momentum before and after collision is equal to zero. Now suppose that one of the cars is a large truck weighing twenty times as much as the car. The initial velocities are still the same but the momenta are not. It turns out, in fact, that the momentum of the truck is twenty times that of the car. The momentum before collision is far from zero, and it is unchanged after impact takes place. As a result, the truck is hardly slowed down by the collision with the car. Instead, the direction of the car's motion suddenly reverses as it is pushed along backward at about 27 miles per hour. The truck, on the other hand, receives a minor jolt as its speed is reduced slightly by the collision. The fact that momentum is always conserved in such collisions is of little satisfaction to the unfortunate occupants of the car.

How does infrared photography locate underground springs?

There has been much research in recent years into the use of infrared photographic devices to learn more about the earth. Infrared scanners, for example, produce images that show the temperature variations in the region being studied. Abnormal earth temperatures discovered in this way can provide valuable information on crops, pollution, and even sources of fresh water.

Infrared sensing from aircraft and spacecraft has become an important tool in various geologic studies. In Hawaii, for example, infrared images have been used to pinpoint places along the coast where freshwater springs flow into the ocean. The island of Hawaii has few well-developed streams because most of the rain water sinks quickly into the porous volcanic rock of the island. It eventually passes from the rocks into the sea. Because fresh water is less dense than salty ocean water, it rises to the surface and "floats" out to sea. In addition, the ground water from the island is about 9°F cooler than the ocean water. Infrared film faithfully records this temperature difference, and the image of the coastline can be used to locate places where fresh-water springs feed into the ocean. More than 200 valuable springs have been located in that way.

Infrared photography has also been used to determine differences in rocks and soils, to locate sources of pollution, to determine geologic structure, to find ground water, and to study volcanic activity. Unlike conventional photography, infrared photography measures the amount of energy *emitted* from the ground, rather than reflected by it. For that reason, it can be used at night as well as during the day.

Are all stars yellow?

If you examine the night sky closely, it is easy to see that stars differ in color. Some stars are red, like Antares; others are white like Canopus. It turns out that a star's color depends on its temperature— a red star is "red hot," and a white star is "white hot."

You can convince yourself of that relationship by grasping a pin or needle with a pair of pliers and holding it in a gas flame. As the metal gets hotter, it progresses from red to yellow to white. The colors and temperatures of all pieces of matter, including stars, are related in the same way. Yellow stars are hotter than red stars, white stars are hotter than yellow stars, and blue-white stars are hotter than white stars. Astronomers can measure the wavelengths of light given off by a star and calculate how hot it must be. By studying this light, scientists can also determine which chemical elements are present in a star.

To understand how this is done, suppose that a chemist adjusts a gas flame until it is essentially colorless. He then puts a bit of matter

277

in the flame. If the matter contains the element sodium (for instance, if it is table salt, sodium chloride), the flame turns a yellow color. In other words, hot sodium gives off specific wavelengths of light, which we interpret as yellow. Other elements give off different wavelengths.

Chemists can obtain greater accuracy by observing, or photographing, the yellow flame through an instrument called a *spectroscope,* which separates light into the wavelengths that make it up. Viewed through a spectroscope, light is spread out into a *spectrum* of its constituent colors, from red at the long-wavelength end, through orange, yellow, green, and blue, to violet at the short-wavelength end. A simple spectroscope can be made by passing a slit of light through a glass prism. Using such a device, a scientist can identify the wavelengths more exactly. He can then conclude, as in our earlier example, that the bit of matter in the flame gives off precisely those wavelengths that show the presence of sodium.

It is the light, of course, that gives the chemist information about the substance in the flame. The same test can be performed on light from a distant star to discover just which chemical elements are present in the star. In addition, light from a blue-white star produces a spectrum with strong (or bright) wavelengths in the blue part of the spectrum. Light from a red star, on the other hand, has strong wavelengths at the red end of the spectrum.

Actually, one can see stars of all colors in the sky: white, blue, green, yellow, orange, and red. Our sun is a yellow star. Its most intense radiation is in the yellow part of the spectrum. The sun's temperature, therefore, is between that of an orange star and a white star. The following table gives the approximate surface temperatures of a few representative stars of different colors.

Star	Color	Surface Temperature °C
Rigel	blue-white	12,300
Sirius	blue-white	10,700
Canopus	white	8,200
Sun	yellow	5,530
Capella	yellow	5,200
Arcturus	orange	4,230
Antares	red	3,200

Once a star's temperature is known, it is possible to calculate its size. The only other information needed is its actual brightness. Let us see how a star's brightness is determined.

When we look at the nighttime sky, we notice at once that the stars vary considerably in brightness. Over 1800 years ago, a Greek astronomer named Ptolemy, who worked in Alexandria, Egypt, classified the stars by their brightness. His system used six different degrees of brightness called *magnitudes,* stars of the first magnitude being the brightest. With the invention of the telescope and other instruments, his method has been refined and expanded to include stars too dim to be seen with the unaided eye. Ptolemy's magnitudes, of course, merely describe how bright a star *appears* to be. It is more accurate, therefore, to speak of the *apparent magnitude* of a star—its brightness as seen by an observer on earth. The more distant a star happens to be, the dimmer it seems to us. Because astronomers have other methods of measuring the distance to a star, they can convert its apparent magnitude to its real brightness—the intensity of light that is actually given off. This true brightness is called a star's *luminosity.*

We are now ready to see how a star's temperature and luminosity can give a clue to its size. The sun is almost twice as hot as the red star Antares, yet the luminosity of Antares is nearly 2000 times greater than that of the sun. Since the sun is considerably hotter, a square foot of its surface area gives off more light than a square foot of the surface of Antares. In order for Antares to give off so much more light than the sun, it must be much greater in size. Astronomers have calculated the diameter of Antares, and it turns out to be about 390 times the diameter of the sun. Its volume is so great that it could contain almost 60 billion stars, each the size of our sun! Betelgeuse is even larger than Antares. These red stars are called *red giants.* Other red giants are Beta Pegasi (113 sun diameters) and Aldebaran (35 sun diameters). At the other end of the size scale, some white stars are as small as the planets in our solar system. These so-called white dwarfs are thought to be near the end of their life cycles as luminous stars.

How does lightning help fertilize the soil?

Proteins, which make up the greatest part of our body's tissues, are compounds containing nitrogen, yet our bodies are unable to make any use of the great quantity of nitrogen in the atmosphere. Unlike oxygen, which is chemically changed by our bodies into carbon dioxide, nitrogen is merely exhaled back into the air. The nitrogen that goes into our proteins comes from plants, or from animals that eat plants.

This seems to be a rather roundabout way to get the nitrogen we need when there is such a plentiful supply in the air. The reason is connected with the great amount of energy needed to split nitrogen molecules into individual atoms of nitrogen. Both nitrogen and oxygen exist in the air as molecules consisting of two atoms. Their chemical formulas are N_2 and O_2. The atoms of oxygen are held together rather loosely by a single chemical bond—one pair of shared electrons. But the two atoms of nitrogen are firmly held together by a triple chemical bond—three pairs of shared electrons. It takes a great deal more energy to break the triple bond of the nitrogen molecule than the single bond of oxygen. Only when nitrogen's molecular bonds are broken can the individual atoms of nitrogen combine with other elements. Chemists call this process of forming useful compounds of nitrogen *nitrogen fixing*.

Whenever there is a thunderstorm accompanied by lightning, some of the nitrogen in the atmosphere falls to earth in the form of nitric acid (HNO_3), a compound of hydrogen, nitrogen, and oxygen. The energy to split the nitrogen molecule into atoms comes from the electrical discharge that we call lightning. Nitrogen atoms then combine with oxygen to form nitric oxide (NO). The nitric oxide then combines with more oxygen and some of the rain water to form a weak solution of nitric acid (HNO_3). The rain carries the nitric acid to the ground, where the acid combines with minerals in the soil to form nitrates. The nitrates are absorbed by plants and used to build complex protein molecules. In this way, lightning actually helps fertilize the soil.

Nitrogen fixing can also occur with the help of suitable chemicals called *catalysts,* substances that help a chemical reaction along without being changed themselves at the end of the reaction. When catalysts exist in the cells of living things, they are called enzymes. Certain bacteria that are found in the soil have enzymes that can assist in fixing nitrogen. Nitrogen from the air is normally found in pore spaces in the soil. Nitrogen-fixing bacteria can take free nitrogen in the soil and change this nitrogen into useful compounds. Nitrogen-fixing bacteria make their home in small nodules on the roots of such plants as clover, peanuts, and beans. Plants with these nodules have a ready source of nitrates with which to build proteins.

How are oil deposits found?

The only sure way to find oil, of course, is to drill a well and see what comes up. Well drilling is expensive, however, so geophysicists do their prospecting for oil with the aid of the seismograph, the same instrument used in the study of earthquakes and tidal waves. In the search for oil, the seismograph records man-made earth tremors, or seismic waves, rather than natural seismic waves. These artificial "earthquakes" are often produced by an explosion of buried dynamite. Vibrations from the blast produce sound waves in the earth, which are reflected from layers of rock beneath the surface. The echoes are picked up and recorded by seismographs located at a number of nearby places. Seismic waves are reflected more strongly from hard rocks than from softer ones, and the times of travel of the waves indicate how deep the various rock layers are buried. Geophysicists then interpret the recordings in a search for rock formations that are likely to contain trapped oil beneath the surface.

In recent years, substitutes for explosives have been developed for setting off the required earth vibrations. One method shakes the earth by dropping a heavy weight, called a "thumper." In offshore exploration, gas under high pressure may be used to discharge bubbles that create sound impulses.

Another method of generating seismic waves has been developed for relatively inaccessible places such as the North Slope area of Alaska. The shock device is mounted on a stand that is light enough to be set in place by a helicopter. Seismic waves are generated by an "exploder," which consists of a chamber filled with oxygen and propane gases. The mixture is exploded by a radio-controlled device, and the impact drives a steel plate against the ground, thereby generating the seismic waves. The echos are then recorded and deciphered as discussed earlier. This method is inexpensive, can be moved quickly to a new location, and can be used on either land or water.

How is the American chestnut tree being saved?

In the short span of just forty years, the chestnut blight destroyed every stand of chestnut trees in America's forests. The mighty tree once dominated upland areas from Maine to Alabama, sometimes reaching 120 feet in height and 13 feet in diameter. Today, only blighted stumps remain, which send up saplings from still living roots, only to have the new growth succumb after a few years to the inevitable blight.

The parasitic fungus (*Endothia parasitica*) that causes the disease first showed up in 1904 in a stand of chestnuts in New York City's Bronx Zoo. For decades thereafter, American scientists had no success in curing the blight. Now, at last, a cure is in sight, and scientists believe that the American chestnut will regain its once great vitality and majesty.

The story of the cure began in 1917, when the blight crossed the Atlantic to Italy. The European chestnut is a close relative of the native American variety, and by 1940 the fungus had devastated chestnut groves in northern and central Italy. By the mid-1950s it had crossed the Alps into France, and the European chestnut tree was about to follow its American cousin to oblivion. French tree surgeons fought the disease by cutting away the bark canker and painting the wound with antiseptic. But their efforts were soon overwhelmed by the rapid spread of the disease.

Then, a piece of exciting news came out of Italy: some of the Italian trees were somehow beginning to cure themselves. Unfortunately, no one knew why. The mystery was finally solved by a French agronomist who took the problem back to the laboratory.

Jean Grente was the director of research at the Clermont station of the French National Institute for Agronomic Research. He took Italian bark samples back to France and discovered that the agent responsible for the cures was a new strain of the virulent fungus. He grew cultures of fungus both from lethal cankers and from cankers whose trees were on the road to recovery. The deadly fungus grew robust, orange strands, but its weaker cousin was white and less vigorous. Grente also grew a sample of each fungus, side by side, in a single dish. As the two fungi grew together, they formed a new kind of strand, the color of milk and paprika. Grente showed that the weaker fungus had infected the deadly strain. By this process, the two strains fuse to form a union called *anastomosis,* and the virulent strain is rendered harmless. When the two come together in a chestnut tree, the union is defeated by the tree's natural defense mechanisms. The new, weaker strain that infects the virulent, or deadly, strain is called a *hypovirulent* strain.

Because of the perversity of nature, Grente found that one hypovirulent strain was not sufficient to transmit its weakness to every virulent one. He solved the problem by producing many new hypovirulent strains in the laboratory. These were then matched to virulent strains of the fungi taken from sick trees throughout France. In that way, an effective hypovirulent strain could be selected for each section of the country.

The cure involves punching small holes around a canker in an ailing tree. The hypovirulent strain is then placed in the shallow holes and covered with masking tape to preserve its moisture. From that moment on, the tree is on the road to recovery. More than that, however, this "blighting of the blight" is transmitted from tree to tree by birds, insects, squirrels, and wind. This means that only a small number of trees in a grove need be inoculated; nature takes care of the rest.

Jean Grente's methods and fungus strains have been used in the United States, but success here has not been as dramatic as in France. American trees do not always respond to the hypovirulent strains that work in Europe. Native hypovirulent strains have turned up in the wild here, and individual trees have been cured, but the cure has refused to spread automatically from tree to tree. American chestnut trees are not cultivated in groves as they are in Europe, but tend to be dispersed throughout the forest. Nevertheless, scientists believe that Grente's methods will save the American chestnut, as better fungus strains and greater efforts are applied to the problem.

Is the world's climate changing?

Year in, year out, climate is one of the more stable and predictable characteristics of the earth. Deserts remain dry, rain forests wet, polar regions cold, and the tropics hot. Yet there is a great deal of evidence that major climatic changes have occurred in the past. Some were minor and short-lived, but others were of major importance and led to fundamental changes in the life forms that have inhabited the earth over its long history.

Long-range changes in climate show up as ice ages separated at irregular intervals by long-lasting warm periods. During the last 600 million years, for example, there have been seventeen known periods of glaciation on the earth. During these ice ages, enormous sheets of ice advanced toward the equator, sometimes reaching as far south as the latitude of New York.

The Pleistocene epoch, covering the last 600,000 years, has been studied extensively by geophysicists, who have dated fossils and other relics of the epoch and have made estimates of the temperatures that existed during their formation. During the four major ice ages of the

283

Pleistocene epoch, the earth's average temperature was about 11°F colder than today's average. Three of the four ice ages lasted about 100,000 years, and the fourth—called the Wisconsin Age—extended from about 40,000 to 10,000 years ago. The interglacial intervals had temperatures about 5°F warmer than those of today. These temperature data show that a temperature change of a very few degrees can have a profound effect on the climate of the earth.

The earth's climate during the last 10,000 years has also been studied quite extensively. The accompanying table gives a small sampling of important climatic conditions during the period.

During the period around 4000 B.C., the earth was 2 or 3°F warmer than it is now, and conditions were optimum for plants and animals.

The most recent cold period, which lasted from A.D. 1500 to 1900, is called the Little Ice Age. During this period, the climate was cool and dry, and glaciers grew in size. Beginning in 1890, a warming trend began over all the earth, producing an average temperature increase of about 1°F by 1940. Glaciers began to retreat once again, and the level of the ocean rose a small amount. Since 1940 there has been a gradual cooling of about one-half degree, and glaciers have begun to grow. It appears that the changes in climate that have taken place throughout the earth's history are still going on.

Some scientists believe that the earth's climate is related to the energy output of the sun. At present, the average temperature of the earth is close to 58°F. In the past, it has been as high as 72°F and as low as 42°F. Attempts have been made to correlate these changes with nuclear processes in the sun, but to date the results are inconclusive.

Another theory suggests that dust from volcanoes might account for the ice ages. The basic idea is that volcanic dust in the air would reduce the amount of solar energy taken up by the earth, and result in lower temperatures. Unfortunately for that theory, particles in the atmosphere can result either in warming or cooling of the earth, depending on the characteristics of the particles, the altitude at which they float, and the reflectivity of the earth.

Some scientists have suggested that climatic changes are induced by the variation in carbon dioxide (CO_2) in the atmosphere. Before the industrial revolution, most CO_2 came from volcanic eruptions. Most scientists, however, believe that unrealistically large variations in CO_2

284

Climate of the Earth During the Past 10,000 Years

Year	Region	Climate
B.C.		
9000–6000	Europe	Cooling to 7000 B.C.
	Southern Arizona	Warm and arid.
6000–2500	North America, Europe	Cool and dry, changing to warm and moist. Then dry by 3000 B.C. (optimum climate.)
2500–500	Northern Hemisphere	Warm and dry with intermittent heavy rain and drought.
500–1	Europe	Cool and moist, glaciation in Ireland and Scandinavia.
A.D.		
300–600	U.S.A.	Glacial advance in Alaska. Drought in southwest of U.S.A.
600–800	U.S.A., Europe	Europe and Near East very dry, Black Sea frozen, glacial advance in Alaska.
800–1200	U.S.A., Europe	Glaciers retreat, North Africa cold, ice in western U.S.A.
1200–1500	U.S.A.	Glacial advance, periods of wetness and drought in the west.
1500–1900	U.S.A., Europe	Cool and dry, several glacial advances, drought in the southwest in the sixteenth century.
1880–1940	U.S.A., Europe	Temperature increase of 3°F in winter, reduced glaciers.
1942–1960	U.S.A., Europe	Temperature decrease, glaciers stable.

levels would be needed to account for the known changes in climate.

Another theory behind variations in climate has to do with the exchange of water between the Atlantic and Arctic oceans. At present, about 10 percent of the earth's surface is covered with ice. This represents a relatively small area when compared with past interglacial periods. It is thought that water from the Atlantic warms the Arctic Ocean slightly and melts some of its ice. This allows evaporation to take place, and water vapor enters the Arctic air, eventually falling as snow. The snow adds to the amount of water locked in Arctic glaciers and other forms of ice. There is a shallow rock ledge between the two oceans between Norway and Greenland. As the ocean level drops, the flow of water from Atlantic to Arctic Ocean is blocked and the temperature of the Arctic region becomes lower. The Arctic Ocean then freezes over, and the earth enters a new ice age.

With the Arctic frozen, evaporation of water is reduced, precipitation is reduced, and the glaciers start to melt. The sea level rises again and the Atlantic begins the flow into the Arctic and warm it once again. The ice recedes, and the cycle is complete.

There is some evidence that this sort of effect has taken place in the past. During the last ice age, the sea level was about 330 feet lower, and the earth was from 7 to 14°F colder than at present.

None of the theories outlined above are accepted universally. At last count, in fact, there were forty different theories advanced to explain the changing climate. It seems likely that a workable theory will have to take into account not just one or two factors but dozens before a better understanding of our climate is achieved.

INDEX

289

Fossils, 66
  and lengthening of the day, 258
  and prehistoric fire, 115
  in rocks, 17
  micro-, 18
Fourth dimension, 184
Franklin, Benjamin, 37, 74
Free radical, 40
Freezing temperature, lowering of, 4
Freon, in air cooling, 99
Frequency of light, 141
Friction
  and fire-making, 115
  theory of, 84
Frontal fog, 180
Fronts
  warm and cold, 234
  and weather, 263
Fructose, 152
Fruit flies, 163
Fuel
  coal as, 146
  and home insulation, 272
Fungi
  and ants, 196
  and bread, 1
  carnivorous, 23
  and cheese, 231
  and chestnut blight, 282
  and enzymes, 1, 109
  killed by heat, 194
  mushrooms as, 248
  orchids and, 66
  and seedlings, 193
  spores of, 197
  and termites, 198
  truffles as, 64
Fungicides, 194
Furnaces
  blast, 86
  electric, 87
Fusion, nuclear, 47

Galactose, 152
Galileo, 206
Galvanized iron, and rust prevention,
  154

Gamma rays, measurement of, 238
Gangue, removal of, from ores, 269
Gases
  from coal, 146
  exhaust, cleaning, 177
  in solution, 210
Gasoline, from coal, 147
Geese, and imprinting, 7
Geiger counter, 239
Genes, 191
  See also Genetics
Genetic changes, and radiation, 239
Genetic code, 192
Genetics, and plants, 101
Geologic time scale, 66
  radioactivity and, 67
Geosynclines, 249
Geothermal energy, 120
Geysers, 120
Giotto, 262
Glaciers, 152, 199
  during ice ages, 284
  melting of, 259
  movement of, 28
Glass, and transmission of light, 164
Glucose
  and dextrin, 205
  and hunger, 179
  polymers of, 152
Glycogen, 152
Gold
  dust, 163
  and rock formations, 230
  from sea water, 112
Grand Atelier, 222
Grand Canyon, 89
Gravitation
  theory of, 184
  and tides, 3
  See also Gravity
Gravitational field, 128
Gravitational force, 3
Gravity, 19
  force of, 127
  and relativity, 183
  and sense of equilibrium, 179
  See also Gravitation

Icecaps *(cont'd)*
    melting of, and sea level, 259
    See also Glaciers
Identification, and race, 202
    prejudice and, 203
Ideograms, in Egyptian writing, 175
Igneous rock, 230
Illusions, optical, 147
Immunity, and influenza, 214
Imprinting,
    in animals, 7, 198
    odor and, 7
Inbreeding, detrimental, and plants, 8
Incest taboo, 8
Indian, American, origin of, 18
Influenza, 213
    in animals and birds, 214
    as health problem, 213
    immunity, and, 214
    pandemic, 214
    See also Virus, influenza
Infrabuccal pocket, in ants, 197
Infrared photography, 276
Ink blots, 236
Insects
    caste system in, 162
    and cold weather, 103
    communication and, 162, 247
    control of, 162
    sex attractants in, 162
    sounds of, 247
    wing beats of, 248
Instinct
    in birds, 13
    human, 220
    maternal, 221
Insulation, home, 271
    effectiveness of, 271
    fuel and, 272
    materials for, 273
Inversion, temperature, and smog, 263
Iodine test, for starch, 205
Ionization, 238
Ions, 39, 234, 238
    and corona discharge, 177
    taste of, 107
Iron, 84

Iron *(cont'd)*
    in ancient times, 269
    and carbon, alloy of, 86
    cast, 86
    catastrophe, 22
    galvanized, and rust prevention, 154
    oxide, 155
    pig, 86
    rusting of, 105
    wrought, 86
Irrigation, 102
Irruptions
    of lemmings, 130
    of locusts, 131
    See also Migration
Isobars, 96
Isolation, and pain, 185
Isotopes, 45
    of carbon, 144

Jail, and crime, 136
Java man, 242
Jet stream, 234
Joule, James, 255

Kelvin (temperature scale), 63
Khârga (oasis), 6
Kikuyu, as pottery makers, 105
Kilauea (volcano), 87
Kilns, pottery, 105
Kilocalorie, 272
Kinesthesis, 179
Kinetic energy, 21
Kite, dangers of, 37

Lactose, 152
Land temperatures, effect of ocean on, 260
Language skills, 199
Lanolin, in suntan lotions, 123
Lapse rate, of atmosphere, 264
Lava, 87, 88
Lead-204, 49
Learners, slow vs. fast, 268
Learning, 173, 217, 268
    social, 220
    while asleep, 206

Lemmings, irruptions of, 130
Length, contraction effect and, 183
Leukemia, 126
Libby, Willard F., 143
Lie detector, eye as, 11
Life
    origin of, 186
        energy and, 187
        lightning and, 187
Light
    nature of, 140
    -sensitive cells, 228
    spectrum of, 278
    speed of, 42, 163
        and relativity, 182
    transmission of, glass and, 164
    ultraviolet, in atmosphere, 24
    year, 170
Lightfoot, John, 176
Lightning
    and airplanes, 159
    cold and hot, 200
    direction of, 79
    and fertilizer, 279
    heat, 109
    nature of, 200
    and origin of life, 187
    protection from, 137
    rods, 200
    striking twice, 212
    See also Thunder
Lignin, 152
Lime, 222
Limestone, and cement, 223
Liquids
    fizz in, 210
    freezing temperature, 4
Little Ice Age, 284
Liver, regeneration of, 125
Locusts, irruptions of, 131
Long-day plants, 251
Low-pressure area, 96
LSD, 35
Luminosity, of stars, 279
Lunar tides, 3
Lye, and soap-making, 94

Mach numbers, and aircraft speed, 42
Magicians
    and observation of eye, 10
    and optical illusions, 147
Magma (molten rock) 88, 230
Magnesium
    and fireworks, 267
    sea water as source of, 113, 268
Magnetite, 270
Magnitudes, of stars, 279
Maltose, 152
    and dextrin, 205
Man
    apes and, 241
    Cro-Magnon, 16
    hominids, 241
    Homo erectus, 242
    Homo sapiens, 243
    Java, 242
    Neanderthal. *See* Neanderthal man
Mantle, of earth, 22
Marble, formation of, 231
Marcasite, and prehistoric fire-making,
        115
Marriage, between brother and sister, 8
Martensite, 271
Mass
    and energy, 244
    and relativity, 183
Mast cells, 60
Mathematics, and the mind, 160
Mating, of mosquitoes, 248
Matter, and energy, 244
Mauna Kea (volcano), 87
Mauna Loa (volcano), 87
Mayonnaise, as emulsion, 235
Measurement, of radiation, 237
Meat tenderizers, 109
Melanin, 123
Melting, of glaciers, 259
Memory
    computer, 70
    permanence of, 216
    protein and, 92
    working of, 91
Mercury
    cell, 109

301

Solar pressure, 261
Solubility, 209
Solutions
  concentrated, 209
  equilibrium of, 209
Sound
  speed of, 8, 42
  waves, refraction of, 9
  and wind, 8
Sounding, of ocean, 89
Sounds, of insects, 247
Space
  and time, 181
  weightlessness in, 19
Spaghetti, cooking of, 205
Spawning, of salmon, 7
Special theory of relativity, 182
Specific heat, 260
Spectroscope, 278
Spectrum, of light, 278
Speed, 210
  aircraft, Mach numbers and, 42
  of light, and relativity, 182
  reading, 103
  of sound, 8
Spoilage, food, and micro-organisms, 84
Sponges, 171
Spores, 2
  fungus, 197
Springs
  hot, 121
  underground, 276
Squalls, 234
Stabiae, 89
Stability, of the atmosphere, 263
Stainless steel, 156
Starch
  and cooking, 205
  iodine test for, 205
  as a polymer, 152
Stars
  age of, 171
  binary, 127
  color of, 277
  density of, 134
  and disease, 214
  dying, 134

Stars (cont'd)
  formation of, 169, 248
  heat in, 277
  luminosity of, 279
  magnitudes of, 279
  neutron, 135
  "seeing", 204
  shooting, 252
  size of, 279
Steel
  and fire-making, 115
  invention of, 270
  making of, 85, 271
  open hearth, 86
  stainless, 156
  tempering of, 271
Steroids, 16
Stomach, upset, and aspirin, 18
Stomata, 24
Stone
  first mining of, 221
  Rosetta, 174
Stone Age, 9, 61
  and flint, 115
  and pottery, 104
  tools, 221
Stones, of ear, 179
Storms
  dust, as cause of oases, 6
  waves and, 15
Stratification, 75
Study, and environment, 173
Sucrose, 152
Sugar
  and food preservation, 81
  sweetness of, 32
Sulfur
  in coal, 146
  dioxide, 24
Sun
  energy of, 243
  formation of, 248
Sunburn
  and suntan lotions, 122
  and ultraviolet light, 122
Sunlight, and plant activity, 251
Supercooled droplets, and electrical

303

305